A. J. Harrison was born and raised in Birmingham, United Kingdom. His passion for writing was born from his interest in military history. Medieval Europe and the rise and fall of the Ottoman Empire are his favourite time periods. In his spare time, he's an avid boxing fan and follows the sport religiously.

A. J. Harrison

Dawn of Destiny

Calhorion Dreams: Volume 1

Austin Macauley Publishers™
London • Cambridge • New York • Sharjah

A CIP catalogue record for this title is available from the British Library.

ISBN 9781528997522 (Paperback)
ISBN 9781398420076 (Hardback)
ISBN 9781528997546 (ePub e-book)

www.austinmacauley.com

First Published (2021)
Austin Macauley Publishers Ltd
25 Canada Square
Canary Wharf
London
E14 5LQ

Writing this novel has been one of the most difficult and enjoyable experiences of my life. Emotions ranged from highs of excitement as both my characters and story developed before my eyes to lows as self-doubt crept in. I would question, is my writing and my story truly good enough? In those instances, I'd like to thank Mathew Davies and Ibrar Hussain, your kind words and enthusiasm for my writing and characters meant more than you knew. I'd also like to thank Lesia for her book cover design and Sarah Shillam for her proofreading.

The Kingdom of Allamantya
HD
2020
Tommelburg
Port of Torken
Flentian Mountains
Falentis Pass
Mountain Coast
Caerholm
Elderon Harbor
Olladrium
Golgia
Balan River
Ethilbar
Blackharrow
Nyah
Whitepeak
Iron Town
Ardenia
Kathoros
Ashfeld
Snowfall Mountains
Ironwood
Golgoron
Oakenhelm
Ocean Song
Mountain Gate of Hamon'dor
Barons Bay
Angel Islands
Antilion
Isle of Rivior
Raven Storm
Southron
Emberhost
Esteel
Red Coast
Doldayne
Blue Haven
The Paws
Yardesa
Bay of Thunder
Jade Stone
Castledon
Narrow Mountains
Kingdom of Darnor

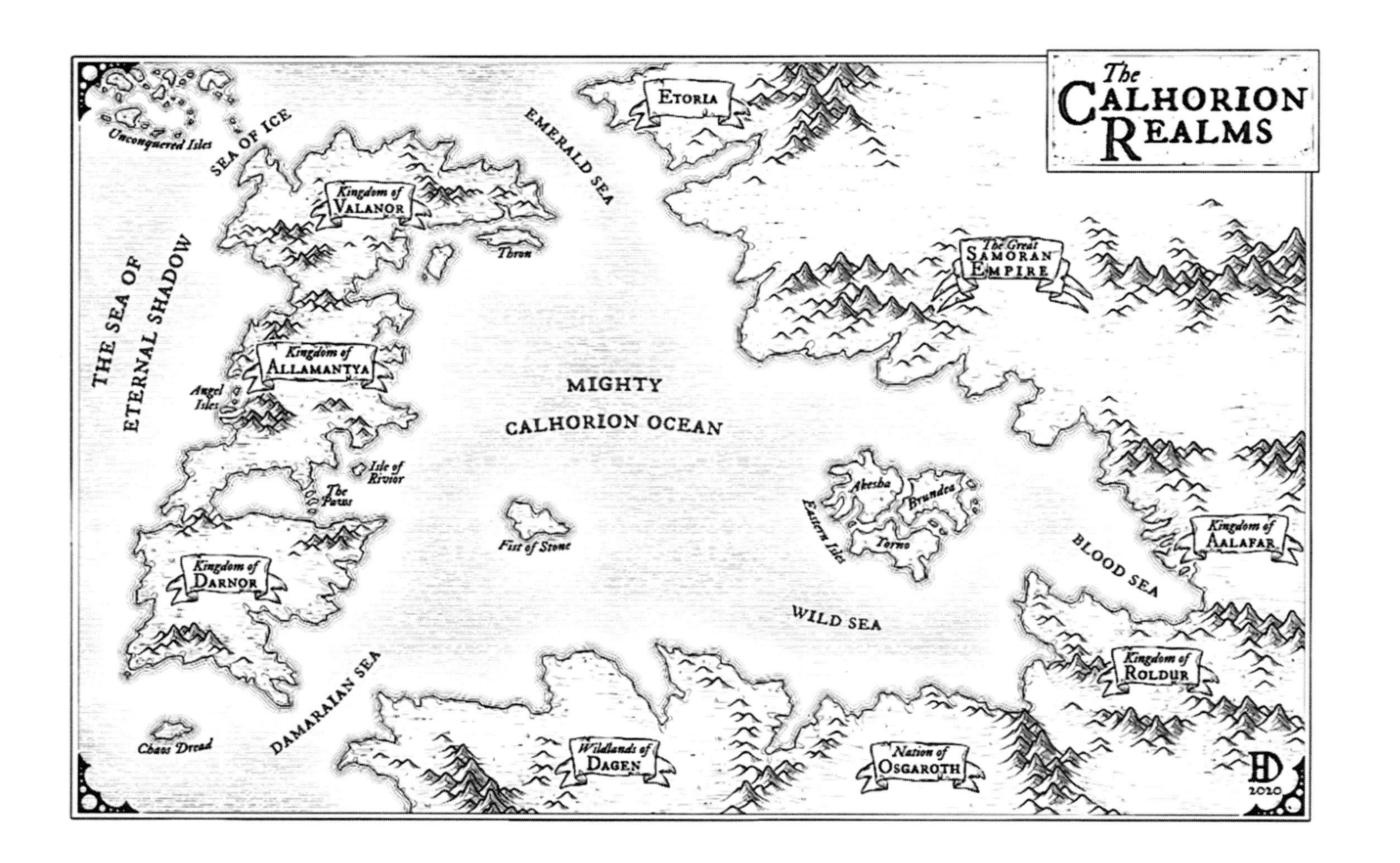

The Calhorion Realms
Etoria
Emerald Sea
Unconquered Isles
Sea of Ice
Kingdom of Valanor
Thron
The Great Samoran Empire
The Sea of Eternal Shadow
Kingdom of Allamantya
Angel Isles
Mighty Calhorion Ocean
Isle of Rivior
The Paws
Akesha
Brundea
Torno
Eastern Isles
Fist of Stone
Kingdom of Aalafar
Blood Sea
Kingdom of Darnor
Wild Sea
Kingdom of Roldur
Damaraian Sea
Chaos Dread
Wildlands of Dagen
Nation of Osgaroth
HD 2020

Chapter 1
For the Good of the Realm

The year is 201G.D
House Da'Menaeon, the Allamantyan Royal family
Heading north through Oalandrium to the Flentian Mountains

"To be king, it takes more than just the name and a crown," King Aristian's hand lingered over his own golden crown. "Andros, listen to me! When it is your time to rule, you cannot just expect to sit upon the throne. Being a king is a great responsibility, not only to oneself but to your people. To wear a crown is a never-ending weight upon your shoulders."

King Aristian looked despairingly towards Andros, who sat with a tormented expression on his face while he peered out of the carriage. The king could feel his son's sadness. He understood why. In a way he felt bad for what he had done, but he knew it was for the best – not only for him but for his kingdom too. Aristian turned and admired the vast landscapes and shades of green that passed them by. The grass was bright and healthy, the river Balan was flowing to his left, the sounds of the birds and the water were relaxing. The scorching sun shone down from the sky, reflecting off the armour of the knights who followed them. The harsh light forced the king's eyes away and back into the dimness of the carriage. He squinted; the bright rays of sun had burnt into his ageing eyes. His short grey hair showed his age and the wrinkles on his skin looked like old leather that had seen better days. He was never going to be a maiden's dream, but his wisdom was second to none.

"I'm listening, Father," Andros replied suddenly.

"He knows what he has to do," Princess Arrabella interrupted, clearly irritated by the conversation.

Aristian turned to his daughter. Her long beautiful brown hair and fiery look in her pale blue eyes reminded him instantly of his wife, Sonja. He missed her greatly.

"I don't see why I should marry her," Andros snapped. "I've never seen her – she could be fat and ugly."

Arrabella laughed. "It's not the fat or ugly part that concerns you."

"Be quiet," Andros snarled at his twin. "When I'm king you won't dare talk to me that way."

King Aristian laughed to himself. The pair had never got along even as children and now, nearing their twentieth year, they still bickered over the smallest detail. By the time he was twenty he had defended the kingdom from invasion and been crowned king. What had his son Andros done? He could barely ride and not once had he defeated an opponent in the training yard. *Being a strong warrior doesn't make a king.*

"Why does the wedding have to be so soon?" The prince clearly seemed anxious. "From the first time I see her it will have been only four new moons before we are to marry."

"I agree, Father." Arrabella showed her first sign of interest in the wedding since they had set off from the capital three days ago. "Why should things move so fast? They don't even know one another."

Aristian looked at his children, twins but ever so different except in one way. Neither had inherited his brains or logical way of thinking.

"These things happen fast," he replied. "I had never seen your mother when my father told me I was to marry her. I didn't want to but I did as he commanded. Our love wasn't created at first sight. It takes time; in fact, she hated me when we first met. I have a habit of always being right, and she couldn't stand it. Eventually we grew to love one another. Vincinicus and I have agreed we both will rule our kingdoms together, learn from each other. Then we will pass this knowledge over to you and Tilia." *But will he listen?*

The carriage passed through the waters of Balan, and the clear blue river gently crashed onto the wheels. The armoured knights, numbering close to three hundred, were guarding them either side. *One would think we were marching through enemy territory.* However, it was his brother, Prince Daemar, who had demanded the protection. He was very doubting of Valanor, but he was loyal. Loyalty was needed when ruling. You needed your soldiers and your people to trust you. You needed to be able to inspire them. Aristian saw none of those qualities in his son, but wondered if maybe it was his own fault. He didn't push him enough and allowed him to become what he was.

"Keep those horses moving, damn you!" a voice bellowed from outside the carriage.

Aristian peered out to see Sir Dolfan Greenway riding by. He was first commander of the red sword legions and one of the kingdom's greatest swords. The silver armour covering his thick chest flickered in the sun as he rode by. He wore the royal colours of Allamantya: the red sword of Tyranian sitting upon a field of green. The visor of his helmet was raised, showing his thick ginger beard and his intense blue eyes. His voice boomed like a drum as he yelled commands to all those around him.

Would all these knights who had served him so faithfully stay loyal to his son when he died? Aristian doubted it. That's why he had done what he had, to ensure his son would be safe and to keep his kingdom and empire secure. Many doubted his choice, but he was the wise king. He had been named that for a reason and he was going to make sure he lived up to it.

The journey was long, the carriage uncomfortable and the king's old bones began to ache. His legs were numb and the back cramps became almost unbearable. The heat didn't help. It was one of the hottest summers in years. His rich leather stuck to his chest and he found it hard to breathe. He took his crown off; he never liked wearing it and whenever he could, he removed it. *I must ignore my pains.* What they were doing would change the kingdom forever. A few aches and pains were nothing for what the rewards would be at the end.

The carriage clumped and banged as it rode up the bank, back onto land. Andros's head bounced back and forth. The anger built up in his face but to the king's surprise, he stayed calm, adjusting his red and green silks and brushing his short brown hair back off his narrow face. The prince was tall, standing nearly six feet, but he was slim and ungainly. Above his weak chin, the prince wore a faint look of surprise. Not quite the warrior image that his father had hoped for.

"Father, what is Princess Tilia like?" The prince carried a rare bit of humanity in his voice.

The king looked back at his son. "I hear she is beautiful, strong and loyal. Many of the finest men in Valanor asked for her hand. She chose you, my son."

Andros stared intensely at his father, as though trying to read his thoughts. He couldn't.

"It's her brother, Prince Gabriel. I hear he is the beautiful one," Arrabella chipped in, rolling her eyes slightly at the rumour and looking out upon the vast lands around them. "Son of a god they say, shining hair of gold, his eyes sparkle like diamonds and his ability in war is rivalled by none. Women from all over pray that he may grace them with his touch but once in their life."

Aristian smiled. "Legends don't often live up to their stories." Though this was true, he knew Prince Gabriel was said to be a formidable warrior, one he wouldn't like to go to war against. Aristian ruled the five regions of Allamantya from his capital of Antilion. Two hundred years ago, when his ancestors, twins Prince Artendaus and Princess Valenya were born, the gods had seen fit to curse the land with blood and terror. Both thought it was their right to claim the throne: Valenya because she was first born and Artendaus as he was the eldest male heir. Valenya, however, was forced to flee north, taking a few noble families with her. She travelled over the Flentian mountains to Northrum, to form the Kingdom of Valanor. For two hundred years the wars had raged on. Aristian knew that the peace he'd been able to garner for the past twenty-five years had been a blessing. But he wasn't a fool. He knew that it was wearing thin and soon war would break out once again if something didn't change.

The match between Andros and Princess Tilia had been a clever one. After long thought and against the advice of those closest to him, most notably the members of the High Council, Aristian had offered his first-born son to wed the eldest daughter of his long rival, King Vincinicus I of Valanor. Despite Andros's shortcomings, the offer was accepted and now, six months on, they rode to meet each other on the borders. It wouldn't be easy and the hardest part was yet to come.

The carriage came to a halt and the door opened, a summer breeze rippling through and catching the king as he waited to be greeted. The cool air wrapped around his face like the cool touch of his wife. He liked it.

"We are here, Your Majesty," Sir Dolfan said as he held open the door.

They had pulled up on the fields of Balross. The grass was green and healthy, a beautiful sight to behold. One would never believe that this field once held the bodies of over ten thousand dead and dying men over a hundred years ago.

"This is a good place to make camp," the king replied as he leant out the carriage, Dolfan taking his hand. His thick steel gauntlet started to burn into his flesh. He ignored the pain and placed his feet onto the ground. Thick dense forest covered them either side, the river to their back and the only entrance was straight ahead. *No chance of an ambush.*

Andros and Arrabella were quickly helped out of the carriage by other servants as Sir Dolfan stood ready for his orders.

"Have my tent made ready, sir." Andros glanced up at the hot blaring sun, admiring its beauty. "I don't wish to look like a beetroot for my betrothed."

"Yes," Arrabella jutted in, "As that will be another thing to put her off. That pretty little face of yours will be like a tomato." She smiled sweetly as she walked off with her handmaiden.

Andros scowled and placed a hand on his cheeks. "Hurry," he snapped.

"As you command, Your Highness," Dolfan replied obediently. Andros stalked off, flanked by two soldiers as he headed for shade, leaving his father to slowly make his way to the centre of the camp.

Soldiers and squires alike, as far as the eye could see, were pitching up tents. The hot sun was blaring down on them. The king watched from the shade, with his son and daughter either side of him. All three were resting on an old wooden stand that made his back ache. Arrabella had a mirror in one hand and her handmaiden was braiding her thick brown hair. Her red and gold dress twinkled like stars in the night sky. As always, her dress emphasised her breasts, tightly fitted around her waist, complementing her frame.

Aristian was wiping sweat from his brow, sulking in the heat. In front of them three men and a young boy were trying to erect his tent. It was bright white with a rich green and red trim. They pulled with all their might to lift it up. Just watching made the king feel tired. To his right, heavy goods wagons were bringing up food supplies, and he could see baskets full of fruit: bright red gleaming apples, large sweet looking oranges and grapes as large as walnuts. He was looking forward to his meal tonight.

The king had always liked the hustle and bustle of an army encampment, the noises, ranged from chatter and shouting from the men, the laughter and screams of the camp whores and finally to the crackling of the camp fires. The smells of rich red wines to bitter ales, from smoking roast pork to freshly boiled soup wafted over. As a boy he would walk around his father's encampments, interacting with all his subjects. You could meet all sorts of characters: fat blacksmiths sharpening weapons, obedient squires who would be running about from place to place and knights praying to the gods of Ollaria'h for glory and their eternal place in the night sky.

Aristian loved it all, except for one thing. An army encampment usually meant a battle. The last time the king had been present at a camp as large as this was during the rebellion of the Mountains Clans of Golgia, nearly sixteen years ago, when the sounds of laughter had been replaced by the screams of the dying, and the calls for wine had been taken over by those of men pleading for their mothers or their wives with their last breaths. The thought of such things encouraged a dark cloak of sadness to drape itself over his shoulders, and for a fleeting moment he felt all the happiness in the world had drained away. He had to remind himself that he wasn't riding to battle. This time he was riding to peace.

Suddenly the ground began to rumble, and the king's feet began to shudder against the wooden stand. Across the bright green plains, and through the rising heat, Beyorn approached. He was running as always, two riders flanking him either side. He was the king's champion and a mountain of a man; he was as tall as three men and as wide as two; he wore two thick leather belts across his torso which revealed his bulging chest. He looked as if he had been carved from stone by the gods themselves. His arms were larger than most men's legs. Just the sight of him put fear into everyone who glanced up at him. Long thick black hair fell loose from his head and most of his face was covered by his well-groomed beard.

"Are you well Your Majesty?" Beyorn's voice echoed as if it spoke from within a cave.

"I think I am feeling better than those four over there." The king pointed towards the four men still struggling with his tent.

"I have word from Prince Daemar. He and Prince Arteus were scouting the area for the northern savages."

Aristian was quick to interrupt. "Savages? They will soon be kin to us all. There will be no more talk of that."

Beyorn offered no reply except to bow his head in shame. His dark soulless eyes closed ever so briefly. He was so used to talking about the people of Valanor in such a manner when he was in the company of Prince Daemar.

"The young Prince Arteus will make a fine warrior one day. His skill with horse and sword improves daily." Beyorn rarely spoke, but when he did, he often complimented the young prince, who was as different to his brother Andros as the sun was to the moon.

King Aristian admired Beyorn, as most did. The beast of Golgia they called him. The rumours said devils created him. Aristian wondered if he would have any luck in training Andros on the battlefield but quickly shook the thought from his head. Andros had tried the patience of many a good warrior, and none of them had taught him to wield a sword with much success.

"My brother was always more interested in horses and swords," Andros said loudly. "That is why he will be a soldier, and why I am to be King and Emperor of the Calhorion Sea. I enjoy the finer things in life."

The king noticed Andros's irritation and tried to calm him. "Certainly," he agreed, "Arteus is gifted with both horse and sword. But I do hope in the times to come there will be no more use for the latter. He should be taught how the use of his brain can be mightier than any weapon."

The king knew teaching Arteus to use his brain and to study was as likely to happen as it was teaching Andros how to wield a sword. But he continued to dream.

Andros shot up from his seat and spat angrily onto the dry ground beneath his feet. "What the hell are those men doing? I should have them flogged for their stupidity!" He flew from the shade, pointing towards the men still struggling with his tent. All four of them immediately stopped what they were doing. The youngest of the group – a skinny young boy of fourteen at most – started to shake at the outburst, the rope he held beginning to slide around the grass like a snake.

"I should show you how to do it myself!" Andros shouted as he stomped towards the boy, Aristian and Arrabella watching on with interest.

One of the men stepped in front of Andros's path and blocked his way, possibly the boy's father. "I apologise, Your Highness," he said, his bald head glistening with sweat. "Pip – he is only young and still learning. He isn't used to this heat. We are from Baron's Bay, the weather there is wet and—"

Andros scoffed, stepped round the man and pushed his son to the floor. "I don't care for his name or where his whore mother shat him out. All I want is my tent up, so I can get out of this heat." Andros grabbed the rope from the boy as Aristian watched him carefully from the shade. *I would like to see him attempt this; I haven't had a laugh in a while.*

As the prince leant back on the rope, a group of knights rode into the camp. "Wait, Your Highness," one of the knights called cheerfully from his horse as he began to dismount. "It would be a dishonour to see you work while these peasants sit back and enjoy the sun." The young handsome knight was Sir Lyon N'Dai, son of Latimor N'Dai, the Marshal of Kathoros. He was dressed in silver clad armour with a white tunic, with his family emblem of the red war lion upon his chest. His long thick brown hair was half tied up and half down. His five knights were behind him, known across the land as his *pride*. All dressed identically, they clanked along in heavy silver armour.

"Let me do the honour." Lyon held out his arm to the prince, who seemed so entranced by the knight's rich brown eyes that he obediently let go.

Lyon was a well-built man, standing at a strong six feet. His shoulders were broad and his jaw fine cut, like he was made from stone. He gripped hard on the rope and leant back, pulling with all his might and yet still the tent didn't move. A sense of embarrassment took hold of him but he kept pulling. Arrabella looked to her father and the two shared a secret smile.

Just as Andros started to frown again at Lyon's seeming lack of strength, the five knights dismounted to lend a hand. All together they pulled and launched the tent into the air. The cloth of the tent flapped loudly as the tip was erected, forming a slight breeze which caught them all in the face.

"Bravo, Bravo," Arrabella shouted as she stood up and walked towards Lyon N'Dai, clapping her hands furiously. "What a knight you are," she said, her voice breathless. "My brother should be honoured to have a man as strong as you looking over him." She ran her hand across Lyon's cleanly shaven face, while all the time smiling at her brother. The king could see the anger building up inside of Andros. He knew that look. It was the same one he had when he was a child, before he would attack his sister.

Lyon, however, never sensed the princess' sharp sarcasm; his arrogance blinded him. "Your Highness is too kind," he said, taking Arrabella's pale hand and kissing it three times. "You are truly the most beautiful lady in the realm. I will never forget this moment, to have such a fairer hand as yours to touch but a humble knight such as I." He turned to Andros. "My prince knows I am here for him. To help and serve in any way I can."

Arrabella smiled sweetly and turned back towards her father. "What an honour," she murmured again, causing the king to smother a loud laugh.

The day slowly drew to a close across the hustle and bustle of the camp. The bright sun had dimmed its light and the intense heat had finally cooled, allowing for food to be served in the royal tent which had been erected and fully furnished. A huge dark red and green rug had been placed along the floor, from the entrance to the centre of the tent; its embroidery was the Allamantyan coat of arms, the sword of the god Tyranian. At the centre stood a round table, adorned with a sheepskin map of the Calhorion world. A large oak table at the back rose up so those sitting at it looked down on anyone who entered; it was near twelve feet long and almost three feet wide. The colour and the grain of oak were warm and appealing, and on top were plates full of meats and fruits that filled the entire tent with a rich scent.

At the table sat the king, wearing thin red silks that made him feel cool and relaxed. To his left was his daughter and two empty chairs, one for his youngest son Arteus and the other for his brother Daemar. Both still hadn't returned from their scouting mission. Next to Prince Andros sat the king's father-in-law, and the prince's own grandfather, Devon Hohjan. Beyorn the beast of Golgia stood silently behind the king.

A large stuffed pig with an apple in its mouth was the main course. Everyone tucked away into their meal, chatter filling the tent and lifting the atmosphere after the intense heat of the day.

"I wonder why they put the apple in the pig's mouth," Andros said rhetorically as he sat stuffing his face with the rich tender meat. The juices began to run down his chin – an image that Arrabella didn't think was fit for royalty.

"It is to keep the jaws of the swine open, Your Highness," Devon Hohjan, the Darnaion lord, leaned in and explained with an air of arrogance in his voice as he held out his cup of wine to be filled. "When the pig gets roasted, the jaws would lock shut if not for the apple." He drank his wine down in two large gulps. The old lord was nearing his seventieth year and was dressed in dark purple robes that hung loosely from his body. He was old and frail, with a thin face that had deep wrinkles carved into his skin like scars. He was also a known alcoholic; the king only really put up with him due to him being the father to his dear departed wife Sonja.

"I see you know your food, Lord Hohjan," the king added with a smile on his face. He wasn't one to get involved in a conversation unless he knew he was right. "In the fall, the farmers fatten their pigs on apples. So, when roasting the pig, they would put fruit in the pig's mouth. It is a way of portraying the life and death cycle so that the pig would be eating the apple in both life and death. Also, the pig's snout is not the most beautiful thing to look at." The king poked the pig's snout with his fork, as though to emphasise his point.

Arrabella looked over to her brother. "Maybe we should do the same to you, Andros. If we put an apple in your mouth, it might make the Princess Tilia find you more appealing."

Before Andros had any time to react, his grandfather Devon Hohjan burst into hysterics, knocking his wine all over the floor.

Suddenly the two soldiers at the entrance announced, "Prince Daemar is approaching!"

Everyone looked up, except Andros who turned to Hohjan. "I wouldn't drink too much, Grandfather. It could one day be the death of you." His hand tightly squeezed the old man's wrist.

Daemar entered the tent with some haste, dressed in light mail and armour, his silver breastplate showing a golden sword carved at its centre, and a green cape that hung loosely from his shoulders. His left hand as always was placed on the tip of his sword. He was an average sized man, but strong and imposing. He had aged better than his brother; his skin was smooth and his hair still a light brown. His face, as usual, sported rough stubble scattered across his jaw. He wasn't a man to fuss about his appearance.

He walked straight over to the table and poured himself a large glass of wine. He gulped it down in one go. Some of the wine ran down his cheeks and he wiped it away with his hand. He then looked up to his brother, bowed his head and placed his right fist over his heart.

"Your Majesty, our foreign friends are less than a day's ride north. They had just passed through the Falentis pass when I last saw them. Maybe a thousand in total, more than double the men we have with us." His voice sounded concerned.

The king smiled. "You sound worried, Brother. I would be too if we were riding to war. Luckily for all of us here we are going to a wedding not a battle."

Andros suddenly butted in. "A thousand soldiers! We should send word back to the capital to call for more men."

Daemar looked up at his nephew, who he never had much time for. He was too weak and spoilt for his liking. "My prince, it is a two-day ride back to capital and two back. There would be no time to call for aid. Luckily, I was prepared; I sent word to the Marshal of Ardenia, Varrone DeVeil. He, along with eight hundred men, are camped just a few hours south of our position."

King Aristian was a little irritated by his brother's over-cautiousness. "Thank you, Daemar, for protecting us all. I feel, though, those eight hundred may have just got themselves a lot of needless exercise and maybe a nice tan in this summer heat." He wasn't in the mood however to argue with his brother, so he changed the topic of conversation. "Where is Arteus?"

"I am here, Father," Arteus said happily as he strolled into the tent. The youngest of the king's children and only a boy of fourteen, Arteus was handsome, strong and large for his age. His short brown hair reminded the king of his own in his youth. He too was dressed as a knight in the same attire as his uncle. “We saw them, as far as the eye could see, knights dressed in silver and blue. They look fierce.”

“It is always good to have fierce allies,” the king added.

“Did you see the god-prince? Is he as beautiful as the legends say?” Arrabella sounded like an excitable child.

“Yes, Gabriel was there; a great looking warrior he was, on a white horse at the front of his men.”

Arteus was quickly cut off by his uncle who added, “Where all leaders should be.” Daemar looked towards Andros with disgust.

Andros replied with an arrogant tilt of his head and a roll of his eyes before he drank down some more of his wine.

“Please sit down, Brother.” King Aristian looked up to Daemar. It wasn’t a suggestion; it was a command. He pointed towards the roasted hog in front of him. “Have some food with us all. The pork is particularly good.”

Daemar glanced at the food, but instead of sitting down he turned and walked back towards the entrance of the tent.

“I’m afraid I haven’t the time, Your Majesty. A soldier’s rations are all I need.”

The king’s eyes narrowed at his brother’s supposed piety.

“Preparations need to be made, and the guards need to be alert and changed every few hours. I rode in here today unchallenged. If we had been the enemy, this camp would be overrun by now.”

“Who is this enemy you speak of?” the king replied with a hint of sarcasm in his voice. When Daemar didn’t respond and walked away, Arteus turned to follow him.

“Arteus, my boy. Where are you going? It is late, you should eat.”

“Sorry, Father, I must see to the men with Uncle.” Arteus could barely be heard as he quickly scuttled off after Daemar.

The king would always forget that his son was a boy of fourteen but had the strength of mind and body of a man of twenty-five. Arteus never cared for the luxuries in life, such as fine food and a warm bed like his elder siblings. He was happy to sleep outdoors and fight all day – something which made him incredibly popular with the small folk.

Slowly, in small groups of twos and threes, the company in the tent began to filter out into the inky darkness outside, their chatter floating up into the wind. All that eventually remained was King Aristian, his son Andros and a couple of other soldiers who were talking quietly whilst they finished with their wine. The king was still eating. He took his time; he liked to savour his meals. He believed that good food was to be eaten slowly, to enjoy each bite, taking in all the different flavours and textures. It also helped his indigestion.

“Andros, what makes you different to that boy, Pip?” the king asked as he cut up the final piece of his pork. He wanted to teach his son something.

“The boy?” Andros was confused. He never had the best memory. Especially for people he thought of as inferior. He’d stood up and was lingering in the centre of the tent, running his fingers over the large map of Allamantya and its empire which, one day, would be his realm.

"The one you pushed to the ground. What do you think makes you and him different?"

"He is a peasant; I am a prince, a future king and emperor, destined to rule. *He* is destined to wallow in mud and piss. To be forgotten." The prince's fist began to tighten on the map.

"You are wrong," Aristian said slowly. "Yes, you are of royal blood. You are my son and heir to the throne, whilst that boy is born of the common people. More than likely he will be forgotten by the mortal man. That isn't what will make you different, however." The king leant forward and lifted a cup of wine and washed down his pork. The sweet taste almost took him away from his conversation and back to happier times with his dear departed wife.

"So you are saying I am no better than a peasant?" Andros looked tense as if his blood was starting to boil.

"The gods, in their White City of Ollaria'h judge all men equal when they arrive at the golden gates. A king and a farmer are deemed the same. Their name and who their fathers were count for nothing. It is the deeds you do every day that will decide whether you are worthy. What we do in life will be remembered, maybe not by the common man but by the gods. The actions you take in life live forever."

Andros stood silently as if he was taken aback by his father's words. His fist loosened and he wiped his palms on his silks. "I will try, Father. I hope to make you proud one day. I am sorry I am not what you wished for." His voice was tinged with sadness.

The king smiled as he finally stood from his chair, the servants relieved to at last be able to begin their clearing of the tent.

"Every day you make me proud. I have loved all my children, from the day they opened their eyes until the day when the gods decide I should finally close my own."

He walked towards Andros and wrapped his arms around him. As they embraced, for a brief moment, the king could feel the love a son should have for his father. Maybe it was his own fault as to why his children struggled to show love. His own father, King Alector, had been a cold man.

"One day you will make a fine king, one that will deserve his place among his ancestors." The king's words were powerful but Aristian wondered how much truth there was in them. "It is getting late and we have an important day ahead. Get some rest. These old bones of mine are not what they used to be." The king turned and walked to his room, stretching his old weary arms out wide and ready to fall into a deep sleep.

****

The sun had set, replaced by the largest great white moon anyone had seen in years. The bustling sound of horses, men and armour was now replaced by light chatter, the crackling of campfires and crickets in the long grass. Prince Andros stood alone near the forest edge. It had seemed like it had taken an age for his father to fall asleep. He could hear him tossing and turning, even muttering to himself. It wasn't until he heard the snores that he knew it was safe to get up.

He looked up and admired the sky, dark and never-ending. Imprinted on the night sky were stars, the god's tribute to fallen heroes so their memories could shine on forever. He thought back to his father's words, trying to recall the odd phrase here and there. No matter how much they irritated him, he knew they had meaning and wondered if he too, would one day go on to have a star of his own.

His hands were sweating. He felt excited and guilty, as he always did when it came to nights like this. Both feelings were like an inner fight inside of him, constantly trying to outdo the other. He rubbed his hands down on his silks. The bright white tunic he wore had become sweaty; the patches were starting to show under his arms. He noticed dirt on the wrists of his tunic. He hated white, it always got dirty and it didn't suit his pale complexion. He was jealous of Arteus, his younger brother; he had olive skin, better suited to the sun like his mother.

I have been cursed with my father's looks and my mother's brains.

It was late; the moon was high in the sky. Andros's excitement had been replaced with frustration and he was about ready to leave when he heard rustling in the grass. He turned to see Sir Lyon N'Dai slowly making his way to where Andros stood waiting. Lyon's eyes never left the prince's as he paced forward, his fingers stretched out sliding through the long grass in front of him.

Andros was clearly irritated. "I am to be your king. I shouldn't be kept waiting."

Lyon brushed off the prince's irritation with a swift laugh. "I had matters to attend to, Your Highness. Your uncle, he is distrusting of our northern cousins. He wants guards every fifty metres, changed at two-hour intervals."

"My uncle is a suspicious fool; since his wife died, he is ever so paranoid. He needs a new wife to keep him busy."

"The king and his family are our greatest concern. We are here to keep you safe." Lyon lowered his head, his dark brown eyes looking up at the prince's sullen face. He'd reached Andros and the two of them were inching closer. Lyon slowly raised his head with a smile. "We are here to protect and serve Your Highness."

The prince interrupted, "To obey."

Suddenly, Lyon pulled the prince towards him. Their lips met, and their hands started to explore. Lyon, with his strength, pushed the prince back onto the wagon behind him, causing both of them to catch their breath. Andros could taste the sweat on Lyon's lips; the prince could feel himself hardening as Lyon ran his hand up his tunic, over his chest and around his throat. His lover's free hand slid inside his trousers.

Lyon whispered into his ear, "What would you have me do?"

“Take me!” Andros commanded, his voice hissing sharply in the darkness. Before he knew it, Lyon had turned him over so that his face pressed against the hard wood of the wagon. Lyon’s hard kisses across his neck sent a cold shiver up his spine.

For a brief moment, Andros didn’t care about his family, his honour or his desire to be king. Finally, the prince had got what he had been waiting for.

Chapter 2
Heading South, into the Unknown

Splintered faction of House Da'Menaeon, royal family of Valanor
Heading south across the borderlands towards the Flentian Mountains

"Rumour has it, the Antilion women don't shave. They let it grow thick and bushy. I hear it is because their husbands are more interested in books and boys than in their wives. They prefer little cocks to big plump tits." Prince Lucian smiled at his elder brother.

"I think their husbands will love you then, little brother, and if that rumour of yours is true then we shouldn't find many men down south at all." Prince Lassander laughed. "They will all be dying out."

The brothers looked almost identical, yet they were separated by nine months. Each had shining blonde hair down to their necks, teeth as white as pearls and slender faces. They looked younger than their twenty-one years. Both were fully dressed in Valorian armour, clad in single steal cuirass breast plates, each with carved images of a muscular torso embroiled onto them. Their Phrygian style helmets were of a crystal blue, with a waterfall of silver plume, which fell from the crest of the helmet to the soldiers' backs.

Angered by his brother's reply, Lucian shot back, "When we get to Allamantya and then to Antilion, their women will be dying to get their hands on this." His left hand grabbed between his legs. "They have never experienced a real man before; we know men of Valanor are equal to two of Allamantya."

"Aye that is true, Brother. But what of that dear young maid you left back home? What was her name again? Frona. Won't she be devastated, you marrying an unpruned southerner?" Lassander smiled as he directed his horse around some rocks in front of him.

"Frona? She wasn't one of mine. She was that girl from Varia, the one who wore that chastity belt. Bloody good job she wore it too. I tried for nearly an hour to get it off before I gave up. My balls were the size of my fist by the time I left."

"I bet she wept until her heart's content," Lassander replied with a hint of sarcasm in his voice. "So who is the lucky lady that you have been courting these past few weeks?" Lassander was always forgetting which girl his brother was seeing. He moved from one to the other like food at a buffet.

"Euterpia is her name. Pale skin, green eyes and a figure even a priest of the gods at the White City couldn't turn down. Oh, and those red lips… like roses they were, thick and beautiful… Mighty talented she was with those lips." Lucian thought back to those intimate moments they shared together.

"She sounds a fine lady to me. One our dear mother would be proud to see you wed."

"You are telling me you aren't interested in their women in the slightest? Uncle Damidar told us to enjoy everything life has to offer; he said the gods are cruel and cut our lives short. So it is down to us to bask in the moment, no matter how short." Lucian felt proud in the way he had replied to his brother.

"Enjoyment to you is bedding a different girl every week, a noble's daughter, a fisherman's wife or even an unflowered priestess of the gods. To me, enjoying life to its fullest is to spend time with my wife and son, watching my Melaina smile, seeing my son, Zander, walk for the first time. What you didn't realise when uncle told us that, is that he meant for us to enjoy life in our own way." Lassander's reply made Lucian lost for words; he had no answer for his brother's comeback so he opted to bring the conversation back to Euterpia.

Lassander was third in line to the royal throne of Valanor, his mother Lorella was the younger sister to King Vincinicus. He, by now, had become a little bored of his brother's escapades with his latest female conquest, so he was admiring what was out in front of him. Far on the horizon, were hills of yellow sand, rocks and desert flora. Behind that horizon was Allamantya, a land only his ancestors talked about, a realm of hatred and evil. *I guess soon I shall see how evil they are.* Behind him a sea of blue and silver followed; however, this was a sea that wasn't made up of water, but soldiers.

On the horizon, he saw a rider heading towards them. His brother was still talking about Euterpia. "Lucian, Lucian, look." He pointed out in front of him. "Prince Gabriel, he's back."

****

Gabriel was clad in starlight blue armour. A breastplate hemmed with diamonds and pearls. His grieves rose from his ankles to his knees. He wore no helmet. Long blonde hair floated from his head as he rode towards Lucian and Lassander on his white horse. The smooth defined muscles on the horse could be seen as it galloped towards them. A mighty beast, one fit for royalty.

Lassander and Lucian spoke at the same time, "My prince." They then placed their right hands over their hearts and bowed their heads.

"Gabriel, we were starting to get worried, you had been gone awhile. I thought maybe you had run into some trouble with those southerners." Lucian had a genuine concern in his voice.

"Fear not cousin, it would take more than a southerner to do away with your prince." An air of arrogance came from Gabriel as he spoke. He knew himself to be a formidable warrior and he would always let others know it.

"The road ahead is clear. No signs of an ambush," Gabriel said as he turned his horse around and rode alongside his cousins. All three were as close as brothers. From their youth they had fought, studied and flirted with the young girls together. None of them had struggled with the opposite sex. Gabriel turned his head to look back over the army that followed, near a thousand men. All loyal, battle hardened warriors. *If it had been up to me, I would've brought double.*

"The wars had raged for over two hundred years between us and Allamantya. We hate them yet none of us have ever seen what they look like. The old nurse maids spoke of them as demons, who come out only at night to drink the blood of little children. The philosophers with all their wisdom said they are warmongers who despise our way of life and live for nothing more than our destruction. Our father spoke of them as merciless invaders. Yet, in all my twenty-one years, I have never been to war with them. Maybe they aren't so bad after all." Lassander turned to Lucian.

"You sound nervous, Brother. Have no fear, my sword will protect you." With his right hand, Lucian grabbed hold of his sword and drew it from its scabbard. His weapon was a single-edged blade that pitched forward towards the point.

"Put that away, before you hurt yourself. I am curious that is all, curious to see what our new brothers look like. I suspect I will be mightily disappointed." It was clear Lassander was getting annoyed with his brother; he could be a fool at times.

Lucian quickly responded, "I am curious too, to see what their women look like between their legs." He started laughing before adding, "Gabriel, talk some sense into Lassander, he sounds like he wants to be their friends."

Gabriel angrily replied, "My father says we are to be allies, so that is what we will be. I may not trust them or agree with his rational thinking, but a loyal son is what I am. Unless a Valorian is harmed in an unjust manor then I will not fight. I am my father's son, his word is law." He turned his horse away from his cousins and rode back along the column past his soldiers. He was already in a bad mood. All he could think about for the past months was that his sister, Tilia was to marry a foreigner. A man none of them knew but only by reputation, a weak, arrogant prince who some said preferred the touch of a man to the company of a woman.

Earlier, when he had ridden ahead of his men, he hadn't really been scouting along the pass for the old enemy. He knew if there was to be some kind of ambush it wouldn't be in his own lands. He just wanted to be alone, time to think. He and his sister Tilia had been close, as close as siblings could be; he had always loved her and wanted to keep her safe. He remembered the day his father announced she would marry Prince Andros; he pictured it like it was yesterday.

He had walked into the great throne room, the chamber of kings and queens. Earlier that day he had been bedding the wife of a Flarian noble. The man had dishonoured him in public, saying he was a prince not worthy of remembrance, one blinded by his ego and infatuated with his own fame. He had wanted to kill the pompous old man but his father wouldn't allow it. The Flarian's wife though, had been a beautiful thing, petite but feisty. He saw his father, King Vincinicus, bargaining his sister and heir to the kingdom like she was some whore at a brothel. Maybe it was the gods punishing him for his sinful acts. *Thy shall not take my brother's property, whether of material or flesh.*

Along the column he could see the faces of his men; each one looked at him as he rode past. Young and old, he knew they loved him and he loved them too.

"The god-prince," they whispered.

Gabriel looked each of them in the eyes. *I wouldn't remember their faces if we were to meet again.* He directed his horse up a small bank. The tiny stones rolled down the slope as the horses' hooves drove into the ground. Once up, he looked out in front of him. He pushed up into his stirrups and leant forward to get a better look. He could see soldiers on horseback in rows of two by two, each clutching spears in their right hands. Then he noticed a large starlight blue flag flapping softly in the cool breeze. A silver rose was at its centre, a rose given from the gods, a sign of strength. He sensed a feeling of pride whenever he saw his country's coat of arms.

Behind the flag bearers he saw the royal carriage, a mighty thing made from silver that was forged from the ancient rocks at Verginium. It was being pulled by four great war horses, huge animals built from nothing but muscle. Inside was his father, King Vincinicus, and his sister, Tilia. Then suddenly a sickness hit him in the stomach as powerful as any punch he had ever felt before. *It is my sister who will sacrifice everything, her home, her family and her honour to a foreigner. So why is it I who feels sick with pain?*

****

"You look anxious, Father. What is the matter?" Tilia, the beautiful princess of Valanor, looked at her father, King Vincinicus. Watching him, she could tell he was not the man he had claimed to be in his youth. His harmless tales were always full of hollow truths, whether they were of his conquests in the bedroom or on the battlefield. As the years went by, they had taken their toll. He was only a small man, barely standing five feet and six inches, and he had grown wider with each passing year. His large round belly stuck out like a sore thumb. He now claimed he was too old for battle, leaving the matters of war to his younger brother, Damidar, and his son, Gabriel. All that was left for him now was to eat, and my, did he enjoy eating! Being a king was boring, he always told her.

"If anything goes wrong, Tilia, anything at all, head north to the Dantford hills, then west until you reach Jerome Riordal, Lord of the Marsh." King Vincinicus sounded concerned. His face was round and his cheeks were covered in a thick grey, well-groomed beard. Sparkling blues eyes still shone from his now ageing face, the last reminiscence of a once handsome king. Grey silks clung to him like a babe to its mother; they gave him little room to breathe and, in this heat, they stuck to his flesh.

"Why would anything go wrong? We are here for a wedding." Tilia was worried by her father's remark.

"Everything will be fine; we are here to make peace. But we cannot be too careful. No matter what happens, you are our main priority." The king placed his hand on his daughter's knee. She was his first born, two years older than Gabriel and heir to his kingdom. In Valanor, whether you were male or female, it did not matter. If you were first born, you had the right to the throne. Tilia, in return, wrapped her tiny hands around his. She felt safe with her father so close. Whenever she was scared as a child all her father had to do was wrap his large hands around hers and look into her eyes, and whatever it was that scared her was wiped from her mind.

"What about Gabriel, is he not your concern too?"

"Gabriel can look after himself. No matter what I tell him, he will do what he sees fit. Do you remember, child, what I am telling you?"

Tilia was loyal to her family and had a great sense of pride and love for her people. She wore a turquoise blue dress, well fitted, with a silver flower pattern running up the side. Her long blonde hair was tied back away from her face. She was petite in frame but strong, a beautiful princess in every way. It was obvious why many had called for her hand in marriage. Not only was she a princess, but a fine woman too.

"Yes Father, I know what you are saying. The Riordal family have been loyal to us since the retreat from Battle at Falentis. Lord Gerold Riordal and his two sons gave their lives so you and Grandfather could escape. I have seen it hundreds of times on the map. You would tell the story to me and Gabriel every night as children." She always remembered what her father told her. Gabriel loved the tale, of how three men sacrificed themselves for the old ways. Tilia, however, was never interested in tales of war or death, of how men killed each other like it was an act to be proud of.

"Lord Jerome Riordan, however, is not his brother. Not the warrior type, he is like food, gone rotten with age. He has no love for us but he hates his own Allamantyan people more than anything, sees them as a disease that you can never be free of. He won't greet you with open arms but he will keep you safe. That, I'm sure." Vincinicus leant forward and kissed his daughter on the head. He sat back and closed his eyes.

Tilia knew the last time he had headed this far south was twenty-five years ago and it was to war. Two battles were fought in the last war; the first was the clash at the Three Fords which was the proudest moment of her father's military career. His father, her grandfather, the mighty Lycinious, destroyed the invading Allamantyan army. Their king, Alector, was left distraught and disgraced. The largest Allamantyan force ever assembled was decimated. The other battle however was a defeat, one riddled with shame that would haunt the Vincinicus name forever. Until the day he reached the golden gates of Ollaria'h, the pass at Falentis would be her father's curse.

Tilia briefly watched her father as he slept. His heavy breathing amused her; his large belly moved up and down. Not even the dumps and bangs of the rocky ground outside woke him from his sleep. He looked so peaceful, yet she knew the heavy burden that rested upon his shoulders. Across the pale sea lay the nation of Etoria, the current enemy of Valanor. The invasions had begun to take their toll and his popularity with his people had begun to wane.

The fighting core of the Valorian army was its battalions of Delloria, each made up solely of warrior women. King Vincinicus had slowly been reducing their numbers, keeping them away from the battlefield. For the last ten years they had been left to guard the capital at Verdina. Tilia dared not question her father but she knew his decisions had not gone down well with his Flarian nobles.

Tilia looked away and out of the carriage to see a flock of birds flying above, beauteous white doves moving elegantly through the sky. She loved the finer things in life. The birds reminded her of home where she would watch the sun set over the mountains at Yarona. It was relaxing and peaceful. She may not have enjoyed tales of battle and death but she loved nothing more than to hunt and ride. Mounted upon her glorious red horse, Flame, was when she felt happiest, riding with the wind in her hair, the sun on her back and the clean air filling her lungs. Riding was not her only talent, she was fine archer too, a dead shot with a bow. Whatever she killed, she ate. It was never a sport to her but it gave her a sense of excitement, a thrill.

"Your Highness, Your Highness!" An excitable voice could be heard from outside the carriage. Tilia looked back to see a young knight, clad in a pale blue cuirass breastplate. His matching helmet was held under his left arm, his right hand gripped the reins of his grey horse. It was Sir Kaian Vadius, a young man with short blonde hair, slim features, and brown eyes. He was cleanly cut and had pale skin, one of her two sworn swords.

It was Valorian custom for every princess to have two knights sworn to protect her from the day the gods decided she was a woman until she was married when, from then on, it was her husband's duty to protect her until his dying day. Sir Kaian may have only been young but he was brave. Sir Byro Levanis had been his predecessor, an old knight of fifty when the gods saw fit to take him to the White City.

Sir Kaian pulled up his horse alongside the carriage. "We are nearing the border. The road ahead is harsh and unsettled. Would you prefer your horse, Your Highness? The sun would do you some good. The gods have blessed us with fine weather, a good omen."

"Or it is summer and, from what I recall, the sun always shines bright this time of year." A harsh voice cut off the young knight. It was Leylan. "Move along, good knight, I am sure the princess is in no need of your protection today. There is many a good warrior here willing to do their duty for our glorious soon-to-be queen."

His cocky arrogance immediately annoyed Tilia who wanted nothing more than to command Sir Kaian to cut him down where he stood. Leylan was her bastard brother, a man over thirty, but of his actual age no one knew. Her father had taken many mistresses over the years. Leylan's mother, however, had died before Tilia was old enough to remember her, yet the rumours said she was of Allamantyan blood. Leylan wasn't blessed with the natural good looks of her true brother Gabriel. Yet he had a way with words and a confidence which allowed some to be seduced by his charm and others to despise him. He was slim of face and body; his narrow shoulders didn't fit well within his breastplate. This was the first time Tilia could recall seeing her bastard brother in armour. He looked uncomfortable as he scratched beneath his breast plate. Thin brown hair was brushed back off his face. Leylan's yellow hawk-like eyes looked intensely at her; sometimes she could feel his hatred.

"My dear little sister, I hope you are well. This carriage isn't uncomfortable, is it? If your arse is sore, I don't mind rubbing it down for you." Leylan smiled, revealing a large set of white teeth. A sort of sinister smile that made her feel uncomfortable, like the ones he gave her as a child.

"Dishonour! You don't talk to the princess with vile remarks such as that." Sir Kaian, pulled hard on his blade and pointed it towards Leylan. The tip of the sword pressed against the bastard prince's chin, drawing blood. Leylan smiled at the young knight; no fear was shown. Tilia had never seen him show emotion, all he did was smile. A harsh tension filled the air; it made Tilia's stomach turn.

"Please, Kaian, put away your sword. It would be a bad omen to draw blood when the gods have blessed us with a day such as this." Tilia knew talk of the gods would ease the young knight's thirst for blood. Ever so obedient, Kaian put away his sword without hesitation.

"I wish my dog was as acquiescent as your man here. Maybe you can teach my hound your talent for being so feeble, sir knight." Leylan's arrogance was enough to rile anyone; he pressed his middle finger on his now-blooded chin. "My first scar, I will wear it with pride. My first taste of combat. Do you think the gods will think me brave?"

Tilia ignored her brother's remark. "Sir Kaian, I will be fine here. Thank you for your thoughts. I am grateful for your concern."

"As you wish, Your Highness, I won't stray far." Kaian pulled back on his reins, turning away from the carriage.

"Yes, young knight, don't run off too far. We don't want to lose a dog as talented as you." Leylan's never-ending smile stopped suddenly as the knight's back was turned. He then brought his attention back to his sister. "Dear Tilia, what a frightful start to the day." Leylan adjusted his breast plate. "These things are mightily uncomfortable; you would've thought the blacksmiths might make these so they don't rub the flesh. Us royalty are not meant for such things." He was always taking digs at the royal family. One would think her father had disowned him. No laws stated her father had to take in a bastard child and raise him his own, but he had.

"What do you want, Leylan? Isn't there some other unlucky person you can grace your presence with? I am not in the mood for you today." Tilia leant back into the carriage so she was out of sight. Before she had time to think, Leylan had flung himself from his horse and through the carriage door. He moved gracefully like a cat. He wasn't athletic in build but he was nimble and moved quickly, with agile and cunning.

"Your words cut deep, dear sister. One would think you have a dislike for me. I will struggle to sleep tonight knowing you will marry another man and that your thoughts of me are so cruel." Leylan twisted his neck to the left and then the right, cracking his bones as he made himself comfortable.

"Since when did you care of my marriage?" Tilia refused eye contact, always looking away.

"Tilia, how can you say that, when we were ever so close as children, the fun we used to have?" The comment made Tilia's blood run cold; a sickness hit her in the stomach. She turned to see that ever so spiteful smile, wide-grinned and menacing, but before she had time to reply, Leylan looked to their father with disgust. He was still fast asleep and snoring. "What a fine man our father is, the great Vincinicus, the wise, the conqueror, the ravager… So what do you think of your groom? I have heard many tales of Prince Andros. None of them were very flattering. Weak, spoilt, paranoid, indecisive, oh and rumour has it, his carnal pleasures are that of sin and unrighteousness in the eyes of the gods."

"That is what they are, rumours. Tales and small talk from his enemies and our sceptic philosophers who believe the old ways are the only way. Their pig-headedness leaves no path for change." Tilia didn't want to reply but she was compelled to, if she ignored him, he would soon leave but he had a way of always getting a response from her. She knew the tales of her soon-to-be husband but she never let anyone know how they frightened her.

"I wept for days when I learnt you were to marry such a fiend. Why would the gods allow a man blessed to rule the two greatest kingdoms in the world with such sin in his soul? I feel sorry for you, sister, I really do." Leylan looked at their father, who was still asleep, before leaning forwards towards Tilia, showing his teeth. "Don't you remember as children, when we were alone in your chambers, we would speak of love, family and marriage?" His hand touched her knee; it gave her a sense of fear and sickness. She quickly pushed him away.

Tilia quickly leant outside and shouted, "Sir Kaian, Leylan wishes to leave and wants to be escorted to the back of the column with the whores and stragglers."

In a flash, Sir Kaian was at the carriage entrance. To his left was her other sworn sword, Sir Dajax Feilos. A well-built man nearing his fortieth year, his face was covered by his helmet, only showing his brown beard. He couldn't speak, born a mute, but like Kaian was obedient.

Leylan smiled that ever so menacing smile as he sat up and opened the carriage door. His horse was still trotting alongside. "Oh, don't stop the carriage, I will be fine getting on my horse from here." His sarcastic tone was plain for everyone to hear. He leapt from the carriage onto his saddle with ease. "It has been a pleasure talking with you, dear sister. I hope to do it again soon before your marriage." He kicked his spurs into the horse and slowly trotted ahead.

"Wait, prince, the whores are the other way." Kaian pointed behind him as Dajax grabbed hold of Leylan's reins. "This heat must be confusing you; we will escort you all the way to the rear."

"How kind, my own personal escort. How royal I feel." Leylan smiled and pulled his reins away from Dajax as the two made their way to the back of the column. Kaian looked up at Tilia, and the two shared a smile before he rode off behind his sworn brother and Leylan.

Leylan's mention of marriage made Tilia think; she was never short of men calling for her hand. Flarian nobles had always offered their sons and gave great reasons why they should be chosen over the next suitor. Ludicrous bravado statements such as Gerhardt Linos stating his son, Evandinor, had killed a bear with only his hands; Cassius Jove that his son, Kanutus, had the genitalia of a horse, perfect for breeding strong sons and daughters. Then there were offers from Cato Balbus and Domiol Vude, with gifts of land and soldiers – two things she would have control of even without their fat cumbersome bodies on top of hers every night.

The list had gone on and on and, with her nearing her twenty-fifth birthday and still unwed, her father was in trouble and she knew it. Before long she would have no choice but to marry and to give birth to heirs. She had always wanted to marry for love but she knew it was unlikely. She had heard tales of people wishing they had been born into royalty but the dream was far from the reality; the common man or woman may not wear silks from Akesha or drink wines from Yorno but they married who they loved, not who their father chose.

At one point her father had almost chosen her cousin Lucian for marriage. The thought made her smile; the two had fooled around as teenagers. Heading out into the gardens, they had lots of fun kissing where no one could see. She now knew, though, he wasn't the man for her, plus he would never be faithful. She remembered him telling her she was the most beautiful girl he had ever seen; her beauty had stolen his heart. Later that same day he said the same words to her best friend, Helaina.

If they had married, he would stray from his marital vows and he wasn't as smart as he thought. Rumours would spread and eventually he would be executed for dishonouring the queen. The last thing she would want was for her dear immature cousin to be killed on her orders.

I wonder what Andros looks like? She thought to herself. *Are the tales true? Is he really that cruel and weak, or is he strong?* Soon she would find out. She had had many a sleepless night thinking of the day they would meet, but she knew it was the right thing to do, for her father, for her people and maybe in some way for herself too.

Loud coughing suddenly brought her back from her thoughts. Her father was finally waking. Sickening chokes came from her father's mouth; he always woke like this. He raised his right hand to cover his lips and his left held his belly. He was clearly in pain. Sadness came over Tilia; she hated seeing her father like this.

"Father please, let me call for the wise men, they can help you." Tilia moved along the seats closer to her father.

"Don't fret over me, child, I am fine. I have fought more battles than the years you have been alive. I can handle a little illness." Vincinicus wiped away the phlegm from his mouth with a cloth. Tilia saw it was stained with blood, thick and nearly black in colour. She had first noticed it five days ago; his coughing fits would come and go but now they were more intense and it was clear he was in agony. He quickly put the cloth in his pocket as if Tilia could not see.

****

Gabriel sat and watched a soft breeze blow against the sands. A swirl of gold sand surrounded the hooves of his pearl white steed. Seeing his bastard brother climb into the royal carriage had made his blood boil and his muscles tighten. He knew his sister felt uneasy around Leylan. "Sewer snake," he and his cousins had named him for he was always lurking beneath the crypts of Verdina as a child.

His uncle, Prince Damidar, commander of the royal guard, had taught him to think before reacting; he found it hard but he was learning. His heart thumped and his hands trembled as the golden swirl of sand and encircled him faster and faster; only did it ease when he saw Leylan escorted to the rear. He hated the sewer snake, a deep hate; he wasn't his true brother. Lassander and Lucian were more like brothers to him. *It is said Allamantyan blood runs through his veins, he cannot be trusted.*

Once he had calmed, he sat peacefully watching the royal column rode by, admiring the view. He always loved watching soldiers on the march. He could see how few they were, such a small force to be entering enemy territory. His father claimed the main army must stay behind to defend against Etorion invasion, yet what of the battalions of Delloria? He refused to even acknowledge them.

Suddenly he realised he was nearing the back of the column. His men liked to see Gabriel at the front, leading them, inspiring them. It was an image he loved; he hated those lords and kings who sat and watched as others rode into battle. He swore to his men he would never ask them to do anything he wouldn't do himself. He turned his horse and headed to the front, to be back beside his cousins.

It had been nearly an hour since Gabriel had resumed his place at the front of the column. Everyone was beginning to tire from the sores from sitting on those thick leather saddles, the heat on their skin and weight of the armour on their bodies. His father had given orders that they didn't stop until they reached the end of the Rylor Valley, then they made camp in the land of their *old enemy*. Gabriel stopped suddenly, pulling hard on his reins, forcing the soldiers behind him to ride around. A cold shiver ran up his spine like a winter chill; deep into his bones he felt it.

Lassander pulled his horse up alongside him. "Gabriel, are you okay? What is wrong?"

The prince looked out in front of him; what was over this mountain pass was forbidden. A truce was made twenty-five years ago after the Battle at Falentis. No man from Valanor or Allamantya would step over these mountains. If so, it was treason; the penalty was death, even for a prince. He had been here hundreds of times as a child. Some days he, Lassander and Lucian would ride to the border and tell tales of what each believed was out there. Giants, demons, monsters and every foul creature the mind could conjure.

Some nights he came alone, to play out his dream, the one he dreamt every night. The great warrior prince who did what no king or queen before him could do: conquer the great realm of Allamantya, sworn enemy of Valanor. He had seen it a thousand times, standing on the crumbling castle ramparts, broken rocks beneath his feet. Hundreds of his enemies had fallen to his blade, as he raised his country's flag high in the air. His name was to live forever on the lips of the mortal man, yet he wasn't happy; something was missing, a deep sadness filled his heart with a pain worse than death. He didn't know what it was but it scared him.

Finally, Gabriel replied, "We are doing what we said we would, all those years ago." He smiled. "Heading south, into the unknown." He kicked his spurs into his horse and took that first step. The furthest he had ever been away from home.

The Falentispass was harsh and unrelenting. Red sand embankments covered the pass on either side, large stone rocks formed perfect hiding spots for an ambush. It was an uneasy time for everyone as they rode through. Soldiers and horses alike were restless, the slightest movement from the loose rocks above caused horses to stir and soldiers to panic and look up, expecting the worse, to see the *old enemy* clad in green and red, swords in hand to deal them all the death blow.

They were all in unknown territory; no one really knew what lay ahead. Even the most experienced of Valorian knights had never used this path before. Usually it was heavily guarded but they had passed adisused barracks a few miles back, a small fort that, due to its location, could repel an entire army. All they found was wood and stone, the gate to the fort had been pulled down and, as King Aristian had promised them, no soldier was found inside. Gabriel had found it an eerie place. Ramparts that once held men were bare, the drill square was silent, the only noise was of the marching of feet on sand and the light sound of the valley breeze.

"It's so hot; my balls feel like they are on fire." Lucian removed his helmet to reveal his pale face and long blonde hair. His once shining hair was now dark and wet. When it was cold, he called for heat, and when it was summer, he wanted it to cool down. "I cannot wait for a glass of cool wine when we make camp." Just the thought made Lucian's mouth feel as dry as the sand beneath his horse's hooves.

"It mustn't be long till we are out of this cursed valley," Lassander replied, putting his fingers on his throat, imagining the wine his brother had just mentioned.

Lucian turned to the soldiers behind them and shouted, "When we make camp, boys, the wine is on me!" The soldiers all let out a cheer and raised their spears to the sky.

"Brother, the wine is free," Lassander replied, smiling at Lucian.

"I know that, but they don't," he said with a huge grin on his face.

Sweat was dripping down Gabriel's face, tiny beads slowly running over his well-defined cheeks. With his forearm he wiped them. "There will be no drinking tonight; we don't know what to expect in the morning but if all goes well, we will have all the wine we wish for at the pre-wedding feast." He looked high into the sky, admiring the great vastness above him. It was a crystal blue ocean, never ending, not a cloud in sight.

"Those Antilion boy lovers best not kick up a fuss. I would rather drink wine and bed their women than fight." Lucian was looking the worse for wear, his arms were bright red where the hot sun had burnt his skin.

"You sound like you want to be their friends; a change of tone from earlier on." Lassander gave his brother a little smile.

"Listen, who wants to fight in heat like this? All wars should be cancelled in the summer; the heat is for sitting in the sun, getting pissed on fine wines, while watching the beautiful ladies walk by." Lucian closed his eyes and began to wipe the sweat away from them.

Gabriel looked up to see a single rider sat alone on the embankment ahead. He was no more than twenty metres away; he wasn't a knight that was for sure, he wore no armour. He was atop a large black war horse; behind was a smaller black horse which had a large chest and saddle bangs draped over it. He wore a white poplin tunic that had a faux leather shoulder strap; the tunic came down as far as his deltoid on his right arm and revealed all of his left shoulder. His large, muscular arms were ripe with veins that stood out on his biceps like small winding rivers. Around his waist he had a wide brown faux leather belt which had decorative gold-tone studs.

His hair was thick, jet black, brushed away from his face and shaved short on the sides. He wore no coat of arms; he just sat watching unwavering like a statue. A sword was hung across his back; it immediately caught Gabriel's attention. He knew this man was a fierce warrior. He could feel it in his bones.

"Look, an Allamantyan knight, a spy; they have come to see what we bring with us; do we prepare for an attack?" Lucian pointed out in front towards the unknown rider.

"He could be a scout, seeing our progress, not one planning an ambush," Lassander replied.

"He is no scout and he is no knight. I don't know what he is, but he is of no concern for us now. He has a pack horse, he isn't going anywhere in a hurry." Gabriel was still looking up at the man as he replied. He felt like they would meet again but he didn't know why.

"I am going to see what our new friend wants." Lucian quickly pulled his horse away from Gabriel and Lassander, but before they had time to reply, the rider kicked into his horse and rode out of sight down the embankment.

Lassander started to laugh. "Just seeing you, brother, made him think he was about to visit the White City." Lucian, too, joined in with his brother and began to laugh.

Gabriel, though, didn't even grin; he just thought to himself and wondered. Life would never be the same. For better or for worse, he didn't know, but everything they had known was going to change forever.

Chapter 3
A Girl of Emerald Green

Region of Oalandrium
City of Tomellburg, north eastern Allamantya

"Griffin! Griffin!" Danaka yelled from her porch. It was early morning and the hot sun was beginning to rise. "Where are you, boy? Come here." She did this every morning; she would wake as the sun rose, call to her most loyal friend, Griffin, and begin her work. For hours she would plant the seeds and gather in her wheat and vegetables. Most of what she grew, she ate, but some she would need to sell at the town market; she hated going there.

"There you are, good boy, good boy." Danaka dropped to her knees as she saw Griffin running at full pace towards her. He was big and strong with long thick sable and white hair; the tanned part of his fur looked almost golden in colour. Griffin jumped up at her as he always did. She wrapped her hands around his large face as he began to try and lick her cheeks. He was a tall dog, the breed she never knew. She had thought he was part sand lion but her aunt had always rebuffed those claims. Danaka had found him as a stray when he was a puppy in her garden. He had been her closest companion for the past five years.

Danaka was young, only nineteen, but she lived alone. She was slim and athletic, maybe that came from all the physical work she had to do. Her clothes, she made herself; her Aunt Heidi had taught her everything she knew. She chose to wear a long thin brown dress today, not very appealing on the eye but it was perfect for this summer heat and her work. It allowed her to move freely and it didn't cling to her body too much. It did, however, have a tear down the left side, revealing her skin, but she had no one to impress so it didn't bother her. It was her eyes, however, that glowed like emeralds. A beautiful green that twinkled in the summer sun; warmth shone from inside of them, a beam of both innocence and sadness.

Danaka stood up as Griffin continued to jump up at her excitedly; she pulled back her sandy blonde hair and tied it up in a bun. She had a pretty face but it was usually covered in dirt so it wasn't the most obvious kind of beauty.

"Come on, eat your food." Danaka pushed the bowl of meat and water towards her friend, who began to wallop it all down in one go. She smiled. *You would think he hasn't eaten for days.*

Stepping down from her porch, she looked out onto the little bit of land she owned. Well, what had become her land when her aunt died nearly a year ago. She had two eight-metre vegetable patches that ran parallel to each other with a strip of grass in between them, leading to her wheat field which was near enough fifty metres in length.

Looking behind her, she admired her home, a small wooden cabin which her Uncle Otis had built himself nearly twenty years ago. It was only a single floor home which had two bedrooms, a small kitchen and a living area. It was very cosy in the winter months, sitting by the log fire. The only entrance was a small red door, flanked by two hanging baskets with bright, blossoming flowers of all sorts of colours bursting free: blues, pinks and oranges. The location of her home was perfect; it was just on the outskirts of Tomellburg, a decent sized town which was rich in trade. She wasn't too close to hear all the noise of the locals but not too far away to travel in when she needed privations or to sell her crops. The main entrance to the village was visible from her porch; many people would pass by her house, she saw all sorts: traders, knights, squires, lords and even whores sometimes, although they never lasted long before they were driven out. Tomellburg was a very religious town; its lord, Franco Tomell, had allied himself with the religious group, the Guardians of Thelonia. In return, those knights guarded Tomellburg and spread the faith of Ollaria'h with an iron fist.

It was then she noticed it, the word she hated more than anything. *WITCH!* It had been painted in blood which dripped down the dried wood of her home. Danaka and her family had never been the most popular people in Tomellburg; it had been a couple of months since they'd done this, Danaka had hoped the drunken locals would've given up by now.

"Bastards!" she angrily screamed out. Griffin responded with a growl; he could always sense her emotions. "I don't have time to clean that off now. I will do it later, after my work is done." She picked up her sack and sickle and headed towards her wheat field. She enjoyed having Griffin around, as at least she had someone to talk to, even if he never replied.

Her work was hard. Even if she had been born a man it wouldn't have been easy. Harvesting the wheat she would sell at the market took its toll; she had been on her hands and knees filling her sacks for nearly two hours now. She was exhausted and her body begged for rest. She still had to take all her sacks into town which was no simple task, especially as she owned no horses.

Danaka slowly stood up and stretched out her back, which was beginning to stiffen and ache, before wiping the sweat from her brow. The summer heat was getting to her; the rays that burst from the sky were like spears of fire, burning into her flesh. She slowly trudged over to the well and pulled up the bucket. Even doing that, which she did every day, was hard work; her muscles began to ache. She plunged her cup into the cool clear water and gulped it down. It wasn't very ladylike as the water ran all down her face but she didn't care.

"Pretty, pretty, come here to Walter," a loud, slobbering voice bellowed from behind her. Before she had time to react, she felt a hand squeeze hard on her bum. Danaka quickly spun round and pushed him away. She had more strength than she gave herself credit for and he stumbled back.

"What do you think you are doing? Get away from me. What would your wife say if I told her you were here again?" Griffin started to growl; he was up, alert and tense. He revealed large sharp white teeth; he never liked strangers and he had cause not to. Danaka quickly began to pat his head, trying to calm him. She knew Griffin would tear him limb from limb, something that would only make her situation in Tomellburg even more difficult.

"You wouldn't do that to me, witch." Spit flew from Walter's mouth, he clearly had been drinking. He must've been at the town's festivities last night; they were celebrating the union of the two kingdoms. Something she had no interest in.

Walter wore a red tunic that was undone down the middle which revealed a dirty white shirt covered in red stains. His skinny face was not easy on the eyes; he had a wart on his chin and had two front teeth missing where, rumour had it, his wife beat him up for sleeping with one of those passing whores who never lasted long in town.

"Get off my land!" Danaka replied angrily. Griffin stepped forward, growling louder.

"All I want is you to be nice to me." He stumbled forward, just about keeping his balance. The stench of alcohol and sweat made Danaka's stomach twist with a deep sickness.

"You young whores are all the same, cock teasers, showing your flesh, urging us on." He ran his saliva-drenched tongue over his lips as he stared down at Danaka's breasts; one was partly on show as her dress was so loose.

Danaka quickly realised and covered herself. "If you don't leave, I will tell Lord Franco; you know he will have you banished to Isle of Dread." She turned and quickly started to walk away.

"Everyone knows what you did with Terrence's son!" Walter shouted.

Danaka stopped, frowning. He was on about Jorian. He was a skinny boy, who had ginger hair upstairs and down; she remembered that had made her giggle. That was four years ago, nearly five in fact. Jorian's mother caught them in her barn. She had her son sent away because of it, so Danaka's sinful ways couldn't lead him from the path of purity.

"That was years ago and nothing happened, not that it is any of your business." Danaka turned around to face him; she didn't want to give him an answer but she was very opinionated, and she had to have the last word.

Walter stumbled towards her. "Lies, don't tease, show me what you did with that pretty mouth of yours." He ran his finger over her lips before pulling her hand towards his cock. She could feel it was hard; it sent a gut-wrenching sickness to her stomach. She stepped back and shoved him to the floor. Walter hit the ground with an almighty thud. Dirt sprayed out from around his body, most of it stuck in his hair, well, what little hair he had. He sat up quickly, as if the fall had sobered him instantly. He clambered to his feet, his eyes cold and sinister. Suddenly Walter stopped. A beautiful tune played out, whistling softly but deadly.

Danaka turned, following the music, towards the dirt path that ran next to her home. There was the finest horse she had ever seen, a beautiful thing, as black as night. It was tall and powerful and its muscular frame gleamed in the sunlight.

On top of the horse was a man, one she had never seen before. He had deep dark tired eyes, jet black hair pulled back and a strong jaw which sprouted dark stubble. A white poplin tunic was all he wore, which revealed his entire left shoulder and covered half of his right arm. The only decoration was a faux leather shoulder strap. The white of the tunic showed the dirt and sand of a long journey. On his back he carried a large sword. Behind him was a smaller black horse, which carried two large wooden chests and numerous saddle packs. Danaka felt sorry for the smaller horse, it must've been hard for it to carry all that weight in this heat.

The rider was blowing softly into his pan flute. The haunting tune played over and over. Walter was scared, she could feel it. He spat at Danaka's feet and walked off, holding his head. He would have a bad headache in a few hours, and he deserved it. Griffin suddenly started to growl and this time moved towards the stranger, arching his back as if he was ready to strike.

"Stop, boy, it's okay," Danaka said. As she stroked Griffin's head, his barks fell silent.

The man lowered his flute then kicked into his spurs and headed for town. He never turned back. Danaka stood there for a while, watching him ride away until he disappeared into town. It had felt like an age that she and he had been looking at one another, but in reality, it had only been a few seconds. *He must be here for the market.*

That incident with Walter hadn't scared her; she had many run-ins with lonely desperate men who thought that, as she was young, they could have their way with her. It was her Uncle Otis who was always there to protect her, but now he was gone, she was alone. The stranger looked fierce, more fierce than Walter or any of those other men. If he had wanted to take her, she knew she wouldn't have been able to fight him off, but she never felt in any danger; he didn't look like he was in need of a woman's company, maybe more in need of a soft bed.

At noon everyday Danaka went to the graves of her aunt and uncle. They had been a poor family so the headstones were simple rocks with engravings carved into them. She would sit there with Griffin and water the pink and white flowers she had planted around the headstones. Sometimes she would sit in silence and other times she would talk. Today she spoke.

"Heidi, why am I still here? There is nothing for me in this town. All I have is this land and our home. Yours and Uncle Otis's home; he made this with his own hands for you as a wedding present." Danaka was feeling down. She sat running her fingers through Griffin's thick sable coat. "I can't just pack up and leave, where would I go?"

Death is easy for the person who's dying, but hard for the ones left behind. Those were the words Heidi had told Danaka when she was dying of cold fever. She couldn't have been more right. Her aunt had been distraught when Uncle Otis had died – he had been rebuilding the roof when he fell and hit his head. Not even her knowledge of healing could save him. However, when she was bedridden, she seemed happy; maybe because she thought she would see her husband again.

It was bad enough for Danaka when her uncle had died, but when her aunt left her, she felt completely alone, with no one to turn to when she needed advice or comfort. The house was silent. She had always wanted her own space but now she had it, it was too quiet; you could hear the sound of a pin drop, the creaking of the floorboards and the rustle of the wind outside.

Her aunt had taught her so much; how to make clothes, how to cook and, most important of all, the art of healing which most people in Tomellburg thought was witchcraft and sorcery. The locals believed in the old ways, the teachings from the book of Pure Souls by Elbar Jefferson. His main source of healing came from bleeding out the impure sins and eternal prayer.

"Griffin, come boy. We need to get to town; we can't sit here all day." Danaka turned to Griffin who replied with a growl of disapproval. "Hey, I don't like going there as much as you, but how else am I going to buy goods, unless you fancy going for me?" Griffin tilted his head; a look of confusion spread across his handsome face. Danaka smiled as she looked back into his deep dark eyes.

With her big empty cart behind her, Danaka slumped into town. Griffin, as always, was only a few paces behind. The sound of the squeaky wheels had been annoying her as she drudged along the dirt path towards the town gates, at least now the noise of the town would block them out.

Walking through the gates, the noise hit her hard, like a gush of wind to the face. Laughing, shouting, swearing, everything you could imagine from a bustling market place. The market was on a long slope with stalls either side that ran parallel to one other. They would eventually lead to the large open square, where there were taverns and inns, and where legal matters such as trials and executions would take place. The stalls would sell all sorts of items, from swords and shields to fruits and vegetables. There were also hand sewn clothes which they claimed came from Akesha, which was part of the Eastern Isles, but that was a lie and she knew it. They looked no better than the ones her aunt would make for her.

Danaka tried her best to pull along her cart through the busy crowds but it was no easy task. People would knock into her and not even utter a single word of an apology. Foreign traders from the Eastern Isles of Yorno, Akesha and Brundea were very common in Tomellburg. Its location, near to the northern Allamantyan port of Yorken, meant it was the first place for anyone to settle if they were allowed to leave their ships.

As she struggled up the pebbled slope, the smells of sweat, wine and food were overpowering. At times she struggled to hold her breath but she kept on going. The muscles in her legs began to burn. The rays from the sun reflected off clear grey pebbles in front of her. Danaka could feel the beads of perspiration running down her cheek. Up ahead she could see a Yornish man pacing towards her. He was large, overweight, with dark brown skin. He wore tatty leather trousers, no shirt and he had more hair on his chest than she did on her head. Danaka knew he wasn't going to move for her and she was right as he bashed right into her side. The impact of his weight shook her entire body, taking her breath away. The Yornish man didn't even look back; all he did was shout some obscenities to his kin folk who were working on his wine stall. Griffin, though, snarled and growled.

"Come on boy, we have no time for arguments. I want to be out of here as soon as possible." Danaka turned to Griffin who, in response, jumped into the cart and lay down. "Ah great, so now I have to pull you along, too. You aren't light you know." She smiled to herself.

She could feel her shoulders were now starting to ache; her muscles were burning. *At least going home, it is all downhill.* Each push was harder than the last. She remembered why she rarely came into town – not only did the people annoy her but it was bloody hard work too.

"Danaka, Danaka, come, come see what I have today!" A loud, bubbly voice with a distinctive accent caught her attention. She turned to her right to see Irban, a pottery salesman from Akesha. He was small and slim; he had black hair that was receding at the front and light brown skin. His dark eyes were always warm and friendly. "Please, look, this one came in this morning." He lifted up a beautiful pot. It was cream with bright purple decoration, and it had an Akeshan lion on the front which reminded her of Griffin.

"Irban, it is beautiful." Danaka pulled her cart out of the walkway and towards Irban's stall. She took it from him with both hands and admired its beauty. She could tell it was good quality, heavy and strong. Danaka loved decorating her garden with pots and flowers. "I cannot afford it though, but maybe one day." She placed it back down on his stall which was covered in all sorts of pots and clay statues; some were of knights, animals and even of King Aristian himself.

"No, it is a gift. Please, you take it." Irban leant forward and placed the pot back in Danaka's hands.

"A gift? For me, why?" She was confused. Wasn't often she was offered something for free; usually there was a catch of some sort.

"Your aunt, bless her soul. She save my baby when she caught the red fever." He placed his hands on his heart. "Please, you will take." He pointed towards the pot.

Danaka remembered clearly, as if it was yesterday. Irban and his wife, Azra, had arrived at their house begging for help when the wise men's prayers had done nothing for their daughter. She was a tiny thing, innocent and sweet. She had beautiful brown eyes but her skin looked as if it had begun to boil; it had bubbled up from her neck to her toes. The skin had turned as red as blood and the slightest touch was followed by screams of pain.

Her aunt Heidi, though, she knew what to do. Danaka had caught the disease herself as a baby, not that she remembered any of it. Heidi had placed the baby in a cool cloth and rubbed moss, lavender oil and salt gently over the skin. This was followed by allowing the baby to breath in the sweet Sandalwood incense Heidi regularly burned to cleanse the soul. The same procedure would follow for the next five days until the skin began to cool and loosen.

"That was nearly two years ago, a long time, Irban."

“I had to pay. This was made back in my village. Takes a long time to get message back home. Little token for your aunt’s kindness to my family.”

Danaka smiled and took the pot. She wrapped it in some cloth and placed it beside Griffin who decided to sniff all around it. *Maybe everyone here isn’t so bad after all,* she thought to herself as she made her way up the last part of the slope. *Still, this isn’t the place I want to spend the rest of my days.*

The top of the market slope opened onto a large square, with taverns and inns all around. The open space made Danaka breathe in a big gulp of fresh clean air. It was very claustrophobic walking through that crowded market. The floor was laid with bright white clear slabs, with a large fountain at the centre. The water sprayed out from between two large sand lions who were clawing at each other; the lion’s manes were large and their teeth fierce. The water looked cool and clear; it was refreshing just to look at. It made Danaka’s throat feel as dry as the dusty path between her home and Tomellburg. Two small Akeshan children, wearing nothing but their birthday clothes, climbed all over the two lions, allowing the water to soak them through. They looked like they were having a lot of fun as they screamed and laughed together. Danaka couldn’t remember a time when she had been so happy.

Directly beyond the fountain stood the council building which was also home to Lord Franco Tomell, the governor of Tomellburg. His family had ruled this city for as far back as the record books went, even before the great divide of the two kingdoms.

Lots of shouting and laughter brought Danaka back from her thoughts. To her right she could see a tavern wench bringing a large flagon of ale to a group of men who were sitting around a table enjoying the summer sun. In front she could see four men on horseback; they were part of the religious order known as Guardians of Thelonia, a militant group who swore their souls to Ollaria’h. Danaka thought their beliefs bordered on lunacy but she was smart to keep her thoughts to herself. The Guardians had many people burnt at the stake for their blasphemy. The knights’ glistening white armour sparkled like jewels; the carving of a sun flocked by three doves decorated the centre of their breast plates. Her aunt said their sigil was a reference to the three doves of the Ollarium angel, Thelonia. Even with their faces covered by full face helms, they looked fierce. The four men didn’t even give her a second glance as they rode by.

Just as Danaka headed towards the local store, something caught her attention. It was her mystery man, the stranger she had seen earlier that day on horseback. He was wearing the same dirty white poplin tunic as before, and his sword was still strapped across his back. He had dismounted and was talking to the local store owner, Harad Joyn. She felt a hint of embarrassment as she walked towards them.

Do I thank him? Do I say nothing at all? She slowly trudged towards them. Her heart rate started to increase, thumping inside her chest like a little drum. She didn’t know why she felt so nervous; her palms began to feel sweaty as they tightly gripped the handles of her cart. She never normally felt like this; maybe it was because no one had really done anything to help her before. Well, not that this man had actually helped her. *Maybe he doesn't deserve any thanks.*

The man looked a lot bigger than Harad. Not that it was hard to look bigger than Harad, who was nearing forty and barely pushing five feet. As she got closer, she noticed her mystery man's back was broad and the muscles in his arms and legs were defined, just like those of his horse. A fine match they must be together. Harad was handing him a flagon of ale, some bread and meat. She watched the stranger place the bread and meat inside one of his saddle bags and turn away.

"Thank you, sir knight, for earlier... I..." Danaka blurted out. She even noticed a bit of spit fly out of her mouth and land on the bigger of his two horses. *Oh shit, now I've done it, Danaka, you fool.*

"I am no knight, little girl," he replied in a stern tone. His voice was deep and powerful. It sounded like an echo in a dark empty cave. Before Danaka had time to utter another word, he had pulled his horses past her and his back was turned.

"He isn't very talkative, that one," Harad interrupted, without even looking up from his palm as he counted the coins in his little hand.

"Who is he?" Danaka watched the man walk by.

"Just a man. Maybe a soldier, an explorer, a mercenary. Who knows and who cares? Long as he pays me, that is all that matters. He was looking for someone – Claris or was it Clarence? Look, this coin is from Dagen." He held it out in front of him and towards Danaka's face. The coin was red and worn, showing two small daggers instead of the traditional Allamantyan currency which showed the face of the king.

All Harad cared about was profit. He collected coins from all over. With all the money he made, you would think he could at least pay for a bath. He smelt of sweat; it was dry and hot. He was a plump looking man, with long greasy grey hair that fell to his shoulders. His white tunic was wringing wet, patches formed under his short thick hairy arms and around his neck. Not the type of man you would want to buy food from, but he had the best stock in the village.

"I want three bags of seed, a sack of flour and some cheese." She reached into her dress to find her coins.

"Wait here and I'll get the things you ask for." Harad turned without ever really looking at Danaka and headed back into his store. It was a small building, made from wood, with a small stall located outside which sold various fruit and vegetables. The rich shiny bright colours enticed Danaka; for a moment she even considered putting one of those thick dark red apples down her dress.

Loud sickening screams of panic filled Danaka's ears which took her thoughts away from the possibility of becoming a thief. She turned around to see a large overweight woman dressed in a plain pale blue dress with a white gravy stained apron over the top. In her arms she held a small child before she collapsed to her knees in the middle of the square.

Without a second's thought, Danaka let go of her cart and sprinted towards the woman and her child. Like a cat, she took off, with Griffin, as always, close by. As she drew closer, crowds of people began to form around the woman and her child. She forced her way through the group of people, using all her strength to fight her way to the front.

"Help me, someone do something!" The woman screamed before dropping down beside her child. She looked up helplessly.

"Move! Give me some space!" Danaka yelled as she pushed through the crowd. Using strength she never knew she had, she thumped her palms into a large man's chest, knocking him back. She turned to see the child was a young boy, of maybe four or five years of age. He was laid stricken on the white slabbed floor; he was small with thin brown scruffy hair. His eyes were closed and he looked as if he was sleeping.

"What happened to him?" Danaka asked as she knelt down beside the boy.

"He just collapsed… he fell… he won't wake up… he… he…" The woman was sobbing and it was becoming hard to make out what she was saying. The skin on the back of her huge arms flapped back and forth as she cried into her hands.

Suddenly the boy's legs and arms began to violently jerk and convulse with alarming speed and strength. His head started to shake uncontrollably and he lost control of his bladder, urinating all over himself and the floor.

"The devil sickness!" Someone shouted from the crowd. Panic and fear spread through them like wildfire, as they all clambered back as if the boy was riddled with plague.

"No! Help him, someone please!" The woman screamed as she began to sob hysterically.

Danaka stepped back away from the boy as he lashed out with his arms and legs. His mother frantically tried to pin her son's arms down as he continued to spasm with shocking strength for his size.

"Stop, don't touch him!" Danaka frantically called as she tried to pull the mother away from her child. During the commotion, the boy's fist caught his mother directly in the face, bloodying her nose.

"Get your hands off me, witch," the woman yelled as she smacked Danaka across her cheek with an all mighty thud. The woman's large rock-like fist crashed into her face like a hammer, knocking her back. Bells rang out in her ears as she struggled to comprehend what had just happened.

"What is going on here?!" A loud booming voice shouted as four soldiers on horseback came bursting through the crowd. Their large powerful horses crashed into people with violent intent. Cries of panic and chaos ensued as the crowd quickly disbanded.

During the commotion, Danaka scrambled to cover the boy, who by now had stopped shaking but had begun to choke on thick white foam that was falling from his mouth. She was able to pull the boy onto his side and open his airway.

"Get off him!" the woman screamed as she pushed Danaka off her son and to the floor. The weight and force of the blow took her breath away.

"Don't touch my son, witch!" a very familiar and unfriendly voice yelled into her ear. Danaka looked up to see Walter who was looking as rough as he looked earlier that morning. She could still smell the stench of alcohol spewing out of his skin. He was still wearing the same red tunic except his white shirt had a few extra wine stains. Suddenly the boy began to wake as he groggily called for his mother.

"Keep that witch away; she has taken away his affliction with her touch of the devil!" Walter's wife shouted as she scooped up the boy in her arms and began to wobble away. Her huge calves, plagued by thick discoloured veins, looked more like tree stumps than legs.

"If you have cursed my boy, I swear by the gods of Ollaria'h I will come for you!" Walter furiously pointed at Danaka as she still lay dazed and confused on the floor.

The day had been long and eventful but thankfully it had drawn to a close. Danaka was finally back home and kneeling on her bed. The hot blaring sun had vanished over the horizon and all that was left was the dark sky and those stars gleaming ever so beautifully from up above. She sat and looked out of her window and admired them. *I wonder if they are really fallen heroes as the holy ones say…? Sounds more like bullshit to me.*

Outside in the moonlight, she could just about make out Griffin as he lay fast asleep on her porch, his big sable coat moving ever so gently as he breathed in and out. She smiled to herself as she looked at him; he was so calm and peaceful.

"Good night, Griffin, sweet dreams." Danaka stretched out and laid back; her aching muscles felt tender as she felt herself moulding slowly into her soft bed. She felt a bruise on her left arm and her face was beginning to swell as if she was hiding grapes in her mouth. *No wonder Walter has no teeth, that woman has the power of an ox!* Danaka ran her hand over her cheek.

Her eyelids were becoming heavier and heavier, as if she had been inhaling her aunt's Sandalwood. As she drifted off, she imagined that man from earlier. *What was his name? What was he doing in a town like this? Maybe tomorrow I will see him again… maybe… maybe…*

Crashing and banging, followed by shouting, suddenly woke her from her sleep. Danaka stirred, still semi-conscious, her heavy eyelids struggling to open. Griffin's violent barks and a man screaming in pain woke her fully. Before she had time to react, a strong cold fist grabbed hold of her hair and yanked her head forwards. Some of her hair snapped as it was pulled from her scalp.

"Get up, witch, sorceress!" a male voice screamed violently into her ear. He dragged her from her bed and she landed with an almighty bang. Her face smashed against the hard, wooden floor. Her attacker was clad in pure white mail and glistening armour; his face was a blur but his breath was hot and dry.

"Sir Tomas, don't let her touch you!" Another soldier stood in the doorway, his voice carried concern for his comrade.

"I won't let this bitch curse me. Thelonia watches over me." Sir Tomas laughed as he forced Danaka to her feet. She was then dragged to the door by her hair. Her head forced forwards and her arms violently pulled upwards behind her back. Her muscles stretched and it felt as though her arms were about to pop.

"What have I done?" Danaka pleaded as she was being constrained and pushed outside.

There she could see three Guardians of Thelonia on horseback, all dressed identical in suits of shining white. Each carried a large round shield and a spear in the other hand. A fourth man, however, was on his knees, clutching his arm, frantically trying to stop the flow of blood which was seeping from his wound.

Danaka, however, couldn't see her loyal companion. "Where's Griffin? Griffin! Griffin! What have you done to him?" Her screams were filled with panic.

Her words were cut off when a violent powerful sickening punch hit her in the gut. The impact instantly took away her breath away and made her choke and splutter. She hopelessly gasped for air. She suddenly felt her head jerked back as Tomas pulled violently on her hair. She could feel his hot breath on her neck.

"You don't ask questions; you're going to jail." Tomas paused slightly as he grinned, revealing brown and rotting teeth. "And tomorrow you will burn."

Chapter 4
Show Me Gold and I'll Give You Blood

Region of Kathoros, eastern Allamantya
Oceansong seaport at Baron's Bay

"Ale, more ale!" Toran boomed as he banged his huge fists on the table. It shuddered under his weight, knocking all the empty clay cups over as if the ground was shaking beneath him.

"Calm down, this is your fourth already. You need to be fit and strong for later," Rhodesha seductively replied. She stood over him and ran her fingertips across his well sculptured jaw line. She then pinched his cheeks together and planted a kiss on his lips.

Toran took Rhodesha by her hips and hoisted her upwards; she in turn wrapped her legs around his waist, squeezing tightly. Rhodesha always felt safe with her man so close. She ran her tongue over his lips and into his mouth; feeling his lips pressed against hers gave Rhodesha a sense of excitement that no man had given her before.

The tavern was full and packed to the rim. Thick wooden beams were visible under the ceiling; they were finely structured giving the building an impressive and warm appeal. Laughter and sin filled the room, just how Rhodesha liked it. It was a lot like back home in Dagen.

Rhodesha breathed deeply, taking in the rich smells of the hickory smoke from the fire, ale and sweat. The ground floor was large, filled with wooden tables and stools, each with large groups of drunken men gulping down their ale. Men showed off with acts of bravado, arm wrestling or games of dice. From across the room came screams of ecstasy as brigands fucked the local working girls where they stood, whether it be over tables, the open stairways or even the floor. Some men only stopped their rampant thrusting to order ale or food.

Eastport, Stormfury and Oceansong were the three small seaports that made up Baron's Bay. The Bay was also known as the Bay of Sin, a name it duly lived up to. Men and women came here to be free, to drink and delve into their wildest desires. The holy men claimed the gods of Ollaria'h had forsaken this land, leaving devils and sin to wash up on these eastern shores.

The screams of ecstasy grew louder, driving both men and women crazy with lust. Hands beat upon the tables and feet stomped, ale and blood red wine flew into the air as men roared and women screamed. The sin that surrounded Rhodesha only fuelled her excitement; she was as wild as they came. She kissed Toran, running her hands around the ginger stubble that littered his jaw line. His large rough hands began to slide up her short leather skirt and around her athletic buttocks. She felt him squeeze tightly.

"Excuse me sir, your ale," a soft quiet voice interrupted. It was a surprise they heard it with the chaos that surrounded them.

Toran adjusted himself, holding Rhodesha up with just his one arm, like a child. A young girl of only twelve stood in tatty brown leather and a white apron with what looked like gravy stains down the front. Her dull russet hair was pulled back, revealing her pale and innocent face. He grabbed the flagon of ale off her and took a huge gulp. Half of it ran down his chin and onto the floor. He reached down and pulled out two small bags of coins and placed them in the hands of the small girl.

"Keep the ale coming all night, child."

"Sir, this is too much."

"My name is Toran, the Iron Bull of Dagen!" He beat his mighty hand upon his chest. "I am no sir. The second bag is for you, but I expect the best." He smiled revealing his sparkling golden tooth.

Toran's kindness to children was what Rhodesha loved the most. This was a huge powerful man, a warrior, a killer of hundreds, but he had love in his heart for children. She instantly began kissing him again running her lips around his chin, licking up the bitter tasting ale.

The Iron Bull stood near six feet and six inches, and was built of pure muscle. His hair was short, almost cut down to his scalp, and he always wore a black thick leather vest which revealed his large arms, which looked more like legs. Rhodesha ran her hands over them and around his biceps. He felt as hard as a castle wall and just as strong.

"Excuse me, my lady, are you from the Eastern Isles?" the girl innocently asked as she looked up at Rhodesha, who in turn looked back and smiled.

"No child, I was born in Etoria. My homeland is many miles north of the Eastern Isles." Rhodesha knew why she would ask such a question. Her skin was as dark and as beautiful as night, not common around these parts. Only people with Etorion blood had skin so dark. Her hair consisted of long plaits that fell past her shoulders and were decorated with gold rings. She was bound to draw attention; Rhodesha had expressed that concern to Garroway the night before they set sail.

Baron's Bay was a small eastern Allamantyan sea port; it was not large or as well monitored as others, such as Yorken, Whitereach or Doldayne. It was, however, a rumpus bustling sea town, which allowed Rhodesha and her kinsman to go unnoticed. The Bay imported goods from all over the empire, mainly the Eastern Isles, but also from the far eastern shores of Roldur and Aalafar, then from the southern lands of Dagen. However, rarely did the Allamantyans allow people from such places as Etorion or Samora to settle. There was no love lost between the lands of Etoria and Valanor, even more so now Valanor was forging an allegiance to Allamantya.

The girl extended her hand and touched the warm skin on Rhodesha's leg.

Toran quickly but playfully swiped her hand away. “Keep your hands off, girl, she is mine. I don’t want to fight you for her. Now quick, more ale!”

The girl quickly scarpered off. Toran boomed into laughter as he returned both his hands to Rhodesha’s buttocks. He then lowered himself down, with her straddling him. His touch immediately wiped away all of Rhodesha’s doubts.

****

“Is that all you have?” Caelan laughed as he mocked his brother, Naleac. The two locked fists together as they tried with all their might to force the other’s hand to the table. It was like looking at a mirror image; both were born to a white Dagari woman and a black Etorion father. Their father they never knew, but they were brought up by their mother at the western banks of Dagen near the sea. The two were identical in every way except one, their hair. Caelan wore his hair in dreadlocks that fell from his head and to his shoulders, Naleac had his thick curly hair tied back in a bun. Both had smooth brown skin that seemed more fitting for a woman than a man. They also had green-blue eyes that sparkled in the candlelight. Both wore leather breast plates, each decorated with the torso of a man. Two belts were strapped diagonally across their bodies.

“Ahh! Come on!” Naleac fired back. He forced the entire might of his bicep and shoulder into trying to pin his brother’s hand to the table.

“Ha, you will never learn, brother,” Toran boomed as he looked over his shoulder at Naleac. “You are defeated before you even start!”

“Keep out of this, horse cock. It is between us.” Naleac struggled to speak as all his effort and strength was directed into his arm.

“He is right. You focus too much on the victory, but not how to get there,” Caelan replied as he began to get the upper hand and twist his brother’s arm down towards the table. His bicep hardened and began to burn as victory was within his grasp.

“What is there in life but victory and seeing your enemy vanquished?” Naleac struggled to reply as his hand came closer and closer to the table surface.

“The love of a good woman,” Rhodesha added as she turned away from Toran and drew her attention to the twins.

Neither replied as they became locked in a bitter struggle for victory, bragging rights and, above all, pride. Naleac could feel his strength waning as his arm became almost parallel to the table. His shoulder started to burn intensely and his forearm began to lock up. Before he knew it, his knuckle had reached the oak table, signalling his defeat.

“Victory!” Caelan laughed as he violently gripped his brother’s hand tighter and began to rub his knuckle against the table surface, causing the knuckle to a leave a slight smear of blood in his path before Naleac was able to yank it free. “Once again, I win! Brother, will you ever learn?” He smiled as he began to fill his cup with wine.

Toran also boomed out his trademark laugh before Rhodesha began to drip ale from her cup into his mouth.

“Do you want a real challenge, boy?” Zaira offered herself as an opponent as she walked towards the table with a flagon of ale in her hand. She was a striking woman; a devilish twinkle sparkled in her eyes. She had curvaceous thighs, a thin waist and abs a man could only dream of having. Her hair was thick and blonde, almost gold in colour; half her hair was plaited along on the side of her head, as the rest fell freely to her shoulders.

“I don’t wish to embarrass you, Zaira,” Caelan replied arrogantly as he began to drink down his rich sweet tasting wine.

“Ha, I bet three coins she wipes the floor with you faster than you beat Naleac,” Toran proclaimed as he reached into his pocket and slammed three Dagari coins onto the table, shaking the ground with a shudder that could be felt at the other side of the tavern.

Naleac moved aside so Zaira could be seated next to him. She slowly began to fill her cup and raised it to Caelan’s face. He returned a smile, showing the white of his teeth. The two locked wrists and tilted their cups towards themselves. The winner would taste their drink first.

“No cheating, brother. Defeat to a woman could lead to everlasting shame,” Naleac laughed.

With all their strength, they pulled at one another’s wrists. Caelan and Zaira both could feel their arms tightening under their power; none of them uttered a word as Toran, Rhodesha and Naleac shouted their cheers of support. The table beneath them began to shake as Toran beat his palm on the oak surface.

Caelan could feel his elbow begin to ache as it began to rub hard on the grooves of the table. Zaira’s eyes were locked on her cup as she tried with all her might to bring it to her lips; imagining the taste of ale compelled her to pull harder. Caelan’s arm slowly began to appear further and further away from him but he would not go down without a fight; he attempted to muster up all his last ounces of strength in a last ditched attempt to swing the contest back in his favour.

Back and forth they pulled at one another, none wanting to give an inch to the other. Both their biceps began to pulsate, veins attempting to burst free. Out of nowhere, Caelan’s arm gave way, his forearm became lose and his hand suddenly plummeted to the table, smashing his knuckles to their weary defeat and spilling his wine all over the table. Zaira’s cup finally reached its target as it rested against her lips and the cool bitter ale slid into her mouth.

“Victory,” she calmly said as she enjoyed her reward.

“Haha!” Toran stood up laughing as he taunted Caelan, “I knew it! She has an arm as mighty as a man.”

“You have given them enough attention, now back to me!” Rhodesha called, as she enticed Toran back to her. She rested his mighty hand upon her firm breast and he in turn began to run his thumb around her hardening nipple. She returned by biting into his lip, locking her eyes onto him.

****

"Young love, do you remember it?" Garroway smiled as he watched Toran and Rhodesha kissing from across the long oak table.

"Do I remember it? I still feel it," Lilah replied as she kissed her man on his scarred cheek and ran her hand through his long beautiful silver hair which was half tied up and half left to fall free.

Garroway was old. Of his own age, he wasn't certain but he could feel it in his bones. He once fought for two days straight at the battle of the Weeping Widows and spent the next night in the nearest brothel. Now, his body would ache even after a few hours of training. Wielding his spear took more effort than it used to but he wouldn't let anyone know it.

Lilah ran her pale slender fingers down Garroway's scared face. He had dual scars that ran parallel to one another; they spread diagonal from his cheek down, across his lips that split through his silver stubble jaw line.

"This will be our last mission; we can all retire after this." Garroway turned to Lilah and looked deep into her seductive brown eyes. Her skin was as pale as milk and her hair was as red as blood. Her body was slim and athletic, naturally built for combat. She wore a brown leather vest which revealed her torso and a short leather skirt identical to Rhodesha's.

"After many years of fighting, you deserve to rest, my love." Lilah held Garroway's rough but strong hands in her own. She had been his woman for twenty-five years, and for each one she had been as loyal as a woman can be. She was nearing her fortieth year, but she did not look it. Garroway knew she loved him with all her heart. It was her love that gave him strength even in the darkest of hours.

"Yes, killing takes its toll." Garroway's yellow coloured eyes were full of sorrow. "I wish to retire not just for myself but for you and them also," Garroway pointed to his *children* across the table.

"What about me?" Lothar groaned from beside him. "Don't forget me, old man."

Garroway looked to see his loyal friend and oldest companion. They had bled together since their youth. In countless wars they had fought side by side. Lothar was his first dragon, a man of Yornish descent. He had dark brown skin with thick black hair that had begun to sprout strands of grey that showed his years. He had a beard to match and he, too, had a scar. His ran from his forehead and over his left eye, which had left him blind.

"For all of us, dear friend," Garroway replied as he took a cup of ale in his hand.

Lothar was slowly swaying his head with his eyes closed as he mumbled and groaned. Garroway looked his friend up and down and peered under the table to see a young girl of maybe twenty; she had thick short blonde hair and sparkling blue eyes that reminded him of pearls from back home in Dagen. She had Lothar's cock in her mouth and was sucking hard as she was rapidly moving her hand around the base. Her eyes were locked on Lothar as he was seduced into a realm of pleasure.

“We are warriors, old friend. We were born to f–f–f–fight, not to grow old in our beds.” Lothar struggled to speak; his words fell brokenly from his lips.

Garroway smiled. “Even warriors such as us need their rest, we cannot fight for ever.”

“I can… I… I… can go… go forever.” Lothar released with loud groans of delight as he exploded into his performer’s mouth. His hands gripped tightly around her head, forcing it down hard until she gagged and had consumed all of his cock in her mouth.

“Clearly not forever,” Garroway laughed as he gulped down his bitter ale. “Where is Maarax? He should be back by now.” His attention quickly turned from laughter to a serious tone. He cared for all his children; he called them dragons.

“Maybe he had trouble finding the horses? I never liked this plan from the start.” Lilah had expressed her doubts before they left home but they had fallen on deaf ears.

“It was simple, it was all prearranged. No haggling, no payments.”

“Fear not, old man. He will be fine. Drink your wine, kiss your woman, and enjoy the night.” Lothar stood from the table; he was naked from the waist down. His leather kilt was still around his ankles and his cock was hanging loose. He stretched both his arms out parallel to him and took in a big gulp of air.

Toran looked over and boomed with laughter, “Do you wish to see a real cock old man?” He stood from the table and began to spread the steel studded leather straps that fell down from his waist.

“I do not wish to see why they call you the Iron Bull, brother. I hear horses cry with jealousy at the sight of you.” Lothar smiled at Toran and the two raised up their cups together and they drank down their ale.

Garroway laughed. He loved how close they all were, as close as family could be. A true bond, unbreakable. “I am going outside. I need to piss.”

“Are you okay, my love?” Lilah grabbed hold of his wrist as he squeezed passed.

“I am fine, drink.” He pushed a cup of ale towards her.

Garroway stood outside the tavern, taking in the cool midnight breeze; it was as welcoming as a woman’s touch, as the air brushed past his hot skin. He looked out in front of him. In the darkness he could make out the row of wooden buildings opposite him. They were cheaply made and not in the best condition but this was the city of vice so it was to be expected. Between him and those buildings was a wide path which was used to bring in wagons full of goods from the harbour at the bottom of the street. It was thick with mud and chewed-up earth.

He was enjoying his brief moment of solitude. He took in a big deep breath of fresh air into his lungs, exhaling slowly. He needed it. Behind him he could hear the screams of sex and sounds of rapturous laughter coming from inside the tavern. Two months ago, he and Lilah stood in this very place but the sounds of life had been replaced with a dead eerie silence that lingered long into the darkness, a situation that would've stricken fear into the strongest of men, but not Garroway.

He had ordered Lilah stay home in Dagen but she would not be parted from him. No matter what he said, she would not take no for an answer. So here they had stood, alone. In his right hand he held the *Titans Bitch*. His most faithful companion, countless times it had save his life. The spear stood over six feet tall, made from pure steel; at the end there was an eighteen-inch curved blade which had a notch at the blade's upper base which was used to catch an opponent's weapon.

Opposite them had stood two hooded figures, clad all in black. They looked like the reapers of death who had come to collect his soul, take him away for all his sins, in vengeance for all those he had killed for coin. Still he stood without fear; he just gripped his weapon, ready as always. One of the figures was large and well-built, the other was small like a woman. He saw no faces; he heard the voice of the bigger figure first.

"*Will you kill for us?*"

"*Show me gold and I'll give you blood.*" Garroway replied with the same words he spoke to every client.

"*A hundred and twenty thousand gold coins for you, leave no trace, leave no evidence, leave no witnesses.*"

Garroway remembered the wind, how it howled, like a woman screaming before the fatal blow.

"I will be the last thing they see before they travel to that White City of yours."

"No, they will burn in the City of Fire," the smaller figure snapped. The tone may have been light and feminine but it sounded more deadly than that of the bigger figure.

It was just the four of them in the moonlight, all alone with nothing but the wind and stars for company. This was the mission that would change Garroway and his children's lives forever. Slowly, both figures stepped back, disappearing into the shadows. A familiar sound brought Garroway back from his thoughts.

"We have the horses, all twelve of them."

Garroway looked up to see Maarax saddled upon the lead horse. He was clad in a thick leather shoulder piece that stretched along his back and up his arms; light mail clung to his neck and his stomach was bare. He wore a leather kilt and his sword was sheathed at his waist.

"They are fine horses; they will see us there and back." Maarax reared up right in front of Garroway. His bald head shined in the moonlight; a long thin black ponytail fell loose from the crown of his head. He was the finest archer Garroway had ever seen.

"Good, now take them all to the Inn." Garroway pointed down the street.

Maarax nodded and rode down the muddied street, no questions asked, no orders refused.

"You can relax now, my love," Lilah said as she stood in the door way to the tavern. She held both the swinging doors open with her arms. "You know I can tell when something is on your mind; I have known you far too long."

Garroway turned to see his woman. He admired her figure, her beauty. The light from the tavern shone around her, like the silhouette of an angel as she stood there. She may have been the most beautiful women he had ever seen but she was also the deadliest. He had shown her how to fight, but to be ruthless, that could not be taught. She could kill without mercy, without a second's thought. She was maybe colder than he had been. *It's a hard world we live in, so we must be harder if we are to survive,* he had told her.

"Come here." Garroway extended his arm.

Lilah smiled and took his hand; it felt cool, and rough, a warrior's hand. He pulled her towards him and stood behind her with his strong arms wrapped around her like a bear. He pulled her tightly to his body; he could feel her warmth as he planted a kiss on the back of her head. Her dark red hair let out an aura of roses. Lilah ran her hands up and down his scarred forearm.

"What is on your mind?" Lilah asked inquisitively.

He slowly replied, "Before I accepted this mission, it had been nearly twenty years since I came to this cursed land. I was part of the hired Dagari mercenaries ordered by King Lycinious II of Valanor to destroy the Allamantyan invaders. I fought at the Pass at Falentis. So many died for nothing that day," he said sorrowfully. "From that moment on, I realised, I would choose when and why I fight." He paused slightly before asking, "How are the others?" The tone in Garroway's voice changed; it always had the sound of concern when he spoke of his children.

"The last I saw, Zaira is still drinking the twins under the table, and Uriah, Roak and Valdar had headed upstairs with whores. I think they are all having more fun than you, my love." She pressed her lips against his rough fist.

"We leave at first light. We have a lot of ground to cover. We must move without causing too much attention."

"You taught us well. We are the Twelve Dragons of Dagen." Lilah smiled.

"All things have landed at this port, but never Dragons," Garroway replied as he squeezed her gently.

"Something doesn't feel right. I fear for you."

"Within the week, we will be gone. This will be no different to the hundred others we have killed," Garroway replied confidently. His words though, were lies. He too could feel it but he wouldn't let her know it. Maybe he should've listened to her before they set sail but it was too late now, they were here and they had a debt of blood to pay.

****

“Oh my god, what is that thing you do with your tongue?” the young whore asked. She was of olive skin with long thick dark hair that ran down her back and over her buttocks. “And the places that you put it.” She giggled in a blushful manner, her head rested against Uriah’s chest.

“I have talents, my little dove, many of them.” Uriah kissed her on her head. Her hair felt warm and had a slight smell of coconuts. “Some men are tall, others have strength. Me, well, I have a magic touch.”

“How did you learn it?” She had a grin from ear to ear and was now running her fingers up and down his stomach. She moved her finger around the grooves of his well-defined abs. Uriah was only small in build, standing near five feet and six inches. What he lacked in height he made up for in speed, and he was deadly with his dual swords.

“Me and my brother, Toran, we grew up in a brothel. On the banks of the river Tyma in Dagen. Those women, they taught us a lot.” He smiled as he began to reminisce of the times he spent there in his childhood.

“They sound like nice ladies.”

“All a boy could ask for.” Uriah’s thoughts brought back sad memories, ones he would rather forget. “Have you ever been to Tyma?” He quickly changed the subject, knowing full well she would never have heard of it let alone seen it.

“No, is it beautiful?”

“Not as beautiful as you, my little dove. I could lay here and talk all night but I need wine and lots of it,” Uriah said as he sat up and pulled back his long brown hair so it hung behind his ears.

The girl watched intently as he stood from the bed, naked. She admired his well-toned buttocks and the muscles in his back as he walked to the entrance of her room. This was as plain as they came: white walls with slight stains of mould in the corners and a tiny creaky bed in the corner. Not the most romantic place but Uriah had seen far worse bedrooms over the years.

Uriah stopped and collected his belongings which were scattered over the floor. He put on his thick black leather vest and mail-studded skirt. He also collected his swords, which were sheathed in their scabbards and joined by a belt which was used to tie around his shoulders. The swords were short weapons, ornate with simple gold trim handles; the blades were thin but strong sharp steel, forged in the mines of Dakkar, deep in the red earth of Dagen.

The girl sat up and covered her petite but beautiful naked body with a thin white bed sheet, holding it up over her breasts as she followed Uriah to the door. He turned and smiled, showing a full set of white and welcoming teeth, and planted a soft kiss on her lips, which gave her butterflies and a quick tingle up her spine. He said nothing as he closed the door behind him.

“Uriah! You little devil!” Roak shouted with his deep and powerful voice. He was standing at the bottom of a very narrow wooden hallway which had small doors either side which were used by the whores for their punters. The hallway was slightly slanted which made Uriah think he was even more drunk than he actually was.

Uriah smiled as he looked at his old friend, a man who had been his companion for over ten years. Roak was completely naked as he stood in the candlelight; he was like Rhodesha, born from Etorion decent. However, he had been captured by pirates as child and sold as a slave in Samora.

His dark body looked as if it had been carved from stone and every muscle had been chiselled to perfection. Under both his arms he had two dark red-headed whores; the one to his left was quite chubby with curvaceous hips. The other to his right was slim but with perky breasts that stood to attention. They looked a lot like sisters but, with poor lighting and the amount of wine Uriah had already consumed, it was hard to tell.

"Why do you please them so? I heard your woman's screams from down here. I could barely hear my own women." Roak squeezed both the girls' heads tightly as he began to laugh. "We pay them to please us. You waste your coin, little brother."

Uriah was not really listening, as he stared intently between the legs of the bigger of the two girls. With the tip of his scabbard he pushed open her leg and looked closely.

"Nope, what a disappointment." Uriah shook his head. "I have always wanted to see if a women's hair was as red down south as it is up top. Women these days, always remove the hair. They should leave it; I like to see it, to feel it. I have been tempted to ask Lilah if hers is as red as it is on top of her head, but I bet Garroway would be none too pleased. Anyway, now listen to me, my big black friend," Uriah said as he changed the subject and beckoned Roak closer to him. As Roak leant forward, Uriah brushed his fingers over the top of Roak's thick Mohawk. "Do you ever wonder why I have so much more coin than you?" Uriah patted the small bag of coins tied to his belt.

"No, why?"

"Now think, I know it may be hard for you, but listen. When I take a woman, I please her, I make her feel how she has never felt before. I make every other man she has been with seem irrelevant. Only I exist once she has had me inside of her. Then, because of my talents, she lets me take her for free and I keep my coin." Uriah threw his little bag in the air and caught it again; the coins jingled as they fell back into his palm.

"Ha! I have the horse cock. That is all these women need." Roak proclaimed as he thrust his hips. The two girls looked at one another with look of disbelief and a lack of enthusiasm.

Uriah looked down towards Roak's cock which looked more like a third leg. "Remember, brother, it is not the size of the sword but the hand that wields it."

Roak didn't stay to reply; he quickly dragged his girls back into his room and slammed the door behind him. Uriah smiled and swayed side to side as he dragged his swords along the floor behind him. Over-the-top screams of pleasure filled the hallway as he slowly made his way to the top of the staircase and looked out in front of him.

He admired what he saw: hundreds of people laughing, drinking and fucking. It brought back all the memories of his youth as he and his brother would sit on a staircase similar to this one and watch the ladies of the night. They would flirt and drink with all their punters. He looked over to the far side of the tavern and saw his brother, sitting with Rhodesha on his lap. Toran was his real brother, but he kept those words only in his thoughts.

Back in Dagen, their mother had been just like the ladies he saw here. She was more beautiful though, a fierce and devoted mother. How he missed her; he couldn't remember how long it had been since he had seen her face. Too long, that was for sure.

"You fucking bitch!" A man screamed out as he dragged a whore from her room. "Laugh at me, you dumb cunt, I'll cut your tits off." He violently pulled the young girl up by her long brown hair and spat in her face.

Uriah turned to see Valdar. Valdar the vicious they called him, and they had every reason to do so, his temper was as violent as they came. He was fully clothed, wearing his thick black metal breastplate, which had two silver horses rearing up at one another. The armour wasn't made for him; he had killed a warrior in Samora and stolen it from him. He lowered his hand to his waist and gripped the handle of his knife as the girl struggled frantically. She was like an animal caught in a trap, trying with all its might to escape its fate.

"Someone's having a good time," Uriah said as he sat up on the wooden beam of the balcony, admiring what was happening in front of him as if he was sitting and watching one of those puppet shows back home.

"Keep out of this, you little shit," Valdar replied without looking up.

"Please sir, help me," the girl pathetically called out. "I will do anything you ask."

"Oh, now that sounds interesting, anything at all?" Uriah replied inquisitively as he dropped down from the beam and walked towards them with his swords flung over his shoulder. "Why would she laugh at you?" Uriah looked Valdar up and down. "Yes, you are a strange looking bloke, I give her that, but your jokes aren't funny."

Valdar was not what you would describe as handsome. He looked older than his years, he was bald with only short grey hair that sprouted from the sides of his head, his face was gaunt and his eyes cruel. Hawk-like in appearance but dark. His left ear held three golden rings and a large scar ran around his neck where he had been hung for rape. Garroway, though, for whatever reason, had saved him from his fate.

"Fuck you, Uriah!" Spit flew from Valdar's mouth landing on the girl's face.

Uriah leant in and whispered in his ear, "Garroway won't like it if you harm her. He wants no unwanted attention."

Valdar stopped as if he was taking in his brother's words. He took in a deep breath and released the clump of hair he held in his hand. Now free, the girl frantically crawled back into her room, slamming the door behind her.

"There are more women than you can count down those stairs." Uriah pointed behind him. "There must be one who can appreciate the smaller things in life." He began to laugh, humoured by his own remark.

Valdar pulled Uriah towards him, grabbing hold of his leather vest and yanking him in. "One day, little brother. You won't have so much to laugh about."

"Yes, when women and wine no longer appeal to me, but be that the day far away." Uriah smiled and forced Valdar's hands off him.

Valdar quickly brushed past Uriah, knocking into his chest, and headed back down the wide staircase that lead onto the tavern floor. The staircase was packed to the rafters with punters and whores alike, crammed together like sardines.

Uriah adjusted himself and slowly followed. Walking to the top of the stairs, he saw Garroway, Lilah, Maarax enter the tavern.

****

Hours had passed and, as the night drew late, the punters slowly stumbled out of the tavern back to their angry wives, and the whores, who felt they had made enough coin, left to retire to their rooms. All that was left was the thirteen and a few men who couldn't handle their ale and had passed out. Their bodies were littered across the tavern floor and over the long oak tables. Mumbles and groans now filled the room.

The twelve dragons sat around their table. Lothar had passed out with a jug of wine dangling from his fingers, and Roak snored wildly, which sounded more like an animal than a man. The twins, Naleac and Caelan, were locked in a bitter battle of strength as their fists gripped tightly against one another, each not giving an inch. Maarax as always was alert and sober; he sat on the far edge of the table, plucking the string of his bow.

Zaira sat at the far end of the table, her eyes locked to the whore opposite. They sat embraced as their tongues slid gently against one another's. The whore had her hand up Zaira's leather skirt, her fingers slowly gliding between her legs, the wetness emphasised how excited she was. As her fingers brushed past Zaira's clitoris, she let out a slight moan of pleasure, and began to bite her performer's lip.

None of the others paid them any attention, with the exception of Uriah, who sat mesmerised by what he was watching. He was like a child, looking into a sweet store, admiring all the delicacies that lay before him. He dared not blink in case he missed but a single moment.

"Is there room for one more?" Uriah asked hopefully as he leaned forward for a better look.

"There is no need for one more, I have all I need right here," Zaira replied without even giving him a second glance. Her groans of pleasure were slightly heightened by the fact Uriah was watching.

"Don't you ever wonder what it is like to have a cock inside you?"

"No…" Zaira stopped talking ever so briefly, as her breath was taken away as the whore's fingers slide inside her. "Men cannot do what a woman can."

"I think you mean, a woman cannot do what a man can, unless that whore of yours has a cock as well as a pair of tits." Uriah leaned towards the whore trying to see between her legs.

Zaira cared not to reply as the whore's fingers began to slide inside her, as her thumb gently circled her clitoris. Zaira gripped the whore's arms tightly, piercing her nails into her flesh as the girl's thumb and fingers began to work as one. Pulsating pleasure began shoot intensely through Zaira's body.

"I wonder what it looks like. Is it as golden as the hair on top of your head?" Uriah took up a cup of wine as he watched Zaira's mouth droop wide open as she moaned louder and louder. "Oh, please no rush, I am here all night," he added as he gulped down the sweet red Akeshan wine.

Her legs began to twitch and shake, as her body became engulfed in the pleasure she was receiving. Nothing else mattered at that exact moment as the whore's fingers moved faster and harder inside of her as she climaxed. Her body began to shake. Single powerful shocks exploded through her stomach and down her legs. Slowly, Zaira began to compose herself, taking in a big gulp of air into her lungs. Before looking directly at the whore, Zaira's chest was still rising and falling like waves on the ocean. She then pulled the girl towards her and gave her a hard and dirty kiss, where she ever so briefly began to suck on the whore's tongue.

"Enough," Zaira said firmly as she pulled away. "You can go now." She pulled out a gold coin and placed it in the whore's hand. As the girl rose from her seat, Zaira smacked her hard on the buttocks, prompting her to move faster.

"Now you're finished, I think you should let me see," Uriah asked innocently as he raised his cup to his lips.

"No, little brother. No man has ever seen or touched this." Zaira pointed between her legs as she poured herself a cup of wine.

Uriah smiled. "None at all? Before I die, I wish to see what no man has seen before."

"Wishes rarely come true," Zaira added with a smile.

"What a fucking night!" Toran boomed as he stepped over the semi-conscious bodies that lay in front of him. "More ale?" he asked as he offered his newly filled flagon to his brothers and sisters.

"We will drink no more tonight," Garroway ordered as he sat with his back against the wall with Lilah resting her head on his shoulder. "We will retire to our chambers down the street. We leave at first light."

A drunken man came stumbling across Toran's path, mumbling to himself as he struggled to walk. "Here, drink friend." Toran laughed as he shoved the flagon of ale into his chest which sent him spewing across the tavern floor as if he had just been hit with a bolt of lightning. Toran howled with laughter. He was obedient as always; whatever Garroway asked, he obeyed, no questions asked.

"Come here," Rhodesha said as she sat up and pulled her man beside her. "I think it is time we leave." She then began to run her hand up his leg and around his cock. As she wrapped her fingers around his thick shaft, she could feel it hardening in her palm, hard as a castle wall.

A huge smile filled Toran's face. "Yes! Ha!" he boomed as he lifted Rhodesha up and over his shoulder. She screamed playfully as he walked with her to the tavern door as if she was as light as a feather.

Garroway turned to the others. "Up! All of you!"

Uriah wet the tip of his little finger and placed it in Roak's ear and began to twist it; it immediately woke him in a state of confusion. Slowly they all began to muster and head to the door.

****

That night, Garroway hardly slept a wink. He lay starring at the ceiling, he watched as a spider crawled across the wooden beams above his head. Big and black it was. Poisonous or not he didn't know, all he knew was that it reminded him of himself and his *children*. It had an objective, a mission in life, and it would fulfil it no matter what the cost, even death. To survive, it killed; no more, no less.

Their room was large and filled with twelve single beds. He wanted them all close; he did not trust this place. *Strength in numbers*. The sounds of snores and heavy breathing filled the room. From his bed he could see out of the large bay window, which looked out onto the street. He could see the stars in the night sky, beaming down onto where he lay. *I wonder if they really are great warriors like the legends say.*

Lilah lay with her head on his chest. He could feel the warmth of her naked body pressed against his own. With her close, he felt whole. He pressed his lips against the top of her head, which made her stir slightly from her sleep. Her light breathing gave her a false aura of innocence. *Maybe I am not as old as I feel*. He ran his fingers across her hips. She was at least twenty years his junior but she had chosen him over all other men. That thought made him smile.

Slowly his eyes began to feel heavy and the darkness began to creep over him, but before he finally gave into the realm of dreams, he mumbled to himself: "Life is easy when you live only for yourself, but living for others is what makes life a little more complicated."

Chapter 5
Dreams and Memories

The roaring of horse's hooves exploding against the ground filled King Aristian's ears; he slowly stirred from his sleep. It was early, and the hot morning sun burst through the flaps of his tent. He struggled to open his eyes as the bright light, harsh and unrelenting, forced him to shade himself with his arms. His old aching back had become as stiff as armour during the night. First, he stretched his arms out above his head in a vain attempt to loosen his muscles. It was then he realised what day it was. How everything he had planned and worked so hard for would come to fruition today; for better or for worse he didn't know. A sickness hit him deep in his stomach, nerves and fear colliding as one, immediately taking away any desire he felt for food.

As he rolled over, he saw Beyorn standing over him, vigilant as always. Tall and strong like a great mountain bear. Aristian often wondered if his champion ever slept – by night he was always by his side. Beyorn's eyes were as black as coal; no emotion lay within his chiselled face. Only the heavy sound he made when he breathed signaled he was alive.

Aristian peered out of his tent, his eyes flinching as the bright light burst through the small gap. He watched as knights rode by with their squires following behind like puppy dogs; he could also see two men struggling to control a wild horse as it whined and brayed as it tried to pull away from its masters. It reared up onto its hind legs, kicking out violently. It was not fully grown but was still full of energy and defiance. The two men tried as they might to restrain their unruly beast as they clung hopelessly to the reins.

"Does Your Majesty wish to rise?" Beyorn asked, his voice deep and slow.

"Good morning, Beyorn," the king replied as he turned his attentions away from the antics that were taking place outside.

Looking up, Aristian remembered the first time he ever saw Beyorn; it was at the Battle at Dantford Hills, when the Golgian Mountain King, Dercindorik, united the three mountain clans in revolt. They began to raid the western mountain coast before laying siege to the castle at White Peak.

What a sight the Beast of Golgia was to behold; the bodies of twenty crippled and dying men lay around him before he finally yielded his weapon. Even then it was only because his king, Dercindorik, had been mortally wounded and called for his surrender.

I feel safer with him as an ally than a foe. Aristian slowly rose from his bed. His back still felt tight and uncomfortable as he slowly walked towards the washing bowl, which was large and made of pure silver and crystal. He caught sight of his reflection in the cool clear water: his face looked worn and battered, the wrinkles had become as defined as Beyorn's muscles and his skin as dry as the scorched sands of the Falentis Pass. Sick of his reflection, he dropped his wary hands into the water and cupped the water between his palms and splashed it across his face. It was cool and refreshing as it wrapped around his cheeks and through his old grey hair.

"Tell Sir Dolfan I wish us all to leave within the hour. Have the horses made ready," the king said as he beckoned Beyorn to leave. He needed to be alone, alone with only his thoughts for company. He imagined if all he had hoped for came to nothing, if all his plans for everlasting peace were destroyed like a ship in a thunder storm. It was best he did not think that way, not now; he didn't need any negative thoughts in his mind. *The wise king, yes that is what they call me and I best believe it.*

More sounds of horse's hooves and heavy metal caught his ears; they clanged and banged together as one, a mighty sound. It was soon followed by shouting and lots of it.

"Get over here, you worms!" one voice bellowed. It sounded like Sir Dolfan Greenway. His voice was very husky and distinctive.

The king smiled to himself. He wouldn't want to be on the end of one of his verbal ear bashings. All the young recruits feared him and they had good reason to do so, he was one of the most fearsome warriors in his army. He was, above all else, loyal. Loyalty and obedience was what Aristian required more than anything else.

"Your Majesty," Daemar called out as he hurried through the open flaps of the tent. As usual, he was dressed as he was the night before, in light mail and armour. His silver breastplate had begun to show signs of dirt along the front. His left hand, as always, was placed on the tip of his sword. He placed his right hand over his heart and bowed his head before asking, "Is it true you wish to leave within the hour?" He sounded concerned.

"Yes, I told King Vincinicus that when the sun rose above the Three Peaks on the third day of the month I would be waiting for him with my son on the open fields below," Aristian replied as he sat down on his bed, looking out past his brother as two maids entered the tent.

They carried in a four-foot oak table and placed it near the king's bed. It was dark brown and expertly hand crafted. Aristian ran his fingers over the carved image of a lion being slain by his grandfather, King Kalidar. He was a man known for his brutality on the battlefield and his thirst for combat. He had died the way he had lived, with a spear in his hand. He was clad in armour from head to toe, his crown placed above his helmet. The lion had been skewered by the king's lance as it reared up on its hind legs. It was not what the king really thought of as viewing material before his breakfast, not that he was hungry. His stomach felt sick and twisted with his nerves chewing up his insides.

“This is the perfect spot for an ambush, how many will accompany you?” Daemar began to rub his eyes. They were red and sore; it was clear he hadn’t slept much last night.

“Only I, Andros and a small escort will be needed,” The king added as he saw the maids begin to bring in his breakfast.

The maids were old and plump with black dresses hanging loose from their bodies and white aprons thrown over the top. Aristian caught the strong aroma of freshly baked bread as the maids placed a large loaf on the table. The bread was golden brown and it had a thick strong crust around the edges. For a moment the king felt hungry again. Next he saw two bowls of fruit. Rich warm colours of green, orange and yellow caught his attention. The oranges and apples looked most appealing as the sun light seemed to sparkle against the fruit. A small bowl of oats was placed in front of him. The king watched as the wave of heat rose from the bowl. Lastly a jug of rich cool ale was brought to his table.

The king was taken aback by the aroma of smells that were overwhelming his senses. The once-bare table was now full of various delights; the violent image of King Kalidar skewering his prize had now been wiped from his mind.

“We must all move together; you shouldn’t be left unprotected.” Daemar began to pace up and down the tent.

“You worry too much. Please sit. Enjoy breakfast with me.” Aristian extended his hand and presented the food in front of him, before picking up his dry wooden spoon.

“I don’t trust them. Everything is running too smoothly. I would feel more at ease riding to battle. At least I would know what to expect.” Daemar’s words began to take away the king’s newly returned appetite. His stomach was rumbling but his hunger was beginning to wane.

The king threw down his spoon as he looked at his brother. “Do you wish for war?” Aristian angrily responded. His mood was already teetering on the edge. Today was stressful enough without his brother’s paranoia.

“Yes, if needs be. I wish for our people to be safe not to be butchered in our sleep.” Daemar stopped pacing up and down. His voice began to rise, like the hot sun on a summer morning.

“War has no prejudice, rich or poor, man or women, it takes who it wishes. What good can come of it?”

“There can never be peace without the everlasting victory. Our empire stretches from the northern Flentian Mountains, over the southern plains of Darnor, across the wild lands of Dagen and Osgaroth, then as far out past the Eastern Isles to the borders of the known world. We have the superior men; each would die to keep you safe. I would too. You are the Emperor, our king; Andros is not fit to rule. He is weak, his mind thinks of song and dance. He is more a woman than a man.” Daemar leant forward and placed both his hands on the king’s table.

Aristian was angered by his brother’s comment; he knew the words he spoke were true, but if he was not of his blood, he could have him tried for treason. He took in a deep breath before replying, “Our kingdom needs this alliance. The desert Yors of Samora have begun to head west, Roldur and Aalafar have fallen. We are next if the Western Realm is not united. Without this alliance we will slowly begin to erode, a strong castle can only stand for so long. Eventually the storms, the sea and time itself will bring it down."

"You went against the advice of the five swords of the high council. They did not give you their blessing."

"Daemar, when have you ever cared what the council thinks? You have never been one to use your head, even as a child you chose the sword over your brain. I am grateful you don't disagree with me in public, that you're smart enough to know."

"You know I would side with you even if I thought you wrong. You're my brother and my king."

Aristian smiled. He knew, above everything else, his brother was loyal. He may not have been smart but there was no finer warrior or battle commander than him. *I only hope he will stay as loyal to Andros as he has been to me.*

"Do you forget Danaus?" Daemar angrily banged his hands on the table. The king startled, as his bowl of oats shuddered before him.

A harsh sickness came over Aristian, deep in his stomach. "How can I forget? And even if I wanted to, Father would not let me! I will hold the grief of that day for the rest of my life. My actions took him away from us." The king suddenly rose from his seat and grabbed hold of his crown and held it out in front of him. "This was never meant for me! You take it if you think you would make a better king." Aristian threw it at Daemar's feet.

Daemar stopped and looked at his brother. It was rare he saw him with any anger; he was always a calm man. He looked old, his eyes weary and heavy. His shoulders had begun to slope and his white bed dressing hung loose from his ever-thinning body. Daemar slowly knelt down and took the crown in his hands. The gold shone bright. The blue, red and green jewels sparkled as he raised it up.

"You are my brother and my king. The Battle at Falentis set about making you who you are. You make a better ruler than he or I could've done combined. You're the greatest king this world has ever seen. Just don't dishonour his memory; he gave his life to stop them entering our lands. Yet you allow them to enter freely without question." Daemar slowly placed the crown on the table and ran his fingers across its beautiful exterior.

"I dishonour nothing. Get out! Leave! I don't wish to see you again today." Aristian angrily pointed towards the entrance of his tent.

Daemar spoke no words. He tilted his head and left. Aristian stood in silence and listened to clanging of his mail getting quieter and quieter until he heard nothing but the sounds of his never-ending thoughts.

Falentis, Falentis, Falentis!! he thought to himself. *How can a deserted, scorched piece of earth hold so much over one man's life? It will forever be my greatest achievement, but there can be no victory without everlasting sorrow.*

King Aristian lay back on his bed and closed his eyes only for a second, but he had drifted into the darkness and he dreamt. He dreamt the dream that held control of his past, his present and his future. The sound of battle filled his ears, the singing of steel as sword clashed with sword and finally screams of the dying. Two mighty armies had collided together, five to one they were outnumbered but in the narrow Pass of Falentis the enemy's numbers counted for nothing.

Falentis was a narrow pass that held sway between the northern lands of Valanor and the Kingdom of Allamantya. The two mightiest nations of the Western realm met head on in one final battle. The pass was flanked either side by steep slopes of jagged rock and red sand. The sun had been bright and ever-burning that day; it was summer but it felt hotter than any he had felt before, as if the gods were punishing them for their sins. Red sands raised high above the ground, forming a cloud of dust as thousands upon thousands hacked at one another. A sickening aroma of blood and sweat fitted perfectly with the screams of death. Aristian was in the thick of battle. Wave after wave of blue and silver crashed against his shield wall of red and green. He had arranged the battle plan: thick shield walls that could withstand attack after attack.

"*Hold them here,*" he remembered Daemar yelling as he drew his shining sword. He had been barely nineteen but he showed no fear in the face of death.

"*If you die, your wives, your sons and your daughters will die. Do not let them step foot in the land of our fathers,*" Danaus valiantly screamed as he stood side by side with his men. He was tall and proud, a handsome knight, a maiden's dream. He was clad in thick shining silver armour, decorated with dragon heads that covered his shoulders. A green and red cape hung from his back. His helmet was decorated with dragon wings and his visor was raised, showing his well sculptured and clean-shaven face. He was twenty-five but full of fire and vanity.

The fires of battle had raged for hours, the three princes led their army bravely. Alector, the king, their father, hid in his castle filled with fear and shame allowing others to die for his arrogance and folly. Shields were splintered, steel was shattered and blood was spilled that day at the Pass of Falentis.

"*Onward, brothers, for Allamantya and eternal glory*!" Danaus shouted as he led his men from the seemingly unbreakable shield wall. Aristian watched helplessly as his brother stood at the vanguard of the charge. His silver armour was painted red with the blood of his enemies, his sword still shone in the sunlight. A valiant knight, fighting for the defence of his people, defending the weak and bleeding alongside his brothers. With his men behind him, Danaus, the heir to the throne, disappeared into the thick cloud of red sand. A shadow formed in the dust, a silhouette of a mighty knight standing alone, overwhelmed by enemies, his sword swung out from side to side as the shadows of demons closed in around him. Many fell by the wayside as his sword hacked out. A lone light shone out from the darkness. It was his blade as it glistened like a great diamond; it flashed and lashed out. Screams filled the air, steel rang out…

"Your Majesty, Your Majesty," a voice spoke. It was mumbled, broken and disorientated. Aristian began to wake; his eyes were heavy and his right fist was gripped tight, as if he had been holding a sword.

"It is getting late, are you okay?"

Looking up, he saw a bright fiery ginger beard and intense blues eyes. It was then he realised who it was. "Sir Dolfan, I thank you for waking me. I think, as my body grows old, the more rest I need," Aristian said as he sat up and rubbed his hands against his head, which had begun to pound as fierce as a war drum.

Aristian walked towards his washbowl, weary and slightly unsteady. He began to look at his reflection in the clear water. He looked young, rings of mail hung from his head, his skin was smooth. As he admired the younger version of himself, he spoke, "I was dreaming. I dreamt of red clouds and black demons in the shadows. We can never escape our past." He paused slightly. "Nor should we want to. It moulds us and finally defines the men that we become today."

****

The flames flickered and crackled. *They are so warm, so beautiful, so welcoming,* Andros thought to himself as he lay naked on top of his bed, staring out at the fire brazier that lay before him. The heat was sweltering yet he just lay there admiring the glowing embers doing their fiery dance. Fire had always excited him but he didn't know why. He watched the beautiful but deadly flames flashing and raising higher and higher. Even the smell of the burning wood captivated his senses.

His cold eyes, pale blue like ice, gazed into the fire. He wanted to reach out and touch it but he dared not. He remembered he had tried to grab the flames as a child and yelped in pain as the fire burnt into his flesh. His sister, Arrabella, had laughed in his face as he cried. *Bitch!*

He turned away from the fire for a moment and he thought of Lyon, his dear Lyon. He wanted his strong arms wrapped around him, making him feel safe and excited. Andros wished he could spend every night with him and not sneak and hide like some kind of outlaw.

It had been nearly five years since they first met. Andros was fifteen years old when his father had taken him to the forty-ninth birthday celebration of Marshal Latimor N'Dai. Their family ruled over Kathoros, the eastern region of Allamantya. They were originally one of the four lion families of Darnor. His mother was Darnaion, maybe that was why he felt a connection with Lyon's roots.

Andros remembered Lyon had stood so proud and strong next to his father. He was tall and beautiful; his thick brown hair fell to his shoulders. Andros could remember it as clear as if it was yesterday. He had worn a red and white doublet, decorated with shinning golden buttons. Oh, how he wished he was back at that party and not here in this tent. He had sat at the end of the great oak table, admiring Lyon's beauty from afar. How he watched Lyon's arrogance as he rejected call after call from all the young girls wanting to dance with him. Yet all the while, Lyon would glance over at the prince and smile. From the moment he and Lyon had first laid eyes on one another, they both knew what the other had wanted.

"Get up!" Arrabella ordered as she strolled into his tent.

"What! Get out! Can't you see I'm naked?" Andros frantically tried to cover his body with his bed sheet.

"Don't fret, it is nothing I haven't seen before. You forget I was unfortunate to share a womb with you once." Arrabella turned to look at the brazier, the flames were flickering brightly and the heat was overpowering, "Why would you need this fire? Haven't you noticed it is summer outside? Or have you been too busy dreaming of your future wife, the beautiful Princess Tilia?" Arrabella smiled as she tipped a jug of water over the brazier. The fire hissed and crackled as the flames slowly died.

Tilia! Andros quickly thought to himself. With all his thoughts of Lyon he had totally forgotten today was the day he had been dreading for these past four months. He looked at where the flames had once stood so proudly, red and yellow glows of power now replaced by chard and blacken wood. The image saddened him.

Arrabella began to hum happily to herself as she pranced around his room. Her dress was elegant and beautiful; it was white and well fitted around her slim and appealing frame. The silks parted around her breasts, showing her cleavage, and tightened around her waist. It had two golden belts, decorated with sparkling green and red jewels; the first was situated under her breasts and the second around her waist. The dress fell loose around her thighs, separating into three sections which stopped by her knees. A very thin and almost see-through silk cape fell from her shoulders.

Andros knew she looked beautiful but he wouldn't give her the satisfaction of a compliment. "Why are you wearing that?" he asked inquisitively as he looked her up and down.

"Why not? We have guests. It is only right we make an impression." Arrabella began to brush back her long brown hair away from her face.

"That isn't one of your dresses." Andros knew the dresses she owned. He had worn enough of them when she wasn't around.

"No, I had this specially made in Akesha in the style of Valorian princesses."

"Why would you want to look like one of them...?" Andros paused for a moment before continuing. "Ha, I know why, for Prince Gabriel isn't it? You want to impress him." He began to laugh as he rose from his bed. "How can you love a man you have never met?"

"Legends are born for a reason; if they were not true then why would people speak of him as a god? There is some truth to every story."

"Father will never let you marry him." Andros poured himself a cup of water.

Arrabella smiled as she walked towards her brother. She began to mess with his thin brown hair. Parts around his crown were sticking up like branches from a tree. She attempted unsuccessfully to push them down. "I will tell you something. Did you know, that if we were born in Valanor, I would be the one getting married today and not you?"

"What do you mean?" Andros replied with a confused look on his face.

"I was born a mere four minutes before you. For those barbarians, as our uncle likes to call them, that is enough to grant a woman as the successor over her younger brother."

Andros quickly rose to anger and pulled away from his sister. "We don't live in Valanor, do we? We live in Antilion and I am to be king!"

"Calm down," Arrabella replied enchantingly as she pulled him closer and brushed his hair behind his ears. "What will you be wearing today for your future bride?" Arrabella turned from her brother and knelt down and opened a large wooden chest near his bed.

"Oh…erm…" Andros sat back down on the bed and wiped the sleep from his eyes. "Father wants me to wear the green tunic with the red cape. He said it will hide my pale complexion."

"Men! They know nothing." She began to throw out all the clothes in the chest. Bright greens, reds, blues, yellows flew through the air it was like an explosion of colour. "No, none of these will do. You want to look strong; a woman likes to feel protected."

"All I have with me is what is in that chest." Andros was beginning to panic; he began to wipe the sweat from his palms. "What will I do? She won't like me now, will she?" He started to pace up and down. He violently kicked out at a small wooden chair in front of him. Arrabella slowly rose to her feet and smiled. "Wear that." She pointed towards a suit of armour hanging from a stand at the entrance to his tent.

It was beautifully polished, golden in colour with two silver phoenixes clawing at one another across the breast plate. The shoulder protection was designed in the shape of a silver phoenix's face with the beaks sticking out like sharp spikes. His helmet was equally impressive; it was white and gold. The visor was curved towards the base with a swirling pattern for decoration. Two great golden wings were attached to the visor, and silver plum hung elegantly from the top of the helmet.

"Armour fit for a king," Arrabella said as she ran her fingers across the breastplate, admiring her own reflection in the well-polished steel.

"I have never worn it before. Uncle Aymar had it made for me, but…"

"Today is the perfect day. Wear it. You will look like a princess' dream." Arrabella began to smile as she ran her finger over her own reflection. She quickly turned to her brother. "Now get it on, we don't have much time." Arrabella quickly left the tent, like an excitable child.

Andros could hear her outside, ordering the squires to assist him in getting it on. He looked at the armour with a lack of enthusiasm: the hard metal, the rough mail. *How could anyone want to wear such a horrid thing? Give me beautiful silks any day,* he thought to himself.

With the armour finally on, his body had become stiff and immobile. His feet felt stuck in the dirt below, as if they had been consumed by quicksand. The weight was unbearable; his shoulders ached and his arms felt as if they had been strapped to his side. His narrow frame allowed his new dress of iron to fit uneasily around his body. The breastplate was loose and the mail was too long.

"Stop pulling, you idiot!" Andros yelled at one of the squires. "Can't you see I will fall over with all this weight. Imbecile!"

The hands of the two squires were shaking as if they had been outside during a cold winter's night. They pulled and twisted feebly at the straps of the prince's mail. Each looked as if they wished they were anywhere but here. Both were young and dressed in full brown leather attire, each had scruffy brown hair. Beads of sweat began to run down their cheeks. Their hearts raced murderously in their chests.

Andros was admiring himself in a large full-length mirror. His armour glistened in the rays of sun that shone through the open flaps of his tent. For a moment, he looked a valiant knight, like the ones his sister told great tales of. He imagined the look on Tilia's face when she saw him. A handsome prince mounted on his horse. What a fine impression he would make. *I will make my father proud.*

He attempted to raise his right hand to brush a few strands of loose hair away from his face. His arm felt locked and tied to his waist; he didn't let it deter him as he forced his hand up and towards his face. His forearm, and all up his bicep, was burning. An intense hot sensation ran through his muscles as if he had just been in the thick of battle.

"It is ready, Your Majesty," one of the squires said as he pulled tight on the last strap.

"Good, now go," Andros commanded. The two squires quickly left the tent as if they were dogs being called upon by their masters.

On the table beside him, he could see his helmet. Even he could appreciate its beauty. The golden wings twinkled in the sunlight. *One day my crown will sit upon this helm, a god king on earth.*

Andros began moving cautiously towards the entrance of the tent. One false movement could result in him being face down in the dirt. His legs and arms moved together as one, slow and cumbersome. As he approached the entrance, the harsh bright rays of sun caught him in the face, forcing his eyes shut. The hot summer air was humid and dry, his body felt wringing wet underneath his dress of iron.

Whereas his tent had been so peaceful and quiet, outside was an explosion of noise and chaos. Heavily armoured knights rode by, horses brayed as squires tried to control them, men shouted and dogs barked. Andros was disappointed. He had half expected everyone to stop still and applaud, drop down to one knee in amazement, but no one even seemed to notice him.

Directly opposite his tent he could see his father, King Aristian, dressed in gold and red silks, his crown fitted perfectly on his head. He was mounted upon a beautiful white horse. Sir Dolfan was next to him, donned full in battle armour, with a green tunic brandishing the red sword of Draykos.

Andros began to angrily fiddle and adjust his breastplate, which was still loosely fitted around his shoulders. "Fucking, stupid…" Andros spat out only to be cut off by his sister.

"Andros, you look a princess' dream. Tilia will think herself the luckiest lady in the entire realm." Arrabella's voice was full of enthusiasm and warmth as she walked towards him.

"I don't! I look stupid. Those idiotic squires can't even fit a suit of armour," Andros's voice broke as if he was about to cry.

"Don't fret, let me." His sister ran her hand across his face. It felt cool as she wiped the beads of sweat from his brow. He was captivated by his sister's beautiful pale blue eyes; they reminded him instantly of his mother's. How he missed her. "You are almost the perfect knight."

"Almost?"

"What does every great warrior need?" Arrabella paused, waiting for Andros to reply. When he looked back at her as blank as a piece of wood, she answered for him. "A sword."

In her hands she held a beautiful sword; its handle was dark black, the cross-guard shinning gold with phoenix decoration. The pommel at the base was a gold phoenix claw. She placed it in the palm of his hand; it felt heavy and powerful. Andros looked up and, without even having time to admire his new sword, he saw his dear Lyon.

For a moment his heart skipped a beat and his stomach twisted with the feeling of a thousand butterflies fighting an intense battle deep inside his gut. Lyon was dressed in shining silver armour. His family crest of a red war lion on a field of white stood proudly on his torso. How beautiful he looked. His brown hair hung loose. He was mounted with his *pride* behind him.

For a brief moment the world began to move so slowly; the sound of the horses, armour and shouting all became long and deep. All Andros wanted to do was to walk over to Lyon, mount his horse and ride off onto the horizon away from everything and everyone. Suddenly Lyon's smooth and well-sculptured face became tense and distorted, anger filled his cheeks and venom built in his eyes as he looked directly at Andros. Lyon pulled hard on his reins, kicked into his spurs and rode past the prince without a second glance. His *pride* followed loyally.

"Oh, someone has woken up on the wrong side of the bed this morning," Arrabella said as she tightened the last strap on his breastplate. She smiled to herself before adding, "I wonder what could be wrong with him?"

"Andros, come on, we don't have time. The day draws late," King Aristian ordered, as he rode over to his son with a rider-less horse tailing behind. "Those aren't the clothes I told you to wear," he added as he looked his son up and down. He actually couldn't recall ever seeing his son in a suit of armour.

"I-I—" Andros began to stutter.

"I decided, Father. It is what I would want to see if I was to marry," Arrabella spoke up proudly.

King Aristian smiled.

"Someone help me with my horse!" Andros angrily shouted as he struggled to get his foot in his stirrup.

"Bring me mine!" Arrabella shouted.

"No, Arrabella. Just me and Andros will greet them." Aristian leant down towards his daughter.

"Father… I should be by your side." Arrabella tried to change her tone, to seduce him into changing his mind.

"I have spoken. You stay here and make sure everything is prepared for when they arrive. Find Arteus and make sure he is ready." Aristian turned his horse away from Arrabella and rode back towards Sir Dolfan.

Anger rose in Arrabella like a tidal wave. Her fists tightened and her nails dug deep into her palms.

"Don't worry, I will tell you if Gabriel is as beautiful as your legends say." Andros laughed as he struggled to turn his horse. It backstepped and brayed before finally obeying, and Andros then feebly chased after their father.

****

Beautiful dark seas of green lay before King Aristian. Fields as far as the eye could see, the long strands of grass swayed slowly and elegantly in the light summer breeze. The fields rose slightly and eventually formed hills, smooth oval mounds, each overlapping the other. Birds sang their song as the riders entered the paradise in front of them.

The riders rode in a diamond formation. Sir Dolfan took the lead; his armour twinkled in the sunlight. Behind him, King Aristian and Prince Andros rode side by side. Next followed two men at arms, clad in dark silver armour over rings of mail. The visors of their helmets were raised, allowing them good peripheral vision in case of an ambush. They carried green shields with the red sword of Draykos at the centre and long spears in their right hands. At the back rode a single soldier. He too was dressed in armour, but he carried the Allamantyan flag high in the air; the cloth blew beautifully for all to see.

"The armour is very becoming," Aristian said as he looked Andros up and down. They had hardly spoken a word since they left camp. He had just watched as his son sat uncomfortably, fidgeting from side to side. He knew he was nervous.

"It is heavy and rubs against my skin," Andros replied as he pulled the mail away from his neck.

"A small sacrifice for the rewards that lie before you. All great kings have to make them." He tried flattery; he knew Andros was suspect to it.

"How long until we are there? This saddle is beginning to give me sores."

Aristian took in a big deep gulp of fresh summer air, ignoring his son's never-ending calls of complaints. The smells of grass, leaves and the vast never-ending sites of beauty took him back to a happier place. "Did you know it was a place like this where I first met your mother?"

Andros looked up, eager to hear more. "No, were you scared?"

"I couldn't sleep the night before. I tossed and turned. When we arrived on the shores of Darnor, I thought I would collapse. Then, the moment I saw her, I remember it as clear as a summer's day. She was beautiful, all a prince could ask for. She had enchanting brown eyes, smooth skin and long hair down past her waist." Aristian smiled, "Longest hair I had ever seen, but all my worries were wiped away the moment I first laid eyes on her. She though, was harder to impress, very opinionated, very…" The king suddenly stopped, realising the rest of his story might make his son far more anxious.

"How do you make a woman love you?" Andros asked with concern in his voice.

"I was never a man who had a way with women. That was always one of your Uncle Danaus's talents. Women loved him. I, however, couldn't bring myself to look at one, let alone talk to one. Love isn't something that you force, it will happen naturally. It is like a flower. It takes time to grow. You nurture it and eventually it blossoms; it spreads its petals into the most beautiful thing imaginable. A thing words cannot describe."

"Will she have to know everything about me?"

Aristian turned to his son. "Some things are best kept secret. The past defines who we are but sometimes it is best those things are left behind." The king knew what his son spoke of, a deep dark day, one full of disgust and sorrow. One he chose to forget, yet he could not forget his own secret. One which would haunt him until the day he died.

"Your Majesty, there is a man up ahead." Sir Dolfan raised his right hand. Within seconds the two guards who rode behind the king suddenly appeared either side of Aristian and Andros, their spears pointing towards the man that lay before them.

On the brow of the hill was a man, sitting on a fallen tree, one knee raised sharpening his sword. The blade glistened in the sunlight. A large muscular grey horse was beside him. Andros noticeably began to look uneasy, looking all around him.

"Fear not, Sir Dolfan," The king smiled. The six of them continued riding, and as they approached the fallen tree, he spoke again. "I did not expect to see you here."

"You knew I would be here, before even I knew it." Daemar stopped sharpening his sword and looked up at his brother.

"We will not have need for that sword."

"I will keep it anyway. Better to have it and not need it than to need it and not have it." Daemar stood up and mounted his horse. "They are encamped over there." He pointed behind him towards the Three Peaks.

There were three large green hills each joining the other. The centre hill was the largest. On top was a sea of silver and blue, tent after tent as far as the eye could see, Valorian flags flying high. The silver rose blossoming proudly.

"The last time you and I rode together and saw this many barbarians, we were riding to war." Daemar paused before adding, "Now we ride to peace."

Aristian replied, "I hope you're right."

Chapter 6
A Prince Who Will Never Be King

Again! Again! Gabriel slashed as he stepped forward; his spear and body moved as one: a single fluid movement. His blade crashed against the oak tree that stood before him. Splinters of shattered wood flew in the air as his blade elegantly cut through its target.

Gabriel sidestepped and attacked again, slashing and moving. Each time the wood broke and split as his spear violently crashed against it. With each movement he imagined the tree was an enemy, a southerner armed to the teeth, clad from head to toe in thick iron, a man with the sole purpose of killing him, wiping his name from memory, denying him his right to enter the night sky. He would not allow that.

He stopped suddenly and stepped back, admiring his work. The oak tree was slashed and broken. Where it once had stood so proud it was now a hacked and battered mess. He breathed deeply, trying to catch his breath, filling his lungs. He could feel the sweat running down his half-naked body, the droplets working their way down his chiselled torso.

The hot rays of sun shone through the leaves above him. He could feel the heat burning into his naked flesh, his back felt loose and his muscles warm. He was ready if they came for him today. If they had betrayal in their hearts, he was ready to fight; he would not kneel to a king from the south. He had sworn it in front of the gods themselves. *Only when my heart beats its last, shall I fall before a foreign king.* He wore only a brown and gold skirt that fell from his waist down to his thighs. It was decorated with the head of a lion at its centre. He preferred to train without armour; he felt free.

He was alone in foreign land. Yet he felt at peace, just him and his thoughts. Gabriel stood in a circular open space, surrounded by dense forest. The land was slightly raised, forming a bank. The trees blew softly around him, the leaves rustled under his feet, the birds sang beautifully. It was a calm place, a little paradise. Not the demonic hell he had once imagined as a child. So many shades of green and brown filled his eyes. The air was clean and pure, refreshing his lungs with every breath.

Gabriel admired his spear. What a weapon it was, standing six feet tall, with a large blade at the top which widened at the base before narrowing in the middle before sliding back out and tapering again at the tip. A beautiful weapon, designed for one purpose, to kill. A thick base of silver plume rested at the base of the blade, which was followed by tassels of deep dark blue which would glide elegantly whenever the blade moved.

The spear had been his weapon for nearly eight years. He was only sixteen years old when he first tasted battle. King Fulgar the Ferocious of Etoria had begun to raid the Eastern bank, taking slaves and ravaging the farms and sea ports. Gabriel rode out to meet them, just him and a thousand spear maidens of Delloria against twice that number. There had been no fear in his heart, just a thirst for glory. They had all said he was too young, even his father had laughed at him. Gabriel knew his father only gave him the Dellorian women to shame him. How he was wrong, they were all wrong.

They had held the field of Elysia and, before the day was done, his enemy knew the taste of Valorian steel. He killed nine men that day; it would be no easy task to send him to the night sky. The ninth was the biggest man he had ever seen, skin as dark as night, eyes pale white, and the spear, what a beautiful spear it was. Gabriel wanted it and he made sure he took it. He was born in battle that day. Prince of the plain they called him ever since. Even with his enemy scattered before him and their army in disarray, his father offered no praise. He just congratulated the young commander, Hyandrei Milo, for being the man who had slain King Fulgar in single combat, knighting him for his swordsmanship.

There had been no sleep for Gabriel last night. Whenever he slept, he dreamt of a demon, a monster from the City of Fire. Fiery eyes, slimy skin made from scales, teeth as sharp as razors. It had come for his sister, dragging her away, far from his protection. His body was immobile, stiff and frozen; there was nothing he could do as his dear Tilia was taken.

I must be awake and alert. He wiped the sweat from his eyes. *They will not take her.* He thrust forward again, one swift god-like movement, and this time he carried anger with his attacks. The muscles in his arm and back tightened as he lunged forward, his right arm carried the blade as he extended it out. Keeping his balance as always, his legs dipped, his quads began to burn as they generated the power of his attacks.

The leaves around him began to rustle, soft crunches, like feet on snow. His senses were heightened; he was in battle mode, in his zone. Again, the leaves crunched, echoing amongst the trees, then he realised they were not his own steps. Again and again he heard them. *One... no, two people approach.* Like a cat he listened, his ears twitched. With each movement, he pictured them as they came near. First he thought they were assassins, paid with blood money to take him to the White City, but then he realised.

"Gabriel, you know trees don't fight back. Try your hand with me, dear cousin." Lucian approached. His grin was wide and friendly, his pearl-like teeth sparkled in the summer sun. Lassander followed behind. Both wore dark blue breastplates cast from hard iron. The chiselled torso of a man was carved at the front. They wore light blue undergarments which fell down to their knees. Their athletic arms were bare, small diamond shaped shields were strapped to their backs.

"Our prince likes to stay in shape," Lassander added. "He would be lost without his spear."

"He is right, we are not safe this far south." Lucian looked around him. "I hear demons linger in these parts."

"I fear no demons," Gabriel replied firmly as he turned and walked towards his horse.

"That is your problem, my prince, you fear nothing," Lassander added as he followed behind his cousin. "Fear keeps you alive."

"This keeps me alive." Gabriel held out his spear before sliding it back into the scabbard attached to his saddle. He then began to wipe down his body with a white rag, running the cloth over his chest, shoulders and the back of his neck.

"You need rest. Go back to camp; we need you at your best."

"I am fine; you need me awake if they come."

"You could sleep for a whole year knowing we are here protecting you." Lucian's self-confidence was regularly heard.

Gabriel took the bait; he was always one to accept a challenge. He pulled out three wood training poles from alongside his saddle. "These should do." He threw them at his cousins.

"Two against one?" Lassander smiled.

"He underestimates us." Lucian began to spin his pole between his hands.

"Come see if your hands are as fast as your tongue." Gabriel looked at Lucian before walking away, giving himself a distance from his cousins.

"How long has it been since we fought against one another?" Lassander asked as he and Lucian began to step away from each other.

"Too long, but in a few moments, you will see why you have waited so long to challenge me again." Gabriel continued spinning his pole between his hands. His eyes locked on his cousins as they continued parting. He knew they intended to attack him from different angles. *They listened well to the words of Uncle Damidar in the training yard.*

Lucian and Lassander began to circle Gabriel, like two lions eyeing up their prey. They kept their distance, knowing it would be difficult to defend attacks from opposite sides. Gabriel listened to each step they made, the crunching of the leaves beneath their feet, the slight breeze that blew through the trees. He envisioned their every movement, where they would step next, the position in which they would hold their training pole, even their next breath.

He knew Lucian was the most eager and over-confident, he would attack first. Lassander would follow suite, knowing his brother was exposed. With each step, they got closer to their fate. Gabriel ran his hands along the smooth wood; he felt its texture beneath his fingertips. He parted his legs so he had good balance. He moved onto the balls of his feet. He was ready.

Like he predicted, they attacked; like a moth to the flame. Lucian came first, lunging out with his pole. Gabriel, like lighting, lashed out, deflecting the coming blow before quickly turning his attention to Lassander who had already moved into striking distance. Gabriel brought his own pole back, intercepting

Lassander's attack and rapidly moved away from in between their pincer movement.

Now they attacked together, moving forward as they swung out with their poles. With each attack, Gabriel moved back, giving away ground as he deflected each blow with ease. He moved like a god as he ducked and dived. Side shifting from left to right, all the while he moved back, giving them a false sense of security, waiting for the right moment to counter.

With two hands, Gabriel now held his pole out horizontally in front of him; he defended against the two lots of attacks that his cousins rained down towards him. Suddenly, unexpectedly, he moved his own attacks south, catching Lassander on the back of his leg. The wood slashed against his calf, knocking him to his knees. With his next attack Gabriel smacked the base of his pole into Lassander's forehead, snapping his neck back violently.

Then he noticed, just for a millisecond, that Lucian's eyes moved away from his target and to his brother who had fallen to the floor. In that moment Gabriel brought his attack up, knocking Lucian's pole flying in the air before striking his own pole straight into his gut, winding him instantly.

As Lucian clambered for breath, Gabriel dropped down low, spinning as he descended, and extended his leg out as he spun a full three hundred and sixty degrees, taking away Lucian's legs. The force of the spin-kick launched Lucian off his feet and onto the floor. He landed with a loud thud as he lay dazed with his eyes rolling into the back of his head.

"What just happened?" Lucian called out as he shook his head.

"We got our arses kicked," Lassander replied as he rubbed his hand against the lump that was beginning to form on his forehead.

"Just like when we were children, you two never learn." Gabriel smiled as he extended both his hands, pulling his deflated cousins back to their feet.

The loud sound of hooves and metal approached the bank. The noise echoed powerfully amongst the trees. From below, a patrol of armoured horses appeared, eight men clad in dark blue breastplates, decorated with a silver rose on their torso. Their faces were covered with full helmets, showing only their eyes and mouth. Long beautiful silver plumage fell from the top of the helmet down to their backs. Each carried dark blue kite shaped shields in their left hands and long spears in their right.

The rider at the centre dismounted and made his way over towards Gabriel and his cousins. The three golden haired warriors stood silently as the rider approached.

"My prince, your father, King Vincinicus, wishes to speak with you." The rider removed his helmet and bowed his head. It was Sir Hyandrei Milo; he had been a brave soldier who had worked his way up from a squire all the way to commander of the royal guard. He and Gabriel had fought side by side since their first taste of battle at the Banks of Elysia.

Sir Hyandrei Milo was a man of average height, with dark brown hair, cut short on the sides. His eyes were a shade of yellow and hazel. His cheeks were well sculptured and his face was clean shaven and narrow along his jaw line. He was a handsome knight in his own way.

"I know my father's name, Sir Hyandrei. What does he want?" Gabriel was clearly irritated by the command he was being given.

"It was not my place to question my king; he just demanded that you come right away," Hyandrei replied in his usual slow and articulate tone.

Demanded. Gabriel did not like that word. Even as a child he was against being given orders; from the moment he could walk he rebelled against his father's words. "I best not keep my father waiting; he might have something important to do, like eat his breakfast, drink his wine or to shit." Gabriel walked away and mounted his horse. In one fast and fluid movement he was on its back. He looked down towards his cousins and Sir Hyandrei.

"Lucian, I thought it must be you. On your back in the dirt as usual," Hyandrei spoke as he walked back to his men, clearly revelling in his comrade's defeat.

"Oh, please do tell your wife next time you see her, I prefer sweet wine in the mornings not ale." Lucian smiled as he rubbed the back of his head.

Gabriel kicked into his spurs and rode at full haste out of the forest.

****

Tilia sat and watched as a small beautiful doe and her fawn grazed peacefully in the field opposite her. The mother who was petite in frame and had a light brown coat with circular patches of white, ate the rich green grass below her hooves, while her child moved unsteadily around her. The two deer seemed content with their simple and peaceful life. *If only mine was that simple.*

Her lady in waiting, Cassandra, stood behind her, braiding her soft and smooth blonde hair. Long strands of yellow gold fell from her head: a golden princess, shining in the morning sun. The two of them were about one hundred metres from camp. Tilia wanted to be away from the hustle and bustle of the army encampment. It was too loud and she had started to become irritable.

It was still early but the sun was bright; its powerful rays lit up the valley below. Behind her was a silhouette of the dark mountains of Rylor Pass and an endless ocean of green fields lay before her. To her left, maybe one hundred metres away, lay a dense forest rich with oak trees and thorn bushes. It was a beautiful sight to behold and she knew one day it would all be hers. It was peaceful to look out at. The land and animals, they took her mind away from what would happen in the next few hours.

The fiery sun's intense heat had produced one of the hottest summers in years. Tilia was sweating yet she had barely moved. She wore a silver tight fitting dress that was situated above her breasts and clung to her petite body before stopping around her knees. The jewels and diamonds on her dress sparkled in the sun. The beads of perspiration ran slowly down her neck and over her shoulders.

"Cassandra, can I ask you a personal a question?" Tilia asked inquisitively as she wiped the sweat from her palms.

"Of course, Your Majesty," Cassandra replied as she continued to braid her hair. She was a young woman, maybe in her early twenties. She was of pale skin with long dark hair; she wore a loose fitting pale blue dress to conceal her large frame. She had a pretty face and a very large curvaceous body.

"I want you to speak to me now as your friend and not as your princess." Tilia looked up at Cassandra. "Have you ever been with a man before?"

Cassandra began to giggle. "Will Your Majesty think less of me?"

"No, answer truthfully, please. I will too."

"I have, many times."

Tilia smiled. "Many times? Cassandra!" Tilia began to giggle too.

"Once I have it, Your Majesty, I just want it more and more." Cassandra continued to smirk.

"How do you know you are doing it right?"

"Just confidence and practice, Your Majesty. I believe you only live one life, so I try to have as much fun as I can."

Tilia smiled. She knew, being a princess and a future queen, she didn't have such luxuries. She could not go from man to man fooling around. She had a reputation to uphold; the lords and ladies would not follow a queen they believed no better than a whore.

"What is it that men like more than anything else?" Tilia asked as she looked out at the deer in front of her. "I want to make sure I please my king on our wedding night."

"I can't say." Cassandra giggled again.

"Please tell me, no one can hear." It wasn't often Tilia could have such carefree conversations; almost always, she was followed by her two sworn swords, Sir Kaian Vadius and Sir Dajax Feilos. She could not see them but she knew they were near; they kept a close eye on her. It was their sworn duty to keep her safe and to keep her pure.

Cassandra lent into Tilia's ear and began to whisper as if they were surrounded by hundreds of people, she even covered her mouth with her small chubby hand.

Tilia gasped. "Cassandra, you are a dark horse! I never expected such things from you. We will talk more later. Now carry on with my hair." Tilia began to smile.

Tilia was both excited and then frightened to her very core at the thought of sex. She had only a few memories of sexual contact and each one filled her heart with sorrow and disgust. It was nothing like she had heard people talk about, no pleasure, no connection just an eternal sadness and self-loathing. Would Andros know her secret when he entered her? She began to think about it over and over. Would she bring dishonour to her family? She prayed she would not.

All her life, Tilia had dreamed of marrying a wonderful man and having a beautiful wedding. She knew most certainly she would get the latter. Her wedding would be the biggest and most spectacular event the world had seen for the past three hundred years, but would the man she married be fit for the occasion?

Leylan had told her such terrible things about Prince Andros. She had pretended none had bothered her, but each word that fell from his lips was like a poisoned dagger piercing her flesh. The scars from his words stayed on her body, never leaving.

"The god-prince." Cassandra's words brought Tilia back from her never-ending world of unanswerable questions.

Tilia looked up as Gabriel appeared on the ridge; he was riding at a brisk pace. His horse forced the two deer to jerk with panic. The mother moved like lightening, running away from the oncoming beast. Her child scampered behind her, trying frantically to keep up. She felt sorry for them both, they had been so peaceful.

She could tell he looked angry; his handsome features were distorted as his hands gripped tightly to the reins. He never looked over towards her. Tilia's heart was full of sadness. It had been so long since she and her brother had spoken. They had been so close once. As children, he would follow her every step. Now he seemed happier the further he was from her.

"Oh, what I would do to him," Cassandra mumbled under her breath.

"Cassandra! Less of that talk. He is my little brother." Tilia playfully slapped Cassandra's hand. Her smile slowly turned to sadness as she saw Gabriel disappear out of sight into the wall of silver and blue tents.

"Sorry Your Majesty, but he is very handsome. We all talk about the god-prince."

"I know, I hear all the gossip about my brother. There is more to Gabriel than his appearance, though. He has a soft heart; he just doesn't show it."

Tilia remembered how her brother had been such a happy and innocent child. They loved each other so much but, from the moment he was born, her mother was never the same again. She claimed to have been raped by a god and that Gabriel was not the son of her father. Slowly her mother's warm heart turned cold. She would not bond with Gabriel and always left him to be tended by the wet nurses. Maybe that was why Tilia and Gabriel were so close. He would climb into her bed at night and she would tell him tales of love and heroism until he fell back to sleep.

Tilia's eyes felt sore and she just wanted to close them. She had hardly slept last night, tossing and turning, each time thinking of a man she had never met. How could one name cause her so much anxiety? Soon it would be over, she would tell herself. But was it true? Meeting him would not be the end, it would be the beginning.

"Do you think of your wedding?" Tilia knew she needed to talk to keep herself awake and away from her thoughts.

"I do, Your Majesty, but what woman doesn't? My wedding would not be as glamorous as yours, though."

"That is true, but your wedding will be to a man you love and who loves you. I am not blessed with such luck," Tilia replied with sadness in her voice. "The man I am to marry is said to be every vile word you can think of."

Cassandra could tell Tilia was feeling down. "When I was a young girl, there was a boy in our village. He wasn't very popular and he was different to other people. They called him a freak, an outcast, a bastard, but to me he was beautiful, kind and loving. Every person has their opinion, but all that matters is your own."

Tilia took in her words; she knew Cassandra was right. She spoke the truth; it didn't matter what others thought or said. For their opinion was their own and might not be the same as the one she would have. She had made her decision and she must live with it.

"Thank you." Tilia smiled and she looked out at the world before her. *There is no room for sorrow in such a beautiful place.*

****

Gabriel slowly rode into the encampment. Either side of him he could see rows and rows of silver and blue tents. Each one was big enough to hold three men. Outside the tents there were fire braziers and suits of armour being polished by squires. It was a crowded place. Knights and men-at-arms strolled from one side of the makeshift path to the other. It was only when they realised who he was, that they all stopped still, frozen like great old statues before bowing their heads.

He could feel their eyes on him, sense the pride and loyalty each man had for him as he rode by. The whispers travelled softly to his ears like a butterfly elegantly travelling from one place to the next: "Look, look it is Prince Gabriel!"

"The god-prince!"

"The Prince of the Plain!" The endless calls and chatter amongst the men. Although there was one that he knew they called him: "The prince who will never be king." But he didn't care.

Although he showed no emotion as he rode through the camp, he liked the attention and the love they had for him. He too loved them, not individually but as a nation. The love he had for his people and his homeland was what he held most dear.

As he made his way through the camp, the smells of burnt wood and sweat filled his nostrils. The summer heat only added to the claustrophobic feeling of an army encampment. The men slept side by side; the water they had was for drinking not washing. The aroma of hot sweat and leather was overpowering but it did not bother him. The smells made him feel at home; he was born in battle. He was not made to sit back and enjoy the finer things in life.

Up ahead, at the centre of the camp, stood a very large carousel spoke-wheel pavilion tent which was connected by a hallway. Beautiful flags, with a silver rose on a sea of blue, flapped proudly above each of the joining tents. It was pure white in colour which reflected the sun; the bright light forced Gabriel's eyes shut.

A row of eight soldiers stood vigilant outside; a dark blue carpet stood between them which lead to the entrance of the tent. Gabriel dismounted and made his way along the carpet; each guard he passed raised their right hand over their heart and bowed their heads. He could hear loud rapturous laughter coming from inside the tent. He closed his eyes and took in a big heavy gulp of air before he entered.

"Ha! Leylan, you know how to make your father happy! More wine, yes, pour more wine," King Vincinicus ordered as he stood admiring himself in a large mirror being held up by two struggling servants. He was clad in shades of silver and red; the robes were tight, showing the bulge in his belly and the woman-like breasts he had begun to develop. His hair, which had once been a god-like gold, was now a dull grey. His beard, which was the only part of him which he seemed to take pride in, was well-groomed and filled his large puffy cheeks.

"A little early for wine," Gabriel spoke with a tone of disapproval. He hated it when his father drank. He could only just about bear him sober, let alone with a glass of wine in his hand.

"That is the luxury of being a king; it is never too early to drink, especially on a day as glorious as this," Leylan spoke in his sly and smooth demeanour as he handed a silver goblet of wine to his father. He was still wearing his ill-fitting breastplate and a small sword hung feebly from his side.

King Vincinicus turned to Gabriel. "I may drink, but at least I have the dignity to wear clothes. Strutting round the camp half naked, no better than a whore." He then lifted the wine to his lips before taking a huge gulp.

"Brother, can I tempt you?" Leylan held out a newly-filled goblet to Gabriel. His arm was thin and weedy; it came towards Gabriel like a snake slithering towards its prey. His yellow hawk-like eyes were as piercing as arrow heads.

Gabriel ignored his bastard brother's offer and sat himself down on a small wooden chair. "You wish to speak to me?" He looked at his father with an air of shame. How could a king allow himself to fall into this deep barrel of despair? He should be inspiring a nation, not shaming it.

"Yes, you will not embarrass me today, you will..." Suddenly, King Vincinicus began coughing uncontrollably. He knocked over his wine and placed both his hands on the table as he choked and spluttered. Tears coursed down his round face. His cheeks began to redden as he coughed over and over again.

Leylan began to overact and patted his father's back. "Father, please, you must see the wise men." His sly grin was blatant and obvious as he looked over at Gabriel; his white teeth filled his small face.

"Leave me, I am fine." King Vincinicus pushed Leylan away. "All of you, go!" he bellowed as he still continued to cough violently. The two servants quickly scarpered out of the tent, carrying the mirror between them. Gabriel stood up and was about to follow them out. "No, you stay," the king ordered as he pointed to Gabriel with his left hand. With his right, he wiped away the blood that had begun to form in his mouth and concealed the cloth before anyone could see.

Gabriel turned and walked towards his father. "Why are you so stubborn? See the wise men, they can help you. If not for yourself, do it for Tilia." He had an air of compassion in his voice.

"Give me the wine!" King Vincinicus called out to Leylan, who walked over ever so obediently and handed him the goblet. Leylan's grin was from ear to ear. "No, the jug, then out with you."

The king's order took Leylan by surprise; his large white eyes began to bulge out of his head. "Ah, yes, anything you command." He pushed the jug closer to his father's hand. He looked at Gabriel and smiled arrogantly before leaving.

"You shouldn't drink so much. I have never had a taste for wine." Gabriel sat himself on the table closer to his father.

"You think yourself better than me because I have vices. I drink so I can forget, but then again, I also drink so I can reminisce." The king stood up straight, wiping away the phlegm from his mouth and beard. He coughed once more as he refilled his goblet. The deep red wine fell from the jug beautifully, like a waterfall of blood. "You don't remember your mother, do you?" The king then swilled his mouth with the strong Brundean wine.

"I have only a few memories of her." Gabriel's voice sounded soft. It wasn't often he spoke of his mother.

"She was a magnificent woman, so fierce and proud. What a warrior she had been. She could best all of us in the training yard. She gave me a bruise or two I can tell you that."

Gabriel smiled, only a small one which he concealed well. He had never known she had been such a good fighter. Maybe now he knew where he got his talents from. No matter what his father told him about his glory days gone by, he would never believe those exaggerated tales. "What was her weapon of choice?" Gabriel asked.

"The spear. Never have I seen such a fighter. She was deadly, yet she was so elegant about it. If she had not been a prince's wife, she would've followed me into battle." The king took a huge swig from his goblet. The wine fell from his mouth and dried into his beard.

Gabriel closed his eyes, shook his head, and looked away.

"Ha, she had that same look when she was angry with me! I knew it!" King Vincinicus laughed loudly.

"What was it you wished to speak to me about?" Gabriel asked quickly, wanting to finish the conversation.

The king replied as if Gabriel had not even spoken. "Then you were born and her beautiful face became full of sadness. The life she once loved so dearly evolved into an empty void of darkness and sorrow." He smashed his fist on the table. "Raped by a god, she said; delivering me a god-prince, she said." Anger brewed in his heart; the tone of his voice began to change like the storm brewing across the eastern sea. "Later, you will do as I command; you will stay quiet and speak only when spoken to. Stay close to your sister. Do you understand?" Venom coursed through his words. His small chubby hands gripped the goblet tightly as he stared directly towards Gabriel.

Gabriel stared right back at his father. He breathed deeply so as not to say something he knew he would deeply regret later on. He nodded slowly and walked towards the entrance of the tent.

"You will not shame me boy!" his father suddenly bellowed.

Gabriel quickly turned to his father, taking the bait. "The only shame will be what you bring on our house and our nation." His father began to cough, regurgitating up all his wine. It sprayed from his mouth and onto the table. Gabriel looked him up and down. "Oh, what a man, a great king. What legends the storytellers will say of Vincinicus, son of Lycinious, when you die. The king of wine, the father who sold his daughter."

"Out with you!" The king smashed his hands on the tablet, knocking his wine everywhere. "So many times I wanted to smoother you in your cot for what you did to your mother!" Spit flew from the king's mouth. His rage exploded like a volcano. His face was as red as blood and his eyes bulged from his head. "I would banish you back to Verdinia to serve under your uncle, but you would disobey me as usual. But, by the gods in their White City, I will be dammed before I allow you at the meeting. You stay here!"

But Tilia, she needs me! Tears began to form in Gabriel's eyes. He said no words but he turned and walked away from his father and out of the tent. He heard a loud crashing behind him as he left; he knew his father was taking his anger out on furniture. As he made his way along the carpet, he could hear the king coughing once again. One single crystal-like tear slowly fell from Gabriel's cheek.

****

"Oh, it looks beautiful, thank you, Cassandra!" Tilia spoke with a huge smile as she held out a mirror in front of her. Cassandra held out a small mirror behind Tilia's head so she could admire her new hair. It was braided with two thick lush golden locks on both sides of her head which joined together at the back, forming a single pony tail.

Cassandra put down her mirror and felt the princess' shoulders. "Your Majesty, you feel as hard as a castle wall." She then proceeded to run her thumbs across Tilia's shoulders. With each movement she could feel her muscles crunching, like feet on top of fallen leaves in Autumn.

"You don't know how much I need this. Is this how you would seduce all those men of yours?" Tilia closed her eyes as a sensation of pain and relaxation ran through her body. With each movement of Cassandra's fingers over her shoulders, her body began to tingle.

"If I may be so bold, the men do say I have magic hands." Cassandra began to smile as she forced her thumbs harder into Tilia's shoulder and then down across her shoulder blades. Her thumb ran smoothly around the tense muscles, and with each movement Tilia would groan.

Suddenly Tilia began to feel uncomfortable; a cold sickening cloud hovered above her. The warm Allamantyan sun was no more, there was just an internal darkness only she could sense. Up ahead in the long strands of a grass, a shadow emerged. It stood still. It was Leylan, his face cold and emotionless. His eyes examined her with a sadistic glee. He enjoyed tormenting her. *Leave me, be gone foul demon.*

Ever since Leylan's mother had died, he would haunt Tilia's steps, moving in the shadows, watching from afar. He would never blink his eyes, absorbing every inch of her. One night she awoke to find him standing at the foot of her bed, a demon in the darkness. His thin branch-like fingers sliding over her bed sheets, "Be quiet," he hissed as he slithered beside her. "I only want to play." It was not the last time he would visit her. A jolting sickness forced its way up her throat; her nightmares would never leave, always they lingered ready to be lived out over and over again.

"You look beautiful." Gabriel appeared; he walked proudly out of the long grass. He oozed confidence as he stood, blocking Leylan's cruel glare. It was as if he was intentionally shielding her from his evil gaze. Gabriel's long golden hair was now tied back in a bun. His torso, though, was still bare; his sweat made his skin look as shiny as silver.

"If you have come here to have a go at me, I don't want to hear it." Tilia frowned as she looked up at Gabriel. Her words did not reflect how she felt; a happiness swept back over her like a warm summer breeze.

Gabriel smiled. "You will never be alone again." He stepped forward, taking his sister's small hand in his own. "We need each other now more than ever before. I will keep you safe."

Tilia looked him in his sparkling blue eyes. The way he came to her reminded her of when they would argue as children. Gabriel was always the first to break their silence.

A strong breeze blew through the valleys; it was uncharacteristically strong for this time of year. The grass swayed in the wind and a few strands of Gabriel and Tilia's loose golden hair began to hover beautifully from their heads. The breeze was refreshing as they both closed their eyes and felt the cool air on their warm skins.

"The gods send their disapproval," Leylan spoke as he appeared beside them.

"Since when did you speak for the gods?" Gabriel replied angrily.

"There is more to me than meets the eye."

"Maybe he is right; it could be a bad omen. The gods may be against us." Tilia's little hands began to shake ever so slightly.

"With or without the gods blessing, you have made your decision. You carry the fate of a nation on your shoulders; allow me to carry it with you." Gabriel pulled his sister close to him. She could smell his sweat and feel the heat from his body but it did not bother her, this was the safest she had felt since she left the capital at Verdinia.

"There are some things I must carry alone," she replied with sadness in her heart.

"Oh, look, we have guests." Leylan's voice was as unwelcome as a winter cold.

Gabriel and Tilia looked up. On the horizon, six riders appeared. A sigil of a red sword on a field of green blew proudly as the riders drew closer. Tilia could feel the thumping of Gabriel's heart; she felt his arm squeeze her tightly.

"When the wind blows through the valley and the animals scatter to their burrows. It is then we all must rally, for death will come with the face of a friend when southern wolves approach. Behind them darkness follows and then only sorrow lies ahead." Leylan smiled as he watched the riders inch closer and closer.

Chapter 7
The Fire or the Sword

Screams echoed through the darkness; they were sickening calls of pain and pleas for help. Each one had fallen on deaf ears but the walling never stopped. The sounds were driving her insane. All night Danaka had hoped someone would come and open her cell door and set her free but no one did. First, she had stood with her head peering through the small opening of the cell door, her tiny hands wrapped around the thin iron bars of what she would now call home.

All she could see down the narrow corridor was darkness and shadow. Fires on the walls flickered, offering the only light; even then it was virtually impossible to see. In between the screams and crying she would hear the clanging of metal and the rattling of keys and the odd mumble between the prison guards. Yet still no one came.

She remembered the words, the words of hate and disgust, "*And tomorrow you will burn.*" She could still feel his hot dry breath on her neck, even now. Why did he hate her so? She had never seen that man until that moment yet his words carried venom and he seemed to revel in her pain and fear.

"I'm innocent!" she had screamed as they had thrown her into her cell. She collapsed face first onto the cold hard stone floor; her head rang like the bells of the city watch as she lay disorientated. No one replied; there was just the sound of laughter as the keys jangled and the heavy wooden door of her cell had creaked shut with an almighty thud.

It had been hours since Danaka had stopped screaming for her release. Her throat had begun to feel sore and dry; she knew she was wasting her time. It was only when she realised she sounded as pitiful as those in the cells next to her that she decided to stop. When they wanted her, they would come.

Danaka had tried to sleep but all she could think of was the trial tomorrow and what had happened to her dear friend Griffin. The last she could remember was hearing him barking; he always would at intruders but when she was dragged from her home he was nowhere to be seen. He would never have allowed her to be taken by such force. "I will kill them all if they have hurt him," she mumbled to herself as she threw an old clay pot against the cell door. It shattered into pieces, just like her life had a few hours earlier.

A witch had been burnt when she was a child. Her aunt had been able to shield most of it from her but the images still stuck strong in her mind, as clear as a summer morning. The girl must've been around the same age Danaka was now; she had been stripped naked for all to see. Her body was thin and bruised and her hair was short and scruffy like a boy. It had been hacked at by those religious fanatics who had wanted to shame her before their gods.

She had been tied to a long post in the middle of the town square; bundles of branches and sticks had been tied together and placed around her. The crowd had heckled and thrown rotting fruit at her as she stood with her eyes closed, knowing what terrible fate would befall her. It was at that point she remembered her aunt yanking at her arm and pulling her away from the crowd. Danaka didn't know why but she was compelled to look back. Bright light began to appear between the huddles of people, smoke began to rise, then the screams followed – sickening vile gut-wrenching pleas as the flames engulfed her. The flesh was scorched from her bones; her pale skin became black and charred.

Those images had stayed with Danaka for the rest of her life. Her hands began to shake at the thought that she might face a fate as bad as that poor girl's. Her stomach turned and twisted as she retched onto her cell floor. Nothing but phlegm came up. She took in a deep breath and tried to compose herself but all she inhaled was a strong smell of urine which filled the room.

Her cell was dark and claustrophobic; it was just big enough to house two people. The walls were cold and dirty. She didn't know how far underground she was. It was summer but here it felt like winter. Shivers ran through her body as she huddled in the corner trying to keep warm.

Danaka could make out deep scratching on the stone in front of her. She had counted twenty-seven lines; each must've counted for a day a previous occupant had spent in the cell. Danaka hadn't been in here one day yet and she felt like she was going mad.

Eventually she began to drift off, her heavy eyes slowly closing as her head slumped into her knees. Creaking and banging awoke her from her nightmares, dreams of flames and death. As she slowly raised her head, her eyes felt sore and overwhelmed by the bright light that entered her cell.

"Up with you, witch," the prison guard shouted as he squeezed into her cell. He was fat and sweaty; he wore nothing but a torn leather waistcoat which revealed his large and hairy belly. His head was bald and he had nothing but three brown teeth in his mouth. His brick-like hands grabbed a chunk of her hair as he pulled her to her feet. "Move, bitch!" he yelled into her face; his breath stunk like a concoction of ale and rotting fish.

Outside stood two mail-covered men at arms. Danaka and her escort began to walk down the dark and narrow corridor. When she was first brought in, she was too disorientated to notice what was around her, everything had happened so fast, but now she could take in her surroundings. The corridor was littered with identical cells doors, maybe five on each side. She caught sight of a face peering through the bars. All she had time to see was that his skin looked brown and beaten and that his beard was black and scruffy. His eyes looked hopeless and full of sorrow.

At the end of the corridor was a narrow spiral stair case which was wide enough to hold only one person at a time. It was made of pure stone and the flickering of a single fire hanging from the wall was the only light.

Her feet felt sore and she began to take small steps as she tried not to fall, but a pain exploded into her back as one of the soldiers rammed his shield against her. Danaka's head snapped back and her breath was taken away.

"Don't stop," he said angrily. His voiced echoed through the cold walls.

"Where are you taking me?" Danaka said as she tried to compose herself. She didn't know if she wanted to break down and cry or to stop and attempt to fight her way free. *Fight, what an embarrassment that would be. Death by sword is better than death by fire.*

No voice replied as she was taken up countless steps. Eventually they came to a single wooden door; a small square was situated at the top. For a moment she thought she was being escorted to a new cell and then she noticed a ray of light bursting through. It was just like the sun shining down from the heavens. Danaka knew now she was heading outside. The door flung open as if it had been caught by a sudden gush of wind. The bright light exploded into her eyes, forcing them shut. An overwhelming mixture of shouting, screaming and laughing crashed against her.

Danaka's eyes slowly opened as she was forced forwards by the soldiers. Hundreds of people stood before her, all heckling and screaming, baying for her blood. Some spat at her as she tried to make her way through. The phlegm began to run down her cheek and down her chest between her breasts. She wanted to stop, curl up in a ball and cry, but she forced herself onwards, defiant as always.

"Clear the way," one of the soldiers commanded as he forced his way in front of Danaka and began to knock the crowd back with his shield. Some of the people began to push her, knocking her from side to side but she stayed strong and was able to stay on her feet. *I won't let them see me on my knees*! A single tear droplet fell from her cheek.

The hot sun was blaring down; she could feel it burning into her flesh. The smells of sweat and ale were strong and overpowering as she forced herself onwards. A sudden shock of pain shot through the back of her head and then another against her arm, it felt like rocks raining down against her but it was two young half-naked Akeshan children throwing apples, possibly the two she had seen playing in the fountain the day before. The apples stung as they bounced off her, leaving bruises the moment they smashed against her skin.

"Away with you, you scum!" One of the soldiers yelled as he thumped one of his boots into a child's arm, knocking him to the floor. They quickly scurried away like rabbits.

Up ahead, she could see a small wooden dock with two more soldiers standing vigilant either side. She knew that was where she would stand. Behind the dock, and slightly higher, stood a newly erected wooden stand which was about fifteen feet wide and around six feet off the ground. All it had on top were three empty seats. The middle chair was highly decorated with a red cushion on the base and at the back. It was clearly meant for someone of high importance.

The soldiers forced her into the dock and one started to tie her hands. He clamped her hands together with a vice-like grip. The heat from his mail began to burn into her skin; she flinched in pain but didn't pull away. The rope was bound tightly around her wrists; there was no way she would be able to pull her hands free.

Suddenly she felt anxious and tense. She could feel the burning stare as hundreds of eyes latched onto her. She turned to face the crowd. A silence fell over her. All Danaka could hear was the sound of the bird's wings flying above. The hostile crowd stared at her with hatred and malice. She could see their mouths moving – brown and rotting teeth were exposed and their hands gestured violently towards her – but she heard no sounds. They all had judged her guilty, yet half would not even know why she was on trial.

"Here enters Franco Tomell, Lord of Tomellburg, in service of Marshall Guy Bailen of Oalandrium!" Mayor Benedict Darris bellowed for all to hear. He was standing on the platform looking out towards the crowd, clearly enjoying his moment in the spotlight. He was small in height and overweight; blue and yellow silks clung to his body. His hair was brown and curly around the sides of his head, whereas his scalp was as bare as a baby's bottom. It shone in the bright sunlight.

The crowd cheered loudly as Lord Franco Tomell appeared on the platform. He was an old man and frail. His hair was grey and very thin; it was brushed back away from his forehead. He wore a long black robe that was decorated with gold stripes that ran along the edges. He was helped to his chair by two servants. A knight soon followed, clad from head to toe in battle attire. His armour was shiny and silver, and underneath his steel plates he wore rings of mail to protect his vulnerable spots. His face was completely covered by a large great helm. It had only two small slits for sight and a few circular holes near the base so he was able to breathe. A long blue cape hung from his broad shoulders. He stood, vigilant, behind Lord Tomell.

"Silence!" Mayor Darris commanded, clearly wanting everyone to hear what he now had to say. His little chubby hands held a script which he was reading from. "Ladies and gentleman, young and old, from near and far. Today we are here to try a young girl for witchcraft and attempted possession of an innocent child!" He pointed towards Danaka as if he was an actor on stage.

The crowd roared with excitement as they shouted obscenities towards her. Danaka couldn't make out any exact words as the sounds all collided as one, but she knew they wouldn't be compliments or words she wished to hear.

"Over there stands Danielle, the accused. Witnesses say they saw her trying to absorb a child of its illness."

The crowd began to mutter amongst themselves.

"First of all, my name is Danaka, you fat oaf! I was only trying to help!" Danaka yelled, suddenly forgetting herself. She knew the trial was a sham but they could at least get her name right.

"Be quiet, girl! You will speak only when spoken to." Darris pointed towards one of the guards standing beside her. The soldier grabbed the base of his spear and rammed it into Danaka's gut, taking her breath away instantly as she began to retch. She felt light-headed and started to sway as her legs began to feel loose. Her vision became blurred and disoriented. *Stand up; don't let them see you on your knees.* Danaka took in a big deep gulp of air and stood up straight. Tears filled her eyes.

Lord Franco Tomell rose from his seat and raised his hands. The crowd slowly began to quieten as they peered up towards their lord. "Let the girl speak. There are two sides to every argument. Speak, child." Lord Franco beckoned Danaka to have her say.

Danaka smiled and slightly tilted her head; she felt a sudden build-up of nerves as she began to speak. "I was only trying to help the boy. He was having a seizure; he needed space and time to ride out his affliction. I absorbed him of nothing."

"The boy has been weak ever since you touched him. You took his illness and drained him of his lust for life," Darris replied with air of arrogance to his voice.

"He will be weak, his body has been through trauma. He needs proper medical attention. I have herbs to make him feel more comfortable."

"More witchcraft! The gods will save the boy. Your potions, mixed with the devil's touch of the City of Fire, will do nothing for him." His voice raised louder when he spoke of the City of Fire. The crowd followed with him as they screamed towards her.

"I hear the girl has someone to speak for her," Franco Tomell replied as if he was sick of hearing Mayor Darris's voice. "Let him come forward."

"Yes, my lord, she has someone." Darris flicked his wrist towards a solider standing below him.

Danaka watched in confusion. Who would stand for her? She had no friends. Then she suddenly saw Irban walking towards the stand. He looked scared and tense as he looked around the volatile crowd. He was uncomfortable with so many eyes on him. His hands constantly moved around his wrists. Irban looked up and gave Danaka a smile that was filled with sorrow and sadness. Danaka, however, smiled back.

"Speak," Darris commanded.

Irban jumped as he replied. "I–I… Danaka she is good girl. Her family they good people. They save my daughter. She had the red fever, she is cured now." Irban pointed towards his wife who was holding their baby in her arms before she held it out for all to see. "She would not harm the boy!"

The crowd began to chatter amongst themselves.

"So you believe her innocent?" Darris countered.

"Yes, with hands on my heart. By the book of the Winged God and his children." He placed his hand across his chest. People of the Eastern Isles did not believe in Ollaria'h, they worshipped the Winged God, Dalackis.

"Your god does not live here," Darris proclaimed.

"We have heard enough. Bring in the witnesses," Lord Franco ordered as he sat uncomfortably in his seat. Soldiers took Irban away from the stand; he glanced over at Danaka hopelessly.

Danaka looked to her right as Walter and his wife made their way to the stands. They looked a funny pair. He was as a thin as a rake and she was as wide as a house. His wife seemed to be dressed the same as yesterday in her pale blue dress. Yet, this time, she had made an effort to tie back her hair and she must've left her gravy stained apron back home. Walter wore white shirt and dull-brown trousers. He swayed a little. He looked as if he had been drinking.

"Please, this will be difficult, but I ask you to try and relive that terrible ordeal you went through yesterday," Darris said with a hint of humanity in his voice, which was clearly an act. "In your own time." He dabbed some beads of sweat from his forehead.

"That witch tried to take my son. Her hands were all over him, my poor baby. When I tried to save him, she smacked me across the face and broke my nose." The woman pointed to her now crooked nose.

"That isn't what happened! Your boy did that to you when he lashed out!" Danaka furiously yelled.

"Silence. I have told you once." Darris pointed to one of the guards who stepped towards Danaka with his spear. She immediately flinched and moved back, waiting for the blow, but none came. The guard smiled at her and moved back to where he was standing. "So you are saying the accused drained your son of life and then attacked you as you tried to save your boy?" He paused slightly before adding, "As any mother would for her child." The crowd began to cheer loudly as if they were watching some sort of game not a trial.

The hot sun was blaring right down where Danaka was standing. She could feel the sweat dripping down her face and the beads running down the curve in her spine. Her eyes began to squint as the sun rose high in the clear blue sky. She stopped listening to the lies and twisted truths Walter and his wife were spouting. She knew the trial was not going her way and no one would believe her. Not even if those gods of theirs came straight down from that White City and proclaimed her innocence.

Beautiful white doves flew overhead and perched on the fountain she had admired the day before. They looked elegant and their feathers were smooth and clean. She drained out all the shouting and hatred and admired the birds and the cool clear water as it sprayed from between those two great lions. All she heard was the cooing from the birds and the splashing of the water. Oh, how appealing it looked! Danaka wished she could just walk over and lie in the crystal-clear water, wash away all her dirt and sweat and be awoken in a different place and time. Just her and Griffin in a green field away from this cursed place.

"She is a girl of sin. She always would try to seduce me with her body. Look at her now, exposed to tempt us all." Walter words brought her back from her happy place.

Danaka looked down and could see her dress was torn and ripped. Her breasts were barely covered. There was nothing she could do to try to cover herself. Even Lord Tomell began to shake his head with disgust. He was a very religious man. It was he who barred all whores and images of temptation from the village.

Once again she took herself away from the trial. Danaka looked down at her hands. Her wrists looked red raw as the thick tight rope dug deep into her flesh. She wished she was strong like those warriors she had heard people talking about; she knew no names but she wished she had their strength. She would break free and kill all those who had wronged her. Never had she felt anger like this before.

To her left she noticed a man carrying a bundle of branches over his shoulder. A fear hit her in her stomach; a sickness began to curdle deep in her gut. Her hands began to shake as she saw rows of men carrying branches and wood. Further away she could see a tall wooden pole being erected. A priest of the White City, clad in pure white silk with golden trim, was giving out directions.

She knew at that moment they planned on her death. This trial was just for the crowd, they may as well have just killed her in her cell last night. Danaka's legs began to feel weak at the knees; she wanted to collapse and be swallowed up by the ground. *No, they will not see me on my knees; they will not have that satisfaction.* She wiped the tears and sweat from her face.

The guard to her right was standing beside her, unflinching. She noticed his sword in his scabbard; it was nothing fancy, just plain. It had an all-black grip with a silver pommel and cross guard. The scabbard had a silver locket at the top and chape at its base.

Maybe that is my only hope. The Fire or the Sword. I won't give them the pleasure of hearing me scream. Danaka took in a big deep breath and closed her eyes. Her heart began to beat thunderously like a drum inside her chest. She tried to speak but her words broke as they shamefully tried to fall from her lips. She composed herself and took in another big gulp of air and breathed out slowly.

"I demand a trial by combat! I choose the sword!" she screamed at the top of her voice. Her words cut through the crowd like a knife through butter. A slight summer breeze blew through the streets and the sound of a cat yelping was all she heard.

Walter and his wife looked at one another, confused, unsure if they were to carry on talking or not. Mayor Darris, for once, looked lost for words as he turned towards Lord Franco Tomell who seemed to be awakened by Danaka's demand.

"A woman cannot fight in a trial by combat," Darris replied as he nervously wiped the sweat from his palms.

"There is no such law. The law of the White City states any person may fight to prove their innocence." Lord Franco extended his arm and called Danaka towards him.

Danaka nervously walked towards Lord Tomell. Her heart was still beating murderously inside her. She struggled to breathe as she walked up the few steps. She could feel herself welling up inside but still she fought it.

"Come, child, sit."

Danaka knelt before her lord.

"Are you sure this is what you want? If you are found guilty, I will have the executioner make it a quick death. There will be no fire if you so wish it." Lord Franco's words were full of sorrow. The old man had seen his fair share of death; Danaka could tell he was a good man.

Danaka paused, slightly unsure of her answer. A quick death sounded better than to be feebly cut down by the lord's champion. "No, my lord, I choose the sword," she replied quickly with defiance in her voice.

She was struggling to her feet, but Lord Tomell stepped forward and offered her his hand. "I will pray for thee." Lord Franco turned towards Mayor Darris and nodded his head signalling that there would be a trial by combat.

"Great people of Tomellburg. This matter with be decided by the sword."

Danaka stood alone in the town square. The hot sun was reflecting off the bright clear slabs that lay beneath her feet. She had been given a sword; it looked just like the one she had admired earlier on. It felt heavy in her hand; she knew she would need to swing it with two hands if she was to carry any weight behind her blows.

The dock where she stood had been taken down and the crowd had been pushed back, giving space for the combat that would soon follow. Lord Tomell was still seated on the platform giving him the best view of the action.

She could still hear the crowd chattering and mumbling behind her. *Don't make a fool of yourself, just a few swings and this will all be over.* Her heart was still thumping in her chest; each beat was harder than the last.

The heavy thud of metal against slab could be heard as her opponent stepped forwards. With each step, she could feel the weight of his armour. The knight seemed to shine in the sunlight; his armour was clearly well taken care of and polished regularly. He came up and stood by her side but didn't utter a word, he just stared. In his left hand he held a heraldic shield, which was seamed with bright silver with golden trim and a half moon at its centre. He looked average in height but still taller than Danaka, and with all that armour he was clearly a lot stronger too. The knight unsheathed his long sword, the point facing Danaka.

"The moment has come. Now the gods in their beloved White City will decide if the accused is innocent or guilty!" Darris shouted as he paced up and down the platform. "Danaka, the accused, stands before you, ready to fight for her life against the lord's new champion – a great warrior ordained by the gods to fight for his lord. I give you, Sir Claris Moon!"

The crowd roared as the knight turned to face them before he raised his sword to the heavens. He looked an imposing figure as he stood tall and strong with his sword held out in front of him. The steel flickered in the sunlight, forcing Danaka to close her eyes.

Danaka took a big gulp as she stepped back, ready to accept the fate that lay before her. *Soon it would be over.*

Sir Claris Moon began to swing his sword over and over. The wooshing sound sent a shiver down her spine as she watched his blade swinging effortlessly from side to side. She couldn't see his face but she felt he was revelling in her fear.

A whistle, a haunting tune, began to play. The soft tune silenced the crowd. Danaka turned towards the crowd. Slowly they began to part as a large figure began to emerge. Broad and confident, a man stood in the sunlight. Two black horses flanked him either side, their muscular frames were enhanced by the rays of light shining down from the heavens. The man was dressed in a white poplin tunic and his large sword was draped across his back. His face was down, showing his thick black hair. The tune continued to play; the man blew effortlessly into his flute.

Suddenly Danaka began to realise who it was, and her hand began to shake. It was her mystery man from yesterday morning. A thousand thoughts rushed through her mind.

He slowly began to tilt his head and look towards Sir Claris, revealing his intense and menacing face. His eyes were dark and full of hatred. Once he stopped playing, he spoke, “I will fight for the girl.”

Chapter 8
Death Will Always Hunt the Living

In a few days it will all be over. Just focus on the target, the gold. Garroway knew this would be their last mission. The coin they had been offered was more than enough for them all to retire three times over. Their last assignment had been in the Desert Realm. They had been paid one thousand and two hundred gold coins by an Aalafarian noble to kill Yor Bazaba one of the Samoran chieftains. Garroway would always charge that price: one hundred coins to himself and each of his children.

Yor Bazaba was a vicious, heartless killer who led the Dulgar blood warriors on a rampage across the borders of Samora and Aalafar. It was once said that he would eat the hearts of his victims. It was no simple task to kill this fiend but they carried out their mission to the finest detail. Twenty-five blood warriors fell to their blades that day and not a single scratch on him or his children. A job well done but, oh, his body ached for days after the combat had ended.

So why did he feel so unsure of this mission? It was no different to any other; something felt different this time but he was not sure what. Maybe it was because Lilah had been so hesitant at accepting such a task. The money was good but the risk was far greater.

They had left Baron's Bay at first light. No one in the town had been awake. The sun had slowly risen from behind the great eastern ocean, lighting up the dirty downtrodden streets before them. They were to follow the Silver Spear River west until they reached the Ironwood.

Garroway was at the front, his beautiful Lilah to his right as always. She could not be too far from his side. The others followed loyally behind in rows of two. Only Maarax rode alone at the back of the column. They had been riding nearly four hours. The day was bright, casting the birds above them into dark shadows against a sky of the palest blue. Not a cloud was in sight; the air was fresh and welcoming as he breathed it into his old lungs.

The path they followed was made of light sand; to their right were oceans of grass. Up ahead, along the brow of the horizon, was the Ironwood. Strong thick woodland that was once said to have held home to trolls and giant spiders – tales for small children to keep them out. Now it was ruled over by Lord Glynn Harron, in service of the N'Dai family. Garroway knew nothing of this man except that he was suspicious of foreigners, so they were to keep a low profile until they were far from his lands.

"When do we stop, my love?" Lilah spoke with her soft voice.

Just the sound of her light tones made Garroway feel summer warmth deep in his heart. "We do not stop." Garroway turned to Lilah admiring her pale milky skin and blood red hair. She wore a short leather skirt which connected to a thin leather breast plate that stopped around her breasts. "We have a lot of ground to cover; we must be at the Black Ale Inn in two days. It is there we meet our guide."

"This guide you speak of, Dillian Howard, you say you know nothing of this man?" Lilah was concerned. She liked each mission planned to the finest detail.

"I know only of his appearance and where to find him. My sources in Dagen knew nothing of this name. He is either of low birth or, as I suspect, a traitor posing under an alias to go unseen. If this goes wrong, he will want to slip back into his old life."

"We have never needed guides before. Hundreds of times we have stood together, we are all you need." Lilah pointed to their children. "This name – Dillian Howard – makes me feel uneasy."

Garroway sensed the shiver that ran down her back, as if it was as cold as the touch of the death. "I know very little of this land. The map I have takes us only so far. He will guide us the rest of the way and make sure we have safe passage. This is a tense time for all who live here, so we must tread carefully and not arouse suspicion." Garroway leant over and ran his old rough hand down Lilah's soft forearm. "Trust me, I have not led you all this way to fail you now."

Lilah smiled. His touch was all she ever needed. "You could never fail me. We all owe you our lives."

Garroway thought back many years ago, to when he was a young warrior, a solitary man who sold his sword to the highest bidder and went to war. His life had no meaning, yet his only talent was killing. He was the finest warrior he had ever seen but war was not for him. Short action was more his style. One-on-one fighting, where he could use his speed and agility to out-manoeuvre his opponents. Battles were chaos and, during the carnage, even those fighting alongside you could kill you by mistake. He liked to know his surroundings and to trust those fighting beside him.

It was not until he met Lilah twenty-five years ago that his life changed forever. He could remember it now. It was as clear as the pale blue sky above him. She was so beautiful, her muscles as defined as they were today, her body slim and powerful. Her brown eyes were enchanting, seducing all that looked upon her. She had been only young, maybe twenty when he first laid eyes on her beauty. Lilah had been in the midst of a battle of strength with a local brigand back in Dagen. Garroway remembered how he admired her pride, her cunning and her confidence as she fought so hard against her opponent. She may have been beautiful but she never needed to use her womanly charm to get what she wanted.

The only women Garroway had come across until that point were whores and Lilah was certainly no whore. Her charisma and charm were nothing more than elegant and she knew how to use her fists that was for sure. That brigand never knew what was coming when she let loose with a three-punch combination that left him with his front teeth on the floor and his pride beside them. It wasn't long after that she became his second dragon.

Those memories brought a smile to the old man's face. All thoughts of how he met his children made him happy. When all twelve of them were together, that was when he felt content. All he needed now was the gold and to be safe home across the sea, but for now he had a job to do and his mind needed to be clear. *Blood for gold, death for life.*

Up ahead the thick dense forest drew near, the large thick oak trunks were as wide as five men side by side. Their great shadows were cast far and wide across the green grass that lay so humbly beneath them. Two tall flags were flying high at the entrance to the forest, the Allamantyan colours.

"All of you listen." Garroway turned to his children. Within an instant, all their chatter turned silent and their horses pulled to a halt. "From this moment on, we are acrobats, circus performers, here to perform at the royal wedding. If confronted, I will do all the talking." His voice carried power. He knew when he spoke, they obeyed without question.

****

"I hate this fucking country. All I see is green. I hate green." Valdar spat, and then began to run his tongue around his gums where one of his front teeth used to be. "I can't wait till we are back on that ship and heading home." He began to adjust his breastplate.

"Make up your mind, Valdar. A few days ago, all you did was whine and bellyache that you wanted off that cursed ship," Naleac replied with a smile on his face. His green eyes were at full beam in the summer sun. His brown leather tunic fell from his shoulders down to his knees.

Valdar quickly shot back, "You were the one bitching about a sore head this morning. Don't drink wine if you cannot handle its fire."

"If you had drunk what I had, you would still be back in Baron's Bay in some ditch." Naleac leant back into his saddle bag and pulled out a small leather pouch. He untied the end and began to drink down the cool clear water from inside. His throat felt as dry as scorched earth until the liquid made its way past his lips.

"He will be complaining he has no water soon." Caelan spoke with a smile identical to his twin brother's. He brushed his long dreadlocks away from his face. Small beads of sweat slowly trickled down his cheek.

"All you men are the same, you are never happy unless you have something to complain about." Zaira turned her head and looked back at Valdar and Naleac and joined in their conversation.

"No one was talking to you. Turn around, bitch." Valdar angrily flicked his wrist out in front of him.

"You will hate this country even more if you talk like that to me again." Zaira's voice rose in anger. She pushed herself up in her saddle. The definition in her arms was as clear as water on a bright summer's day. Her half-plaited blonde hair shone in the short rays of light that burst through the leaves of the mighty trees above their heads.

"Listen to me, my pretty friend," Uriah, who was at the back of the column, shouted to Valdar. "Don't anger her; you struggle with the fairer sex as it is."

"Fuck you, you little weasel! Come up here and say it to my face!" Valdar's voice exploded like a volcano. The birds sprang from their trees and the leaves rustled in the wind.

"It is a long ride and I am feeling a little tired but, if you wish to talk to me, by all means come back here and I will converse with you." Uriah's grin was ear to ear.

"All of you, shut up!" Lilah shouted. "You will bring us all unwanted attention if anyone is near. If you can't talk quietly then don't talk at all." Her voice sounded like a mother scorning her children. Silence fell over them like naughty delinquents.

****

The twelve assassins rode steadily through the forest. The sunlight flickered between the trees, lighting up the path before them. Hours had passed since they had entered the Ironwood and there was not a single sight of anyone. The place seemed silent and peaceful, just them and nature. Surprisingly, they had all kept relatively calm, no bickering, no fighting. Maybe the thought of rest and food was what kept them all so quiet. Maarax rode ahead of the column and out of sight.

"He is happiest when he is alone," Lilah said.

"When you have family, you will never truly be alone." Garroway smiled as he watched his son disappear. Maarax was the finest archer he had ever seen. He could hit a bullseye at one hundred metres. He was only sixteen years old when Garroway first laid eyes upon him; a defiant and proud boy – living alone did that to you. Back in Dagen, Maarax had been hunting on forbidden land; he'd killed a lord's deer and was being beaten by three soldiers, until Garroway appeared and severed their heads. *"Ride with me boy, and you will never be on your knees again, that I can swear to you,"* Garroway told him. In that moment, Maarax became the fourth Dragon of Dagen. Maarax was as loyal as a son could be, no questions asked, no orders refused, blood for gold.

A narrow winding river was to their left. It was green in colour and moved swiftly like a snake over the pebbles and between the banks. The banks were covered in roots that had become wilted and weak over the years. The blade-like leaves that hung feebly to the branches had become yellow and discoloured where they should be lush green and hanging proud.

It was more a stream than a river; the harsh summer months had caused the days to go by dry and without rain. Yet the river was impassable by horse. A large fallen tree now lay in the way for all those wishing to cross. On the far side of the bank, great fallen stone statues littered the path before them: huge faces of once-great rulers now left to decay and break away like they never existed. Moss and weeds intertwined around the crumbling rock. Dirt and excrement from passing animals stained the tributes to the fallen kings.

"Who were they?" Naleac asked as he directed his horse around a heap of rubble that lay before him.

"Who knows? And who cares?" Toran replied in his usual booming voice. He spoke as he began to scratch at his fiery ginger stubble.

"Kings want their names to live forever so they build monuments to themselves. The vanity of men is their curse," Zaira replied as she looked down at the fallen rock, seeing a squirrel scurrying underneath.

"These knights worry too much of the afterlife and not enough of their current life. What use to them is their name and rock when they are long dead? I live for today not tomorrow," Uriah added.

"Same here, little Uriah. I will use my coin to buy me a fine house and maybe a pretty little wife, too!" Roak shouted as he slapped Uriah on his shoulder, the force of the blow almost knocking him from his horse.

"I would at least like to have time to spend my coin, so if you wouldn't mind keeping your big bear paws off me, I would be very happy!" Uriah replied calmly as he pulled himself upright in his saddle. His shoulder began to throb but he showed no pain. "Anyway, us Dragons of Dagen, we don't have wives! No time for them."

"I had a wife once," Valdar added as if he was talking to himself and not the group. A hint of sorrow flowed with his words.

"Horse shit!" Uriah paused. "Really?"

"We weren't married long."

"What happened?" Uriah asked, genuinely interested.

"She died," Valdar said, bluntly.

Uriah suddenly stopped and began to think, slightly regretting goading his brother. He had known him for nearly ten years and not once had he spoken of a wife.

"Yes, I will get me a beautiful wife with my coin. Have me some kids too, they can work on my farm," Roak suddenly blurted out before wiping the sweat away from his head. The sun was beginning to reflect off the shaven sides of his mohawk. His large, dark well-defined body was beginning to shine due to the sweat seeping out of his skin. "Lothar, what will you do with your coin?"

Lothar looked back at Roak and Uriah, who were behind him riding side by side. His deep thick scar which ran down his left eye was always the first thing someone would see when he looked at them. His blinded eye was as pale as ice. "By the sounds of it, I will be spending a lot of my time at your farm, if your new wife is as beautiful as you say."

"Ha, my wife would have no need for you, old man, not with little Uriah showing me his tricks." Roak turned to Uriah, brandishing his large cheesy grin before flapping out his huge tongue.

"Put that away!" Uriah flinched, and then with his fingers he pushed Roak's tongue back into his mouth. "Women want to feel it, not see it. Especially not yours, either." Uriah twitched and shook his shoulders. "That thing's like the tongue of a buffalo."

"Even with these magic tricks you speak of, you will still be baffled at the sight of your children." Lothar now had a large grin on his face.

"Why would I be baffled?" Roak asked back.

"Because you would be thinking, why all your children look like me?" Lothar began to laugh, soon followed by Uriah and Roak.

"What? They would all look old and grey with shrivelled cocks and one eye," Zaira added.

"Ha, be careful what you say little sister, I have my eye on you!" Lothar closed his good eye before looking towards her with his blinded one. They all began to laugh; even Valdar and Zaira forced a little smile.

"Everyone, stop!" Garroway shouted. He raised his right hand in the air and everyone suddenly stood still; they knew something serious was happening.

Tension filled the air; the once peaceful forest became a turbulent hell. The sound of the birds stopped dead. The wind appeared to blow harder and branches began swirl; the sound it made mimicked that of a scream, of a woman's howl as it burst through the bushes and around the mighty tree trunks.

Maarax had turned his horse and was riding full speed towards the assassins. His left hand was gripped tightly to the reins like a baby to its mother. His right hand was out wide, almost perpendicular to his body. His long pony tail blew out behind him.

The assassins all brought up their horses so they stood side by side, each was ready for what was about to happen. They had all seen it a hundred times before; they knew what the others were thinking and they would fight as one.

"What do you hear?" Garroway asked Maarax. His voice was calm as always; panic was not a word that he understood. Maarax began to reply with his hands: he held up four fingers, then beat his hands on his chest and waved his right hand over his face. Toran leant down towards his saddle and began to draw his huge double handed broad sword. Garroway quickly turned. "Put that away, no weapons. Four knights approach; I will do the talking."

Suddenly, as if by magic, four heavily armoured knights appeared in the clearing, the loud thudding of their horses' hooves heightening the sense of danger. Each man was clad from head to toe in cast iron armour. Each piece of metal was polished until one's reflection could be seen. Underneath were rings of thick mail which rose up to their necks. Each had the visor to their helmets raised and none was decorated with plume of any kind.

"Allamantyan knights," Garroway spoke softly. "We must tread carefully here."

Three of the four knights rode grey horses and the fourth, who was at the centre, was seated upon a large black horse. His helmet was different to that of his company – his visor had what appeared to be three matching steel leaves sprouting from both sides of his helmet. He was clearly the leader. All four slowly began to ride towards the assassins, clearly interested in the twelve strangers that lay before them.

"All of you, stay here. I will speak with them," Garroway ordered. He began to ride towards his unwanted guests.

They watched helplessly as Garroway kicked into his spurs and slowly rode off. Lilah's heart began to thump in her chest and her palms were beginning to sweat; she wanted to be by his side. Silence gripped them all as they watched Garroway greet the knights. They could hear chatter but no words could be made out.

"What are they saying?" Naleac asked, trying to lean forwards as if that would help.

"I can hear nothing with your voice in my ear," Caelan replied abruptly to his brother.

"Both of you, be quiet," Rhodesha ordered. It had been the first thing she had spoken since they left Baron's Bay. It was clear her mind had been on other things.

"I say it would be better to kill four today than twenty tomorrow," Lothar said as he ran his index finger over his scared face before turning to Lilah.

"Garroway said we wait, so that is what we do." Lilah's words carried the same conviction as Garroway's but she was favouring Lothar's less diplomatic approach.

Still they spoke; the four purple knights had formed a semi-circle around Garroway. The tension was becoming too much to handle, the heat was beginning to rise like flames. The horses beneath the assassins were stirring; they could sense the unrest in their riders. Their hooves began to claw at the dirt, they brayed loudly causing one of the knights to look up. The knight's eyes glazed over, suspiciously, watching the twelve riders meticulously. He looked them all up and down like they were nothing more than meat for sale in a butcher's shop.

"I can't take this much more; give me the word and this will all be over," Lothar said as he felt the hilt of his short sword.

Lilah's heart began to race, beating faster and faster. She could tell Garroway was in an awkward position. He had two knights opposite him and two on either flank. He would struggle to deflect blows from four different angles.

"Lilah?" Lothar pleaded.

"Let him do it," Zaira added.

"No, Garroway ordered us to wait here," Toran shot back.

"There are four of them!" Valdar sharply joined in.

"We need to decide quickly." Naleac reached down and squeezed the base of his sword between his fingertips.

"I am with you whatever you choose," Rhodesha said reassuringly.

"Kill or die." Caelan's eyes never left the knights before him.

"Decisions, decisions." Uriah raised his highbrows in quick succession.

"Wait, everyone, wait." Lilah began to panic; the heat rose inside her body, sweat began to pour from her skin. Her hands started to shake as if she was outside on a winter morning.

Suddenly Garroway turned his horse and began to ride back towards his *children*, the knights steadily following behind him. He was riding slowly and calmly; it was hard to read his facial expressions as he was so poker-faced. As he got closer and closer, the tension began to lift, the birds began to sing once again and the temperature began to drop to a bearable level.

"All of you, follow me." Garroway spoke without emotion before turning his horse back around. Obedient as always, his *children* followed quietly behind him; none knew what to do or to think. They all followed in single file, each looking straight ahead.

Lilah could feel the eyes of the knights staring intensely towards her. It seemed like they never blinked as they watched each of them ride by; she could feel the unrest and the uncertainty in the eyes of those metal chested riders.

Only Lothar stared back, catching the leader straight in the eye. The knight was around forty but clean shaven; his face showed his years and he was a man of average looks. Beads of sweat ran down his high cheek bones. His eyes were deep and he had an aura of arrogance and over confidence as he watched Lothar with a look of both disgust and suspicion.

"Do you like what you see?" Lothar asked with a seductive tone.

"Insolence! How dare you talk to his lordship!" One of the other knights reared up, raising his voice and grabbing the hilt of his sword.

"Calm yourself, Sir Wallace," The lord ordered, raising his left hand. "Peasant, do you know who I am?" He looked Lothar up and down.

"I'm afraid not, but I have a feeling you're about to tell me." Lothar smiled as he slowly reached round his back to grab the handle of his dagger.

"I am Lord Glynn Harron's son, Jenson Harron. It is wise not to cross me, old man. I can see why you look so pretty with a tongue as fast as yours!" Lord Harron looked at Lothar's blinded eye before dropping his head and spitting on Lothar's sandal. The hot saliva ran down between his toes. Lilah could feel the anger building up inside of Lothar, she knew his temper. It would not take much for his blood to run cold. "Ha, he is all talk this one, boys. Let's go, it is better I not stain my steel with the blood of the old." Jenson kicked into horse, riding off the way the assassins had just come; his three companions followed behind, laughing.

"You fucking idiot! You could have ruined everything," Lilah shouted when she saw the knights were out of sight.

"Calm yourself, woman. If I had wanted them dead, they would be food for the crows." Lothar avoided eye contact, just looking down as his foot.

"We haven't time for this, let's keep moving," Garroway ordered.

All the assassins began to ride, following behind Garroway just as before. This time though there was no idle chatter; each was silent, looking out around them. They no longer felt at ease. It was as if at any moment their cover could be blown so they had to be ready. Each was highly skilled in the art of death and they were ready to paint their masterpiece.

****

Hours had gone by and night was drawing in; the mighty summer sun had begun to fade. Darkness was creeping over the land, so Garroway had ordered them all to make camp. The place he chose was a small clearing a few miles west of the Ironwood; it was surrounded by dense rose bushes and tall trees. It gave them good cover from passing soldiers and enough space for everyone to laze about freely. The ground was hard but it was nothing they weren't used to, living on the road was their life.

A single fire was at the centre of their encampment; the flames flickered and crackled as a deer lay skewered over the hot bed of red and yellow embers. The meat had become crisp and tender; the juices had begun to run freely down the side of the once mighty animal.

Toran sat so close to the meat, watching it intensely like a small child waiting for the order from its mother to be allowed to devour the delights in front of it. He was a big man, bigger than most, so he loved to eat. His stomach had started to rumble, as loud as if the gods had started to shake the land beneath him.

"I can't wait to taste you, baby." Toran's voice was low and husky as if he was trying to seduce some beautiful princess. He began to run his hand around his empty stomach.

"Cooking is like pleasing a woman, an art, something that cannot be rushed; you must take your time and embrace the flavours and smells that are before you." Uriah stood over the meat, slowly turning it as if he enjoyed teasing his elder brother, "Let the urges build up inside of you, let the meat take hold of your senses, let it control you and excite your thirst for its flesh." His voice was enchanting and as smooth as ice.

"What are you on about?" Zaira walked towards Uriah. Her athletic and slender body was enhanced by the flickering of the camp fire. "Step aside and let me finish." She pushed Uriah away, who laughed in return.

"When will it be ready?" Toran asked, his eyes never leaving the meat.

"Soon," Zaira replied. She began to turn the meat while adding newly plucked herbs.

"Where is Lothar? Has anyone seen him?" Garroway sounded taut as he walked through the camp. He looked around at his *children.* Valdar sat with his back to a mighty oak tree, sharpening his dagger. Rhodesha lay on the ground staring up at the darkening sky, her mind elsewhere. Roak was wrestling with the twins, overpowering them with relative ease.

"I haven't seen him since we made camp," Lilah replied as she too began to look around.

Garroway looked around frantically and then saw Lothar riding at full speed. Within seconds he was in the clearing and hastily dismounted.

"Water, someone give me water," Lothar ordered, before helping himself to a large sheep skin flask that lay beside Rhodesha. His face and body were wringing wet, rays of heat lifted from his body like a layer of fog. Smears of blood stained his face and chest. It was not his own.

"Where have you been?" Garroway's voice rose, as anger began to build inside of him.

Lothar was slow to reply; he lifted the flask above his head and began to pour the cool water over himself. The water splashed against his hot, sweat-filled body, washing away the blood that stained his skin. "I felt a little sorry for those poor knights," he said as he swilled the remaining water between his teeth, before spitting it out, "There was one of me and only four of them."

"You killed them?" Roak's face was full of shock.

"Are you sure they are dead?" Garroway's voice cooled, he now sounded more concerned.

"Well, unless you can live without a head, then I am pretty sure they are dead." Lothar turned and look at the meat roasting over the open fire. The rich smells of cooked flesh took hold of him. "Ahh food! I'm fucking starving." He began to walk over towards the deer.

"You idiot, you could've ruined everything," Lilah snapped, grabbing hold of Lothar's arm and pulling him back.

"They knew something was up. I did us all a favour." Lothar angrily pulled his arm away. "By morning they would be back with a hundred men. I saved you, woman."

"We have faced worse odds, old man." Uriah walked towards the nearest tree, before kneeling down.

Lilah quickly turned to Garroway, "We should head back. What will happen when that lord doesn't return home? Knights will be swarming these forests by dawn."

Garroway stopped still, contemplating his next move. He knew they were both right. After letting the knights go, he half knew they did not believe his story and it was only due to the royal emblem he held that they allowed him to pass. He had, for a moment, thought about killing them himself, but he knew what the consequences would be.

"The meat is done!" Zaira spoke, hoping to ease the growing tension.

The twelve swarmed the dead animal like a pack of wolves, tearing at it like a horde of savage beasts; they wildly bit into the juicy tender meat, devouring it as if they had never eaten before. The sound of chatter was swapped with a grotesque noise of chewing and cooked flesh being pulled apart.

Toran seemed to be sucking the meat from the bone, barely stopping to take a breath. Roak gnawed furiously at the chunk of meat he held before him, only stopping when his teeth cracked into something hard and inedible. He moved his tongue around inside his mouth until he pulled out an arrow head. He looked at it with an air of confusion; his big white eyes bulged out of his head before he flicked it away.

Loud belching filled the empty forest as one by one they finished their meal. They all sat in a circle around the camp fire, the bright flames reflecting off their faces, giving them all a red glow as they intensely tucked into the meat before them.

"What a meal! Some things are just born to be eaten," Toran's deep voice echoed through the trees. He lay back as he spoke, looking up at the night sky.

The stars sparkled like diamonds, little yellow twinkles on a bed of eternal darkness.

"Well, death will always hunt the living. No matter who you are, you will never escape its clutches." Uriah's voice was slow and intense; he flicked out a bone into the fire. He concentrated on the flames flicking and crackling as it wrapped its fiery embrace around it. The red glow forming on his face only enhanced the seriousness of the words he spoke.

"When did you get all philosophical?" Zaira inquisitively replied, turning to her *brother.*

"No, he is right," Garroway spoke; he slowly raised his head, looking out at each and every one of his *children.* "From the moment we are born, death searches for us all. With each passing day, whether we realise it or not, we have eluded its cold embrace." The eleven of them listened intensely, their eyes never leaving him. All that mattered at that exact moment was the words he spoke. "Many years ago, I made myself a promise; I would be the one who decides the day it finally finds me." Garroway rose. "I have been thinking, it is not safe that we all ride together. I cannot take the risk of us being led into an ambush. I will ride ahead alone and meet with this Dillian Howard. If all is safe, I will send word."

"No!" an array of voices called out.

"We always have ridden together."

"We will not separate." It was not clear who was speaking, the words crashed against his ears like hail shattering against the ground.

"We bring too much attention in such a large group. The Black Ale Inn is but a few hours ride west of here. If it is not a trap, I will send for you." Garroway stood up, stretching out his old back.

"No, I go where you go." Lilah shot up, standing beside him. She took his rough hand in her own and pulled him close. "For twenty-five years we have never been apart." Her seductive eyes drew him in. The beautiful shade of hazel took hold of his soul, as if trying to turn the tide of his thoughts.

"You are wrong." Uriah poked at the fire with a small stick. "This Dillian Howard you speak of, he would have your description, right?" Garroway looked down at him, clearly interested in what his *son* had to say. "If it is a trap, as you suspect, then is it not safer that I go in your stead? He knows not who I am."

A silence took hold of the forest; a slight night breeze blew softly through the trees and around the bushes. A cooing called out and the fire crackled and hissed angrily. Garroway knew he was right; he could enter the tavern unnoticed. Dillian Howard, or anyone waiting for them to arrive, would have no suspicion of a single rider. But letting his son ride alone in a foreign land was something he could not do so easily. *I promised to keep you safe, to shield you from harm and fight beside you.* Garroway thought back to the first words he uttered to his *son.*

"No, if Uriah goes. I do too." Toran's loud booming voice shot out as he rose to his feet. "He needs someone to look over him." He looked towards his brother and smiled, his gold tooth sparkling.

“It is settled then; me and the Iron Bull ride out in the morning. So, on that note, I need my beauty sleep.” Uriah began to yawn as he lay back next to the fire, curling up in a ball like a small child.

Lilah looked intensely at Garroway, running her hands up his forearm. Her soft touch was welcoming and much needed. He spoke no words but he just nodded before planting a kiss on her blood-red lips.

****

Hours had gone by but Rhodesha did not sleep. She had watched Lothar pray in his Yornish tongue before he slept. Every night he would fall to his knees and pray to his Winged God, Dalackis. He would utter the words, “Valla hathraen, Valla sehaer. Valla eskalar Yorgala.” He told her it meant, “My sword, my life for my god and family.” She liked the words.

It wasn’t long before she was the last one awake. Loud snoring from the others seemed to echo throughout the forest. The fire had virtually died out, just half flames flickered feebly between the last few pieces of charred wood. They all slept in a circle; if anything was to happen, they would all wake and fight with their backs to one another.

Rhodesha felt a cold shiver run through her spine. A sickness began to twist in her stomach, as if her heart was being pulled from her chest. In all the fifteen years they had been together, she had never spent a day apart from Toran. From the very first moment she saw him, she knew she loved him. She wrapped her hand around Toran’s mighty arm. Her fingers clung to his huge bicep. For a second, she felt safe again, knowing he was so close.

“Toran, my love, there is something I need to tell you.” Rhodesha’s voice was soft and innocent, an aura that did not sit so easily with her. Her left hand lowered to her bare stomach, resting below her belly button.

“Not now, I must sleep.” Toran kissed her softly.

Maarax appeared out of the shadows. He was patrolling throughout the camp; his steps were soft and silent. Even a cat would be jealous of his stealth. His bow was gripped tightly in his right hand, an arrow perched on his finger. Rhodesha closed her eyes for a moment and, when she reopened them, he was gone. She smiled briefly to herself.

She laid her head on Toran’s rock hard chest; his heavy breathing made her head move up and down with every inhale and exhale he took. The movements were relaxing and peaceful; she wanted to make the most of every minute she had with him. His large hands held her tight, pulling her close to his body. Feeling his skin against her own made her body feel loose and tingle with excitement. He smelt of sweat but she liked it, having his aura on her made her feel safe.

Do I tell him before he leaves? She had, had her suspicions during their trip across the Calhorion Sea, but she thought it could be the journey that made her sick. However, it was not until she woke in Baron’s Bay that she knew for sure. Everyone was still asleep when she had rushed outside to choke up her guts; she was not a big drinker like the others but she knew this was no hangover. Her mind was clear and her body was full of life.

No, his mind must be clear. His thoughts should be on the mission and nothing else! she defiantly told herself; there were more important things right now. She slowly ran her fingers down his naked torso, first over his chest and then down his stomach. His body was big and his muscles hard, but they were not defined and ripped like the others. He was built for power not speed, yet he had a gentle touch.

She began to kiss his chest, tasting the sweat around his pectorals and over his nipples. Slowly she started to work her way down his body, running her fingers through the little bit of hair that sprouted down his lower stomach. With each kiss she took, her heart began to beat faster and faster. She could feel her excitement building as she unclipped his belt, revealing why he called himself the Iron Bull of Dagen. Slowly she ran her tongue down the shaft of his penis. Even flaccid, it was large; it was more of an arm than a cock. She kissed the tip before taking it in her mouth. Only then Toran began to stir; he groaned slightly as she seductively began to suck. She angled her head and started to move up and down, before she slid him further down her throat.

She could feel him hardening; he quickly began to fill her mouth. As she forced him further in, Toran moaned loudly as he woke. First, he was startled, then he stared down at her and began to smile. He cupped her small head in his large rough hand.

"Shh!" Rhodesha replied as she released him, her voice smooth and enticing. *I will make the most of every minute I have with you.* She grabbed hold of his rock-hard shaft and slid him back inside her mouth.

Chapter 9
Two Kings, One Kingdom

The summer sun was high in the sky. Not a single cloud filled the ocean of blue above them. King Aristian was nervous; the fear of the unknown weighed heavily on his shoulders. He and his son, Prince Andros, sat side by side on their horses, looking and waiting. The green field they stood upon seemed ever so quiet. Not even the birds were singing and the light summer breeze had faded away. Just a humid air lay between them.

"When will they move?" Prince Andros's voice was ripe with fear. His words broke like thin glass. His heart raced murderously in his chest; his body felt like it was consumed with fire. His skin boiled inside his suit of armour. Sweat poured down his bony cheeks.

"Relax, my son." King Aristian placed his left hand on Andros's wrist. "Stay calm. Everything we have ever known changes in the next few moments." His voice was reassuring but Andros could sense he was just as nervous as him. His father wiped the sweat from his palms.

Prince Andros stared intensely, admiring the six riders that stood only fifty metres from him. Their blue armour sparkled and the mighty Valorian flag was flying high in the sky. His hands quivered and his stomached twisted. *Lyon, where are you? Come and save me from this living hell.* For a moment he thought of turning his horse and fleeing south, casting aside his right to the throne. Letting other men take heed of the burden he didn't wish to bear. Whether it was his lack of strength or thirst to please his father, he had followed him like a loyal dog. He briefly turned back, hoping to see his dear Lyon appear through the trees, declaring his love. Yet all he saw was the ugly sweaty faces of Uncle Daemar, Sir Dolfan and the three men at arms.

Under Andros's right arm he held his great helm. He thought for a moment to place it over his head and to cover his face, as if to hide himself from the outside world. His body began to sway, as if the dried earth beneath him was a great magnet pulling him down. He defiantly gripped his reins, digging his feet hard into his stirrups. To fall from his horse at such a time would not only shame himself but his father too. *Not this day.*

The king's horse began to stir beneath him. "Steady." He patted its white coat gently.

The six Valorian riders stood still, not a single movement between them.

"Father… I—" Andros stuttered as his horse stirred back and forth.

"Become what the gods intended you to be! Not a scared child!" King Aristian's voice was hard and snappy.

Andros froze; small tears began to fill his pale eyes.

"Just follow my lead, and sit up straight." His father quickly changed his tone, speaking calm and slow.

****

"My king, they are there. Should we not move?" Sir Kaian Vadius spoke, pointing out towards King Aristian and Prince Andros, who stood alone. He was dressed in a dark blue breastplate with a light blue undergarment and sparkling silver rings of mail which lay between the two. His Phrygian style helmet covered his head and waterfall of silver plume fell proudly to his neck.

"I am old, Sir Kaian, but I am not blind." King Vincinicus's eyes squinted under the bright sun. He ran his fingers through his well-groomed beard. The king's silver and red silks unflatteringly clung to his body, showing every arch and curve. His shining golden crown, fitted with five sparkling blue ocean gems, was the only part of him that oozed royalty. "Let them sweat." His laugh bellowed out but it was only to be followed by a sickening coughing fit, as if his lungs were attempting to rip themselves from his chest.

Princess Tilia's heart was racing. At any moment, she thought she would pass out. Her head felt light and her vision blurred, but with every ounce of her body she fought it, staying upright on her beautiful red horse. *Be strong, a nation looks to you.* Beads of sweat began to trickle down the arch in her spine. She slowly adjusted her dress, lifting it up higher around her breasts. The silver silk grasped tightly around her ribs, as if it wished to crush her like some great snake. Tilia breathed in deeply, filling her lungs with the hot humid air, as if that would loosen her dress' grip. Even the two braids on the sides of her head suddenly felt constricting and uncomfortable; she tried to adjust them with her hands but to no prevail.

Why did my father banish Gabriel from this meeting? Tilia wished they would see eye to eye but she knew it would never happen. Both were headstrong and neither ready to accept when they were wrong. Yet Tilia knew her brother would not be far from her side; he might not be beside her now but he would be close, watching.

Of the four men who rode with Princess Tilia and King Vincinicus, only two she knew: Sir Kaian Vadius and the mute Sir Dajax Feilos, both her sworn swords and dressed identically. The other two she did not know. One was young, barely a man, but he looked proud as he grasped the flag of Valanor with his right hand.

"Tilia, let's go," King Vincinicus ordered in his deep voice. He softly kicked into his spurs. He rode a huge black horse, one built for battle. Her father looked even smaller saddled on its great back.

Tilia pulled herself up alongside her father; she gripped her reins tightly, straining the muscles in her hand as she made her way closer and closer to the man she would marry. Her body bounced up and down in the saddle. She was a fine rider, cutting a figure of beauty in the summer sun. The small images of King Aristian and Prince Andros slowly became bigger and bigger until eventually they became a reality she could not escape from.

Her father wobbled from side to side, looking slightly tipsy and unsteady in his saddle. His crown was at a slant and his beard littered with drops of phlegm. Then suddenly they stopped.

"Welcome to Allamantya, King Vincinicus and Princess Tilia. It is a pleasure to finally meet you both." King Aristian smiled as he and held out his arm, welcoming them both like old friends. Prince Andros sat silent, as if frozen with fear.

The moment had come; Tilia was now face to face with the man who had caused her so many sleepless nights. She looked at Andros deeply. His thin brown hair was neatly brushed to the side; his eyes were innocent and pale. He was not handsome but he was not ugly either. Not the demon she had dreamt of. He looked as uneasy and as nervous as she did. With that image in her mind, she no longer felt any fear, as if it had been washed away by the tide of the ocean.

"Ah! It is great to be here. Our forefathers were once brothers. Greet me as one!" King Vincinicus rode alongside Aristian and pulled him tight, squeezing him like some great bear. His immense grip took away Aristian's breath. For a moment Tilia felt worried his old bones would break.

Vincinicus was ripe with the stench of wine. "I can see why your house colours are green; I have never seen so much of it since we set foot here."

"I see why so many men wished for your daughter's hand. She is a beautiful woman, and a fine rider too, if I may add." King Aristian looked at Tilia and smiled.

Complimenting Tilia's riding skills meant more to her than complimenting her looks. All her life men had flattered her with compliments of her beauty, yet she believed none. "Thank you, Your Majesty. I hope one day to rule as wisely as you do."

"Enough of these flatteries. King Aristian and I know such things are necessary. Come let us ride with you back to camp. I wish to taste Antilion wine, then we can talk more truthfully!" King Vincinicus voice was overpowering, with his right hand he smacked Aristian on his arm before bellowing out in laughter.

King Aristian paused. "Yes, please. Ride with us."

King Vincinicus raised his hand, signalling for his men to join them. Within seconds, his riders began to approach, their horses' hooves thudding heavily into the ground, like a thunder storm which shook the earth beneath them.

Tilia observed the wise King; she could tell he looked concerned. Tilia knew he was wondering why Gabriel was not there. The situation left her feeling uneasy. She tried pushing those thoughts to the back of her mind.

"You lead the way, my lord." King Vincinicus extended his short chunky arm. "Let our children ride at the rear, they have much to discuss."

"I agree." King Aristian turned to his son, beckoning him to talk to the princess.

Andros flinched, as if he saw a great fist heading towards his face. He turned to Tilia and smiled awkwardly. "My princess, I—"

"You have a fine smile, Andros." Tilia spoke quickly. She could tell in that moment her voice seemed to calm Andros. His rigid body began to loosen, his shoulders relaxed.

Andros returned a smile.

The two groups slowly rode back towards the Allamantyan encampment, the two kings, Aristian and Vincinicus engaging in idle chatter. Tilia could hear them both talking of days gone by and the old wars, yet both made it obvious to avoid the battle at the Pass of Falentis. The conversation between Andros and Tilia had died before it had even begun. By now, they both sat silently. Andros fidgeted constantly with his armour, all the while trying to stay in his saddle. Tilia watched him, not knowing whether to laugh or help him. She chose to do neither as both would dent his pride. Instead she chose to admire the vast landscapes around her. Soon it would all be hers to enjoy. She wondered about the hunting, what animals there were for her to hunt and where to find them.

"Andros," Tilia asked as she looked to her right, seeing him pulling frantically at his breastplate. "Where would you advise I go hunting?"

"I care not for hunting," he replied abruptly. "My sister, Arrabella, she can tell you."

"Oh, I will look forward to meeting her."

Andros offered no reply as he wiped the sweat from his forehead.

Tilia continued to examine her soon-to-be husband. He did not look an evil man, more a spoilt boy who did not know the true hardships of life. *But then*, she thought, *neither do I, for am I am royalty too. Although neither of us will marry for love, love however does grow like a flower over time. Yet some flowers are not able to grow, cut down before they are able to blossom.* Andros was tall but slim in frame, not built to be a warrior. His pale eyes however showed more to his soul than he would reveal. She knew there was more to this man than a crown and royal blood.

The Princess could feel the heat on her back, the beads of sweat slowly trickling down her body. She hoped patches would not form on her dress; she did not want to put Andros off at this early stage. Tilia noticed, however, that Andros had not once enquired about her or what it was like back in Valanor. Maybe he found her ugly? Then, suddenly, Leylan's cruel words stuck in her mind – was she good enough to be a queen? Was she, in fact, beautiful or were the compliments she received hollow truths to gain her favour?

Suddenly the column came to a halt. Each pulled on their reins, stopping their horses from moving. Andros pulled too hard and almost fell back, just about keeping his balance. Tilia released a small smile, sweet and innocent. Andros surprisingly smiled back, maybe through embarrassment more than anything else.

Aristian extended his arms. "It is said King Artendaus and Queen Valenya would spend hours picnicking in the sun when they were small children so I saw fit to honour our meeting in a way that would please both our ancestors."

Tilia knew all about Valenya, she was the first queen and ruler of Valanor. She had once been an Allamantyan princess who was promised the throne, yet when the nobles favoured her younger brother, Artendaus, she was forced to flee north over the mountains. Brother turned on brother, father killed son, and for two hundred years the blood flowed. *Let it stop today.*

Tilia looked out in amazement. The royal feast was full of wonder. A magnificent long oak table at the far side of the field rose up, looking down towards the five rows of smaller tables, ten in all, which littered the grass. A few men at arms stood at each end of the feast, while maids laid the tables with rich fruits. There was a vast array of colours and smells to please all the senses.

Seven great handcrafted chairs stood proudly behind the king's table. Each one had been perfectly designed for this occasion; thick engravings of the highest quality had been carved into each one. A mighty sword entwined with a single rose climbing its blade, the ancient sigil of their family, the royal house of Da'Menaeon. Each long rectangular table was full of meats and vegetables. Roasted pork and hot cooked turkeys were laid out; the meats were ripe and the juices fell freely. Large jugs of wines and ales were placed on each table; it would not be long before each man would be struggling to stand. The smells captivated everyone, and their stomachs rejoiced in the delights that lay before them, a mighty feast, a royal picnic for all to enjoy.

As the group made its way towards the feast, they all dismounted. Tilia was eased down by Sir Kaian as he held her waist and lowered her gently, like a fine piece of glass.

Andros sat like a spoilt child waiting for men to help him to the ground. "Come, I do not wish to be here all day!" he yelled out.

Tilia flinched at his tone, but she chose to ignore it and walk away. She ran her small delicate fingers over the smooth oak tables, each one identical to the other. Dark in colour but thick and strong. This morning her heart was full of fear but now all she wanted was to taste those exquisite meats. Fifty metres behind the royal table she could see the Antilion encampment, a row of green and red tents. Knights and men at arms were riding up and down. As she made her way up between the two columns of tables, she could hear her father's loud overpowering voice as he waddled up behind her, his echo draining out King Aristian soft and gentle tones. *If only Gabriel was here now,* she thought as she imagined him sulking in his tent.

"You must be Princess Tilia. I am Princess Arrabella." The voice was articulate and confident.

Tilia turned to see Princess Arrabella walking towards her. Her movements were smooth and fluid, with each step her body followed freely. Her elegant white dress was well fitted around her slim and appealing frame. The silks parted around her breasts showing her enhanced cleavage and tightened around her waist. It had two golden belts, decorated with sparkling green and red jewels; the first was situated under her breasts and the second around her waist. The dress fell loose around her thighs, separating into three sections which stopped by her knees. A very thin and almost see-through silk cape fell from her shoulders. Her shining brown hair was long, falling past her shoulder blades. Each strand shone and glistened in the sun.

"I love your dress; I have one very similar back home." Tilia looked up and down, admiring the eye for detail and fine sewing. She noticed immediately that it was a Valorian style dress.

"I expected you to be taller," Arrabella replied in carefree manner, barely making any eye contact as if disappointed by what she saw. "Queens should be tall." She then lifted up her cape and wrapped it round her arm. Her body was slim and toned, her long legs golden and defined. "Father!" she called out as she brushed past Tilia, lightly knocking her shoulder in the process.

Princess Arrabella embraced her father. Pulling him in tightly, the gesture seemed to take Aristian by surprise. Arrabella then turned to King Vincinicus and curtsied, extending her arms as she lowered herself. The arch around her breasts shone out like gold from a treasure chest.

"I humble myself before you, mighty king." Her voice was smooth and seductive. King Aristian quickly pulled his daughter up.

King Vincinicus took her hand in his and placed a small kiss om it. "The man who marries you will be richer than the gods themselves."

"Thank you, my Lord." Arrabella smiled as if she already knew who she would marry. "Where is Gabriel?" she asked as she looked at the Valorian men who stood behind the king.

"Er..." King Vincinicus paused for a moment, lost for words. "He was not feeling well and so he decided to say at the camp. He will be ready tomorrow when we ride to the capital." For the first time since they met, the king's voice was not loud and confident. He suddenly began to cough violently, retching forwards as if his guts wished to leave his body through his mouth, causing a disgusted Princess Arrabella to back away quickly, covering her face.

King Aristian quickly came to his aid, placing a hand on his back as he continued to cough. "It is you who seems unwell. Please let my physicians see to you."

"No!" Vincinicus angrily pushed Aristian's hand from his back, and Aristian, in turn, stumbled away, struggling to keep his balance.

In an instant, Sir Dolfan Greenway drew his blade, the tip pressing instantly to the young Valorian flag bearer's chin, drawing blood. The Allamantyan men at arms grasped their swords frantically. Sir Kaian and Sir Dajax returned in kind, arching their bodies, protecting their king as they prepared for an attack. In a flash the situation turned from happy to sinister. Each man stood, staring at the other, venom cursing through their veins and hatred boiled in their eyes.

Princess Arrabella screamed as she stepped away. Two men at arms, clad in mail and the colours of Allamantya, came to her aid. Each clutched six-foot spears and large circular shields, their blades pointing towards King Vincinicus and his men.

The chaos caused Prince Andros's horse to jerk. The prince stumbled back in fear as his horse reared up against him, both front legs kicking out violently. The whites in his eyes consumed his face as he tried to keep his balance. His arms waved out around him like two windmills before the weight in his armour brought him crashing to the ground. He thudded loudly on the dirt, the impact taking away his breath and rendering him silent.

"Father!" Princess Tilia yelled as she turned to see the commotion. In a flash she ran back to him. Her tight fitted dress restricted her movement but like a loyal daughter she was there to comfort and protect her father. King Vincinicus continued to cough, clawing at his gut before spitting both blood and phlegm to the ground. Tilia began to softly stroke his back as she held his chubby hand in her own.

"Ease your swords!" King Aristian frantically ordered. Sir Dolfan removed the tip of his blade from the young flag bearer's chin and sheathed his sword instantly. The men at arms still grasped at their weapons. "Stop!" the king pleaded.

Sir Kaian and Sir Dajax gripped their swords even tighter, all the while never taking their eyes off of their targets. Both men were ready to die, to protect their king and princess. The gods welcomed such warriors to the night sky.

Out of nowhere, the young Prince Arteus appeared. He launched himself onto one of the oak tables and drew his sword. He was clad in his Antilion armour, rings of mail clung to his arms and legs. The green tunic fell proud from his shoulders down past his waist. He was only a boy but he showed no fear. He held his sword out in front of him and towards his enemies.

"You heard your king!" Prince Daemar commanded as he rode his horse into the two Allamantyan men, knocking them forwards. They were the first words he had spoken since they had headed back to camp. The Allamantyan men loosened their swords, as ordered, and stepped away. Sir Kaian and Sir Dajax then slowly released their blades and stood up straight. Prince Arteus watched them both meticulously before returning his own sword.

"I am sorry." King Vincinicus stood up, wiping the spit from his mouth. "I need no physicians. It will soon pass."

King Aristian nodded. He spoke no words, as he felt they would break like thin ice; his heart was beating to its full extent. As if, at any moment, it would rip from his chest and escape his old body. "Please, head towards the royal table." King Aristian extended his shaking arm.

"Yes!" King Vincinicus roared. "Bring the wine!" He and his men then headed towards their seats. Tilia slowly followed behind.

Daemar dismounted and then leant in towards his brother. "So you have noticed Prince Gabriel is not here."

"I have," Aristian replied. "Tell those men who are not at the feast to be alert."

"Their swords will be sharp."

"No, I said to be alert."

Prince Daemar bowed his head and walked off with Sir Dolfan.

"Father!" Prince Arteus shouted as he dropped down from the table. "Are you okay? I would've cut them down before they got to you."

"I'm sure you would have." He pulled his son close to him. "Brush your hair." Arteus's thick brown hair was as wild as a thorn bush; he may have only been fourteen but he had the strength and nearly the height of full-grown man.

Prince Andros suddenly woke. "Help me! Someone get me up!" he pleaded from the dirt.

King Aristian closed his eyes and took in a big breath of air as he adjusted his crown before turning to Arteus. "Help your brother up."

****

A few hours had passed since the tense confrontation. Now Kings Aristian and Vincinicus sat at the centre of the royal table. To Aristian's right sat his sons Andros and Arteus, and next to them sat their sister Arrabella. To the left of Vincinicus sat Tilia, and beside her sat one lone empty chair.

The hot summer sun shone brightly, as if the gods too were celebrating, giving their holy blessing on the joyous occasion. The rays of light burst through the heavens and onto each table. Men from both Valanor and Allamantya drank and feasted together like brothers. No hatred was seen, only love and friendship. What wine and ale can do to a man – the image made King Aristian smile. Each table was full, ranging from lords to knights. Directly below the king's table sat the old Lord Devon Hohjan, his frail body slumped on the table, a goblet of wine hanging from his fingertips.

"I hear you cancelled the right for women to fight in your armies?" Aristian asked King Vincinicus as he poured himself a fresh goblet of wine. Two hundred years ago, Queen Valenya broke away from her Allamantyan kin and established her kingdom in the northern part of the realm, now known as Valanor. She had allowed women the right to fight alongside men as equals.

"Yes, I know. Old traditions die hard but battle is for men. I do allow the women to train and to defend our cities in times of war." King Vincinicus stopped talking only to force more meat into his mouth. His small chubby fingers were ripe with grease and strips of turkey as his licked them clean.

"I am glad to hear this. The taste of battle is hard for men, let alone women. Plus, if children are to become fatherless, it is better if they don't lose their mothers too." Aristian raised his cup to his lips. The cool wine slid into his mouth. Its taste was strong and refreshing. "As we agreed, Andros and Tilia will have joint rulership of the Western realm and its empire. I am willing to change our laws and allow their firstborn child, whether boy or girl, to become heir to the kingdom."

"I was hoping you would say that, for that is one tradition our nation was built on." Vincinicus took his wine to mouth, washing down the lump of food which was stuck in his throat.

"For now, though, it is necessary we rule together, until we see fit to give up our crowns." Aristian and Vincinicus raised their goblets, and the gold sang as they crashed together. Loud rapturous laughter called out as men from both sides hailed their kings and called for the new peace.

Aristian, however, only smiled for he knew this was only the beginning. It was hard enough for a single king to rule, yet with two kings and one kingdom… the thought of such things did not fill him with joy.

****

Andros had, by now, removed his armour and was dressed in a fine red and green silk gown, the one his father had recommended he wore. His body felt loose and free, yet his muscles ached and his skin was sore where the hot mail had rubbed.

He poked and played with his food, pushing the thick tender meats around his plate. The thought of food did not please him, yet his stomach groaned for it. He looked up, scanning the feast for his dear Lyon. Yet all he saw was drunk and overzealous men, chanting and laughing. Some were falling over one another, like a mob from a local tavern. He, however, had nothing to laugh about. Although the princess was beautiful and everything a young prince could desire, all he wanted was Lyon the lion of N'Dai.

"Does your food not please you?" Arrabella spoke as if she was revelling in her brother's suffering.

"I am not hungry," he replied without looking up from his plate.

"I think he is overcome with lust, Arteus, don't you?" Arrabella took a small sip of her wine, smiling as she spoke.

"Yes, she is very beautiful." Arteus looked over at Tilia who sat quietly eating her food, taking the small pieces of the meat to her mouth. "I hope Father picks me a wife just like her."

"Oh, he will pick you a far better one than her. She is too small and nowhere near beautiful enough to be queen." Arrabella flicked her head back and brushed her long hair away from her face.

Andros suddenly looked up, anger distorting his face, "There is nothing wrong with her. She is far more beautiful than you could ever be." He leant over, past his brother and towards Arrabella, who pulled away quickly. His voice was venomous but quiet; he knew not to draw attention to himself.

"It truly is love." Arrabella blew Andros a kiss and took another sip of her wine.

King Aristian rose from his seat and raised his goblet. In that moment, the laughing and calls slowly drained out, each stopping to look up to their king. "Listen, I wish to thank the noble King Vincinicus and Princess Tilia for their company. He does us proud gracing us with his presence. Antilion and all of Allamantya shall be even greater knowing we have such strong allies!" The knights and lords raised their goblets and cheered.

Andros, however, was not interested in his father's words. They just buzzed quietly around his head like small bees, for he had seen a lion. A beautiful strong lion, emerging from the trees. His dear Lyon had arrived. A warm happy feeling built up inside him, like his shattered heart had begun to piece itself back together again. Lyon was clad in shining silver armour, his white tunic fell loosely from his shoulders, and the red war lion stood proudly on his chest. His long brown hair, half tied up, half down, shone in the sunlight as he made his way forward. His steps however were not firm and strong, his stature was not full of confidence, his body swayed like an old mast in heavy wind.

"He's drunk," Andros muttered under his breath as he dropped his fork in shock, for he knew what Lyon was like when intoxicated. When they were eighteen years old, Lyon had consumed far too much Akeshan wine and had threatened to tell his father of their love. It was only when Andros took him to his bed that he could persuade him otherwise. Now however he could do no such thing.

Lyon stumbled as he moved; wine fell free from his goblet. The blood red liquid splashed everywhere, staining his white tunic. He just about kept his balance, as he pushed passed a few lords who were far too busy feasting to take any notice. Lyon's face was distorted and angry. His hazel eyes, which were once warm and welcoming, now looked cold and cruel. He locked in on the prince, like a lion focusing in on its prey. Lyon violently threw down his goblet, raising his right hand and pointing towards him.

Andros began to panic as Lyon made his way down the aisle and towards the royal table. His heart beat murderously in his chest, intense single bursts, each one more powerful than the other. His hands started to shake and a painful sickness grew inside of him. His stomach twisted and turned. *Please no!* he pleaded, shaking his head.

Arrabella looked up; her attention was caught by the fear that had consumed her brother. Her eyes grew wide, her face full of shock.

"Treachery!" a panic-stricken voice screamed out. "My king, treachery!"

The words took hold of everyone, draining out the joy and laughter like a dark cloud sent by death itself. Each knight and lord looked back, feeling the rumbling beneath their feet.

In shock, King Aristian rose from his seat. Looking out before him he saw a sea of blue heading towards the feast. Rows of Valorian cavalry spread across the field like a great blue snake. Their armour sparkled in the rays of golden sun.

Sir Dolfan Greenway rose from his table, grabbing hold of those men closest to him, quickly trying to form some kind of shield wall.

"Treachery!" that lone voice yelled out once more.

Chapter 10
A Clash of Steel

For so long she had been alone, existing day to day, no future to aim for. All she had was to hope that each long drawn-out day would be better than the last. Yet now a man who she did not know was willing to lay down his life for her, *but why?*

Danaka's fist slowly loosened and the sword she was holding began to slide through her hand as her fingertips parted. The blade clanged as it smashed against the white slabbed floor. She stood in shock, still trying to comprehend what was happening.

"Who is it who calls to fight for the girl?" Mayor Darris shouted.

The mystery man slowly walked away from the crowd and into the centre of the square; all the while he never broke eye contact with Sir Claris Moon, who stood motionless. Just the sound of his slow heavy breathing inside his great helm could be heard.

The man looked up at Mayor Darris and Lord Franco Tomell before he spoke. "My name is Duro of house Bel'Rayne," he claimed in a proud deep tone.

The crowd gasped and they all began to chatter amongst themselves. Mayor Darris started to whisper into Lord Tomell's ear.

Duro Bel'Rayne? I've never heard of him before. She looked and admired him as he stood before her. He was tall and broad, and his muscles were defined. He had an aura of confidence about him as he stood silently, waiting for Lord Tomell to reply.

"Do you accept this man as your champion?" Mayor Darris asked.

"I–I–do," she stuttered as she replied, nerves once again taking hold of her.

"How will you pay for his sword?"

"I don't know, have no coin."

"You have your farm?" Mayor Darris added.

"I will accept neither coin nor dirt," Duro butted in as he turned and walked back towards his horses.

"Danaka, do you know the law, what the consequences will be if he defends you and you cannot pay this man?" Lord Franco sounded concerned.

Suddenly Danaka remembered the law of the White City. *The blood debt.* If a man shall stand for you and no payment is arranged, you will become his property until the day comes when the debt is paid. For moment she didn't know what to do. Should she allow him to fight for her? Or should she face Sir Claris herself? She looked at her opponent; he looked slightly unsteady, not as confident as before. Yet he was still a powerful specimen, his armour and great helm gave him a sense of villainy, a faceless demon.

"I accept," she suddenly blurted out. *A life with this Duro cannot be any worse than facing the sword of Sir Claris.*

Duro silently walked back towards her; now he was carrying his sword in his left hand. It was still in its scabbard, which was made from grey and white fur with a thick leather strap winding around the shaft of the sword.

"It has been a long time, old friend. I thought you were dead," Sir Claris spoke as he removed his great helm and pulled back the mail that covered his head. Sir Claris was of olive skin, he looked handsome and clean shaven. His eyes were dark and enchanting, not the eyes of a killer. His hair was short and jet black, his cheeks were well sculptured.

"I am dead and soon you will be too," Duro coldly replied as he unsheathed his sword. "I travelled a thousand miles to kill you." The steel sang as it was drawn free.

"I knew this moment would come. I have seen it in my dreams." Claris took in a deep breath.

"I linger not in dreams, I exist only in nightmares." Duro turned to Danaka, "Step back." He threw her his scabbard, which she clumsily caught before she stepped away. Her back was to the fountain, far from the combat that was about to take place.

Danaka's heart began to race, beating fast and intensely inside her chest. She felt more nervous now than she had when she was to face Sir Claris herself. Her hands began to shake, her knees quivered and her palms began to sweat.

"Duro, of the once-great house, Bel'Rayne, shall face Sir Claris Moon, the sworn sword of Lord Franco Tomell. May the gods decide who is just." Mayor Darris signalled the fighting to begin.

The crowd drew silent as the two opponents stared intensely at one another; just the sound of the water from the fountain splashing and bubbling behind her could be heard. Neither broke eye contact, not wanting to give the other a psychological edge. The tension was killing Danaka inside; she wanted to wish Duro good luck but no words fell from her lips. Then, before she knew it, it had begun.

Suddenly Duro lashed out, stepping forward and swinging his sword. Danaka knew nothing of fighting but she knew Duro's style was very unorthodox. He held his sword by the handle with the blade facing away from its target. He attacked with a demonic intensity; his sword smashed and crashed against Sir Claris's shield. Bits of broken and splintered wood flew high in the air. With each swing, Duro changed the way in which he held his sword, switching from the traditional way of fighting to the unorthodox, to confuse and keep Sir Claris unbalanced.

Sir Claris, though, was no pushover. He deflected the blows well as he covered up, using his shield to take the brunt of the attacks. Suddenly he struck back, forcing Duro to deflect the oncoming blows. The steel rang out as the blades danced together, over and over.

Duro wore no armour so he was more mobile. He used the balls of his feet as he moved in and out of range. His attacks were quicker and more precise as he rained blows down on his target. It was clear he harboured great feelings of hate for Sir Claris; each attack was full of malice and cruelty. He had the intention of causing as much damage as humanly possible. The swords clashed together, each blow harder than the last. Sir Claris was the stronger of the two, his armour was heavy and he was forcing Duro back whenever they exchanged.

Sir Claris lashed out, forcing Duro to sidestep and pivot to his right to avoid the oncoming attack. He then pulled his sword back before thrusting it forward, hoping to take advantage of Duro's lack of armour. Duro however took a half step back, before deflecting the blow. It was beginning to show that the extra weight Sir Claris was carrying was beginning to wear him down. He could only exchange a few swings at a time before he stopped to draw breath, taking in big gulps of air.

As Sir Claris stepped back, just for a moment's rest, Duro pounced on him like a lion springing out against his prey. He unleashed a hellfire of fury as his blade exploded against his shield, and the wood shattered as it collapsed under the weight of his attack. Sir Claris threw down the remains of his shield and gripped his sword with both hands.

"You fight better than I remember." Sir Claris smiled uneasily as he wiped the sweat from his brow.

Duro offered no reply as he attacked once again. Sir Claris defended well, holding both arms out to deflect each horrific blow coming his way. Duro began to switch his sword from his right hand to his left, each movement keeping Sir Claris on edge and uneasy, unsure of where to defend himself next.

Danaka felt queasy and unsteady. She had never enjoyed violence but now two men were fighting to the death because of her. She took in a big gulp of air and sat back against the fountain step as she watched these two warriors hack away at one another.

The crowd began to scream and shout as the two exchanged blows; steel clashed against steel. For the first moment in the fight, it seemed that Duro was beginning to take charge. Sir Claris was beginning to swing wildly, hoping his attacks would find his elusive target. Duro bobbed and weaved as he avoided the sword that slashed before him.

Sir Claris raised his sword high in the air, conjuring up all the force he had left inside him, as he brought it crashing down towards Duro, who in turn sidestepped to his left, bringing his own sword up which slashed violently under Claris's armpit. A fountain of blood sprayed out from his wound. His silver mail quickly turned deep red.

A roar leapt up from the crowd as if they were excited and aroused by the sight of blood. Danaka looked at them with disgust – a few moments ago they were all calling for him.

Sir Claris yelled as he grabbed the mail under his armpit to stem the flow of blood. He stumbled forward, but somehow he managed to hold onto his sword as he quickly turned back to face Duro. He was clearly an experienced knight, one who had seen combat many times before. The blood began to run down his armour and drip slowly onto the white slabs below.

Duro smiled. "Blood for blood." He began to spin his sword in his hand.

Sir Claris was clearly in pain; his face grimaced in agony as he slouched forward. He held his sword out in front of him, clearly not ready to give up just yet.

It's over, stop the fight, she wanted to scream it but she knew it was no use.

"Again, old friend, one last dance." Sir Claris spat the blood from his mouth.

Duro nodded, offering no facial expression as he waited for his opponent to stand up straight. It was clear he had hatred for Sir Claris but there was respect there too. The two slowly stepped towards one another, their eyes locked together. Nothing existed in that moment but their opponent and their sword. In a flash, they both began to exchange blows. Duro pressed the attack, stepping forward with each swing as he forced Sir Claris back. It was as if an indestructible monster raged inside of him. He seemed impervious to the attacks from Sir Claris, each swing of Duro's sword shuddered through his opponent.

Sir Claris valiantly defended himself, but that was all he did, defend. He struggled to get off any attacks of his own as he fought with his left hand gripped tightly under his armpit. He offered no pleas for surrender or mercy. Sir Claris brought up his sword to protect himself from one of the many hate-filled blows that were coming towards him, but at the last moment Duro switched the angle in which he held his sword. The blade was now behind Duro as he slashed his sword up and across Sir Claris's torso, splitting it like a melon. The mail broke and the armour shattered before the sword exploded through his flesh. The knight gasped and yelped as he slumped to his knees. A loud thud echoed throughout the courtyard as his iron covered body crashed to the slabs below. Blood sprayed freely from his body; he knelt in a river of red as he looked up towards Duro. He coughed and choked as blood began to fall from his mouth.

The once loud sadistic screams from the crowd were suddenly erased; silence gripped hold of them as if they never expected this moment to come. Just the odd mutter could be heard as Duro knelt down in front of Sir Claris, pulling him tight.

Danaka could see that they were talking, quietly whispering into one another's ear. Duro's hands cupped his once hated opponent's face, holding him close. Sir Claris held Duro's shoulder trying to keep himself upright. She wanted to walk over and listen. *What would they have to speak of at a moment like this?*

Slowly, Sir Claris began to sway from left to right as his life bled out before him. Duro lowered him to the floor, cupping his head as if he was a new born baby. Sir Claris's mail-covered hand slumped heavily to the ground, and the clang of the metal rang out as he lay motionless. He was dead.

Lord Tomell slowly rose to his feet. "The fight is over. The gods deem Danaka innocent. There will be no celebration tonight. Sir Claris was a good knight and loyal subject." He turned to Mayor Darris who still seemed shocked at the outcome of the contest. "Have his body prepared for his journey to the White City."

Duro slowly stood up straight and began to walk towards Danaka. He left footprints of blood as he made his way over to her. She gulped heavily and her hands began to shake as he stood beside her. His body produced intense rays of heat, an aura of sweat and his skin was wringing wet. The white poplin tunic he wore was stuck to his body. Large patches had formed down his back and along his stomach. The sweat seemed to make his muscles shine as he ran his large sword through the fountain water. The blood was slowly erased from the steel as the clear sparkling water turned red.

"We are leaving." Duro spoke slowly and abruptly as he took his scabbard from Danaka's hand and returned his blade to its home.

Danaka didn't know what to say, she just followed him like a dog behind its master. She watched as the crowds parted before him, like a god they seemed to fear and admire him. She could feel the hot burning stare of a thousand eyes as they made their way through the crowd. Danaka didn't look up, she felt too ashamed and embarrassed. She could just see the red foot prints in front of her, each step bringing back the horrible violence she had just witnessed.

His two beautiful black horses followed loyally; the clang of their hooves echoed behind her as they stepped on the white slabs. She could hear the muffled calls from Mayor Darris as he addressed the crowd. She didn't care for what he had to say but as they walked further and further from the courtyard his voice began to drift away. No words were spoken as they walked through the market place and down the slope out of town.

With each step, the flashes of steel burst before her eyes. Loud echoing screeches, as the steel scrapped together, rang through her ears. She saw the images of the clashing swords, the blood, the screaming and the sadistic demon-like faces of the crowds as they looked on like rabid dogs, drooling at the feast before their eyes. Her legs felt weak and loose. She wanted to be sick, and her stomach was in knots, rumbling loudly. She had the urge to curl up and heave but she held it together. *Stay strong, it's over.*

"Get your things, only what you can carry. I will wait here," Duro ordered.

With all the thoughts racing through her head, she hadn't realised they were outside her home. She watched as he mounted the larger of the two horses. He moved with ease. One fluid movement and he was on its back. He looked strong and handsome as he gripped the reins of his horse.

Danaka slowly made her way into her home. It seemed so empty and quiet. The once-warm friendly walls now felt cold and uninviting. Sadness came over her as she looked around the living area. She imagined her Uncle Otis sitting at the dining table, carving wood, always a smile on his face, then her aunt cooking her hot meat pies. A single crystal-like tear fell from her cheek. She had wanted to leave this place for so long but now the time had come to finally go, she didn't want to. Her stomach twisted and turned. She collected a few healing herbs, clothes and blankets, and she packed them in her leather bag which she threw over her shoulder. Each item she saw, whether it be an old clay cup, chair or a flower, all had meaning and carried a memory of its own.

Walking back outside she felt the hot summer sun on her skin. She stood on her porch, looking out on the land before her. She knew that when she left, it was unlikely she would ever see this place again, and if she did, the locals would tear it down.

"Griffin! Griffin!" Danaka yelled as she looked out over her farm. She stood in hope that her most loyal friend would appear, sprinting towards her like he did every morning. Yet all she got was an unhappy silence. The soft summer breeze blew through her wheat field. It swayed gently. A deep sadness came over her. A thump began to form in her throat, and tears welled in her eyes. *Where is he? Please be safe.*

"Danaka! You safe! The Winged God gave you protection," a loud bubbly voice called out.

Danaka looked over to see Irban and his wife standing before her. She was holding their daughter in her arms. He was clearly a lot older than her; she was young slim, and underneath her tired eyes and slouched body she was pretty. Both were small in stature but had a warmth to them. They wore tatty brown leather overalls, covered in dust and hardened clay. She wiped a small tear from her eye and swallowed hard before replying, "Irban what are you doing here?"

"We couldn't watch, but I knew you would be safe. He protects his children!"

"I want to thank you for trying to help me." Danaka smiled. "It was not this Winged God who saved me but him." She pointed towards Duro who sat watching her intensely from the dirt path. He was in exactly the same spot as yesterday, when he first laid eyes on her.

"No, the Winged God controls everything. He put him in Tomellburg. It was destiny." Irban looked up towards the clear blue skies.

She didn't really know what to say; she had no love of religion and knew nothing about it, but what she did know was that out of everyone in the village he was the only one who had come to her aid. No matter how many people her aunt had saved, none had stepped up for her.

"I must leave; I don't know when I will return." She knew she wouldn't be back. Danaka fought back her tears as her voice began to break. "Please, I want you to take this." She handed Irban a metal key.

Irban took the key from her. His hand was small, dry and rough; it felt like sand paper. It was the feel of a man who clearly worked hard for a living. She knew his family were poor and that they lived at the northern part of town, in the run down and overcrowded shacks they called home.

"What is this?" Irban was confused and he looked at his wife, unsure of how to answer.

"The key to my home. Your home, Irban." Danaka knew she had no need for it anymore. The people of Tomellburg would ruin her house the moment she left. "Please don't refuse. I have just one request of you."

"Anything," Irban struggled to reply, tears welling up in his eyes.

"Look after my aunt and uncle. Take care of their graves." Danaka looked over at the graves; she knew if she was to go over to them, she wouldn't want to leave. Not that she had any choice in the matter. She was now Duro's property, and he could do with her as he pleased until the blood debt was paid. She would keep the memories of her aunt and uncle in her heart, where they belonged.

Danaka closed Irban's fingers around the key and walked away. The quicker she left the better. No sad drawn-out goodbyes. She heard Irban calling out to her but she refused to look back. She just slowly made her way back over to Duro, who was still watching her intensely. His eyes never left her, ever watching like a hawk.

She walked over the soft warm dirt until she stood directly below him. He gazed down at her with his deep dark eyes; she saw sorrow in them but didn't dare ask about his past. His face was well sculptured with a strong jaw line. He looked far different to the Walters she was used to coming into contact with. Being this close to him, close enough to touch and smell, made her nervous.

"It's time we left. We have a lot of ground to cover." Duro's voice was deep and straight to the point. He pulled his horses away from Danaka and began to slowly trot away from town.

"Where are we going?" she asked.

"We head south and to…" Suddenly his voice was cut off, like a knife had slit his throat. He turned quickly to his right.

Loud enthusiastic barking rang out; happy vibrant calls of joy filled the air. Danaka turned to see Griffin, her most loyal friend, charging at full speed towards her. He moved like lightening as his feet rapidly moved beneath him. Sand and dirt formed a dust cloud around him. Danaka's heart melted as Griffin made his way towards her. His large frame and long thick sable and white hair made him look a beautiful specimen as he moved swiftly across her garden.

"Griffin!" She screamed as she fell to her knees. The hot dirt burnt into her skin but she didn't care as her companion jumped all over her. His warm fur was thick and soft; his tongue was wet as it ran across her face. Griffin leaped all around her like an excitable child. "Where have you been?" she asked as if he was going to reply. "You had me so scared!" Tears of joy began to fall from her eyes. She kissed him over and over.

"What's that?" Duro asked with the first real signs of expression, as he raised his eyebrows.

"A dog? My dog," she added firmly.

"We don't need a dog, let's move." Duro pulled his horses away from Danaka. Griffin began to growl, his large fang-like teeth exposed.

Danaka quickly stood up and replied defiantly, "He goes where I go; if he doesn't go then I stay here." In a split second she suddenly realised what she was saying. She knew nothing about this man or his temperament.

Duro stopped and pulled his horse back around. He stared directly at Danaka, his deep dark eyes looking her up and down. She stayed strong, matching his stare with an equally intense defiant look of her own. She could feel her heart beginning to thump in her chest. Her hand was beginning to shake but she gripped her fist in a feeble attempt to hide it.

"It looks as if I now have two travelling companions instead of one." Duro closed his eyes and took in a slow gulp of air.

"Thank you, thank you! You won't regret it. He is loyal and a great guard dog. He can hunt too. I once saw him catch a young deer," Danaka replied excitedly. She didn't know whether she was so happy because he had allowed Griffin to come or because he hadn't killed her.

"I am starting to think I should've left you to face Sir Claris," Duro replied with a half-smile as he began to slowly ride away.

But you didn't. "Come on, boy," Danaka spoke to Griffin as she happily jogged after her new master. As they ran along the long dirt path, made from red sand and flanked either side by long open and lush green fields, she looked back, admiring the small town that was Tomellburg and the strong grey ageing stone walls, with two small matching towers which formed the entrance. The one she would pass through every day, when she would make that long dreaded journey into town. The sky was clear blue, the sun high and bright; for once the town looked beautiful. Never would she ever have thought she would think those words.

"Look at it, Griffin. This will be the last time we ever see it." Danaka slowly stroked Griffin's sable fur. The summer breeze blew ever so elegantly. The light air blew around her cheeks; her long brown hair began to sway from the back of her neck. "Our old life has ended, our new journey begins now."

Chapter 11
Two Sons of a Whore

"Caelan or Naleac?" Uriah excitedly asked as he brushed his long hair away from his face. The summer heat was intense, his neck was ringing wet and he could feel the sweat running down his back.

"Caelan, he is the stronger," Toran replied with his usual deep booming voice. His dark black leather tunic only emphasized his pale skin. His huge arms resembled tree trunks, thick and strong.

"No, no big brother. I have to disagree. Yes, Caelan is the stronger of the two but strength does not always win a fight. Naleac has the edge in speed. Speed over power any day." Uriah smiled.

"You would say that as you have no power. The big man will always defeat the small one." He beat his hand on his chest which resembled the sound of a beating drum, before looking down at his brother. "Do you want to put your speed over power to the test?" He smiled, and his gold tooth sparkled.

"It is in your best interests if we don't fight. We need you in good health for when we meet this Dillian Howard." Uriah's voice was light and playful.

The brothers had been walking for nearly two hours. They pulled their horses behind, giving them the rest they deserved. Uriah and Toran looked a strange pair; the top of Uriah's head barely reached the chest of his brother. From a distance they would appear to be father and son. They were polar opposites in appearance but they were as close as brothers could be.

The narrow path they followed was made of red sand, wide enough for only two men to walk side by side. They were no longer protected by the leaves of the trees so the heat from the sun was taking its toll. It was still early morning but the sun was bright, its great beams of light lighting up the land before them.

Uriah could feel the rays burning into his flesh; he pulled frantically on his black tunic. He was trying to allow some cool air onto his body. The heat however was nothing new to him or Toran; they had grown up in eastern Dagen near the river Tyma, the summers there were harsh and unrelenting. Yet still their skin was pale and rarely did it change colour.

Toran's almost bald head was pouring with sweat; the small beads slowly made their way down his large cheeks and through his ginger stubble. "I like this place," he said randomly. He looked out around him, admiring the green landscapes and the smooth hills on the horizon.

"Why?" Uriah replied with an air of confusion. "It is just like any other land we have seen. Roldur, Samora, Etoria, all the same to me."

“No, it is different here. There is more green and the air is clean.” Toran allowed the fresh air fill his huge lungs.

Suddenly Uriah let rip; a loud powerful trumpet like sound exploded into the air. “The air is not so clean now.” He began to laugh uncontrollably; he held his stomach as he leant forward before wiping away a few tears that began to well up in his eyes.

Toran yelled as if someone had just struck him with a brick; he quickly held his nose as a violent whiff of rotten eggs and decomposing rodent flesh entered his nostrils. “You little shit.” Toran’s arm shot out with unexpected speed for a man of his size; it extended like a snake snapping at its prey. He grabbed Uriah by the scuff of his neck and lifted him up off his feet.

“Out the way peasants!” A voice floated with an air of disgust.

Toran instantly dropped his brother. The ground beneath them began to rumble, as if the gods had begun to the shake the earth. The vibrations began to tingle in their feet and work their way up their legs and shake them at the knees. Looking behind, a column of armoured knights rode towards them. As far as the eye could see, Knights in rows of two charged at full speed. They were clad in thick, heavy plates of sparkling white. The rider at the front carried a flag, decorated with a sun flocked by three doves. Their kite shaped shields showed the same coat of arms.

Toran and Uriah frantically pulled their horses off the path and onto the grass; it was clear if they did not move, they would be trampled to death. The knights roared past like an arrow flying through the air. The noise of the armoured horses was almost deafening, like thunder it crashed against their ears. Bits of dirt and sand flicked up from the hooves; some pieces of grit hit Uriah in the face. As the final rider passed them by, the intense overbearing sounds began to ease off, slowly fading away as the knights charged further and further towards the horizon.

Uriah had seen that sigil before; back home in Dagen the Guardians of Thelonia were a common sight. The Allamantyan knights who had joined this group had ridden from city to city, converting non-believers either with the sword or the word of the gods. For a moment Uriah thought they were coming for him and Toran but he was grateful they weren’t; no matter how deadly he and his brother were, there was no way they stood chance against that many foes. Not that Toran would accept it, his overconfidence bordered lunacy at times.

“You still love this country?” Uriah began to rub his eyes, wiping away from the grit and the dirt from his face.

“There are cunts everywhere you go,” Toran replied as he brushed himself down.

“Some places have more cunts than others.”

Uriah looked out in front of him as the saw the last rider disappear. *Where were they heading? And why in such a hurry?* Maybe he was getting paranoid, allowing Garroway’s over protectiveness to plague his mind. Garroway was one of the oldest men he knew, being wary clearly had allowed him to live longer than most in his profession.

He and Toran had left the others at first light. There had not been any emotional goodbyes but it was clear his *brothers* and *sisters* were concerned, the tension was tight and uncomfortable. Uriah had just wanted to leave; he had never been one for showing his emotions. He remembered watching Rhodesha hold Toran so tightly, like she never wanted to let him go. Their love was deep; he knew she needed Toran in her life. Seeing them together would make him smile, a smile he would not let the others see.

"Remember boys, we kill today so we can live tomorrow." They were the last words Garroway uttered to him and Toran before they left, he remembered them loud and clear. No matter how much he loved the sound of the coins clanging together, *our lives are more important than coin.* He reached behind and felt the small leather pouch tied to his belt; he felt the texture of the smooth round coins between his fingers. He liked it.

"You will not see us, you will not hear us, but fear not. We will not be far behind." The words rang out in his head; he knew the others would be close but how close was the question? He was not nervous but cautious, it was best to do as Garroway said.

The two made their way down a hill; the red sand beneath their feet turned to rock and stone. The rubble crumbled and rolled freely down the slope. The horses brayed and pulled back, frightened at what lay ahead. Being patient was not a word Toran understood; he growled and yanked hard at the reigns puling his horse behind him. It seemed his animal feared him more than the unsteady ground.

At the bottom of the hill stood some ruins. The structure of a once tall building now lay charred and burnt; the wooden beams were black and broken. Small waves of dark smoke glided softly up into the sky. The windows were shattered; the crystal-like shards still stained the floor. For a moment it reminded Uriah of home. A small stream flowed nearby; the cool clear water sparkled in the summer sun. The sounds of women's laughter and children playing filled his ears.

Two young boys played in the stream, one was big and strong, the other small and fast. The bigger brother playfully lifted the smaller above his head and ducked him under the water. It was a happy sight; a warm feeling took hold of him. A smile slowly filled his small face as a beautiful young woman appeared, cursing her sons, pulling them both out the water by their ears. The boys squealed like girls. She wore a long red sequin dress that emphasised her breasts, her long shining black hair fell to her waist. What a woman.

"Uriah! Come on," Toran's loud booming voice called out. Like an echo in a cave, it rang out in his ears over and over. As the sound took hold of him, his eyes flashed and the two children and their mother were gone. Just the empty stream and broken ruins lay before him; the smell of burnt wood was potent and unsettling.

The smouldering building seemed dark and unhappy. A feeling of unrest and sadness took hold of Uriah as he looked out before him. By his feet there were stains. Red smears of blood sprayed freely across the plains. He looked closer and in the folds of grass lay a body, a woman's body. Her dress was torn and her long dark black hair covered her face. Her pale skin was bloodied and bruised, her legs and arms contorted, spread out in unnatural positions like strings of spaghetti.

"I'm coming," Uriah replied as he slowly turned away, leaving his memories behind.

They had mounted their horses and ridden for half a mile before they saw the inn. It stood alone. It was situated in a narrow valley, surrounded by trees and a path that forked near the entrance. The path then proceeded to flank the building either side. It was a perfect location for weary travellers wanting to stop off for shelter and food. The inn was made of hard clay and painted pure white. Thick strong black beams ran down the side of the building. The roof was thatched and filled with dry vegetation.

A sign was held out by a single thick metal beam. Bronzed rust had begun to form on the end of bar; two thin chains dangled loose with a kite shaped piece of wood clinging to the ends. The sign read, *The Black Ale Inn,* in thick black paint. The sign creaked and swayed softly back and forth in the cool breeze.

"This is the place," Uriah said confidently as he strapped his two short swords to his back. He fastened the two belts tight around his chest; the leather straps wrapped around his body like the embrace of a mother for her son. With his swords so close to him, he felt whole. He was ready for whatever was waiting for him. "I will do all the talking." He pulled his hair back away from his face and tied it in a pony tail.

Toran grunted as he withdrew his huge double handed broadsword from his saddle. Its length was almost the height of Uriah. The handle was made of pure metal, forged in the slave valleys in Dagen. Thick red straps entwined around the handle, allowing a more comfortable grip. The scabbard was made of strong plain brown leather. Toran was not a man interested in the decoration of his weapon. *A fancy sword does not make a great warrior,* he once said.

The two slowly made their way down the narrow winding path. Everything seemed so quiet, so peaceful. Only the birds singing and the thud of their horses' hooves on the ground could be heard. The sound of leather creaked as Toran tightly gripped the handle of his sword. Uriah watched as Toran's hand twisted around the leather straps; the veins in his forearm were ready to explode.

Uriah's eyes flicked from one side to the other, looking from left to right, scanning the area in front of him. Garroway's words suddenly came back to him: *"Dillian Howard will be seated on the fourth table to your right, looking out the window. He would have seen you long before you would've seen him."*

"Remember, he can see us," Uriah spoke as if he was a ventriloquist.

Toran looked towards the Inn; a large bay window was at the far side of the building. The window panes were dark and misty. "I can see nothing." He gripped his sword even tighter.

They both pulled their horses up outside the inn. Uriah lifted himself up in his saddle and looked around him and into the trees, but still he saw nothing. Just leaves and bushes. It was ever so silent, even the birds had stopped singing. He was waiting for the moment treachery would strike, when the arrows would loose and hordes of men would pour from the trees to hack them to pieces. But yet nothing happened, the paths either side of the inn were empty. Not a soul was in sight.

A loud crash exploded and their horses brayed in fear. Uriah's lifted back onto its hind legs and kicked out frantically. Toran let out his huge war cry as he drew his sword. The steel sung beautifully as it was set free. The blade sparkled in the summer sun.

A woman screamed hysterically as she stumbled back, losing her balance, dropping a keg of ale on the ground. She was as tall as she was wide; her large body was covered in a dirty white overall which was stained from top to bottom. Her hair was dull and knotted, her roots had begun to sprout stems of grey and her eyes looked old and weary. "You cunts gave me a fright!" she shouted as she dusted herself down. Her voice was deep and common; she was clearly not brought up around royalty.

"Forgive us," Uriah spoke as he tried controlled his horse, "but where is everybody?"

"It's those dirty foreigners, sprouting shite about some winged god and his children. It is not safe out on these lands today. They have already burnt down old Margie's whorehouse!" The woman knelt down and lifted up the old keg and waddled towards a heap of wood before tossing it onto the pile like it was nothing more than a half-eaten apple. "Not that I give a fuck about Margie mind you. Stuck up bitch; just because she had some coin, she thought she could open a whorehouse. Takes away all my customers she did! Men prefer the taste of cunt to ale these days."

"As much as we enjoy the taste of our women, we will not say no to some refreshments," Uriah said in his smooth tone.

The old woman's weary eyes lit up, like torches on a dark night. "Oh, yes, come in, come in." She excitedly waved her arms, the excess skin flapped furiously back and forth. Before the woman disappeared inside the inn, she added, "I have the finest black ale in all of Kathoros."

Uriah and Toran looked at each other with a sign of relief. Each took a deep breath and slowly dismounted before walking towards the entrance.

"Don't worry about the horses." The old woman suddenly reappeared, sticking her head back out of the door. Closer up, her round face was wrinkled and worn. The bags under her eyes were deep and dark and she reeked of ale. "My daughter will take care of those." She suddenly yelled back inside, "Helga, get out here now! We have customers… Fuck's sake, expects me to run this place single handed she does." The lady quickly disappeared back inside.

The brothers entered the inn. An aura of old wood and spilt ale took them by surprise as they made their way inside. The hallway was narrow, wide enough for only one man to pass at a time. Once they were into the main seating area, it was dark and poorly-lit but it opened up and was larger inside than it appeared. Various empty circular tables were spread out in what seemed to be no order.

As they made their way towards the bar, a strong smell of warm freshly boiled soup took hold of their senses. In front of them, near the hearth, was a large steel pot. Furious red flames engulfed it, roaring away as rich smells of vegetables and herbs filled their nostrils. The soup was bubbling angrily; small bubbles expanded and popped one after the other. The sight instantly made their stomachs rumble and groan, as if it was begging their masters to allow them to taste it.

"I think we passed that whorehouse you spoke of," Uriah asked, hoping to get a little more information.

The old woman appeared once again, the loud thumping of her steps on the wooden floor echoed. She carried with her two large jugs of black ale; each was overflowing. Ale spilled over her hands and down her arms as she banged them down on the bar in front of her.

Toran stood silently, holding his huge broadsword upright between his legs. His eyes never left the jugs of ale. The yellowy coloured froth called out his name enticing him to bring it to his lips.

"Yes, good riddance if you ask me. She nearly ran me into the ground. Don't get me wrong, I hate these religious cunts just as much as the next person but they did me a favour when they burnt her whorehouse down." The woman looked up at Uriah, admiring his face, "What brings you to these parts?"

"The legend of the Black Ale Inn spreads far and wide," Uriah added with his seductive tone. "What stops these followers of the Winged God coming for you?"

"This!" In a flash she slammed down a short two edge battle axe. The sound thudded and echoed as it crashed against the bar. The two jugs of ale shook, spilling even more of its dark delights. "Let them come! I will give them a taste of true Allamantyan steel. Think they can come here and kill me in my own home. They have another thing coming. Sir Lyon N'Dai is meant to guard these lands but he is too busy sucking cock. His father, Marshal Latimor, governor of Kathoros, is real a man, brave and honourable. What I would do to him if he came here." Her voice turned seductive, her old grey tongue sliding from inside her mouth and around her dry broken lips.

"Well, he would be one lucky man." Uriah closed his eyes as a shiver ran through his spine; he then proceeded to lift his jug and allow the bitter ale to pass his lips.

Toran followed suit. The sound of loud gulping filled the inn as both brothers tilted their heads and drank down the dark liquid. It was strong but refreshing; not a single drop was wasted. When finished, both placed the jugs down peacefully onto the bar. An eerie silence crept over them as the brothers stared intensely at the old woman. Until suddenly Toran let out with a huge belch which shuddered and shook the furniture like a mini earthquake. The smell of ale and an empty stomach hit the woman hard in the face, forcing her eyes shut.

"Two more please, my fine woman. The rumours are true." Uriah smiled; his welcoming face enticed and flattered the woman who quickly poured two more ales. "So what is wrong with this Lyon N'Dai?" he added as he wiped away the froth from his upper lip.

"He is as weak as this once noble land you stand upon," a sharp strong voice shot out.

Uriah and Toran quickly turned, looking down the inn. In the far corner by the bay window sat a lone figure. He was old and clad from head to toe in a black cloak. A single sword lay in front of him.

"Who is he?" Toran asked the old woman, unaware of his froth filled moustache.

"He came here yesterday. I don't ask names. Long as they pay the coin, I am happy," the woman replied half-heartedly as she looked up towards the damp ridden ceiling. "Helga, where are you, damn it?"

"Boys, come here and sit with me," the man asked. His voice was old and well spoken. Still his face never looked up.

Uriah nodded and walked forwards, his eyes never leaving the target.

Toran quickly placed his sword under his armpit and picked up both jugs of ale. Before moving, he spoke, "Two pots of that soup!" He looked down at bubbles popping, his stomach groaned. "Make them big ones."

"I believe you are looking for me." The man looked up as he spoke. His head was virtually bald; lines of thin silver hair were brushed back in a poor attempt to conceal his scalp. His skin was smooth and his eyes a sparkling blue; a strong aroma of Jasmine surrounded him.

"Oh, am I?" Uriah asked as he made himself comfortable at the man's table. "For all you know I am in search of the most beautiful woman in all the land. And I am afraid to disappoint, you are not beautiful and by your appearance I do not believe you are of the fairer sex, although you do smell like one." He leant forward breathing in deeply.

Toran sat himself down at the table, intentionally banging both jugs down heavily. Ale spilled out, splashing the man across his face. Small beads of yellow froth littered his cheeks; he slowly raised his hand and wiped his face with a small white cloth.

"I am Sir Dillian Howard," he replied angrily. "And by your appearance and lack of manners, you are the men I seek." He looked at Uriah and Toran with an intense glare. His eyes carried a feeling of disgust; the sparkle in them began to fade.

Suddenly the woman appeared, breaking up the uncomfortable atmosphere that had begun to develop. She placed down two large pots of soup; the waves of steam began to rise. The hot smell of herbs replaced the sweet overpowering odour of Sir Dillian Howard. Two loafs of crusty bread soon followed; both were thrown to the table without a care in the world. They sound like rocks hitting wood as they landed.

"So, who are you then?" Uriah asked. With his middle finger he pulled one of the bowls of soup towards him.

Toran gave Uriah a gloomy look, one like a child who was having its favourite toy taken from him. "Oh, I didn't know you were having any," he added.

"You know who I am."

"No, I'm asking who you really are." Uriah ripped off a piece of bread. It felt hard and dry, before dunking it into his soup. The liquid was the darkest of green, like an autumn vegetable garden. He swirled his bread in the soup, while staring at Sir Dillian Howard.

The harsh sounds of slurping filled the air. Toran ate with a ravenous hunger, filling his gaping mouth with large chunks of dried bread. Drips of soup began to run freely down his chin; he cared not for his appearance, just the meal in front of him.

Dillian Howard took his eyes off Toran before looking back at Uriah. "I am a man who seeks change, to stamp out the flames before they consume us all."

"I see no flames." Uriah smiled before exchanging an intense glare. He then proceeded to slip a small piece of bread into his mouth. The tension began to build; from his demeanour Uriah knew this Sir Dillian Howard was not a man he would like to spend his evenings drinking ale with.

A young girl around eleven years old ran down the narrow wooden stairs that appeared beside the bar. She looked sweet and innocent; her brown hair was tied back and she was dressed in white throw over and a pale blue dress. The noise of her light steps echoed through the inn, bringing Sir Dillian's attention away from Uriah and to the girl; he watched her like she was slice of cake at a bakery, admiring every piece of her.

"I heard there were twelve dragons in Dagen, not two." Dillian retracted his eyes from the girl as she disappeared outside.

"We rode ahead, to make sure everything was safe." Uriah watched him with meticulous eye. His whole aura was sleazy and untrustworthy. *If you do not trust him, kill him where he stands,* Garroway's words called out to him.

For a moment Uriah imagined withdrawing his short swords and slicing his poisoned throat. *To kill a snake, you remove its head.* It was the simpler option, quick and easy, no witnesses. The innkeeper would be no bother; he and Toran could meet back up with the others and be back on the ship in less than two days.

"You insult me boy. You were given our word there would be no treachery. It is not safe to linger here; the land you stand upon is breaking away like old bread. Leaches from the east pour in, eating away at her flesh, draining her. Now Valorian scum flood our borders. If we fail, this land is destined for ruin but I will not be here to clear away the ashes. I will head east across the Calhorion sea." Dillian's voice rose harshly. His hand gripped the scabbard of his sword.

"Where will you go?" Uriah calmly replied as he dunked more of his dry bread into his soup.

"To the hot sands of Etoria."

"I have been there; it is not that nice. Pretty ladies though." Uriah filled his mouth with the moist bread, tasting herbs and the texture of vegetables as the soup made its way down his throat.

"Can I get you anything, my lord?" Helga suddenly appeared; her voice was as sweet as fruit on a summer's day. She was small, barely Dillian's height while he was seated. She stood by him holding a small brown clay pot.

My lord? Uriah thought to himself.

"No child," Sir Dillian replied, his voice unpleasant to the ear. He began to slide his hand down the girl's back, his smile widening as he gazed at her.

A huge shatter echoed through the inn. Shards of glass flew through the air, the small sharp pieces crashed against their table. Uriah and Toran raised their arms to defend themselves as Dillian dragged the small screaming girl in front of him to protect himself. Loud booming chants soon followed.

"Yakash Mudra, Yakash Mudra, Yakash Mudra, Yakash Mudra!!" The voices were rhythmic and unsettling. Hate filled their calls. The words shot out over and over again.

Through the broken window, people began to appear like ghosts. Over twenty men clad in black formed a mob outside, still the chants screamed out. They began to bang their spears on the ground. The floor beneath their feet began to rumble.

"Fucking scum! We give them our land and yet they curse us for it!" Sir Dillian violently yelled out, as he struggled to hold the petrified young girl in front of him as she kicked out wildly. "I would've burned the Eastern Isles to the ground if I was king." More glass flew through the air.

Stones and bricks began to fly towards the inn. More glass shattered as they crashed against the windows. Uriah felt a slight stinging pain as his forearm started to bleed. Thin trails of blood began to flow down his arm like little red streams.

Toran roared like a mighty lion as he stood up, drawing his huge sword. With his left hand he grabbed hold of the table and flung it up against the window. The sound of stone crashing against the wood could be heard seconds later. Within a flash Toran lifted the young girl up onto his shoulders and carried her towards the bar, moving her to safety. "Fear not, little one, the Iron Bull of Dagen is here." He turned to face the entrance, throwing tables and chairs against the door, barricading it as best he could.

"Get up!" Uriah ordered as he drew his swords. Sir Dillian obeyed as he scrambled frantically to his feet. Uriah watched him in disgust as he feebly tried to grab hold of his sword. He then turned and peered through a small gap between the table and the wall. Outside he could see the men. They were clad in black from head to toe; some of them you could only see their eyes. Others were topless and wore tatty torn leather on their legs. A ravenous mob, ready to kill.

"I am Hazar! By the will of Dalackis! Burn this place of sin!" a man screamed out as he paced up and down the row of chanting men, their fists beating the sky. He must've been their leader; in his hand he carried a spear. On top was a black flag with the image of two white wings. He was small and thin; his eyes were dark and empty. His cloak was pulled away from his head; his face was covered with a thick beard and he had a shining shaven head. Hazar held out his spear towards the inn. "Let the flames of Lawgiver wipe out their sin, Yakash Mudra!"

All of his followers began to scream louder and louder, as if his words had possessed them even more. One man screamed uncontrollably; spit flew from his mouth, the veins in his neck began violently pulsate and his eyes bulged from his head, turning red.

"How many?" Toran called out. He gripped his sword with both hands.

"Too many for you and I," Uriah replied as he scanned the mob.

"Ha! My sword begs for blood!" Toran's voice was powerful and without fear. "Let them come!"

"No!" Suddenly the innkeeper came barging in behind Toran. Her voice was high pitched and sharp. She was a little stumpy thing, with her arms flailing about like a flag in heavy wind. With an axe swinging around wildly in her small chubby hands, she screamed, "I will kill them all!"

"Move aside woman." Toran pushed her hard with his right hand, her body came crashing to the floor. Like a sack of potatoes, she thudded against the ground face first. "Stay down!" he ordered. The woman lay motionless on the ground, groaning in confusion.

The chants outside suddenly began to stop. Heavy thudding sounds of hard-boiled metal rumbled against the ground, like an earthquake shaking the land. Next, slashing and steel carving its mark into flesh took over. Men began to call out and scream sickening pleas for mercy.

"In the name of the king and the holy city of Ollaria'h!" a voice yelled out.

Uriah looked back outside to see chaos. Armoured knights charged through the mob, each clad in full battle attire. With shining armour and huge steel swords they crashed against their helpless victims like a raging tidal wave. One man had his head taken clean off as a rider charged by; his stump sprayed a fountain of blood as his hands clung to his neck. Others were hacked down like weeds as they tried to flee the flood of knights roaring through them. One rider skewered another man with his spear. The blade cut into his back and then exploded out of his chest, lifting him off the ground as he screamed in agony. Some of the mob turned to face the knights, sticking their spears into the ground in an attempt to hold off the oncoming attack. Their bravery or stupidity was short lived as the knights rode over them like grass.

"Guardians of Thelonia, the gods are with us!" The knight dismounted; his face was covered with a full helm. Not even his eyes were visible. In his left hand he was brandishing a small kite shaped shield with an Allamantyan coat of arms and a long sword in the other hand. He took on two members of the mob; their poorly made spears broke against his armour as he cut them down, slicing open their chests and emptying their guts on the ground. One of the injured men attempted to crawl away, but the knight pinned him to the floor with his heavy mail-covered foot before ramming his sword into his back, killing him instantly.

Uriah watched intensely at the carnage. The slaughter was one-sided, not one knight lay dead or injured. He saw Hazar, the ringleader, standing in shock. He was flanked by two of his followers; both were big burly men with dark skin and thick hair clinging to their chests. They were away from the danger in the forest, hidden by the trees. Hazar's face was full of anger, his eyes as red as the devil's.

He tried charging towards the slaughter in a futile attempt to aid his fallen comrades. The two large men grabbed him by his arms and pulled him back, they slipped away into the bushes and out of sight.

"We must leave now and quickly." Sir Dillian's voice was ripe with fear.

Uriah sheathed both his swords and headed to the back of the inn.

"What about Garroway and the others?" Toran lowered his sword.

"They will find us," Uriah replied. *Well, I hope they do.*

The three of them quickly made their way to the back of the inn. The sounds of combat, the screams of dying men and of steel clashing together, slowly began to fade away. Toran, with one mighty kick, lifted a door off of its hinges; it cracked and snapped like a twig under his immense power. Outside, they found their horses. In a flash both Uriah and Toran were mounted and ready. Sir Dillian slipped as he tried to put his foot in his stirrup. He began to panic and fluster as he frantically tried to climb his animal.

Toran rode past, grabbing hold of him by his cloak, and lifted him to his saddle. "You ride like an old woman."

"Let's go!" Uriah shouted as he kicked into his horse and rode out into the forest. Toran and Sir Dillian followed behind.

They rode intensely for a few miles, making sure no one was following them. The three stopped on a small stone bridge, wide enough for three riders to pass side by side. The stone was grey and old; bits of rubble broke away with each passing step. Green weeds began to sprout from between the mortar. Behind them was the forest but on the far side of the bridge lay a vast open space of long grass and fields of gold; the wheat swayed softly in the cool breeze.

Uriah leant forward, wiping the sweat away from his horse's neck. "We should be safe now."

"How will Garroway find us now?" Toran asked as he looked down from the bridge at the narrow stream. The water flowed ever so silently underneath the bridge and around the small rocks.

"Maarax will track us, we will just move slowly."

"You fool." Sir Dillian laughed as pulled out a small cloth and began to wipe the sweat from his brow. He unclipped his black cloak, revealing a fancy plate of armour. It was white and decorated with a silver sword at its centre. Silver rings of mail covered his arms, stopping at his wrists. Golden circular shoulder plates were fitted to his mail. "If you had taken my word, we wouldn't be in this mess and you," he then pointed to Toran, "Don't you ever lay your hands on me again, you son of a whore." Venom coursed through his words.

Toran retracted his head away from the stream and slowly rode over towards Sir Dillian. His eyes locked on him, like a lion to its prey. Fear began to rise in Sir Dillian's face, his eyes widening and his mouth beginning to droop open as if all he wanted to do was roll over and cry.

Uriah quickly kicked into his horse and stopped Toran in his path. "In fact, we are two sons of a whore," he added to break the tension.

Sir Dillian looked at them both with a confused eye, observing them both. Uriah was small and well-toned; his hair was long and brown, his eyes a pale blue. Toran was the opposite, tall and slow with the muscles of a bull. He was virtually bald with dark eyes and a large thick jaw, filled with sprouts of ginger stubble.

"Different fathers and, yes, before you ask, mine must've been the more handsome," Uriah added as he gestured Toran to back away. "We must continue to head west."

"Without my protection the others will not get far before they are challenged. We must reach the mountain gates of Hamon'dor within the next three days." Sir Dillian looked flustered, looking around as if he was surrounded by wolves. He suddenly began to mumble to himself, "This whole thing is getting out of hand, I should never have listened. Power and lust blinds them both."

Uriah and Toran watched him as he turned his horse and slowly rode across the bridge. Uriah looked behind, peering down the narrow dirt path they had just ridden down. The trees were thick and the bushes sharp. He hoped Garroway and the others could pick up their trail. Looking out in front he watched Toran following behind Sir Dillian as they headed towards the golden wheat fields up ahead. The bright summer sun made for a beautiful sight.

Maybe those knights had already cut them down. No, don't be silly, we are the twelve dragons of Dagen, death will not claim us so easily.

Chapter 12
A Brother's Love

"If betrayal is in their hearts, I will paint this field with their blood." Prince Gabriel watched helplessly. His sister had been his rock growing up; she kept him close when their mother died, raised him when their father cursed him. Yet now he could not repay her kindness. She was out of his reach and away from his protection. His father, the king, had bargained with her life like she was nothing more than a common whore. "How can my father be so stupid? He brings only four men with him into an enemy encampment!" *No wonder he was defeated at Falentis!*

Lassander squinted, raising his hand to shield his eyes from the hot sun. "Calm yourself cousin, they look friendly enough."

Gabriel did not reply. *How could he ban me? Why would he? He believes I shame him but I am the one who defends our kingdom. I spill the blood of our enemies to keep his crown safe.* The prince stirred in his saddle, back and forth. He could feel the sweat building in his palms.

King Vincinicus and his sister, Princess Tilia, had met up with King Aristian and Prince Andros and ridden out of sight. All Gabriel could do was look down from the Three Peaks, helpless to do anything to protect her. His heart beat powerfully within his chest, he felt restless, agitated and powerless. What was he to do? As the days passed by, he knew he drew closer and closer to his destiny. Whether it was to death and destruction or to everlasting glory he did not know.

An hour before, he had watched his father saddled on his horse. His overzealous attitude had only fuelled Gabriel's irritation. It had taken all his might to stay calm; one more mistake and his father would banish him from his presence and send him back to Verdinia. That, he would not allow. As much as his army needed him back in Valanor, his sister needed him more, he would not abandon her.

"What shall we do now?" Lucian asked as he wiped the sweat from his brow.

Lassander replied firmly, "We wait."

"I am Prince Gabriel, I do not wait." Gabriel pulled hard on his reins.

Lucian and Lassander turned to one another; shock began to grow on their faces. Gabriel rode away from his cousins and towards the row of Valorian soldiers who sat mounted behind them. Their glistening blue armour sparkled like diamonds. Gabriel looked like a warrior angel; he was clad in his finest armour, a white breastplate, decorated with blue gems and a light blue cape. His white greaves rose from his ankles to his knees. Around his waist he wore a decorative skirt of leather strips; each was fitted with blue jewels. He cut a magnificent image. His long golden hair was pulled back away from his face, tied in a bun with a few strands falling loose.

"I am your prince, will you follow me?" Gabriel pushed up into his spurs. The Valorian cavalry responded with a cheer of approval. "Since I woke this morning, oh my stomach has groaned. Are you hungry? I sure am. They are heading to a feast! So why shouldn't we?" Gabriel extended his arm past his cousins and down the hill. "Do you not wish to experience true Antilion hospitality? Well, ride with me and I promise you, you will have your fill of it!"

The soldiers roared as loud and as proud as lions.

"I knew this would happen." Lassander turned to Lucian. "Keep your eyes open and your sword close."

The ground broke and rumbled, the mighty sound of armour and horse, a beautiful noise, the call of battle. Gabriel rode at the front, his armour shining like a star from the heavens. He could feel the warmth of the summer air on his skin. Feeling strong and alert he ran his fingers down the shaft of his great spear. He was ready.

Either side of the prince were his cousins, Lassander and Lucian, and then behind them was the Valorian cavalry in rows of two. They all descended down from the Three Peaks like a great snake of blue and silver. Along the great plains they rode; the sound of armour and horse clashed beautifully together, the song of battle that sung out so gloriously.

As the horses ground to halt, they spread out wide across the field. The prince and his cousins rode a few paces forward and stopped. Across the field Gabriel could see the Antilion encampment. Tents of red and green spread as far as the eye could see. Out in front lay rows of tables. The royal feast awaited him.

"What will your father think?" Lassander asked with concern in his heart.

"What of him? Did he care when I lead our people to victory at field of Chaperon? When I sent the Etorion fleet to the bottom of the Emerald Sea? Or when I faced Al'Kyram the wild in single combat? I have learnt there is no pleasing him. By the will of the gods he is my father and my king, yet no love flows through these veins." Gabriel leant forward; the leather of his saddle creaked. "But it was not I who wished it so."

Gabriel could feel the hot sun against his neck. Taking a deep breath, he kicked into his spurs, and his beautiful white horse began to move. Steady and calm. The prince's cousins and the Valorian soldiers followed, loyally. Gabriel could feel his heart thumping in his chest for now it was his time. His destiny had brought him to this place, he would not falter now. The wide-open field was smooth and steady; the Antilion encampment got bigger and bigger as he approached. For a moment he wished to turn his head and see the faces of his men. He knew they would inspire him, their love and respect for him was greater than any reward a prince could receive. But he dared not. He kept his head forwards; they should only see him strong and proud.

Like little ants the people at the feast began to scatter, moving in all directions in state of panic. A few soldiers clad in green had begun to form a wall. A rider on a grey horse stood behind them; he was bellowing out instructions.

Gabriel smiled before lifting his hand. “Raise the flag!”

“Raise the flag!” Lassander repeated his prince’s command.

Instantly a Valorian rider lifted a white flag. It raised high in the air, clear for all to see. Gabriel pulled a little on his reins, slowing his horse down to walking pace. If he approached too fast, they might panic and who knew what may happen. A few metres before the Allamantyan shield wall, he stopped and waited. The soldiers looked scared and tense. Their spears began to shake as they pointed towards him.

“You fool! Damn you boy!” King Vincinicus voice rose as powerful as a storm across the Calhorion Sea. The soldiers parted so the old king might pass. “I command you to get down. I will not look up to you. You know what you could’ve done?”

Gabriel dropped down from his horse.

Vincinicus quickly pressed his face against his son’s, cutting Gabriel off as he tried to speak. His breath reeked of ale. “You push me too far boy, you will go back to…”

“So this is the magnificent Prince Gabriel. I have longed to see you in the flesh; it is a pleasure to finally meet with you.” King Aristian appeared, his voice soothing. He was stood straight with his arms behind his back.

Gabriel leant around the ball that was his father and towards the wise King; he could see he was a slim man and his face old. His hair was short and grey; his skin wrinkled but friendly warmth passed with each word he spoke. Gabriel looked Aristian in the eye and bowed his head.

“Please, let there be no fighting on this glorious day. Come and join us.” King Aristian extended his arm, pointing towards the royal table.

King Vincinicus stared intensely at his son. “One incident and you will be gone, do you understand?” He turned slowly before walking away.

Gabriel watched as his father headed back to the royal table; his heart beat with anger. He breathed deeply.

“That was an entrance to match your reputation little prince. So this is the man who puts himself before family and god.” Daemar appeared, looking down from his horse with suspicious eyes.

“You are?” Gabriel replied as he looked up.

“Prince Daemar, brother to King Aristian.” He dismounted and walked alongside Gabriel.

“It was you who cut down Delanios, my grandfather’s bodyguard, at Falentis?” Gabriel eyed Daemar up and down, just like he would any potential opponent. Daemar’s reputation with a sword had spread far and wide. For a moment Gabriel imagined clashing steel with him.

Daemar smiled. “I did.”

“He was an old man by the time he reached Falentis.”

“Well, he aged not a day more when he tasted true Antilion steel.” Prince Daemar stopped, his left hand squeezing the hilt of his sword. “I will leave you here. I have a feeling we will talk again." Daemar smiled, mounted his horse and rode away. A few Allamantyan soldiers followed after him.

Gabriel watched him leave before walking down between the rows of tables. With each step he took he could feel the sting of wandering eyes burning into him. Gabriel knew they all had heard of the prince of Valanor. Looking up, he could see his father's hate-filled eyes, cursing him as he approached. However, it was his beautiful sister, Princess Tilia, that erased his father's hate. She was sat beside him, petite and innocent, but as always, she looked as magnificent as a Valorian princess should. Tilia smiled and to his surprise she looked happy and at ease, not in need of his protection. He smiled back as he stepped up and sat himself beside her.

"Gabriel, you shouldn't have come," Tilia whispered into her brother's ear. "But I am glad you did."

Gabriel took his sister's small hand in his own. "I swore to you, that you would never be alone again, and I never break a promise."

As the day went by, the festivities grew louder and louder. Men who were once sworn enemies feasted and drank together like brothers. It was not blood that stained the grass this day but wine. A royal band and dancers lay out on the plains, a joyous occasion without malice or violence. The hot sun was glorious, as if the gods themselves praised the union of both Allamantya and Valanor.

Gabriel, however, was silent; he sat, listened and watched. He had seen Lucian drape his arm over an Antilion soldier, pulling him close. The two laughed and filled each other's goblets. How wine can change a man. Lassander was less zealous but he too still seemed up beat. For Gabriel however it was different; he wanted to be happy but he could not. He could feel something was not right, as if this happiness was only the beginning of something dark and sinister.

As the sun began to fall, King Aristian had moved the royal families to his tent. Inside, Gabriel stood staring. Looking up at the king's table he could see Tilia handing Andros a small lock of her hair. It was Valorian custom for any woman who is to marry to give her betrothed her hair as a symbol of their union. Gabriel then turned and looked down, running his fingers over the sheep skin map of Allamantya and its empire. Its power was undeniable; its mighty arm had spread east over the vast Calhorion sea and south over the plains of Darnor. Valanor however had no domain to speak of; it had been over one hundred years since his country had an empire. It was when the Valorian warrior, Queen Korinnia I, had conquered both Etoria and Goshdel. Now neither nation was under his kingdom's control. Yet the wars between the three nations continued. King Vincinicus never allowed Gabriel to take his armies across the Emerald Sea and to the lands of Etoria. As a boy, the prince had dreamt of being Gabriel the Conqueror, yet all he had become was Gabriel the Defender.

Suddenly the tent began to fill; lords, knights and maids carrying barrels of wine entered. Loud ecstatic calls followed them in like a wave of laughter crashing against the mountain side. His father, King Vincinicus, roared out, raising his hand in the air and called for more wine.

As the people crowded Gabriel, their laughter turned to screams, their wine turned to blood and the music began to screech like steel crashing against steel. He felt cramped and claustrophobic; bodies bashed against him, drunk faces, screaming and shouting surrounded him. The stench of ale and sweat pushed Gabriel to boiling point. He forced himself forward, fighting to be free. As if he was now on a battlefield, fighting for his life.

Once outside, the cool midnight air calmed him, clearing his lungs. The hot sun had faded and only the moon filled the night sky. He suddenly felt free and loose. Inside that tent, his muscles had begun tighten and the world had started to close in around him. Gabriel's hand was shaking, as if he stood outside on a cold winter morning. He tried to hold his golden goblet tightly, yet the water was swirling and spilling to the ground. He slowly attempted to raise it to his lips, yet what he tasted was strong and warm. He spat it violently to the ground.

He peered back inside the flaps of the tent; through the chaos he could see his father's mouth drooped open, bellowing out in laughter. Wine spewed everywhere, running down his chin and over his red and silver silks. *The Pig King,* he thought to himself. *He sells his daughter then laughs about it. The great rulers such as King Lycinor I and Queen Korinnia I must look down in shame at what we have become, a nation of whores.*

To the left of his father he saw his sister, Princess Tilia. She sat quietly drinking her wine and chatting away with Prince Andros. He could not make out what they said but it seemed awkward and broken.

"What must I do to keep her safe?" Gabriel's voice was soft and low as if he whispered the words to himself. He spoke as if he wished for a reply, for a voice to call out to him, to tell him what he was to do. Yet no words came, a dark silence.

Gabriel turned his head, wishing to remove the images from his eyes. He looked out around him. The night seemed dark, darker than any he had seen before. The stars had dimmed their great light; gods and fallen heroes looked down in despair at what the mortals had done to the world. He walked away from the great tent, standing by a brazier of flickering red flame. The warmth it produced offered him no comfort; he turned his golden goblet into the light, red and green jewels sparkling before him. He angrily threw it into the fire, seeing the flames consume it; his reflection flickered in the gold.

"That was made for King Kalidar. The Lion Slayer," a light youthful voice called out.

Looking back, he saw Prince Arteus standing behind him. His short brown hair looked as wild as pile of hay. His youthful face, full of wonder, seemed to calm Gabriel. "I asked my father to give it to you."

Gabriel was unsure how to reply. A rare sense of guilt took hold of him. "Why would you want me to have it?"

"He was a great warrior, just like you. Will you teach me to be great?" His voice now seemed upbeat and playful. Arteus walked forward. His suit of armour clanged loudly with each step. His green tunic of Antilion hung proudly from his chest. He then unclipped his belt and extended his sword, the scabbard resting on the palms of his hands.

"I prefer the spear." Gabriel took the sword from the boy prince. Unsheathing it, he could tell the steel was pure and strong. His face reflected off the blade, Gabriel's blue eyes staring deeply into his own soul. "You must be strong to wield such a sword." His words were not used to flatter the boy. The sword was heavy; he knew Arteus must carry much strength for a boy of his age.

"My uncle Daemar says the spear is no good for close combat. A true knight fights with his sword."

"My enemies never get close enough to have me at a disadvantage." Gabriel leant forward slightly, so he was eye to eye with the boy. He was impressed by Arteus's size, he was broad and tall. "But then a great warrior also fights with this little prince." With his index finger, Gabriel tapped his head.

"My uncle tells me that too. But I find thinking harder than fighting."

"I feel we are the same."

Arteus smiled. A huge grin from ear to ear, "So you will teach me then."

"Yes, when we reach the capital." Gabriel pushed down a few strands of the boy's messy hair.

"Arteus!" A loud dominant voice called out from the darkness.

Beyorn stood in the shadows; the beast of Golgia slowly walked forwards. The red flames from the braziers reflected off his muscles. The ground rumbled with each step he took. Gabriel looked up as if he was staring to the top of a mountain. He stepped back, never had Gabriel seen a man that size. Beyorn was an imposing figure, a beast built from brute strength. "Your father said you were to sleep." The giant placed his huge hand on the boy's head, consuming it like it was nothing more than a grape. "Come."

Arteus solemnly nodded as he walked away.

Gabriel and Beyorn exchanged a long stare.

Gabriel stood alone for a few moments and began to walk around the royal tent. He could see all the soldiers from both nations were still drinking and enjoying themselves. Some men lay on the grass, having drank their full before collapsing. The bright fire braziers offered the only light as he moved through the darkness. Up ahead, he could see a figure moving in the shadows; it leant forward peering through the royal tent. He approached cautiously.

"I have not forgotten, I hear you," the voice of the shadowed figure whispered.

Gabriel grabbed hold of his bastard brother and pulled him back, yanking him to the ground. Peering inside the tent he could see his sister and his father. Both were perfectly in his eye line. Gabriel turned, dropping down and grabbing Leylan by his throat, forcing his head against the dirt, squeezing him tightly. "I see your eyes; they linger too closely. You have plagued her steps far too long." Leylan gasped and choked, fighting to free Gabriel's powerful grip from his neck. "I am not a child anymore. How does it feel to be weak and at someone else's mercy? I should thank you, as it was you who gave me the desire to defend those I love. If my father did not love you so, I would have cut you down many years ago!" Gabriel's face turned red; a demon seemed to summon within him.

"You know not what you see." Leylan's words were broken.

Slowly Gabriel released his grip. Leylan choked as he quickly attempted to draw breath.

"I have seen enough." Gabriel rose, looking down at his kin. "Why are you here?"

Leylan crawled to his feet, dusting down his arms and blue breastplate. "I followed you. I wished to see our new friend for myself. Andros, he looks kind enough, but do you think when he is alone with her in his bed chamber, the devil will rise and she will suffer as the rumours claim?" Leylan smiled.

Gabriel lunged at him, unleashing his anger. The prince's fist crashed against Leylan's jaw at the moment of impact, his legs crumbled beneath him. The bastard crashed hard to the floor. With the heel of his sandal, Gabriel forced it against Leylan's throat, forcing his weight upon his jugular. "Listen and listen carefully. You talk too much and one day those words of yours will get you killed. If I even sense that you will bring any harm to my sister, I swear by the blood of the gods themselves I will kill you. If I condemn myself to the City of Fire for that sin so be it. For I will suffer in happiness knowing it was I who ended your disease."

After a moment of revelling in Leylan's agony, Gabriel released him and began to walk away.

"As a child I envied you." Leylan sat up, holding his bruised throat. "You were a beautiful prince. I remember how the crowd roared when you were born. You had the world at your feet; the girls flocked to you like bees to honey and the lords praised you, and for a time I even wished to be you. Yet now when I look upon you all I feel is pity." Leylan rose to his feet. "When the ashes from your bones have long gone, what words will people say when they speak the name Gabriel? Your glorious father, the drinker of wine, raper of women, will be remembered because he is a king, our beautiful sister will be remembered because she will be a queen, but who will remember the prince, the man who was born never to be king? The prince who was denied his right to conqueror. You are just a man who is destined to be in the shadows of other men's glory." Leylan, his hawk like eyes piercing and poisonous, locked in on Gabriel. He slowly stepped back until eventually the darkness consumed him.

Maybe the enemy is closer to home than I realised. Gabriel stared towards the darkness, the burning red flames from the fire brazier crackling softly in his ear.

Chapter 13
A Journey into Paradise

The flames flickered and crackled, their fiery glare drawing him in. Like a moth he could not escape its beauty. In the fire Andros could see both the faces of Lyon and Tilia. "Are the gods punishing me for my sins? And for the evil I have done?" he whispered to himself.

It was late, and the moon shone brightly from the night sky. The day of festivities had ended. King Vincinicus and Andros's future wife, Princess Tilia, had retired to their private tents which his father had arranged for them. Andros stood outside alone, just him and the single fire brazier in front of him. The night seemed so quiet, just the crackling of the fire and the sound of horses whining. It was peaceful but he did not feel relaxed. His body felt tight and his muscles tense. The last two times he had seen his beautiful Lyon he looked so angry, his face full of jealously and venom.

Suddenly he heard a voice, as if someone was calling to him from the shadows. He quickly turned but saw no one. His heart began to thump in his chest. Not a soul. All he saw was the two rows of red and green tents that ran parallel to one another; they were as far as his eyes could see before they disappeared into the darkness. He turned to the two guards who stood at the entrance to the tent and shouted over to them, "Did you hear that?"

"No, Your Highness. The night sometimes plays tricks," one guard replied in a deep voice. He stood still, emotionless like a statue.

"I heard something, I know I did." Andros was becoming agitated. He quickly wiped his sweaty palms down his red and green silks. His eyes began to scan what was in front of him, yet all his saw was the Antilion tents which sat upon a field of darkness. He turned and hurried back towards his pavilion; he passed by the two guards standing outside and entered his room. He collapsed onto his bed and lay back. He swallowed hard as he breathed in deeply.

A rustling in the dirt came from the back of his tent; the flaps began to move as if strong winds were crashing against them. Andros quickly sat up; he was ready to scream and call for help. Suddenly Lyon slid himself into his room. He wore a dirtied white tunic which was open at the top, revealing his muscular chest. He climbed to his feet and approached Andros. His hair was scruffy and loose, and his eyes red and a strong odour of wine seeped from his body.

"What are you doing here? Get out before someone sees." Andros flew from his bed. His voice was low, fear swarmed his body.

"No, I will not hide anymore." Lyon pulled Andros close to him, his strong hands gripping his arms. "You are mine. I will not give you to another."

"I am not yours to give!" Andros attempted to pull free but he failed, "I am a prince. You will obey. Now leave, what if my father comes in?"

"Let him come, I shall not hide like some dog fetching at the scraps. I want all of you my prince!" Lyon pulled Andros to his chest.

Andros felt warm and safe. Being so close to Lyon allowed all his worries and fears to disappear from his mind. Lyon's body felt hard and his sweat enticing. Andros lifted his head. "Was it you who called to me outside?"

"I did not. I came here hoping to find you." Lyon pushed Andros away from him. "Listen to me, let us take two horses and go east. Head across the Calhorion sea to Dagen. Over there, people like us can live freely."

Lyon's words were soothing and like sweet music to his ears, that was all he had wished for. The Kingless lands of Dagen were open. No matter your religion, the colour of your skin or your carnal desires, each man was equal. Yet without law and order the Dagari wilderness were wild and untamed. Only a scarce few Allamantyan nobles, known as Wardens, governed the conquered nation.

Andros could not cope with the pressure he felt as prince, the expectations his father had for him. He wanted neither of them. Yet now the time had come, he could not leave. Something compelled him to stay, he would not go.

"No, Lyon, I cannot. My father needs me. Tilia, she chose me out of all the others. My father told me so. I am the one who will unite the Western Realm." Andros's words were strong.

"What? Tilia did not choose you. Her father would've forced her hand. Valanor is at constant war with Etoria and Goshdel, they need our armies."

"No! My father he would not lie to me!" Andros began to shake his head, his voice began to rise.

"Andros, we can go tonight. If you leave, Arrabella can marry Gabriel. The kingdoms will still be able to unite; this whole thing does not rely on you. You can be free from it all."

Lyon leant forward and pressed his lips against Andros'. Andros could taste the strong stale wine but as their lips moulded together his body eased up as he fell into his arms. Lyon held him tight, lifting him up and placing him on the bed. Lyon knelt down between his legs.

"No, stop. The guards will hear!" Andros pulled away.

"Why must you live in fear? Prince Nymar did no such thing when he found love." Lyon stood up, with anger in his eyes.

"Prince Nymar? You do know what happened to him when his father King Kalidar found out?" Andros looked at Lyon with piercing eyes, who in turn stepped back, moving his scruffy fallen hair away from his eyes. "Well, I will tell you, Kalidar had his son put to death as well as his lover Damon. He removed both their heads with his own sword. I will not confess my love to die the next day!" Andros's voice rose only for him immediately to stop, realising the guards, or worse, his father, might hear.

"Your father is a better man than his grandfather. Kalidar was a killer, he dreamed of blood. King Aristian has brought change to our land; he would do no such thing to you or I."

For a brief moment, Andros considered Lyon's words. In his heart he knew his father would not have him killed, but he could still not bring it to shame his father again. *After what I did before, I swore never to disgrace him. My hand was on the holy book when I took that oath.* He looked up at Lyon, who was now pacing up and down. *Yet that day when I first saw you, the darkest of evil that lies within me was gone, you cured me of my demons.* Even Lyon knew not of what he thought, his secrets were for him alone to bear.

"Things are now in motion that are beyond our control." Lyon moved forwards towards Andros. "You must listen to me, there is something I have to say…"

Andros however raised his finger to Lyons lips. He could hear someone approaching.

"Is my son awake?"

"I think so Your Majesty. I heard him talking with someone."

"Okay, let me pass."

The voices were faint but Andros recognised one of them instantly. "Quick you must hide."

Lyon quickly moved back to the flap upon where he had entered; however just as he dropped to the ground, outside a loud crashing could be heard as horses rode on by. "Where? There are people outside." Lyon's voice was flustered, his hands shook with fear. His eyes buzzed about his head like little bees. The powerful words uttered only moments earlier seemed as if they had been spoken by a totally different man.

"Under the bed." Andros pointed down.

Lyon dropped to his knees and rolled and, just as he was hidden by the frame and sheets, King Aristian entered.

"Father, you are awake late?" Andros spoke quickly. He attempted to conceal his guilt by turning away; he looked into his mirror and brushed his thin brown hair over with his fingertips.

"I could say the same for you, my son." King Aristian looked his son up and down with suspicious eyes. "I was seeing to King Vincinicus and Princess Tilia, making sure they were settled in properly. Something you should have been doing, too."

"I was feeling tired. It has been a long day, I just needed sometime alone."

"Alone? The guards said you were talking with someone." Aristian looked around the room. "Is everything okay?"

"I wasn't talking with anyone! Those guards need to be changed if they are hearing things."

"Calm yourself, it was just a question. You would tell me if it was happening again, wouldn't you?" The tone in his father's voice was suspicious. "I can bring in the priest if you feel it will help?"

Andros could feel his heart thumping inside his chest. Loud powerful beats that he feared even his father could hear. He wanted this moment to end; it had been nearly two years before anything as close as this had happened. It was a night in the Royal Garden, when he and Lyon had been in the throes of passion, when they noticed a guard. They had stayed silent in the bushes until he passed them by. That instant had been exciting; this one was not. He looked up at his father through the reflection in the mirror. His crown weighed heavily on his head; his curly grey hair sprouted out beneath its rim. His eyes were ripe with mental and physical exhaustion. "I am fine, you must sleep father," Andros said genuinely. *It was Lyon's love that had cured me not your priests.*

"A king must look to others before he looks to himself. Remember that." King Aristian approached Andros, placing a hand on his shoulder and turning him round. "Let me look at you."

Andros looked down at his father, straight into his wise eyes. They were deep and full of wisdom but also heartache. He smiled, a rare smile.

"You made me proud today. That is why I wished to see you."

"Did I?" Andros replied in a child-like fashion. His eyes widened.

"You and Tilia will make a fine couple. The greatest king and queen the Allamantyan Empire has ever seen." Aristian pulled his son close. "Now we both need our rest. It is a long ride back to the capital."

Andros watched as his father left. As the flaps to the entrance of his room closed, his body loosened as if a great weight had fallen from his back. He collapsed to the bed, breathing deeply over and over.

Lyon appeared from under the bed. "Greatest king and queen?" His words were spiteful. "Andros, you were meant for me." He leant forward, kissing Andros's neck before biting his ear.

Andros closed his eyes, imaging all those intimate times they had been together. He remembered that first day they laid eyes upon one another at Lord Latimor's birthday celebration. Oh, how happy they both were. Life was simple back then.

Lyon stood over Andros, looking down at him. He placed a hand on his shoulder. "I have one thing to ask you, how do you expect to consummate your marriage? Let alone produce heirs. Will you have to think of me when you are inside her?"

Andros felt Lyon's grip loosen. He opened his eyes and turned to find him disappearing out of the tent. The prince sat silently before he lay back onto his bed, his eyes weary, his mind heavy and his soul full of sadness. He wished he was not a prince, but he was. He had a duty; *I will not fail my father again.*

****

"Your Highness, you look so beautiful," Cassandra said as she brushed the last few strands of Princess Tilia's shining golden hair.

Tilia admired herself in the reflection. Her eyes sparkled and her skin was smooth yet she did not feel beautiful. Her hair was down; it was long and fell between her shoulder blades. All Tilia could do was to smile in reaction to Cassandra's compliment. She hadn't slept well last night; she rarely did away from her bed. Tilia closed her eyes and for a moment she could feel herself drifting off. She forced them open and watched Cassandra as she did her work. Her small chubby hands gripped the brush as she gently pulled it through her thick hair. Cassandra's skin was pale and her face plain. She was small and her body was as round as she was tall; her white gown was made of poor material and looked uncomfortable. Yet she seemed the happiest girl in the world.

"Are you ever sad?" Tilia asked.

"I have no reason to be, Your Highness." Cassandra smiled. "I see every day as a blessing."

Tilia did not reply as she stared at her reflection. The dress she wore was of red silk; it was tightly fitted around her breasts and waist, and then it loosened off and fell into three separate sections around her legs, stopping by her knees. Silver gems were sown into the silk. It was a lot more comfortable than yesterday's dress.

Cassandra and the rest of the Valorian army had arrived early in the morning. Their loud arrival had woken her from the broken sleep she had endured. Her bed was large and her tent spacious. It had been decorated with a large oak table with a beautifully ornate circular mirror. Around the rim, silver roses entwined with the smooth wood.

"What is Prince Andros like? Did he enter your dreams last night?" Cassandra giggled.

Tilia smiled. He had entered her dreams but not in the romantic way Cassandra had asked. All that plagued her mind was, what did he think of her? Was she a disappointment? Did she not live up to the gossip that would've surely entered his ears?

"He was okay, not very talkative though."

"Some men aren't; they are shy. He will open up the more you talk to him." Cassandra leant forwards. "I find the shyest men are the most satisfying in bed. Those who talk a lot often fail to live up to their boasts."

Tilia laughed. "Less of that talk, Cassandra. My wedding night is not on my mind yet." *Another lie,* she thought to herself.

"Is he handsome?"

"I feel I must know him better. A man's true worth is in his heart."

After Cassandra had made Tilia presentable, she had left her tent and made her way outside before stopping. The morning was hot and the sun bright. The field was crowded as squires and men at arms were pulling down the tents that littered the field. Lords rode by with armoured knights following loyally behind. It was organised chaos. The noise was deafening as armour clattered together and horses brayed and whined. She squinted as rays of sun shone into her eyes, breathing deeply she took her first step across the warm green grass. To her surprise, each soldier clad in the Antilion colours of green and red stopped what they were doing and bowed as she crossed their path.

“They are mesmerized by your beauty,” Cassandra’s words whispered into her ear.

Tilia felt embarrassed but she lowered her head in return. The men seemed to stare at her intensely; their eyes widened as if they wished to take in as much of her as possible. Each soldier smiled, most however lacked teeth and the ones they did have were yellow and rotten. Beyond the hustle and bustle of the encampment she could see Valorian flags flying high in the sky, shinning blue armour glistened in the sun. She could see her father being helped onto his horses. He was surrounded by mounted Valorian knights and men and at arms. As she approached them, she could see her father had a goblet in his hand. Her bastard brother, Leylan, was beside him, filling her father’s goblet with blood-red Akeshian wine. A grin filled his bony face.

“Father, you drink too much,” Tilia spoke with concern in her heart.

“Not you as well. Sir Kaian has already told me this. It is a time to celebrate. The gods gave us wine so we may enjoy ourselves.” He paused, lifting the goblet to his mouth. Red liquid began to fall from his mouth and into his beard. His white and silver silks were already stained with the rich wine.

Leylan stood behind her father, a flagon in his hand, like a devil willing to do his every biding. As always, that sadistic grin was fixed to his face. As always, his presence made her feel uneasy.

“Does Your Majesty wish to ride?” Sir Kaian Vadius appeared before her, holding Tilia’s beautiful red horse, Flame.

“I do.” His beauty automatically made her smile; she ran her hands through his thick mane before being helped onto her saddle by Sir Dejax Felios. Once mounted, she felt complete. She gripped her reins tightly.

“Good morning, I hope you all slept well.” King Aristian greeted them; happiness filled his words. He was surrounded by knights and lords; he was mounted on an old grey stallion. The King was dressed in green silks with a thick brown belt around his waist. His tunic was decorated with a shield flanked either side by two dragons, and at the centre was the red Antilion sword. Aristian turned to Tilia’s father. “We shall all ride ahead; your soldiers may join us while Lord Devon Hohjan stays behind to see to things here.”

She noticed her brother was not around. “Where is Gabriel?” she asked. Sir Kaian.

King Vincinicus butted in, “He hasn’t been seen since last night. Let him sulk.” He raised his newly filled goblet to his lips, and coughed briefly before taking a huge gulp.

“If everyone is ready, it is best we ride.” King Aristian raised his hand. A trumpet soon followed and the entire column began its march south.

Princess Tilia looked back and smiled. Never for over two hundred years had any army from Allamantya and Valanor ever been together like this without hatred in their hearts. The two armies rode peacefully side by side; the glorious Antilion green and the sparkling blue of Valanor looked beautiful together. Just rich green fields and pale blue sky lay ahead. Beautiful white birds flew above. With the lack of shade, the hot sun was relentless, even this early in the morning.

King Aristian and King Vincinicus rode at the front of the column. Behind were Princess Tilia and her bastard brother. Then, further back, were her sworn swords, Sir Kaian and Sir Dejax, and the various Lords and Knights of Allamantya.

"Where is Prince Andros?" The princess asked King Aristian.

The king turned around. "He and his sister are in the royal carriage. His pale skin isn't suited to this summer."

Tilia felt disappointed; she had, in a way, been looking forward to talking with the prince. She was keen to learn more about the man she was to marry. Yet, with him not around, she could relax slightly and make the most of the beautiful scenery.

"I wonder why the prince doesn't want to be around you today. I hope you didn't offend him, dear sister." Leylan's unwelcome voice quietly slithered into her ear.

"Be quiet, I do not wish to speak with you," Tilia snapped back.

"So rude. I only wish to offer my opinion." Leylan pulled at his ill-fitting breastplate. His hawk-like eyes seemed to burn into her flesh, harsher than the rays of sun that shone down from above.

"If you offer me your opinion again then you will be escorted to the rear by Sir Kaian." Tilia's voice was firm and strong. She could tell it took Leylan by surprise; for a moment she felt proud of herself.

They rode for hours; only once did they stop and that was to water the horses. She could tell King Aristian was in hurry to get them to the capital. All around there were wild horses, deer and various birds in the sky. It was the perfect hunting ground. She wanted nothing more than to kick into her stirrups and ride free, just her, Flame and a bow in her hand. With the wind in her hair and the sun on her back, she would be in her element.

A loud crashing of horses' hooves onto dried earth stormed alongside her. Tilia turned to see her handsome cousins, Lucian and Lassander; both were clad in fine crystal blue Valorian breastplates. Their long golden hair was pulled back away from their faces. They held their Phrygian styled helmets in their right hands.

"Beautiful cousin, it has seemed so long since I gazed upon your beauty." Lucian revealed his pearly white teeth.

"It has felt too long since I have heard your kind words." Tilia smiled back. His flirtatious nature was harmless but always welcome.

"Prince Andros does not seem to share in your opinion." Leylan's words were quiet but venomous.

"I am an expert at exterminating rats." Lucian forced his horse between Tilia and Leylan, knocking the bastard prince away. "If Your Highness wishes me to kill one today, she but has to command."

Leylan grinned, knowing when it was best to say little. Suddenly, Gabriel appeared alongside them. He wore his elegant white breastplate with the shinning golden décor that he had been wearing the day before. He looked tired but his eyes still sparkled. A happy warm glow seemed to shine towards her.

Tilia turned to her brother. "Where were you last night?"

"I needed to be alone; I had things to think about." Gabriel pulled his horse alongside his sister. "Fear not, I was always close. Remember, I am here now and I intend to stay."

A few hours went by, and the two armies passed down between two hills as they entered a wide valley that was flanked either side by steep slopes of grass and dense woodland. The goddess, Alcea, seemed to bless the day with clear blue skies, not a single cloud could be seen. Tilia noticed Gabriel rear up; he pushed into his stirrups and raised himself from his saddle.

"What is wrong?" Tilia was concerned. She hated seeing her brother so on edge.

"An army approaches," Gabriel spoke slowly, his eyes staring straight ahead.

Tilia looked down the valley. In front, she suddenly saw a column of Allamantyan soldiers approaching. It was ten men wide; they were all mounted. She could see black and yellow flags alongside orange and blue. The sigils she could not make out at this distance.

"What is this?" Lucian yelled.

"A trap!" Sir Kaian shouted.

"Fear not, little Valorian," Prince Daemar suddenly appeared. He rode past at full speed, his grey horse chewing up the earth beneath his hooves. "These are friends, here to escort us safely to the capital." He pulled his horse closer to Sir Kaian, "If it was a trap you would already be dead." He kicked into his spurs and headed to the front of the column beside his brother.

Tilia did not like Prince Daemar. His tone was always serious and he showed no love for Valanor and its people. He was clad in fine Allamantyan armour; a green cape fell from his shoulders and his left hand rested upon the hilt of his sword. She watched as King Aristian seemed to scorn Daemar with a fiery glare.

The approaching army had stopped; they waited patiently as the royal column made its way to them. Up close, Tilia could see the mounted soldiers were clad in yellow tunics with a black lion on the front.

"Please welcome Marshall Varrone DeVeil, governor of Ardenia." King Aristian extended his hand. "Beside him is his champion, Sir Rolan Bonhuer."

Marshall DeVeil was dressed in black armour; his yellow tunic fell from his shoulders, down past his waist and to his knees. The head of a black war lion was at his chest. DeVeil was of a tanned complexion. Thick black hair was brushed away from his face, and a well-groomed goatee surrounded his mouth and lower chin. He spoke no words, just bowing his head.

"It is my honour that I get to escort you the rest of the way back." Sir Bonhuer spoke, his voice clear and proud. He was pale but tall, his shoulders broad. Shinning silver armour was strapped to his torso. His face was wide and his jaw strong; a scar ran across his nose. Dark auburn hair circled the rim of his head, not a single hair was visible on his scalp.

"These are my closest friends and allies." Prince Daemar spoke proudly. "Brothers since our youth."

Tilia looked back at Gabriel; he watched them all intensely. He offered no courteous replies; it was clear he suspected treachery at every turn.

"I somehow felt safer before they arrived," Lucian whispered.

"I feel safe." Lassander raised his eyebrows.

"What? Why?"

"Because I have the mighty Lucian beside me." Lassander laughed, soon followed by his brother.

The combined armies made their way south. The journey was long but Tilia enjoyed listening to King Aristian talk with such enthusiasm about his kingdom. Even Gabriel listened to each word that he spoke. Whenever they ventured somewhere new, the king named each location as if he was reading the names from a scroll. They travelled passed the forests of Ardenia and over the round hills at Malvaris. Gabriel clearly seemed on edge; as much as he claimed to be fine, his body was tense and he was constantly alert like a caged animal ready to unleash its fury.

When they eventually stopped and made camp for the night, all Tilia could do was watch the prince from afar. He looked shy when their eyes caught one another. Yet, whenever they did catch each other's gaze, he would smile. That smile was all Tilia needed in that moment as reassurance of his acceptance of her. It was like he was scared to approach her; maybe it was Gabriel's defensive mannerisms that had scared Prince Andros away. Gabriel had kept close to Tilia all day and night; he was intimidating even to the most accomplished of warriors let alone a prince who had never tasted combat before. She had half expected Andros to visit her in her tent, yet he did not come.

It was early the next morning when the camp had risen. Tilia had slept better that night, even dreaming of white beaches and pale blue seas. At one point she even had a husband, although the man she dreamt of had looked nothing like Andros. He was shorter, with long hair and cheeky grin, a smile that had offered her warmth and happiness.

After a few hours of travelling, in the distance, across the ocean of green, she noticed the dark silhouetted image of mountains on the horizon. They spread as wide as the eye could see. A cloud of grey seemed to hover above them, stopping the sun from blessing them with its rays of beauty.

"Up ahead you will see the Mountains of Hamon'dor." King Aristian's hand extended in front of him. "Through these mountains, we will take the only pass into Antilion. We will walk the Steps of Avindel. Did you know Antilion is an old Numarian word for Paradise over the mountains?"

Eventually they arrived at the entrance to the Mountains of Hamon'dor. They were monstrous in appearance. The top could not be seen by the mortal eye; they disappeared into a dark mist which hovered softly above. Their rock was made of the deepest black and was as sharp as spear heads. The rich warmth of the Allamantyan fields was now gone; hard rubble now lay beneath them as they slowly made their way along the Steps of Avindel. The vast mountains that flanked them either side were the most impressive she had ever seen; the mountains at Rylor and Yarona looked like tiny hills in comparison to the magnitude of these. The hot sun that had followed them on their journey was no longer present. A chill crept up her spine, sending a shiver throughout her body.

Tilia saw a garrison encamped along the entrance. The wooden fortification rose along the mountain face, and red and yellow flames flickered along the sea of shadow. She heard King Aristian call it the Shadow cliff garrison. The Allamantyan men at arms watched them with cold hard eyes; she could feel their distrust as they glared down at her.

The pass was wide, allowing ten men to ride side by side. Huge fire braziers were placed along the path. King Aristian and King Vincinicus were at the front. Gabriel was beside her; he looked uncomfortable. His nerves were clearly at boiling point; his hand gripped the hilt of his sword.

Tilia leant over and slid her hand around her brothers. "It will be okay."

"It is not me I fear for," Gabriel replied as his eyes scanned the mountains.

They eventually approached the magnificent Mountain Gate of Hamon'dor. Forged into the rock were two huge towers, each standing over one hundred feet high. Tilia's breath was taken away at the sight of the god-like towers. They rose high into the sky; it was as if they scrapped along the skyline itself. They were circular at the top with huge Allamantyan flags flying proudly. She felt Gabriel's hand squeeze hers gently. In between the god-like towers lay a powerful thirty-foot wide gate. The thick wooden drawbridge was lowered, allowing them to pass through.

"This gate was forged by King Avindel, nearly eight hundred years ago. Not once has this gate ever been taken." King Aristian spoke with such wonder. His knowledge of his kingdom was second to none.

"If Antilion women are as dull as this place, I fear I may have made a big mistake coming here." Lucian's face was full of disappointment.

Lassander grinned. "What a shame, as this whole thing was agreed so we may bear witness to beautiful southern women. You will have to make do with ugly ones from now on."

"Ha, I think not. Me and ugly women do not bond well; we are like chalk and cheese. I may not stay long. I bet the Valorian women weep knowing I am so far away."

"They rejoice, more like. Without hearing your whining, I bet they are all the happier for it."

"You are mistaken; it is their husbands who rejoice for they know their wives are safe." Lucian laughed, soon followed by Lassander.

Tilia smiled as she watched her cousins bantering. Their light hearted words briefly brightened this dark place. As they passed over the drawbridge and under the gate, almost total darkness fell upon them. The passageway was narrow and stuffy. The smell of hot sweat and dirt filled the princess' senses. Over the noise of horses' hooves and scrapping of armour was her father's sickening coughs. She could hear him clawing for breath and choking on his own phlegm. The pain he was suffering hurt her deeply. Light, however, shone brightly at the end of the tunnel, offering salvation. Suddenly the ancient words of the holy book came to her, *Beyond the darkness, there is always light. Keep moving forwards, do not stop, do not submit yourself to the shadows.*

The land before her was beautiful; Tilia looked down from the raised slope from which the mountain gate sat upon. It was like she stood at the top of the world; beneath her she saw more fields of green, waterfalls of crystal blue and flowers of various magical shades of purple and yellow. No words could express the beauty of what she was witness too. The bright colours of Antilion seemed to wash away the darkness of Hamon'dor. It evaporated instantly from her mind, a true paradise. Far on the horizon she could make out a white city; it seemed to sparkle like a great jewel. Her heart began to thump, her hands quivered slightly and she breathed deeply for she knew what she saw would be her new home.

Chapter 14
The Eyes Only Reveal What Our Mind Wants Us to See

"Griffin, look it is so beautiful." Danaka looked out, bewildered. The countryside stretched before her eyes like a great quilt of golden, brown and green squares held together by rows of thick hedges. The hills rose and fell like giant waves on a gentle ocean; upon this great sea scores of animals ran freely. Deer and wild horses grazed openly together. The bright sun lit up this magnificent view, and her eyes felt spoilt as they took in the wonders that lay before her.

The delight of the clean air and unspoilt views excited her. The warm feeling she felt was not from the hot summer sun but from the euphoria of escaping the claustrophobia and loveless grasp that Tomellburg had over her. The brief sadness she felt from leaving her home town was immediately washed away. It was if she had broken free from the thick iron chains that had held her back; she felt loose and excitable. Griffin sprinted around her feet, his golden sable fur shining in the bright sun. He was sniffing everything he could, from trees to plants and bushes. Exploring his new surroundings, he seemed as excited and as happy she did.

Danaka felt so blessed, she could barely stop smiling. "What land are we now?" she asked, looking back to Duro who sat playing a soft tune from his pan flute. His horse beneath him seemed to trot to the tune he played.

"This is the region of Ardenia, governed by Marshall Varrone DeVeil from his keep at Blackharrow. From here we head towards Ashfeld," Duro replied bluntly. His horse kicked into the grass as it cantered up the hill; his small horse struggled behind but it wasn't long before they both reached the top.

Danaka looked up and admired Duro; he cut an imposing figure, his broad muscular frame almost blocked out the sun. Once on the brow of the hill he became a magnificent silhouette, a shadow of mystery and intrigue. Danaka and Griffin eagerly sprinted up the grassy slope. Down below were lush green fields and on the horizon lay more hills; however, beneath the valleys stood a lone castle. One long large tower stood at the centre. Next to it were two smaller square stone buildings with turrets on the roofs. They were then surrounded by a circular castle wall, with what appeared to be one entrance. Below the castle was a waterless moat; the drawbridge was lowered as rows of people were entering and leaving.

"Yes, that is the home of Varrone DeVeil's son, Steffan." Duro spoke before Danaka had time to utter a word.

Danaka leant forward with her hands on her knees. Gasping for breath, her heart beat furiously in her chest as she felt what seemed like hundreds of beads of sweat running down her body. The salty drops began to invade her eyes and dripped from her chin. Her long thin brown dress was sticking to her body; patches of perspiration formed along her back and below her arms. A strong smell seemed to surround her, a hot unclean odour. For a brief moment she thought an animal lay dead beside her, one that had been left to rot in the heat. Then it dawned on her and she began to panic, suddenly realising she had not washed for nearly two days. She wore the same clothes she had on when the soldiers threw her in jail, where she had lain on that urine stained floor. At that exact moment she cared not for where they were or where they were going, all she wanted to do was wash.

A hard, stinging pain shot up her arm, a loud thud echoed as she flinched. It reminded her of the hard fruit those young Akeshan children had thrown at her on her way to the trial. Suddenly violent images shot before her eyes, of hundreds of vile screaming faces yelling at her, craving for her death.

"Drink," Duro commanded.

Danaka looked down at her feet to see a small battered and brown water flask. She picked it up and all she could think of was pouring the clean water over her body. Duro brought his flask to his mouth and took a small gulp. She copied, taking a small swig; the water was cool and refreshing as it made its way down her throat. Her mouth begged for more yet she knew the water had to last.

"Come, we keep moving," Duro ordered as he directed his horse down the hill. His horse waded its way through the long strands of Canola grass which were waist high. The petals shone like a chest of gold. With each stride his horse made, it created a makeshift path for Danaka to follow.

As she made her way down the new path that had been especially made for her, Danaka's mind began to wonder. Her thoughts drifted away like a bird into the clear blue sky. Her mind imagined all the wonderful things she had seen since she left Tomellburg: the grass, the hills, the animals and the fresh warm air. She walked carefree behind the rear of the small black horse. Its back slouched underneath the weight of the two boxes it carried on either side. Its muscles, however, were deep and defined, just like its master's.

Duro made his way out of the long Canola grass. As he did, the rays of light shone around him, like the gods themselves had opened the heavens. The light forced Danaka to briefly close her eyes as she made her way onto the open plain. Purple and red flowers blossomed around her feet. Their lush petals opened wide, allowing all to see their beauty.

The ground felt dry and hard underneath her sandals, the summer sun sucking away all the water from the earth. Then, suddenly, out of nowhere, it felt hot and moist. As if she was standing in mud. Looking down she saw what her mind had feared. Deep brown excrement swamped her feet. The huge pile of shit was squashed between her small toes; it rose up past her ankle. The hot mush was embedded in her sandals. The stench made her gag; forcing her to close her eyes and yank her foot free.

"Ahh!" she yelled at the top of her lungs as if she was unleashing all of her frustration in one mighty scream.

Duro quickly pulled back on his reins, sensing danger. His right hand shot up past his shoulder and gripped the handle of his sword. He peered back to see Danaka kicking out wildly. Like a small child playing with an imaginary friend.

"What's the matter?" Duro rode closer towards her.

"What's the matter? What's the matter?" Danaka voice began to rise as she suddenly stopped kicking out, "I'll tell you what's the matter. I haven't washed for two days, my feet hurt, and I have trod in shit. Oh, and I'm hungry, too."

"Hungry? You ate yesterday, didn't you?" Duro replied calmly as he looked down at her shit covered foot.

"Yesterday! Oh, well, I'm sorry I got into the bad habit of eating every single day!" Danaka screamed at the top of her voice. Even Griffin stepped back in shock, not sure what to do next.

Duro looked at her and then exchanged a stare with Griffin before he quickly dropped down from his horse. The speed at which he dismounted made Danaka step back; the thud he made when he landed on the ground made her flinch. He walked towards some dried-out plants; they were brown and crisp, frazzled by the hot rays of light. He yanked at them, forcing them out of the ground. The two roots were thick and white, like small turnips. He brushed them down and hand one to her.

"What is it?" Danaka peered at the dirty object in her palm.

"The Vamiscas root." Duro took a bite. It crunched like a fresh apple as his teeth broke through its hard, outer layer. "Only eat the white ones; if they have red circles, they are poisonous." He remounted his horse.

Danaka looked intensely at the root, making sure there were no red circles. She was still unsure of whether to take a bite. It didn't look very appetising. Her stomach groaned and twisted, and a harsh hunger sickness ripped through her gut demanding she ate. She pressed the dried root to her mouth and took a small bite. It was dry and hard. Yet, past the taste of dirt, it wasn't too bad, edible.

"That should keep you quiet for a few hours." Duro kicked into his horse.

A few hours had gone by and Duro had decided they should rest for a while. They stood on a bend, flanked by two short but steep grass hills. As Danaka perched her weary behind on a large rock, the weight instantly lifted from her aching legs. They felt loose and weak as she stretched them out in front of her. The rock she was seated on was hard and sharp, yet to just sit down was enough to please her for now.

Looking all around, Danaka could see more beautiful landscapes that she could not wait to explore. The sun was still high; the clouds had faded leaving behind a crystal ocean of blue tinted sky. In front of her was a large stone bridge. What was beyond it she did not know. Yet she craved to be on the other side, but not until she had rested first. To her right she watched as Duro unhinged his two wooden chests, relieving the weight that his poor horse had to lump around.

"I feel sorry for him, having all that weight on his back."

"If you want to carry it then you can. I am sure he will be grateful." Duro did not look back as he lowered the boxes to the ground. The weight must've been intense as the muscles in his arm pulled tight.

"What is inside those boxes?"

"Why do you ask so many questions?"

Danaka squinted, as the sun shone brightly into her eyes. "Why do you never answer them?"

A slight smirk pulled quickly across Duro's face. One he quickly removed as he pushed the two boxes away from the path. His horses instinctively followed and began to feast on the rich green strands of grass. As Duro stretched out, she noticed two long scars that ran across his back, thick white tears that started from his shoulder blade and continued down underneath his white poplin tunic and out of sight. She had to hold back her words; she wanted to ask, yet she knew she would get no reply.

"Can I ask you one thing?" Danaka paused. "Please." Her voice was soft and innocent.

"You can ask, yes."

"Why are we heading south?"

Duro hesitated. "There is someone I have to see in Ashfeld." He quickly looked to his left. Like a cat, alert and ready.

Griffin soon followed, his hind legs tightening. His ears twitched. Danaka followed their eyes. She saw nothing, just the empty stone bridge, the cool winding river and trees; lots of trees.

"What is it?" she asked.

"Listen."

The ground began to thud; slight vibrations ran underneath her toes. A tingling sensation ran up her legs. Then they appeared in rows of three. Soldiers on horseback, men clad from head to toe in rings of mail; white tunics covered their chests running down to their legs, a red war lion standing proud on its hind legs stood at the centre. The rider at the front carried the same emblem on his flag. Each wore full helms that covered most of their faces; red and white plume fell from their heads.

They looked like a row of red and white ants as they began to appear from the woods and calmly cross the bridge. They were no in hurry. Each rider held a long smooth kite shaped shield, decorated in red and white. As they got closer, the overpowering sound of hot mail rubbing together fill her ears, then of hard-boiled metal, as armoured horses trotted by.

"House N'Dai from city of Ethilbar." Duro sat himself down.

Danaka suddenly felt nervous with Duro so close. Her heart beat twice in quick succession. She could smell his aura, his sweat. *If I can smell him, surely, he can smell me?* She slightly slid along the rock, moving away from him. The feast of red and white compelled her to look, excited and thrilled by such a magnificent sight. Never had she seen so many soldiers on the march. "Are they going to war?"

"No, the wedding."

All the men looked the same; nothing about each one could be distinguished from the other: same helmets, same tunics, same shields, even the same brown coloured horses. Then something caught her eye: a ray of blue and yellow. Danaka leant forwards looking closely. *They are so beautiful.*

Three ladies, dressed in elegant blue and yellow dresses. Each one rode side saddle, chatting and giggling. The dresses they wore were tightly fitted and pleasing on the eye; they were baby blue with yellow flower decoration that stopped underneath their well perched breasts. Two of the women were young, around Danaka's age. The third was older, perhaps their mother. Each had shining hair, light brown with streaks of blonde that shone like gold. Danaka was instantly envious of their beauty. Their skin looked tanned and smooth, even their stiff upright posture enhanced their appearance. She touched her own hair; it felt hard and dry, knotted and twisted. Feeling self-conscious she pulled her hair back, hiding her broken ends.

Griffin suddenly leapt forwards with lighting speed after seeing a small rabbit peer its small head from out of the bushes. Griffin moved like a cat, darting between the legs of the women's horses, causing them to rear back in panic. One of the younger women screamed, a high-pitched squeal, like death itself had placed its icy hand on her flesh. Danaka ran forwards between the horses, grabbing hold of Griffin by his thick fur. The commotion caused the entire column to stop instantly.

"You stupid bitch! You could have killed her!" The elder woman yelled. Her eyes were a pale green and her hair braided and pulled back away from her pretty face. Her tone did not match her physical beauty.

"Ugly whore, keep your rat under control." The younger lady joined in.

"I'm sorry, so sorry. It was his hunting instincts." Danaka's voice was fast and flustered. She struggled to hold Griffin who began to pull away from her. The women's cruel words cut into her like small blades. A small lump formed in her throat.

"Forgive her, my ladies. She knows not what she does." Duro stood and then casually walked forwards, wiping the sweat from his forearm.

"We are the ladies of house N'Dai. I am Dyana and these are my daughters, Margareta and Yasmin." Dyana was the elder of the three women, maybe late forties but good for her age. Not a wrinkle or grey hair insight. "Is that girl your wife?"

Duro bowed his head. "No, she is mine by right of combat."

"I hope the man you killed was of less worth than her."

"He was," Duro replied bluntly.

"I want her punished, she could've killed me." Yasmin's voice was full of arrogance; her eyes carried venom as poisonous as a snake.

Danaka and Duro exchanged a glance. A brief moment as their eyes locked together.

"No, we have not the time. We are behind schedule as it is. We must be the first house to arrive for the wedding." Lady Dyana looked towards Duro, "Can I trust you to deal out a suitable punishment, sir knight?"

"You have my word."

"Good." Lady Dyana nodded and the column began to move once again.

"Marshal Latimor N'Dai approaches!"

Danaka turned, feeling the loud rumbling beneath her feet.

"What is going on here?" Marshal Latimor shouted as he charged down the column. He was tall and broad, clad in shining silver armour. He wore huge shoulder plates and thick body armour; both were decorated with the head of a golden lion.

"Nothing, dear husband, it is sorted now," Lady Dyana replied as she exchanged a glance with Duro, "Come girls," she added before riding ahead.

Yasmin angrily kicked into her horse. Margaret, however, seemed drawn to Duro, her eyes fixed upon his masculine frame. As they rode off Margaret looked back, taking in as much of him as she could.

Duro, however, was totally oblivious to the girls; he looked up, staring at Marshal Latimor N'Dai. An intense glare glowed from within Duro's eyes. The Marshal was a big handsome man, early fifties but in excellent shape. His hair was thick and grey, pulled back into a pony tail. His face was smooth and covered in a short, well-groomed silver beard. His left hand held the tip of his sword. It was gold and beautifully decorated with red jewels along the handle.

"Don't I know you?" the Marshal asked as he peered down towards Duro.

"We have never met before, my lord." Duro intentionally turned his back.

"I have a thing for faces, I know you."

Danaka watched them both. Her hands still trembled as she gripped Griffin's fur tighter in her palm. After a long stare, the Marshal rode on. Within a few minutes the last rider had ridden by, the noise began to fade and all that was left was chewed earth. Four carriages passed in total, each beautifully decorated with golden lions upon the highest quality oak. The wealth of these lords amazed Danaka, who had spent her life with little more than the clothes on her back and the food Heidi put on her table.

Duro stared intensely at her; his eyes were angry she could tell. He said no words as he lifted his chests onto the smaller horses back before mounting his own and slowly trotting towards the stone bridge. Danaka loosened her grip on Griffin's fur, and he darted after Duro.

I wonder what my punishment will be. For now, I am his and my fate lies with him.

As Danaka and Duro crossed the old stone bridge, they veered right and travelled along the river bank. To her left was a mass of trees and bushes: the black lion forest. To her right was a wide river; the soft sounds of the water and the birds relaxed her as she slowly walked alongside Griffin. Danaka's legs ached and her feet felt sore. Her sandals had begun to rub; her skin was red raw and started to split.

She noticed that the path they were following was away from the road. *Maybe he wanted to travel unnoticed? The Marshal clearly knew his face, and the people in Tomellburg recognised his name. Who is he? He had known Sir Claris Moon when they clashed; he did not fight to save me.* That much she knew.

The old dirt path they followed had faded until it was no more. Light green grass now lay beneath their feet; it felt hot and soft. Duro was ahead; he had dismounted and was filling the water flasks. Griffin suddenly sprinted ahead to join him. Danaka yawned before smiling; she wished she had his energy. They had been travelling nearly one day and Griffin was already getting accustomed to their new companion.

As they travelled along the river bank, the dense trees to their left had begun to disappear; now the land opened up revealing a large field filled with bushes and an array of red petal flowers. On the field near the water bank was a lone horseless wagon. The white cloth that covered the back was torn and hanging loose. Luggage and chests were scattered about.

"Stay close," Duro ordered as he dismounted.

Danaka felt stiff and uneasy. The beautiful landscape suddenly felt empty and silent. A cruel silence ran deep in her bones. She instinctively moved closer to Duro, as he drew his sword from his back. He held it loose, the shining blade gliding across the strands of grass.

They drew closer to the wagon. She could see the chests were broken open; clothes had been thrown to the ground and, to her horror, stains of red smeared the grass around her.

"Blood," Danaka blurted out. He sheathed his sword. "Whoever did this is long gone."

They walked through the camp; pots and pans littered the ground. The white cloth that hung from the wagon had small stains of blood. Duro walked ahead and around the back of the wagon, peering to the floor. A horrible aroma of death swept through the grass, as if carried by a strong wind.

"What is that smell?" A sickness hit Danaka in her stomach.

Duro didn't reply as he scanned to the ground.

"Help," a weak groaning voice pleaded.

Danaka turned to her left. A man lay stricken on the ground; he was old, maybe late fifties. He was slim with bloodied grey hair. His left hand was held across his stomach; blood drained from his wound. She quickly ran to his aid, kneeling beside him.

"It is okay," Danaka reassured him as she placed her hand on his, helping put more pressure on the gaping hole in his gut.

The man choked and spluttered as blood sprayed from his mouth. His wrinkled face was cold and pale. Life was slowly draining from his body.

"My wife, my daughter." The words were broken and quiet. He struggled to speak.

Danaka looked up to Duro who now stood over them.

The man began to cry, perhaps the pain of possibly knowing his family were dead was more painful they the hole in his stomach.

"Who did this?" Danaka asked as she tried to stop the flow of blood.

He tried to speak but he choked and groaned, pain consuming his body. More tears followed.

Duro knelt down beside them and cupped his small head in his hand. “Go to them, old man. Sit beside your family in Ollaria’h. They call your name.” Duro’s eyes were intense and mesmerising.

Suddenly the man’s eyes widened, his mouth gasping for air. His hand gripped Danaka’s wrist with an intense power as he called out in pain. His grip then began to slowly loosen before his face froze like ice. His eyes were deep and lifeless, pale as snow.

Then Duro slowly withdrew a short dagger from the old man’s body. Fresh blood covered the blade. He placed his fingers on the old man’s eyes and closed them.

Anger rose in Danaka. “Murderer, I could’ve saved him.”

“It would’ve taken him hours to die. I gave him mercy. He had nothing left to live for.”

“Didn’t you hear he had a family?”

“I have seen them.” Duro stood and looked over towards the wagon.

Danaka attempted to move so she could see.

“No, you don’t want to look. They cut the women badly, they always do.”

Danaka pushed passed Duro, knocking his arms out of her way. Rushing around the side of the wagon she suddenly stopped, instantly wishing she had heeded the words of her companion. The two women lay naked, face down in the dirt, with their arms and legs pinned to the ground. Their bloodied backs were torn to pieces; deep red cuts were hacked into their flesh. Each had two wings carved into their skin. They started at the spine then spread out, along the back and down the sides of their arms. Looking further down, she could see smears of blood spread across the buttocks of the young girl. A sickness began to rise in her stomach, her jaw began to ache and her head started to feel light. Her legs twitched slightly, her knees started to give way, feeling loose and weak. Before she knew it, Duro was behind her, his strong hands gripped her waist tightly, holding her up.

“I told you not to look.” His voice was angry yet caring. He lifted Danaka up and pulled her away from the horrors.

“Why is the world such a horrid place?” she asked, perhaps not really wanting a reply.

“This world we live in is a loveless place, unforgiving and uncaring. There is no gold at the end of the rainbow.” Duro released her and began to look around, kicking the broken chests.

“A world without love is a world I don’t wish to be a part of.” A single tear fell from Danaka’s cheek.

“See what you can find. His daughter looked about your size,” Duro replied coldly.

Danaka dropped to her knees, suddenly feeling cold. The golden rays of sun offered her no warmth. Griffin cuddled up beside her, his soft fur brushing against her skin. She watched as Duro scavenged through the people’s belongings, tossing clothes aside like they had no meaning. *But they meant something to this man.*

She sat and looked at the old man. She wondered what his name was. Where he was going? He now looked so peaceful, sleeping the endless sleep, far away, lost in his never-ending dreams. *Maybe death isn't so bad after all? He has been set free from the hardships of life.*

"Take these." Duro's voice was stern.

Danaka's thoughts were wiped away as a hailstorm of clothes crashed against her face. Death clearly had no effect on him.

"Put them in my chest, the smaller one."

Danaka cupped the clothes under her arm, an array of red, blue and white dresses. She walked towards the two magnificent black horses. She unclipped the chest and lifted open the lid; the wood was thick and heavy. Inside, a beam of purple caught her in the eye, and looking down she saw a black breast plate with thick rings of mail. A large purple gem was forged at the centre; it glistened and sparkled. Suddenly the lid slammed shut. It crashed like thunder, making her heart skip a beat and her stomach twist.

"I said the smaller one." Duro's large hand gripped the lid tightly, forcing it shut.

"Sorry-I," Danaka stuttered, unsure of how to reply. Duro pointed towards the smaller chest. Danaka moved towards the smaller chest before asking, "How many men do you think there were?"

"Three. Their tracks headed south."

"But that is where we are headed?" Danaka felt uneasy.

"It is," Duro replied without a hint of concern.

Danaka looked down at the old man. "Don't you think we should bury them?"

"There is no need. They believe in the White City; their souls now walk the golden path to heaven. What use is there in burying the bodies they no longer need?" Duro began to fill the smaller chest with a white blanket he had found.

"Don't you believe in Ollaria'h?" Danaka wiped the tears from her eyes.

Duro looked up at her, small beads of sweat slowly trickled down his strong jaw line. "I believe in what I can see. I see neither a White City nor a Winged God. I see only you and me."

She liked his reply; with the exception of her aunt and uncle everyone she knew believed in some form of God. Duro slowly made his way towards Danaka, his white poplin tunic showing patches of sweat. His strong hands suddenly gripped her waist.

"Ah, what are you doing?" Danaka called out as he lifted her off the ground. In one swift movement he launched her onto the back of the larger horse. "I can't ride."

"You won't be walking for much longer either with feet like that."

Danaka looked down; her feet were red and sore. Small cuts had formed where her sandals had been rubbing into her skin. "I will be fine, I—"

"Hold these." Duro handed her the reins. "Just sit still and no sudden movements; put your feet in the stirrups." Duro turned and walked away; the horses followed instinctively.

Danaka griped the reins tightly. The saddle was hard and uncomfortable but it felt good to take the weight off of her feet. She bumped and swayed but eventually she got the hang of it. Forcing her weight into the stirrups, she was able to keep her balance.

They travelled for a few hours, along dirt paths sheltered by dense forest. This was the first time she had ever ridden a horse before, but she was enjoying it. Her skirt however was hitched up, pulled high up her leg, and almost to her waist. With her skirt revealing so much, she felt nervous with Duro so close. Danaka could feel the rays of heat on her long smooth pale legs. If Duro was to turn around, she felt he could see right between her legs.

The land they travelled upon all looked the same; she had no idea how Duro knew where he was going. It was late afternoon and the sun was still bright. She could feel the hot sun burning into her back. Looking ahead, she watched Duro. His large sword looked like it was a part of him, strapped tightly to his back. The handle was large, designed for a two-handed grip. Yet, during her trial by combat, he mainly fought by alternating the sword between both hands.

Eventually they trekked down a narrow winding broken dirt path, flanked either side by mighty oak trees and thorn bushes. The ground was hard, dried up by the summer sun. Large grey stones littered the path, causing the horse to stir beneath her. Danaka gripped tightly. As they made their way over the broken earth, she could hear a loud crashing sound, like water falling from a bucket into her well back home in Tomellburg.

The path opened up into a large clearing; smooth green grass lay before her, and a few metres after that, a wide shining blue river. A mighty waterfall was situated at the far side of the bank with tons of beautiful water crashing down onto the river below. It was a magnificent sight, one she had never seen before. *Paradise*. The birds were singing loudly, the trees surrounding the clearing were rich with shining golden flowers blossoming in the sun.

"We will rest here for the night." Duro stopped, scanning the area before looking back at her. "Let the horses drink."

Danaka dropped down and guided the horses to the river. Without hesitation, they both dunked their weary heads into the water and began to drink. Griffin soon followed, charging forwards and launching himself into the water. A huge splashed followed, soaking Danaka from head to toe. The cool water was refreshing and much needed. She smiled to herself as he swam around in circles.

Griffin made his way out of the river and shook himself dry. Danaka knelt down beside him at the river bank, where she caught a glimpse of her own reflection in the ripples of the water. Her face was dirty and her eyes heavy. Her hair was greasy and drained of colour. She suddenly began to feel sad and self-conscious. "I wish I was as beautiful as those women we saw today," Danaka said, more speaking to herself than to Griffin.

Suddenly in the reflection of the water, Duro appeared behind her. "A pretty face and the finest silk does not make you beautiful." He knelt down beside her.

Danaka could feel her heart thumping. Even with the waterfall crashing heavily in front of them, she felt he would hear the pounding inside her chest. He then raised his left hand and moved a bunch of stray hairs from her face. Slight warmth crept up her back and tingled in her neck.

"The eyes only reveal what our mind wants us to see." Duro looked into Danaka's emerald green eyes. "There is more to you than you realise." He smiled; his teeth weren't perfect and straight but it was warm and welcoming.

"You should smile more often, it suits you." Danaka felt nervous and disorientated.

Duro quickly pulled back; the kind hearted comment must've caught him by surprise. He rose to his feet unsure of how to respond. "Lady N'Dai said I was to punish you."

Oh shit!

"I want you to wash, you stink." Duro headed to his saddle and withdrew a large wooden bow. "I will find us a meal."

"But you gave her your word to punish me?" Danaka replied. *You should've stayed quiet you idiot.*

"Who you give your word to; that's what counts."

Duro walked off, clutching his bow in his left hand and three arrows in his right. His sword was still strapped to his back. Griffin rose, stepping forward before hesitating. He looked back at Danaka with his big innocent eyes.

"Go with him, if you like." Danaka smiled as he sprinted off.

The river sparkled like crystals, a sea of wonder, glistening in the summer sun. Danaka stripped before lowering herself into the water, feeling it rising up past her waist. A cold but pleasurable feeling ran through her body as she succumbed to the enchanting delights the river had to offer.

As the water washed around her skin, she could feel the dirt and filth falling from her body. All the sweat and bad memories were being washed away. The crashing of the waterfall only relaxed her more. She lay on her back, floating softly on the surface like a small duck.

Looking up near the top of the waterfall, she could see Duro looking out. He cut a mighty image, standing in the sunlight with the water crashing down beside him. His muscular frame shone as he lifted his water flask to his lips. Griffin stood proudly by his side. Duro's eyes gazed towards her; he stared intensely as she floated softly in the water. Danaka looked back, unsure of what to do. Then, like a slap to the face, she realised she was naked. He could see everything through this sparkling clear water. Danaka peered down to see her small breasts poking out above the water, the summer warmth beaming down on them. Danaka wanted to cover herself but instead she smiled an innocent smile. Duro offered none in reply and disappeared into the trees.

Danaka watched as Griffin followed after him. She then lowered her head back until the water covered her face. In that exact moment all the stress she had endured in the past twenty-four hours was wiped from her mind. Her shoulders felt loose and free as if a great weight had been lifted from her neck. With her head underneath the water, even the sounds of the forest were gone, just an empty vessel in a cooling crystal blue abyss.

She slowly rose to surface, taking in a big gulp of air. She pushed her hair back away from her face and wiped the water from her eyes. Still she floated on her back, drifting softly like a piece of wood. She dreamed of the outside world and everything it had to offer. As she slowly opened her eyes, the intense bright rays of sun blurred her vision. On the bank she could see the image of a man standing on the edge of the trees.

It didn't take him long. Danaka shook her head from side to side letting her hair fall freely down her back. She rose only slightly so her breasts were covered by the top of the water. As she wiped the last drops of water from her eyes, she saw who was in front of her.

It was not one man but three. Two of the men were big and bulky, both were topless with olive skin, and thick black hair clung to their bodies like the pelt of a grizzly bear. Each held swords in their right hands. Their black hair was scruffy and greasy. At the centre was a creepy looking man. He was small and slim, covered from his shoulders to his ankles in a long black cloak. His head was bald and a long black beard fell from his face. His eyes were dark and soulless. In his right hand he held a spear; a black flag with white wings was perched at the top.

"Yakash Mudra!" The man at the centre shouted pointing his spear towards her, his voice loud and sinister. His dark beaming eyes burnt into her flesh. Hatred ran through his body, she could feel it.

All three stepped forwards at the same time. She knew at that moment these were the men who had murdered that old man and his family and they would do the same to her. Danaka frantically looked around the trees. Not a soul in sight.

"Yakash Mudra! Yakash Mudra! Yakash Mudra!" they all chanted together, louder and louder as they drew closer to the water.

"I am Hazar. The lawgiver has sent us here to wipe your sin from this earth. Dalackis looks forward to meeting you." Hazar smiled, the tip of his spear still facing her. His teeth were yellow, his lips cracked and dry. The men who flanked him either side began to swing their chipped, rusted swords.

Danaka wanted to scream but no words fell from her lips. She froze.

Chapter 15
A Dishonest Knight

The smell of death filled the hallway. A feeling of horror compelled the boy to follow its scent, like an animal hunting its prey. No matter how much he wanted to turn and run, he could not. His heart said no but his legs would not listen. They pulled him closer and closer to what he did not want to see. The hallway was cold, an unearthly winter chill shivered down his body. A foggy mist crept and swirled around his feet. The corridor was thin, the walkway uneven. The old wooden planks creaked and squeaked with each step, in any moment it felt as if they would give way. The walls were white and stained, damp patches littered the paint. Along with the smell of death, a strong odour of sex and sweat floated around him, both sensations he knew only too well.

At only fourteen he had more knowledge of sex and women than most men would know at forty. That is what you got by being raised by ten whores. These were not just any whores, mind you, but the finest known to man and the most elegant and loveable in all of Dagen. The brothel was not just a place of sex and sin but of love and happiness. Each woman loved him and his brother like their own, and each woman they loved like a mother.

Four doors were located on the second floor, one belonging to him and his brother, the other three to Olga, Miranda and to his mother. Oh, what a woman, tall, slim and strong, devoted to her children and a master at her craft. The goddess of the Tyma, the punters called her. When night fell and her mother had visitors, the boys were to stay in their room; *you must sleep while mother works, because by night gold coins grow.*

The boys would never listen though, independent and mischievous. Each night they would sneak to the balcony and watch the punters come and go. Knights, men at arms, drunken farmers and even a prince once came to the brothel at Tyma. Loud euphoric laughter, groans of sex and drunken singing would fill their ears. It was a happy place, a home.

Yet this night was different; he did not know why but he was compelled away from the balcony and down the hallway. The squeaking beds and cries of ecstasy were silent, only the smell of blood and death lingered in the hallway now. With each step, the urgency that he should turn and flee got greater and greater but he forced himself forwards. Screams, sickening blood curdling cries began bellowing out. It was the worst kind, a woman's screams, pleas for help and begging for the pain to stop.

At his mother's door he froze. The old brass handle felt stiff and cold. He yanked and pushed against it yet it would not budge; it felt as strong as a castle drawbridge. With his shoulder he rammed himself against the wood. Pain shot through his body but it only spurred him on. Bang, bang, bang, the noise echoed as he collided with the door.

Suddenly he was pulled back. His brother, elder by two years, flung him to one side like he was nothing more than a bundle of twigs – his strength and size was incredible for a boy of his age. With one mighty kick, his brother removed the door from it is hinges and powered through. The old wood broke and shattered, splinters flew and the old brass handle slumped to floor.

Inside, a horror filled his eyes, a living hell that sent a sickness through his stomach and up to his throat. He did not feel the scream fall from his lips but he heard it, over and over. He knew the sound of his own voice. There was blood, so much blood. The room that had once been pale white was now red; it dripped from the bed and down the walls.

Loud splashing as the winding stream crashed against the bank brought Uriah back to reality and away from his thoughts. He sat alone, on a rock, the warm summer glare on his back as he watched the deep blue water. It looked beautiful, yet deadly; a powerful current pulled the stream over four large jagged rocks and then down slope and out of sight. He had been throwing stones, just like he used to when he was a child, when suddenly he had begun to daydream. It was often his thoughts would go from happy to sad.

Uriah's duel swords were placed next to him. He sat up, grabbing them before he strapped them to his back. He pulled his long brown hair away from his face, tying it back into a bun. No more than a few feet away was Sir Dillian Howard who was half asleep against an oak tree. A few hours earlier he had almost fallen from his saddle. For a man who claimed to be a knight, it was clear he had never ridden far on horse. It was because of Sir Dillian's state they had decided to make camp. The decision suited Uriah though. Garroway and the others would find them a lot easier with them staying in one place.

Sir Dillian began to stir; he rose unsteadily and trudged along the grass. His legs were wobbly, as if he had spent the night drinking ale. As he stood by the water's edge, he fell to his knees, like an exhausted warrior, kneeling before a god. He dunked his head into the water and began to wash his face.

Uriah began to smile a wide grin from ear to ear. He wanted to burst out into hysterics but he held it together. Slowly Sir Dillian began to raise his face from the water. Looking to his left, maybe ten feet away, he could see Toran who stood tall and strong. He was half naked, wearing only a short piece of cloth that was wrapped around his waist. In his right hand he held his cock, pissing into the stream, as the current took the water straight to Dillian's face.

"You dirty son of a whore!" Sir Dillian screamed. He jumped to his feet and began rubbing his hands frantically over his face.

Toran's voice boomed, as he continued to urinate into the stream, "Ha! How did you like the taste, sir knight? Sweet as wine or as bitter as ale?"

Uriah began to heckle, holding his stomach. His breath came in quick gasps between his unstoppable giggles. Tears gathered in the corners of his eyes, threatening to spill over.

"You fucking scum. If we were not bound together then I would cut you down where you stand." Sir Dillian stormed over to his things, grabbing hold of his sword.

Toran charged towards him, intimidating him with his sheer size. He was ready to fight, to squash him like a worm. "I have always wanted to see how these Allamantyan knights fight, haven't you, little brother?"

"I have." Uriah dropped down from the rock and strolled casually over.

Sir Dillian gulped heavily. The sun which shone so brightly over his head was now nothing more than a dark cloud as Toran engulfed him.

"But not yet, brother." Uriah appeared behind the giant that was Toran. He looked down towards his brother's waist. "Put your weapon away."

"I have no sword."

"It is not that sword I speak of." Uriah smiled as he walked past.

Toran looked down and boomed into laughter before covering himself.

The evening was hot; bright sun still lit up the plains. A wide, fast winding stream lay to the right of their camp. Around them were trees, sparsely planted, and fields of open grass. A quiet place but one easy enough to find. Uriah had been leaving heavy tracks and broken branches for Maarax and the others to track. *I hope they find us soon,* he had thought to himself. He had noticed Sir Dillian panic at the sight of those knights. *Why would he fear other soldiers? What was he hiding?*

Uriah leant against a thick oak tree; with a short dagger he was sharpening a stick. All the while, he watched. With hawk-like eyes he observed Sir Dillian Howard. He was a strange man. He moved uneasily within his armour; he scratched at his neck where his mail rubbed him. He caressed oil over his face, hence why his skin looked so smooth and why he smelt so much like a woman. His eyes were bright, yet they offered no warmth. After a while, Sir Dillian had clumsily removed his armour. He now wore a bright white silk tunic with his sword strapped to his waist. It was clear he was on edge; his eyes darted from left to right like a fly and he could not relax. The more Uriah watched him the greater his own paranoia grew. Garroway, however, had once said, *"The vanity of some knights is far more powerful than their sword."*

A few hours had passed since they made camp. For lunch they had eaten fish, the first meal Uriah and Toran had eaten that was not prepared by Zaira. He missed her and her talent for cooking, that was for sure. Uriah felt tired; his eyes were heavy, yet he knew he would not sleep. All he thought about was his *family*. Where were they? And were they still alive? A lonely feeling had consumed him, one he hadn't a taste for.

"I will wait till dawn. If the others have not arrived by then, the mission is over." Sir Dillian forced the last few bits of his fish into his mouth.

"They will come, old man." Toran's voice was sharp. If looks could kill, Sir Dillian would be dead.

"Your lack of trust may have cost us dearly."

"Why are you so scared, old man?" Uriah asked inquisitively before raising his water flask to his mouth.

"Failure will mean more than a loss of coin; my life is at stake."

"If I remember correctly, it is us who will fight, not you." Uriah rose, before turning. "My Lord."

A loud rumbling began to echo through the trees. Horse's hooves crashed against the dried earth. Old wood creaked and turned as metal banged together.

"Someone approaches!" Toran shot to his feet. He was still undressed, wearing only his white cloth that barely covered his dignity.

"We must hide, hide!" Sir Dillian yelled as he scrambled to his feet.

Light, playful voices could be heard, sweet innocent calls as beautiful as birds on a summer morning. Above them, and more dominant, was a deep noise, the sound of a man. Along with the creaking wood and the banging of metal, it sounded like a poorly organised orchestra.

"Sit, old man." Toran grabbed hold of Sir Dillian by his shoulder and forced him back to the log upon which he had sat. "It is the sound of children."

Through the clearing, an old wagon approached. The wood was dark and dry, the white cloth which hung from the roof was dirty and stained. Two brown horses pulled enthusiastically from the front. As the wagon came to a halt, so did the sounds. The creaking stopped, and the pots and pans clanged together briefly before their noise was rendered silent.

"Wohh!" a man yelled from inside the wagon before he quickly jumped out. His actions and mannerisms were as enthusiastic as his singing. Although old, he glided down. A wide smile filled his face. He had short grey hair and a scruffy beard to match. He was dressed in leather overalls and a white under-tunic. "Greetings friends. I am Edgar. Would I be so bold as to ask if we may join you for the night?"

Uriah and Toran exchanged a glance, both unsure of their new guest. He was small but well-built, his hands large and rough. Sweat seeped through his tunic and his arms were dusty.

Edgar leant forward towards Toran, "I have ale," his smile began to widen, "and lots of it, friend."

Before Uriah had time to speak, Toran replied, "Yes! Sit with us."

"We have no need for guests, be gone with you." Sir Dillian's voice was harsh and rude. He looked up at the old man with disgust.

"It is not safe out. Not with all these killings be going on." Edgar looked up at Toran, his eyes pleading for their company.

Uriah looked at Sir Dillian before replying, "It would be rude of us to turn down the offer of ale." His reply was more to spite the old knight than to welcome new guests.

"Thanks friends. You won't be disappointed," Edgar's voice was upbeat. As if each word was the start of a new song. "Dawn, come here. Don't be shy!"

Dawn, a woman in her early forties, dropped out the back of the wagon, followed by a young girl. Dawn was taller than Edgar with grey hair tied back;

her face was slim and bags had begun to form under her eyes. She wore a white dress that fell from her shoulders down her wrists before stopping at her ankles with not an ounce of flesh on show. The top of her white dress was covered with a black tunic which wrapped around her chest; the straps however were undone down the middle. "I hope we haven't caused you all too much trouble." Her voice was light and pleasing; she wrapped her arms around her young girl.

"This is our daughter, Jessabel." Edgar smiled when he spoke of his daughter. A sense of pride took hold of him. "Her voice is as beautiful as anything you will hear."

As Sir Dillian saw the girl, his bright eyes began to sparkle. He rose from the log upon which he sat. "Please, sit." He beckoned the girl towards him. She was young, barely six years old; she wore a smooth white summer dress which complimented her pale skin. Her hair was tied back with a little yellow flower planted in the roots. Innocence surrounded her like a halo.

Uriah watched Sir Dillian with unease. His demeanour was sinister and sleazy; he liked him less and less by each passing minute. As he looked up, he saw Toran and Edgar were at the wagon; moments later Toran had a huge barrel of ale on his shoulder and he was bringing it back to camp.

Slowly the sun had set, and moonlight began to reflect off the water's surface. The crashing stream was peaceful and relaxing. The fire flickered in front of them. Edgar and his wife sat arm in arm. Jessabel sat to the right of her mother; she spoke no words but looked uneasy in the company of strangers. Sir Dillian sat beside the girl, perhaps too close, as he picked at his fish. Toran gulped down his ale while Uriah sat and listened to the idle chatter.

"From your accent you are not from around here; where are you from?" Edgar squeezed his wife tightly, making her giggle.

"We are from Dagen," Toran boomed before taking down more ale. Drops began to spill down his bare chest.

"Oh, I guess with the Empire's open boarders we all may settle where we please."

King Aristian was the first Allamantyan King to allow free travel between the conquered nations. He thought it would bring about peace and harmony between the Kingdoms; for a while it had worked. Now unrest was brewing; it had boiled steadily for too long, and now it was ready to violently spill over and consume all in its path.

"Where are you heading?" Uriah asked quickly before Edgar had time to ask why they were here. He could tell he was an inquisitive man.

"To Castledon, deep south. I am a blacksmith by trade; I hope to find work there. We are from Ashfeld, born and bred, but it is not safe in such places anymore. The attacks are getting worse; our neighbour was murdered but four moons ago. Something must be done about those fanatical supporters of Dalackis. They are evil."

Sir Dillian puffed out his chest. "Things are in motion. Soon the greatness of this country will rise once more. From the fire, the Phoenix rose, so too with Allamantya." He spoke with conviction and a sense of patriotism.

"We have heard the killings are happening all over the country. My sister, she lives in Ethilbar, she told of three attacks in two days. King Aristian should do something; he looks to foreigners from Valanor more than his own people." Dawn squeezed her husband's arm as she spoke.

"Pray to the gods. They will keep us safe until a time when a strong ruler will come to guide us from this hell." Sir Dillian stared deeply into the flames.

It is not the gods who will do your bidding old man but dragons. Uriah rose from his log. "I will leave you to speak of your gods and kings. I bid you all a good night."

As he walked from the camp fire, he could still hear their talks of Dalackis, the people of the Eastern Isles and Valanor. Garroway had never urged any of his children to worship any god, but if they so choose, he did not care as long as they did not force their beliefs on any of the others. Uriah had no interest in religion, just wine, women and his family.

He rested near the base of a great tree. Surprisingly he felt relaxed; he stared out into the darkness and over the river. The moonlight flickered over the ripples in the water. His body began to ache and his legs felt loose. Looking over, he watched Sir Dillian laughing and talking with their new guests; he had looked upon them with disgust when they arrived but now he spoke to them as family. Toran looked drunk; he swayed from left to right as he drank down his ale. Slowly closing his eyes, Uriah faded away, dreaming of blood and death, screams and cries. A voice was yelling into his ear. *Uriah, Uriah! Help me!* Yet there was nothing he could do. He froze. His body twitched and his stomach twisted.

Suddenly, he woke to hear nothing, just the sound of the water and wind blowing through the trees. The camp fire was still burning brightly; Edgar and Dawn were fast asleep. Toran snored as loud as a wild bull. Sir Dillian, however, was nowhere to be seen. Uriah breathed deeply as he rose and approached the camp. To his surprise he could not see Jessabel either.

Standing silently over the flames, he listened. He could hear giggling and words as faint as flakes of snow on a winter's morning. Following his ears, he walked through a few bushes, just like in his dream he was drawn to the sounds. Yet this time, there was no fear. He wanted to follow, he needed to. In a clearing, sitting upon a fallen tree, was Sir Dillian. Jessabel was on his knee. She was giggling as he tickled her.

"You like that don't you, little dove," Sir Dillian whispered into her ear as he pulled her close.

"No, stop," Jessabel laughed, her voice was playful.

"Sing for me; let me hear your beautiful voice once more." His hand then rested on her leg as he ran his fingers in circle around her knee.

"Oh, morning so bright, so strong, so light. Wake us with your glory and send us…"

"Shh, you must be quiet, Mother will be angry with you if you wake her." Sir Dillian's hand began to rise from her knee.

"Not as angry as I will be, if you don't go back to the camp." Uriah appeared out the bushes. His fist was clenched, anger boiled inside of him. "Go child, back to your mother. Now!"

Sir Dillian was startled. His shoulders twitched as he let her go. In seconds the little girl, terrified, sprinted past Uriah and out of sight. "I thought you were asleep, I–I," the old knight struggled with his words as he jumped to his feet. He looked flustered and uneasy.

Uriah slowly walked over and placed his finger over Sir Dillian's lips. "Don't speak, just listen and listen carefully. All my life I have killed to quench my thirst for coin but," Uriah paused as he pressed his finger hard under the old man's chin forcing his head back, "I would get only pleasure from killing you."

"Then do it boy and see how far you get without me."

Uriah released his finger from his chin, "Wake our guests and tell them they are to leave."

Sir Dillian looked Uriah up and down. The smell of Jasmine was potent it only made Uriah angrier. The old knight spoke no words as he brushed past him; their shoulders knocked together before he disappeared through the bushes.

Suddenly Uriah heard a rustling through the trees; leaves crunched and twigs snapped. Turning quick, he saw nothing, just darkness. He stared intensely, gripping the handle of his swords tightly. He waited for a moment, but the sounds slowly began to pass.

Uriah approached Toran as he slowly awoke from his sleep. His elder brother mumbled and groaned like a bear as he sat up, his hands holding his head. "Where has Edgar and his family gone?"

"They had to leave." Uriah offered his brother his hand.

Toran began to speak slowly. "I had a dream last night. I dreamt of a man. He was mighty and godlike, huge wings to his back, a sword of blue fire in his hand. He was battling a shining gold knight. Eventually the god was defeated; he lay in the sand and he turned to me. He called me by name, before saying, "From the ashes we shall rise, from the ruins we shall rebuild, from the sadness we will know happiness." He slowly began to hover, looking down at me. He spoke once more, something I did not understand, "Falahail Delaghara," before he disappeared into the clouds."

"Me and you clearly dream different things, brother!" Uriah laughed.

"What does it mean?" Toran groaned loudly as he rubbed his hands on his head.

"That you drink far too much."

Golden rays of light began to eliminate the darkness. The sun began to rise, signalling a new day. Edgar's family were gone, only the tracks of their wagon and an empty barrel of ale were left. Toran slowly began to dress himself before saddling his horse. His voice was low as he muttered to himself; he moved around like a sulking child.

Uriah had done the same, all the while watching Sir Dillian – the lowest form of man there was, yet for now he was needed. Without him, their mission would fail, and without the debt of blood being paid, no one would receive their coin. Sir Dillian's arms were weak; he pulled with all his might as his lifted his saddle, before forcing it onto his horses back.

"How you Allamantyan knights ever conquered Dagen, I will never know; you struggle to saddle a horse, let alone ride one." Uriah shook his head and pulled the straps tight around his own horse's stomach.

"Allamantya is the greatest nation the world has ever seen." Sir Dillian's voice was ripe with anger. "Dawn has passed and still the others have not arrived. I will not wait any longer. You sons of a whore can stay here and rot for all I care." He pulled himself onto his horse. His silver armour gleamed in the rising sun, yet he looked a funny sight. The few strands of white hair he had remaining were pushed up and his eyes were heavy. He had been tossing and turning all night. Not a man who was used to spending nights away from the comfort of his own bed.

"They will come!" Toran's voice exploded as he grabbed hold of Sir Dillian's reins.

"You have been abandoned! You are alone."

"They will never be alone! For I am Garroway and these are my children!"

Uriah, Toran and Sir Dillian all turned, and by the river they saw a group of silhouettes. Ten shadows standing still as the morning sun shone behind them. The magnificent fiery glare rose steadily, reflecting its light over the river and into the eyes of Sir Dillian, who flinched and raised his hand to shield them.

Slowly Uriah began to smile. The silhouettes began to inch closer, each moving rhythmically until they surrounded him and the others.

"Welcome back little brother."

"The little cunt still lives."

The figure at the centre pulled back his hood. "You both were missed dearly." Garroway revealed his face. His smile was warm and welcoming; he looked as if he wanted to pull both Uriah and Toran close, to squeeze them tightly.

Rhodesha however did not hold back; she dropped her cloak revealing her aesthetically pleasing body. Her leather vest and short skirt did not leave much to the imagination as she jumped on Toran. His huge arms lifted her up as she planted a hard kiss on his lips.

"Oh, I have missed this!" With his shovel-like hands, Toran gripped her buttocks.

Garroway placed his hand on Uriah's shoulder. "It makes me happy to see you again, my son."

A blessed feeling took hold of Uriah as his *father* pulled him close.

The other assassins dropped their cloaks and greeted Uriah. He smiled as he saw the faces of Lothar, Caelan, Naleac, Zaira, Lilah, Roak, Maarax and even Valdar; each one made him happy. They had only been apart one day but it had felt like a life time.

Garroway approached Sir Dillian; his long silver hair sparkled. "So, you are the man who will take us through the mountain gate at Hamon'dor?"

"I will. You are the legendary Garroway. People speak of you as if you are god himself. I hope you are as good as your reputation." Sir Dillian sat uneasily on his horse.

"He is greater!" Lilah responded; her brown eyes pierced into Sir Dillian like arrows. "Get down from your horse, we look up to no man."

"I don't take orders from a whore!"

In a flash, Lilah jumped up. She grabbed Sir Dillian by his breastplate and pulled him hard to the ground. He landed with an almighty thud. His mouth drooped open as he frantically gasped for air. His bright cold eyes bulged from his head.

"I am no whore!" Lilah dropped to her knees and rested a curved knife between his legs. "But I will cut off your cock and make you a whore if you speak to me like that again."

Garroway smiled. "Calm yourself, my love." He extended his hand to Sir Dillian who violently pushed it away before struggling to his feet.

"You will all know your place. I am in command here." Sir Dillian began to dust himself down as he led his horse away from the group. "We must leave now! We have less than two days to reach the mountain gate."

Uriah watched as Sir Dillian mounted his horse and slowly trotted away, leaving his pride in the dust. He then turned to Garroway. "I would like nothing more than to kill that man."

"We all die, but some men sooner than they would like."

Chapter 16
When the Sun Falls

I dreamed of entering this city, the rubble beneath my feet, a conquering hero. Gabriel looked all around; a hint of sadness filled his heart. Antilion, the Allamantyan Capital, was beautiful. Gabriel was spellbound; the city was spread across four cliffs and forged from the purest white stone. The buildings stretched as far as his eyes could see. Each house had a dark red thatched roof. This paradise was made all the more magnificent by the scorching bright sun that shone down from above. Lush green trees ripe with red fruits littered the wide cobbled walkway that sloped up along the edge of the city like a winding snake. To Gabriel's left was a huge drop; beneath that was the most peaceful crystal blue sea he had ever laid his eyes upon. It softly rose and fell against the jagged rock. Pale beaches glistened like gold, darkened only when the sea swept across the shore. Gabriel saw people running and diving into the gentle waves.

As they continued their ascent to the top, he could see the first cliff was joined to a mighty white stone bridge. He wondered if Ollaria'h, the White City, home of the gods, was as beautiful as this. Along the bridge were hundreds of armed Allamantyan soldiers; they stood in square formations and their silver mail sparkled in the bright sun. With the vastly superior numbers of the enemy so close it made Gabriel feel uneasy. Every few metres stood a powerful stone statue. He could hear King Aristian say each one was a tribute to the noblest of fallen warriors, but the names he heard meant nothing to him.

After crossing the bridge, he could see the keep, a stunning building with battlements that stretched along the rim. Red and white roses climbed the walls, beaming out like jewels. Across another white stone bridge was a gigantic tower; it stretched up towards the sky, disappearing into the heavens.

"What you see is the god's tower, four hundred feet high. It's where Avindel, the voice of Ollaria'h and first King of Allamantya, rose to the heavens." Aristian peered up in wonder. "There you will find the holy knights of Hethelyon."

Gabriel knew all about the Order of Hethelyon – knights sworn to guard the faith of Ollaria'h. They were warriors who fought only in holy wars; their allegiance was to the high priests not to any king or queen. Their name came from the golden angel, Hethelios, who visited Avindel before his journey across the shadow sea.

As the column came to a halt, Gabriel could see three white and gold chariots, each were pulled by two beautiful white horses. They wore golden masks that ran down their faces; on top was a small spike with a glorious red plume falling freely. The chariots were decorated with such detail; the base was white with golden trim. The wheels were large, crafted from the finest oak.

"We will ride the rest of the way on these." King Aristian stepped up onto the centre chariot. "King Vincinicus, you shall do me the honour of riding with me. Prince Andros and Princess Tilia, take the one to my right, and Prince Gabriel and Princess Arrabella the left."

Gabriel lifted himself onto his chariot; he felt the wooden frame beneath his fingertips. Straight ahead he could see a huge stone wall, easily the height of ten grown men. At the centre was an arched gateway which was crafted from untainted white stone. The wooded gate was closed, held shut. Eight well-built and muscular men clad only in cream skirts slowly began to push the doors apart. The wood creaked and screamed as it was forced open.

The crowd roared a deafening cheer into the air. People as far as his eyes could see were screaming and shouting. At the far end, after the one hundred metre road, was the huge palace. Eight tall white pillars stood holding the upper level of the palace aloft. On top was the main section of the building which rose high into the sky. The white stone looked magnificent. Forged into the walls were balconies and ramparts. Below the pillars were around fifty long stone steps, which they would to need to climb to reach the top.

The chariot pulled forward as the rider slashed with his whip. The horses' hooves knocked and clanked against the smooth white slabs. The glare from the sun reflected off the slabs, forcing Gabriel to raise his hand to shelter his eyes. The crowd, numbering in their thousands, formed two groups either side; rows of Allamantyan soldiers kept them back. The crowd's hands were waving from side to side, they threw pink and blue flowers onto the white slabbed floor, decorating the path as royal chariots headed towards the palace. The noise of the crowd was louder than anything he had ever heard before.

Gabriel stared into the crowd, seeing the faces of the people as they cheered wildly. "Why are they so happy?"

"The legends of the god-prince have spread even this far south." Princess Arrabella's words were smooth and seductive. Arrabella slid her hand around his, hers was soft but strong. She squeezed him tightly as she lifted his hand high into the air. The crowd howled in approval. When she lowered it, she did not release him; she continued to hold his palm. "Do you ever think of marriage?"

"My life has been only war since I was a boy. I have had no time to think of marriage," Gabriel replied. He stared directly towards Arrabella. Her face was well sculptured, her cheek bones high. This was the first time he had really paid any attention towards the princess. Her long shining brown hair was brushed away from her face. The roar of the crowd and the falling flowers only seemed to emphasis her beauty. The long tight-fitting white dress showed every arch in her body. She knew what her best features were and she was open to flaunting them.

"With the wars over, maybe now you will have more time." Arrabella smiled, her eyes looked up at him.

"Wars never end." Gabriel looked to his right. He could see Tilia. She stood awkwardly beside Prince Andros; her petite frame looked all the more timid with the mighty hordes of people screaming behind her. His father, who was slightly ahead, seemed to love the attention. He raised his hands high in the sky. His overzealous attitude began to fuel Gabriel's anger. Turning back, he could see his cousins and his bastard brother. Beside them was Prince Daemar; for a moment the two locked eyes, neither wanting to pull away before Daemar smiled, turning his head.

At the bottom of the mighty stone steps, the chariots stopped. Gabriel dropped down, pulling his hand free from Princess Arrabella's strong grip. Slowly they made the climb up the steps. The noise from the crowd was still deafening even when they reached the top.

"These steps never get easier; I wish King Avindel hadn't had such scope when he envisioned this city." King Aristian hesitated; he breathed in rapidly as he struggled to speak.

King Vincinicus laughed loudly in response before he burst out into a coughing fit. Gabriel offered his father no comfort as he walked past him. Up ahead, he could see three well-dressed men, each clad in different coloured gowns. One was red, one green, one blue and the other gold. They slowly approached, moving so smoothly it was as if their feet were sliding along the white marbled floor.

"Please let me introduce the wisest men in all of Allamantya, the four members of the High council." King Aristian beckoned the well-dressed men to approach.

"I see only three." Gabriel spoke loudly, clearly showing his distrust.

His father scorned him with hateful eyes.

"Please welcome, Lords Peyton Beldomir, Dellio Greenway and my dear cousin and your blood, Attico Da'Menaeon." Each man bowed his head. Then King Aristian paused, "Where is Lord Mortimer Judaus?"

Lord Peyton stepped forward; he was dressed in a long golden gown. He was slim of both face and body, not a hair could be found on his shiny head. A long thin yellow goatee fell from his chin. "Lord Judaus ventured east; there has been much unrest lately as you are aware, Your Majesty. He promised to be back for the wedding." His voice was feminine and clear.

"What unrest?" Gabriel butted in.

"My son is always speaking out of turn." King Vincinicus stepped in front of Gabriel.

"This will be your kingdom soon; you should know everything. These past months we have been having a lot of trouble with a fanatical group known as the Brotherhood of Ralmalaur. They originate from Samora but their ideologies spread to the Eastern Isles; they worship Dalackis, the winged god. I will tell you more but for now we should not let this dampen our festivities."

Past the mighty white pillars was a wide-open space. At the centre was a huge statue of a naked man; he held his hand to the sky. Beneath him was a lion, dead at his feet. On the ceiling was a painting of the sky, white clouds on a sea of crystal blue. Between each cloud were flying angels, each clad in golden armour. At the centre was a mighty sun, the gateway to heaven. Along the walls stood statues, smaller in size, but they were no less magnificent in beauty. Each was different, from the bodies of beautiful women, to warriors and animals.

At the far end was a thick iron door, twenty feet high, that required four men to push open as they entered the throne room. The marbled floor was painted in bright colours of blues, reds and greens. At the back of the room was the throne itself, moulded from shining gold. Its power was as bright as the sun. For a moment, Gabriel had to close his eyes, shielding himself from its glare.

Lords and ladies flanked them either side as they made their way towards the throne. Gabriel could hear them chatting and mumbling. The women seemed to stare at him with passionate interest; those looks reminded him of court back in Verdina. For a brief moment, his ego enjoyed their wandering eyes.

King Aristian walked up the three steps that were covered in a bright red carpet with golden trim. He beckoned King Vincinicus to join him, who eagerly stepped up, standing by his side.

Like a dog to his master.

"Lords and ladies, I have the great pleasure to introduce our new allies. This is King Vincinicus, ruler of Valanor, and his beautiful daughter, Princess Tilia." King Aristian embraced King Vincinicus. The lords and ladies began to cheer and clap their hands loudly.

The common people may welcome us but these lords do not fool me. The rich like to claim new lands through blood and steel, not with kind words. Gabriel's eyes began to scan the room. Like a hungry lion he looked his prey up and down. He moved towards his sister; he could feel her unrest at so many questioning eyes burning into her.

"Tonight there will be a great feast! For in two days there be a wedding even the gods will be jealous of!" King Aristian shouted. His enthusiastic words were met with a rapturous applause. He turned to Gabriel and Princess Tilia. "My servants will show you to your quarters. From there you may do as you please, explore and interact with anyone in the palace."

****

Princess Tilia made her way towards her royal quarters. She walked casually behind two servant girls, each wearing long green dresses. Behind the princess was her maid, Cassandra. The corridor was wide, the white stone was smooth and clean. Along the walls were suits of armour and fancy paintings, portraits of old kings and queens.

"Your room is here Your Highness." One of the servant girls spoke, her voice light and innocent. "This is the royal quarter; further down this hallway and up those stairs are Prince Andros and Princess Arrabella's chambers."

Tilia looked up; at the far end two lanterns burned brightly; between them both was a darkened stairway leading upwards.

"Behind you is where the princes will stay."

Tilia turned back and saw Gabriel and her cousins, Lucian and Lassander, being led into their rooms. *At least he is close.*

"The royal feast will start at sunset; we will meet you here to escort you to the banquet." The servant girl smiled before closing the door.

The room was large. Inside was a huge four poster bed very similar to the one she had back in Verdina. The walls were white and a large mirror was situated opposite the bed. Although it was summer, she could feel coldness in this room, and a hint of home sickness came over her.

"Oh, it is wonderful, isn't it?" Cassandra's words were enthusiastic. She quickly made her way past the four-poster bed to the balcony, leaning over it. "What a view, you must come and see. My mother and father would never believe I am standing in Antilion."

"I wish I could share your enthusiasm, but I have to agree, Cassandra, it is beautiful." Tilia could see the entire capital, the beautiful white castle walls, then lower down she could see the houses, each with red thatched roofs, then further along on the horizon, the rich green lands and crystal blue water falls of Antilion.

"Why are you sad?" Cassandra asked.

"As beautiful as it is, it is not home. I fear I will miss Verdina more and more with each passing day." Tilia sighed.

"Fear not Your Highness, as queen you may return to Verdina whenever you please."

Being a queen, I will not be as free as you think, dear Cassandra. Tilia offered a smile in return.

Cassandra continued to lean over the balcony, one foot raised off the floor. A loud knock at the door echoed through the room, and before they had time to reply the door creaked opened. Princess Arrabella casually strolled in, her white dress seeming to reflect the bright sun shining in from outside.

Tilia walked back into the room. "Oh, Princess Arrabella, I wasn't expecting you. I—"

"How are you finding the room? Beautiful view, isn't it?" Arrabella swiftly interrupted. "You won't stay here long, as once you're married, you shall move into Andros's chambers. In two days' time, we shall be sisters." Arrabella sat herself down on the bed.

"I had always wished for a sister."

"I didn't but the gods decide what will and won't be."

Tilia hesitated, unsure of how to reply. "Where is Andros? I haven't had a chance to really speak with him."

"Oh, he is always like this, you know how men are. Anyway, less talk of men. Would you be interested in going hunting with me on the morrow? I struggle to find a man who can keep up with me."

"Hunting? Yes, I would love to." A smile filled Tilia's sweet face.

"Great, I believe you will find the hunting here to your satisfaction. I hope you live up to your reputation, we have heard great things of your skill with a bow." Arrabella rose from the bed and walked towards the door. "I will look forward to talking with you later."

Cassandra closed the door before breathing deeply. "I do not like her, Your Highness."

"Why?"

Cassandra's round face squinted. "Her eyes are too close together!"

Tilia laughed. "I think the hunting will be good, a chance for us to bond."

****

The great hall was packed; lords and ladies filled the long rows of tables. Each was laughing and drinking. Vibrantly coloured fruits decorated the tables: purple grapes the size of walnuts, apples as red as wine and oranges as bright as the sun. The noise of the festivities boomed out, loud and happy. A band performed 'Enter the Gods', a joyous theme, played with flutes, vielles and powerful female chanting. The music seemed to pump life into the guests who seemed full of happiness and harmony. The only people in the room not animated were the Allamantyan soldiers, each clad in silver mail, half helms and green tunics with a red sword upon their chests. They were positioned along the walls leading to the mighty wooden doorway.

King Aristian forced a smile; along the table to his left he could see Princess Tilia and Arrabella sitting side by side, and beside him was King Vincinicus, who was happy stuffing his face with tender red meats and sweet Allamantyan wines. Although happy, he had almost achieved his goal. He felt a hint of sadness in his heart. As he scanned the room, he could see all the noble families of his Kingdom: house N'Dai of Kathoros, DeVeil of Ardenia, DeGrey of Southron and Bailyn of Oalandrium. Yet he could not see his Redmond of Yardesa. His dear sister, Drusilla, had married the powerful Marshall Edwin Redmond when he was a boy. Aristian had sent her the invite the moment he knew King Vincinicus had accepted his offer but there had not even been a reply. Since the killing of her son, Prince Varden, she had become a recluse. It saddened him he could not see her today.

To his right was an empty chair. His fist slightly tightened as he reacquainted himself with it. His sadness turned to venom. *How can he do this? After everything I have done.* The king breathed deeply before turning back to King Vincinicus.

"Worry not, my friend…" King Vincinicus began to choke. Pieces of meat spewed from his mouth, wine soon followed, staining his silver silks.

"Father please, the wisemen have said you must eat slower." Tilia leant over, resting her hand on her father's back.

King Vincinicus coughed, throwing up the last piece of half chewed meat. "Damn your wisemen! I am not a child, let me be." He wiped wine and remnants of food from his mouth. "You would think me an invalid, not a king. Are your children the same?"

King Aristian smiled. "Mine are disobedient." He turned back to the empty chair. "Please forgive my son's absence."

"Pre-wedding nerves!" King Vincinicus replied as he bit into a chunk of red meat; the juices ran down the corners of his mouth and into his beard.

"I think you are right; I felt the same before my own wedding." King Aristian thought back twenty years to the eve of his wedding to Sonja Hohjan. She was the daughter and heir to the largest of the four lion lords of Darnor. His wedding, like his son's, was not for love but for an alliance. He felt sick with nerves and his hands would quiver with just the mention of her name.

"My son has no such excuse for his absence!" King Vincinicus turned his head and spat a piece of fat from his mouth. "His arrogance boils my blood. He cares for nothing but his legend, as a child he would tell me he would conquer the world and his name would live on forever." Vincinicus bellowed out with laughter. "Fool!"

The wine and the food flowed freely; the noise and laughter of the guests crashed against the walls of the hall like waves on a sandy shore. The vibes of happiness bounced from one guest to another. Then, suddenly, like the bang of a drum, the aura of happiness evaporated.

"I will kill you!" Marshall Latimor N'Dai roared like a lion as he launched from his seat. "Draw your sword, coward!" His mighty booming voice drained the happiness from the room. His sons, Lyon and Gerold, attempted to hold him back. "Release me!" he thundered.

Marshall Varrone DeVeil goaded him, "Your sons can't save you, old man." He drew his sword.

The ladies of N'Dai screamed as they backed away. Lords and knights attempted to get between the two combatants. The noise from the band was rendered silent. The guests crashed against one another like a stampeding herd. A servant carrying a large platter of food stumbled back, falling onto the table. Food and jars of wine flew into the air and landed on the marbled floor with an almighty clatter. Chaos erupted.

King Vincinicus burst into laughter. "I see some men cannot handle their wine! What is their quarrel?"

King Aristian watched angrily as the two lords were pulled apart. "Theirs is an ancient rivalry. House N'Dai and DeVeil were once two of the four lion families that made up Darnor. In 110 G.D King Nereus II invaded Darnor and allied himself with both N'Dai and DeVeil, defeating the remaining two families, Hohjan and Lannis. After his victory both lords were given lands in Allamantya as a reward. During this time, Lord Elarcos N'Dai was slain by Lord Dorian DeVeil – some say murdered – and lands were taken under DeVeil control. Since then, the red lion of N'Dai and the black of DeVeil cannot be in the same room." King Aristian took a deep breath and a large swing from his goblet.

Marshall Latimer was dragged by Prince Daemar back to his seat. Aristian could see his brother angrily scouring him; his fiery side could strike fear into the most fierce of men. Daemar signalled the band to continue playing.

King Vincinicus sat running his chubby fingers over a small stone engraving. The loud Valorian king suddenly seemed quiet and sad. "Do you ever think of your wife?" King Vincinicus's voice was soft; his thumb pressed against the stone face of what was clearly a woman.

"Every day," King Aristian replied. "How did she pass?"

"Gabriel." King Vincinicus squeezed the stone carving between his fingers. "He took her happiness, her love. He took her from me!"

The words stung a shocked Aristian; he reared up. "Gabriel?"

"The devil cursed me the day he screamed his way into this world. God-prince! Day by day, I watched her die and there was nothing I could do. Her warmth turned cold; her love turned to hate. Her life became nothing but shadow after he clawed his way from her womb."

King Aristian comforted his new friend. "You cannot blame Gabriel for this."

"I do!"

"When my wife died, I felt nothing but pain. I blamed everyone including myself. We cannot question the will of the gods; they decide our fate." King Aristian poured Vincinicus some wine.

He thought back to the passing of his own wife. No death was easy but the way in which his dear Sonja departed this world was both cruel and torturous. He remembered the flames and the smoke, black as the devil's eyes it was. The king and his family had travelled to the western seas at Blue haven for the summer, staying in the sandstone estate at Yardesa. Arteus was only a babe, months old at best when terror struck. The estate was engulfed in hellish flames; they whirled and screamed as they ravaged the royal chambers and down the hallway. Prince Andros was found at the bottom of the stairway in a trance as the fire drew closer towards him. Upstairs was his dear Sonja and their infant baby boy; her screams screeched through the estate.

The king and his men battled as best they could but the flames beat them back; the heat ripped into his flesh. At that point Aristian had wished himself a stronger man. Yet it was Beyorn, the King's Champion, wild with both courage and determination who charged through the fiery wall. He forced his way through the black smoke and red flame, disappearing like a ghost. The king stood hopeless as he watched and listened to crackling of the fire and the rising of the smoke.

Suddenly Beyorn returned, his skin red raw. In his arms he cradled the baby prince. The mighty beast of Golgia screamed with shame that he could only save one life, not two. At that moment King Aristian had wanted to cry too, but he did not; yet he had cried every day since.

****

As the night drew on Gabriel could hear the festivities roaring away, as the laughter and shouting echoed through the castle walls. For a moment he could hear his father's voice; the sound angered him. He was not in the mood to celebrate; he wanted to be alone. He had explored the palace and looked out over the castle grounds; he saw mighty oak trees, fern bushes and beautiful flowers with every coloured petal you could imagine. He hated to admit it, but it truly was the Kingdom of Paradise. As magnificent as it was, he did not feel comfortable. He felt eyes on him at all times, spies watching his every move.

He made his way up a long narrow winding stairway. The guard at the bottom had informed him it was called the Tower of Knowledge. Gabriel was eager to learn more. On the first floor was a single door, and he opened it to find a huge library. Rows and rows of books lay before him. Looking up he saw how the bookcases rose up with the walls of the tower. Mighty wooden steps, each leading to walkways, were spread out along the bookcases. On the ground were five single stands, a large closed book placed on each one.

The first book read, *Love and Harmony by Alwin Blaine.* It didn't interest him. Neither did *The Holy touch: Curing evil by Dalister Flower.* The third book however caught his eye immediately: *Warrior Legends by Borin Bryce*. It was bright red in colour, the title written in gold. Gabriel opened it slowly. He ran his finger along the old pages; they felt dry and brittle and he turned them ever so gently. The writing was beautifully written in thick black ink. He scanned the names yet only a few stood out to him: *Sir Artor Harron, as fierce as he was passionate. Both lover and fighter, loyal to Allamantya and his King, Kalidar I. Undefeated with both lance and sword, killed Sir Cristian Ryon of Darnor and Prince Qhalar of Akesha in single combat. He led the knights of Hethelyon during the failed invasion of Yorno. Singers sung tales of his legend as he climbed the yellow beaches of Amonrak with ten arrows pinned to his chest.* Gabriel smiled. "No man can fight with ten arrows in his chest."

Turning the pages, he saw another name he liked; this one was a king, *King Kalidar I, fierce and wild, lover of both blood and battle. It is said he removed his wife from his martial bed, swapping her for his sword, Dragonfire. It was a great two-handed weapon that could sever a horse in two. He destroyed the southern Darnaion rebellion, killing the pretender to the throne, Kylian Lanis, in single combat. He travelled east, conquering Dagen. His vanity was crushed however when he led the order of Hethelyon on two failed invasions of the Eastern Isles which resulted in the death of his eldest son, Aristos. His final folly was when he called out Valorian King, Lycinor II, in single combat. Both met at the Flentian Mountains and were never seen again. Legends tell of a great thunder storm and two stars appearing through the clouds. It was the gods welcoming their heroes to the night sky.*

Gabriel felt a presence behind him; he stopped reading and turned to see Prince Daemar standing in the doorway. He was leaning against the frame, his left hand perched on the tip of his sword. He was still clad in his Antilion armour.

"I had a feeling I would find you here. Who are you reading about?" Daemar asked inquisitively. He walked towards Gabriel. "Ah King Kalidar. He was my grandfather, you know. Some say he was a conquering hero, others a murdering tyrant."

"What do you believe?" Gabriel looked down at Daemar. For a man nearly forty, he looked young and healthy. His shoulders were broad and he stood with both strength and confidence.

"I believe he was neither, just a man obsessed with his own legend. As a child I always preferred to read tales of this knight." Daemar removed his brown leather glove and turned a few pages back, pressing his finger down. "Read, little prince."

Gabriel looked down. *Sestal knight, died defending Prince Aristos at the Battle of Rakar, where his valour and bravery cemented his place the night sky. On the bloodied sands of Rakar, this unnamed knight stood alone. His mortally wounded prince lay at his feet. The knight took no step back as his enemies closed in around him. The blood from his wounds only fuelled his fury as he fought until his last breath. The Yornish called him the Sestal knight, meaning immortal. For no matter how many times they struck him, he would not die. It was not until his prince was safe that he finally made his way to Ollaria'h.*

Gabriel liked the sound of this knight. *Victory or death.*

"He was warrior who needed no name. A man who fought for his country, not glory." Daemar placed a hand on Gabriel's shoulder before making his way back to the door. "There are some people who say I am the finest swordsman in all of Allamantya; then there are those who whisper that you are the greatest that Valanor has to offer. Did you know that all of the finest warriors the world has produced, each has one thing in common?"

Gabriel watched him intensely, eager to hear more.

"They all at some point had an opponent who was worthy of them. I have a feeling that you will be mine." Daemar disappeared out of the room; just the clanging of his armour could be heard as he made his way down the corridor.

Or you will be mine, old man.

Gabriel made his way back to his chambers; everything now seemed so quiet. All he could hear was the sound of his feet against the stone floor. He slowly walked down the narrow winding staircase to the main corridor to get to his room. As he took the last step, he could hear his father. Loud shouting echoed through the hallway, followed by drunken laughter. Gabriel attempted to step back, not wanting to be seen, but it was too late. His father may have been a fat drunk but he was not blind.

"Gabriel, where have you been hiding?" his father's voice boomed out; he spoke that powerfully, he began to lose his footing. Two Valorian soldiers helped keep him up.

"Leylan! More of that real wine, none of this Antilion piss." King Vincinicus emptied his goblet on the floor, staining the white stone red. Then, like the loyal dog Leylan was, he pulled out his flagon and began to refill his father's goblet. Leylan's smile widened as his father gulped down more wine; it spilled out the corners of the drunken King's mouth. "Why is it whenever I want you, you are never around. Then when I don't wish to see that ungrateful face of yours, you are always there!" His father stumbled forwards, his short chubby arm pointing towards Gabriel.

"All I ever wanted was a father and king I could be proud of. Guess neither of us get what we want." Gabriel could not hide the disgust he felt.

"You are quick with that tongue, boy. The gods curse me with your arrogance."

"Why do you hate me so?" Gabriel quickly stepped towards his father. "Is it because I am the man you could never be? The Valorian people never call your name, yet they rejoice at the sound of my own. I have heard whispers in court, of how our people loved my mother more than you, how she was the true Valorian warrior. Is that why you disbanded the Delloria spear maidens?"

King Vincinicus grabbed Gabriel by his tunic. "You are blinded by your own reflection. You think of nothing but the name Gabriel. You are not a god! I am king; there is more to my life than my name. I have the courts, the lords, the knights, the people to please."

"With you being so eager to please, maybe you should've been a whore not a king."

Vincinicus unleashed a venomous right hand. The impact shock Gabriel to his core; his head snapped violently to his right. Blood began to trickle down his mouth. In that moment, the prince thought of nothing more than beating his father where he stood, to show him the real quality of the prince of Valanor. He breathed deeply, removing his father's hand from his tunic. "No man alive may lay a hand on me but you are my father and my king. But I will tell you now, there will not be a second time. One day you will have wished you kept me close. Leaches cling to your flesh, eating away at you, draining your blood." Gabriel's hate-filled eyes turned towards Leylan, "Yet all you do is drink and bed foreign whores."

"Maybe it is the foreign women who produce the real men, ones who don't kill their mothers!" Vincinicus swung at Gabriel again.

This time the prince stepped back, easily avoiding the blow. He looked his father directly in his eyes. He felt nothing but pity. As Gabriel walked away, he could hear his father's drunken voice, booming down the hallway, shouting and cursing. With each word he spoke, he shamed both his name and his people. Loud choking suddenly and violently cut off his father's words, and gasping calls for breath soon followed.

Whenever Gabriel saw his father, he would always have to remind him of how it was he who killed his mother. Yet he was only three when she took her own life. He remembered it clearly. She rose from her bed on that cold winter's morning, her skin pale, as colourless and ugly as autumn fog. She looked right through him as she made her way to the balcony. For a moment she stood still, her face was gaunt, her eyes dark and empty. Looking up to the clouds she spoke, "*I am going to see your father.*" Then she stepped back, falling from the ledge to her death. It was the only image of her he could remember.

Gabriel slowly made his way up the narrow winding stairway that would lead to his chambers. The hallway was dark, just a few flickering lanterns lit up his path. Princess Arrabella suddenly appeared, like a ghost she emerged from the shadows. She moved in a bewitching mano; he could not make out whether she was an angel or the devil, yet she entranced him to move towards her. Her eyes seemed fixed with passion and fire. She wore a short tightly fitted red night gown which accentuated all her appealing curves.

"I was disappointed I didn't see you tonight at the festivities; one would think you didn't enjoy our Antilion hospitality." Arrabella invaded Gabriel's personal space.

"I had nothing to celebrate…"

Arrabella quickly cut off the prince. "You're bleeding. What happened?" She ran her soft but cold fingers over his bloodied lip. Before Gabriel had time to reply, she leant forwards, pressing her mouth against his.

Gabriel could feel her tongue sliding between his lips, like a vampire she began to taste his blood. Arrabella moaned quietly as she sucked his lip until it was dry.

"Stop, you have been drinking." He could smell the wine on her breath. Looking down, Gabriel could see her large breasts bulging from within her dress. They looked as if they wanted to break free.

Arrabella ran her hand up Gabriel's arm, her finger sliding softly between the definitions around his muscle. "For years I have awaited your arrival. At night you would come to me in my dreams."

"That is not possible, for we met but a few days ago."

"After you won your first victory, all the lords in Allamantya spoke of you. They feared the god-prince, the one who would conqueror. For years after I would hear tales of your heroism, victory after victory, the golden prince who fights without fear in the face of his enemies. I knew then that you were the one I was waiting for." Arrabella leant forward kissing Gabriel as she spoke. "All the men in Allamantya have desired what I am offering you tonight. They would steal, murder and break oaths to bed the daughter of King Aristian. By day they see an angel, innocent and pure. Yet at night, when the sun falls and the moon rises, the devil comes out to play." Arrabella moved up two of the steps before stopping. She turned towards him slowly before raising her right leg onto the next step. She lowered her shoulder straps, and the red silk fell, stopping perfectly just before her nipples. Her breasts looked smooth and firm.

Gabriel froze, his body felt at her mercy. He wanted to rip off her silk and to show her the superiority of a true Valorian man. Princess Arrabella leant forwards, taking his hand; she slid it along her smooth thigh and between her legs. He could feel her excitement, the warmth beneath his fingertips. Arrabella gasped, Gabriel could see her eyes rolling as the feel of him took hold of her.

"My chamber is—" Arrabella's words were broken. "On the left, I don't lock my door." She then pushed his hand away before slowly disappearing up the stairway.

Gabriel could feel the pounding beneath his chest. *To bed an Allamantyan princess, now that would really anger my father*! The thought pleased Gabriel greatly. He smiled.

Chapter 17
Darkness and Shadow

Scream! You fool, scream! Danaka compelled herself to scream yet she could not. Her body began to tremble, causing the water to ripple. Small waves pulsated away from her. A few moments ago, she felt content and happy, yet now a sickness had taken hold. A fear she could do nothing to escape from.

Hazar and his two companions stepped forward; they stood at the edge of the bank. Up close Hazar looked old, maybe early sixties. Thick wrinkles formed under his eyes, his bald head poured with sweat. Small beads of perspiration trickled down his face and into his beard.

"Kalos, take her," Hazar commanded. His voice was cold.

In a flash, Kalos the man standing to Hazar's right, leapt forward. He came crashing into the water like a stampeding buffalo. Kalos grabbed hold of Danaka by her hair; he felt strong and overpowering. She succumbed to his weight as he forced her under the water. She clambered for breath as he held her down; the once beautiful water now seemed dark and deadly as it began to drown her. Danaka clawed at him frantically, but her blows had little effect. He lifted her out of the water and over his shoulder. His body felt slimy and wet. A sickening odour clung to his flesh; he reeked of hot stale sweat.

Danaka slapped at her attacker and dug her nails into his skin. She fought with all her might. Kalos violently slammed her down, and her body shock as she thudded against the ground, the impact of the blow taking away her breath. She gasped in pain; her mouth drew wide, begging for air. The next thing she felt was an almighty pain shoot through her stomach as one of the men rammed their foot into her gut, then another exploded into her back, she wretched and jerked as she curled up in a ball to protect herself.

"Kalos, Zedir, stop!" Hazar raised his hand. "Lift her up."

Danaka felt disorientated as the men lifted her to her knees. Bells rang in her ears as she tried to breathe. She covered her naked body with her arms, hiding her breasts.

"Dalackis, we do your bidding." Kalos knelt down, pressing his face against hers. His hot dry breath stank like the carcass of a dead animal. His receding hair was thin and greasy, as black as coal.

Danaka's head pulled back as Zedir grabbed a fistful of her hair. Both Hedir and Kalos looked like brothers, they were big and bulky. Thick black hair clung to their topless bodies; each was as powerful as a wild beast. With Danaka's head back, her throat was exposed. Hazar stepped forward and pressed the tip of his spear into her jugular. She felt a stinging pain as the skin split, and blood began to trickle down her neck.

"How…how do you know I do not worship the Winged God?" Danaka forced herself to speak; with each word she spoke, the tip of Hazar's spear forced itself further into her throat.

"A true believer does not shame herself for all to see." Hatred consumed Hazar's face. As if the very sight of Danaka disgusted him.

Kalos pinched Danaka's nipple between his figures and twisted it. She grimaced in pain, yet she never called out. Kalos and Zedir began to laugh, booming out together as their sickening breath blew against her face.

"Let the girl go!" Duro's words were calm but powerful. He appeared on the edge of the tree line.

Hazar quickly turned, releasing his spear from Danaka's neck. Kalos stood, lifting his sword and pointing it towards Duro. Griffin growled viciously beside him, his white teeth dripping with phlegm as he snapped towards Hazar and the others. Duro stepped up onto a large rock.

"One move and she dies." Hazar moved forwards, pointing his spear towards Duro. Zedir pulled hard on Danaka's hair, yanking her head back. She could feel his hand trembling. He and Kalos looked uneasy, unsure of what to do. Both looked towards Hazar as if his words decided their next move.

"I am not a man you wish to fight." Duro stepped down from the rock; he untied his scabbard from his shoulder, holding the base of his sword in his hand. "It is okay to be scared; sometimes I scare myself."

"Hazar, what we do?" Kalos was teetering on the edge. His sword hand was shaking.

"Step away from the girl. Release her now or you will see your Winged God sooner than you would like."

An eerie silence crept over this once beautiful paradise, slowly transforming it to a living hell. Kalos and Zedir gripped their chipped, rusted swords. The cruel confidence they once had was slowly draining from their bodies. Hazar, however, showed no fear; he stared intensely at Duro, his dark soulless eyes never left him.

"I will ask you this one last time." Duro drew his sword, the steel screeching as it was set free. "Let her go or die where you stand."

Duro's blade glistened in the sun. The steel was thick and pure, far better quality than the two Zedir and Kalos were holding. Griffin growled louder, his muscles tightened, ready to pounce. Danaka could feel her heart pounding; she stared towards Duro, who stood unwavering. Her eyes were entranced by him.

Duro, gripping his sword tighter, slowly raised his flute to his mouth, gently blowing his song of death. Danaka closed her eyes, listening to his tune. Any moment it would happen. Death was coming, she could feel it.

"Stop, let her go." Hazar raised his spear.

Zedir released Danaka's hair and angrily shoved her head forwards. Kalos breathed heavily and returned his sword to his side.

"We will meet again." Hazar turned his head and spat.

"Pray to your god we do not." Duro sheathed his sword.

Hazar's hate-filled eyes looked Danaka up and down. He stared at her as if to say he would see her again. He released her from his fiery glare and turned, walking away. Kalos and Zedir followed after him. Before she knew it, they had disappeared into the trees.

Griffin charged towards Danaka, jumping all over her and licking her face. His warm fur offered a blanket of comfort as she wrapped her arms around him. Danaka could still feel her heart racing in her chest; the loud intense beats slowly began to ease as she watched Duro approach her.

"Wrap yourself in this." Duro handed her a white sheet, the same one he had taken from the dead family.

Danaka had forgotten she was naked. A sudden embarrassment took hold of her as she quickly took the sheet from him and covered herself. The white cover stuck to her skin, absorbing the water that ran down her body. She suddenly felt cold, and an icy shiver twitched down her spine. She pulled Griffin close to her.

"You should rest, night is coming."

The sun began to sink; its great glow was fading. Even though the rays of light had dimmed, warmth still clung to the humid air. The sounds of the forest echoed and the waterfall crashed heavily. Duro sat beside Danaka; he had undone his poplin tunic so it fell freely from his waist. The light from the fire enhanced his muscular torso. His chest was big and defined, yet it was not the muscles that caught her attention but the small scars that littered his body.

Duro looked into her eyes as he wiped a small tear from her cheek. "You are stronger than you think."

"Will they return?" she asked, perhaps already knowing the answer.

"Rest, do not worry yourself with such things."

Danaka lay back. Her eyes were heavy and her body ached. She could not sleep; whenever she closed her eyes saw the faces of Hazar, Hedir and Kalos. She dared not think what would have happened if Duro and Griffin had not come to her rescue. *Why is this world so cruel?*

Her eyes had closed but she was not sure for how long as, when she opened them, darkness had covered the land and the moonlight reflected peacefully off the river. The fire crackled beautifully, the yellowy red flames shining brightly. Next to her she felt Griffin's fur, as he cuddled up. He was snoring; it had been a long day for him as well.

A soft whistling tune played out over the darkness, beautiful yet sorrowful. Duro was sitting with his back against a large oak tree, his eyes peering up to the stars. One leg was raised, his left arm resting on his knee. His mighty sword was draped across him, the handle against his inner arm. The blade was exposed, the flames from the fire flickering in its reflection.

He must know they are near. Danaka turned and lay back down, staring into the darkness. She imaged their cruel faces, those dark soulless eyes and the tip of Hazar's spear piercing her throat. Danaka chose to close her eyes, as if to shelter herself from evil she was imagining. Slowly her body began to feel heavy and her arms loosened, as she succumbed to the sleep she desperately needed.

A filthy smell began to creep into Danaka's nose, hot, dry and rotten. She started to stir, feeling uncomfortable as her body began to feel weighed down. A sharp pain pushing into her wrists, her legs stretched apart. Opening her eyes, to her horror, she saw his face. The man she feared most in the whole world. Hazar's nose was pressed against her own. His dark evil eyes staring into her soul, his cracked dry brown skin looked as rough as sand paper. His breath stank like rotting meat. She tried to move but she couldn't, as if great chains were pinning her down. Hazar's tongue slid out from in between his lips; she could feel the heat and slime as it ran as against her pale cheek.

"By the will of Dalackis!" Hazar sat up, stretching out with a dagger clenched between his hands. With all his hate, he brought the dagger down as it ripped into her chest.

Danaka screamed as she sat up, and the darkness that had filled her eyes was gone. Hazar was nowhere to be seen. Her heart raced in her chest; she clambered for breath. Danaka's throat was dry and her neck sore to touch. The sun was beginning to rise above the waterfall, the bright ball of orange fire glowing with all its beauty. The fire beside her was out; it smouldered peacefully as the charred wood crumbled.

A great emptiness came over her. She felt alone and scared. Turning her head to the great oak tree, she saw no one. Duro was gone, nowhere to be seen. Frantically she rose to her feet, the white sheet barely covering her naked body. *Duro, Griffin, where are they?* She wanted to scream out their names but she dared not, in case Hazar and his friends were still near.

Heavy footsteps and rustling echoed through the trees. Danaka braced herself, stepping back. Out of the treeline came Duro's two mighty horses, their black coats shinning in the early morning sun. They approached Danaka slowly and stopped before they began to graze on the grass around her. Both were saddled.

"If you're here," Danaka ran her hands across the larger horse's neck. His coat was warm and his muscles hard. "Then he must be too."

The water splashed loudly. Turning, Danaka saw a mighty image, one she had never seen before or was likely to again. Duro rose from the crystal-clear water, the orange glow shone down from the heavens as he emerged, naked as the day he was born. The diamond-like beads of water trickled down his chiselled torso, working their way down the grooves and arches of his muscles. His hair was forward, covering his eyes. With both his hands, he raised them to his head and pulled his hair away from his face, flinging his head back. Small drops of water flicked in her face. Looking down, she began to blush, Warmth swam through her body and her heart thumped like a drum. Excitement took hold of her senses, as she watched it dangle freely.

Duro leant forward, taking his poplin tunic and wrapping it around his waist. "I had planned to leave earlier," he walked past her and towards his horse, "but you needed your sleep."

"Thank you," she replied with a small smile.

"You snore like a wild pig and you have work to do."

Startled, Danaka stepped back. "I don't snore!" She paused. "What work?"

Duro leant into his saddle and withdrew two swords; both were sheathed in their scabbards.

"One day, I may not be here to defend you. So you will learn to defend yourself." Duro threw her one of the swords.

Danaka knelt down and picked up the sword. She could feel its weight; it felt the same as the one she held back in Tomellburg. She took a deep breath. "I have no idea how to fight."

"Soon you will."

Danaka dressed herself, throwing on one of the dresses Duro had taken from the dead family. It was red and to her surprise it fitted well. It was open at the shoulders and loose around her waist, which she liked. The intense heat would not fit well with a tightly fitted dress.

Duro stepped forward and withdrew the sword from its scabbard. The sound the steel made as it revealed itself made her flinch. Danaka copied him, pulling hers free. The blade was dull but she could tell it was sharp. The sword pulled against her wrist as she lifted it up.

"Never stand square on, you will have no balance. Shift your stance; face me with your left foot forwards." Duro pointed towards her feet. "Extend your right foot outwards, ever so slightly."

Danaka looked at Duro as he stood confidently in his fighting position. He pivoted forwards and backwards on the balls of his feet. The muscles in his legs tightened. She mirrored him. She knew Duro was right. She wanted to fight, to learn to defend herself. She did not want to feel like she depended on him. Griffin whined as he sat on a rock with his head resting on his paws. His eyes shifted between them both.

"I will come to you." Duro pointed his sword towards her. "Parry my attacks."

Without a second to prepare, he came to her, swinging out with his sword. Danaka quickly brought hers up to defend herself, and the impact of the blow shuddered down her arm. The vibrations stung and shook through her hand as she struggled to keep hold of her sword. Another attack came, forcing her back as she swung out wildly trying to deflect his advance. He felt so strong as he manoeuvred forwards; each time their swords met, she flinched and stumbled. Then before she knew it, her sword was set free. It flew from her hand and slid against the grass. Her feet then crossed and the next thing she knew she was on her back. Duro stood over her, the tip of his sword pointing down towards her throat.

"Never go back in a straight line, use angles. That is why you lost your balance." He extended his hand to her.

She knocked it away. "I am fine," Danaka replied angrily. Her pride was dented more than anything else. She rose to her feet and dusted herself down. "You are too strong."

“Strength does not win fights. You have speed, you must use it. Now we try again.” Duro picked up her sword and threw it between her feet. It swayed from left to right.

Danaka took in a deep breath. The water crashed heavily behind her, and the sun was rising slowly, its great glow lighting up the paradise around her. The grass was bright and healthy, the leaves blew softly. She suddenly flinched as Duro came at her once again. She swung at him, using all her strength as she blocked his attacks; he first came up high and then low. Each time his movements kept her thinking. Her heart raced as their swords clashed together, loud scraps as the steel screamed. Duro poked out with his sword, the tip flying towards her; she parried the attack and skilfully moved to her left. *Yes! I did it*, a huge smile filled her face. She then bounced around behind him; *maybe I am better at this than I thought.*

Duro smiled. Throwing his sword from his right hand to his left, the quick movement confused her as she now had the sun beaming in to her eyes. He was nothing more than a silhouette as he lunged forwards; their swords collided and she fell back knocking against the rock which Griffin was sat upon so peacefully. The impact took away her breath and once again her sword was no longer in her grasp. Duro’s momentum brought him forwards until they pressed against one another. Danaka lifted up her hands to stop his weight crushing her. They rested against his rock-hard stomach, each muscle felt hard and defined, like the feel of smooth rock beneath her finger tips. She could feel one of his scars; it was raised but surprisingly fine in texture. Sliding her hands further around his waist, she continued to follow his scar; it was like a path she was compelled to travel along. Looking up, she saw his eyes staring down at her, dark and beautiful.

Danaka could sense vulnerability in Duro; he was starring deeply into her eyes. Her aunt had always complimented her on her emerald green eyes, saying they were full of innocence and beauty. Danaka could feel Duro running his rough hands over her soft forearms, as if she had entranced him with a spell. She took in a deep breath, swallowing hard.

Duro then pushed her arms down and away from his body. “You fight well. But you manoeuvred yourself into the light of the sun, an easy mistake to avoid.” Duro stepped away. “Come we will continue.”

For a moment Danaka was frozen, she knew not what to do. Her heart pulsated and her sword hand was shaking. Butterflies twisted in her stomach. It was not a desire for fighting that was filling her heart.

Hours had gone by since both Danaka and Duro had left that little paradise and continued heading south along the river. The sun was high in the sky when Duro took them away from the river and out in the vast ocean of grass. The next part of Danaka’s journey was once again filled with endless sights of beauty and tranquillity. Vast sights of green hills and clusters of trees; the sky was blue and infinite and there was hardly a cloud in sight.

Danaka sat upon Duro’s large horse. His saddle was hard and it rubbed against her buttocks but resting upon it was far easier than walking in this heat. Her dull sandy hair was wringing wet, falling down past her neck and sticking against her back. She could feel the patches of sweat forming down her back and beneath her arms. The mighty horse travelled peacefully, following the exact footsteps Duro was taking. On his back, Danaka had a good view of her surroundings. The horse in ways had reminded her of her uncle, big, strong, and obedient, never uttering a word of complaint. She had named him Otis.

Duro walked silently by himself. His white poplin tunic was pulled up, covering half his body. His mind had seemed elsewhere since they had set off. He was a quiet man but his entire demeanour had given her the impression something was on his mind. Ahead of Duro was Griffin, running around, sniffing everything he could see. He was almost buried in the tall grass that swamped him. His golden fur left a misty glow as he sprinted around like an excitable child.

Danaka's arms and shoulders ached; she and Duro had continued training all morning. She now knew the basics of handling a sword and how to stand. Yet she knew her skills were far off that of being a decent fighter. She lacked both strength and stamina, but she knew with more training both would improve. The sword he gave her was now hers to keep; it thumped and banged against her leg. She felt strong with it strapped to her waist.

The land they travelled was vast. Open fields of green grass surrounded them. Down the hill and in a clearing, between a cluster of trees, she saw three figures, each on foot. Their faces or clothing she could not make out. Three shadows stalking their movements. Like silent hunters watching their prey.

"Duro! Look," Danaka yelled.

He stopped and looked to his left, as if he already knew what she was speaking about.

"They have been following us for the past three hours. I saw them not long before we left the forest." Duro turned away and continued walking.

"You knew!" Anger took hold of Danaka's words. "Yet you didn't say a word!"

"Relax. They will do nothing; soon we will be at the city of Ashfeld." Duro did not turn back.

"What does Yakash Mudra mean?"

Duro replied, "Death to the sinner."

Danaka sat silently as she contemplated his words; she turned her head and continued to watch as the three figures moved on the horizon. They were nothing more than silhouettes but she knew it was Hazar and his two companions. *Why are they still following us? Do they hate me that much?* She would not allow them to sneak up upon her again; Danaka gripped the handle of her sword tightly.

Eventually they travelled along the plains of Doveflawn, a mighty field littered with canola flowers and single trees. Beautiful purple Aubrieta cultorum bushes flanked them either side. Beyond the vegetation and along the open ground was a mighty castle; it was twice the size of the one she had seen at Blackharrow. The walls were at least twenty metres high. Four huge towers were spread throughout the ramparts, each nearly fifty metres in length. The stone was as black as night, dark rock forged from deep in the earth. The drawbridge was down and the portcullis raised. The sight of castle made Danaka nervous; she had never seen anything like it in all her life. She seemed but a fly in comparison to its magnitude.

"Stay close, you do not want to get lost in such a place." Duro stopped before the drawbridge, looking up at the ramparts. "Dismount, only DeVeil soldiers may ride inside the castle walls."

Danaka did as commanded. "Griffin, stay close, you hear. No running off." She took a deep breath as they walked along the drawbridge, past two-armed guards clad in mail and boiled leather. Each held long square shields and spears in their right hands. Neither man blinked or moved, and for a moment she thought them to be statues.

Once they had passed the drawbridge and were inside the castle walls, the noise crashed against her face like the fist of Walter's wife. The impact knocked back her head and forced her eyes shut. Tomellburg had seemed overpowering but this place was something else. People were packed together like sardines, not an inch of breathing space. People forced their way past one another like wild animals; screams and shouts filled her ears. The street they walked upon was wide, yet still she was barely able to move, flanked either side by rows of two storey houses, each made from wood with thatched roofs. Women clad in white rags were shouting as they tossed urine from the windows, laughing as they hit passers-by.

Danaka felt uneasy that Griffin would lose his way. He however stayed close, pressing his fur against her leg. She herself had to grab hold of Otis's tail when she was almost knocked to the ground. Dry sweat swamped her nose and, as much as she needed to breathe, she dared not. Each breath she took made her retch; she prayed soon that they would be away from the chaos. Duro however was calm; he forced his way forwards, even grabbing hold of men and women to clear his path.

At the end of the street it widened, yet the bedlam did not relent. It now seemed more cramped and wilder than before. Taverns and inns encircled them, each with their own strange name, such as The Hung Drawn and Quartered, The Pigs Belly and Ale and Tits. Then there was one that really stood out: The Devils Cunt, with a skinny, sweaty woman sitting outside; her hair was black and twisted, her skin pale and littered with red rash. Her dress was short and her legs were open for all to see; she was tilting her head back and drinking down her ale. Danaka was glad when Duro did not take her in there.

In the distance, on a slope, she could see a mighty castle keep, rectangular in shape with a twenty-metre-high armoured knight crafted from stone standing vigilant over the entrance. Everything here crushed her image of Tomellburg; that place had seemed hell to her but now in comparison to Ashfeld it was heaven. For a brief moment she wished she was back there, before she quickly wiped that thought from her mind.

As Danaka forced her way through the crowd and the sweltering heat, Hazar's evil face appeared and disappeared like a ghost. He moved between the people, gliding in and out of sight. His evil eyes never left her, like a lion eyeing up the meal to come. She flinched and pulled back as panic took hold of her; frantically she scanned the crowd. Yet Danaka could no longer see him.

Suddenly they stopped as Duro asked a small man for directions. She could not hear the words they spoke but where the man pointed, Duro followed. Eventually they manoeuvred themselves away from the hustle and bustle of the crowded streets and down a narrow alleyway. Slowly the noise began to fade and she could now hear the horses' hooves knocking against the cobbled walkway. Eventually the alleyway widened and the air felt fresh and clean. Tall buildings and houses surrounded them.

"Stay here with the horses, I will go inside and find us a room." Duro entered the inn to her right.

Danaka finally felt a little at ease, kneeling down and pulling Griffin close. She breathed deeply, filling her lungs. The heat rose from her body and sweat poured from her skin. Looking up she saw the name of the inn, *The Wanderers Sword.*

All of a sudden, two excitable lads came sprinting past, both dressed in brown leather and broken sandals. *Where are they going in such a hurry?* They turned the corner and disappeared out of sight. In the distance she could hear faint sounds of shouting and cheering. Intrigued, she stood up and followed the noise; around the corner she could see a gathering of people, maybe twenty or thirty. They all crowded in a small circular opening with various narrow alleyways allowing entry from all sides.

Bright sun shone down from between the tall buildings. As if the heavens were giving their light to a tall broad man addressing the crowd, he stood raised on a block. He was dressed in boiled leather and thin rings of mail covered his arms. His hair was black and pulled back in a pony tail; his face was covered with a thick beard and his skin was olive and bright. He was a handsome man.

"I am Elior; I have no fear of these Mudras!" the man shouted, which was followed by a rapturous applause. "Dalackis made this land, the air we breathe and food you eat. These people sin daily; their women show their flesh and taunt us all. They believe in false gods. They should be punished! Dalackis sent us Cesaril to do his bidding. We must unite and wipe these dogs from this land." Elior raised his hands, clenching his fists.

"Rakali, Rakali, Rakali!" The crowd shouted together in one booming chant.

"No!" an elderly woman screamed. She was dressed in all black, her face was old and her hair grey. She had weary eyes but they were full of wisdom. "Do not listen to this man; the Winged God spreads love and harmony. You will burn in hell if you follow him!" The old woman stepped out of the crowd; she was slow like a tortoise and her back was hunched as she leant forwards onto her walking stick.

Danaka kept herself hidden; only peering around the corner. Compelled to listen but not wishing to be seen, her heart beat in her chest.

"Do not listen to her, friends," Elior shouted back. "They burnt our Isles to the ground. Thirty years ago, Akesha lay in ruin; we must reclaim our former glory. I implore you to spread darkness and shadow to this land. In the words of the holy Cesaril, 'Be it the right and obligation of all men to fight evil, until evil is no more!'"

The old women raised her head. "But who here is the evil, young warrior?"

"Quick, we must disperse before we are seen. Tonight we do his bidding!"

Elior dropped down, the majority of crowd following him as they disappeared down the narrow alleyways that joined the square. Only the old woman and a handful of men remained. Danaka began to panic as they looked up. She thought for a second to run but for some reason she stayed her ground, her left hand gripping the handle of her sword.

"Have no fear child," the old woman spoke as she and those remaining approached her.

She may be the oldest woman I have ever seen. Her skin was dry and broken, and thick wrinkles formed under her eyes. Her body was thin and fragile; the man who stood with her held her arms so she did not fall.

Danaka breathed slowly. "I am not scared," she spoke truthfully as she released her sword.

"Dalackis is a god of peace and Cesaril is his messenger of heaven. Do not believe the words you hear for we are not evil," the old woman spoke softly and calm. She then raised her hand and pressed her thumb against Danaka's forehead. "May his holy wings shelter and keep you safe."

Inside the inn, Danaka, Duro and Griffin sat in a far corner. They had a circular table to themselves, and they had eaten their fill of red meat and soup. Danaka felt her lower stomach bloat as if she was pregnant. Duro had positioned himself so he faced the entrance. Every time someone entered, he would peer towards the door. The inn was quiet, only a few punters littered the floor. The only noise came from idle chit chat between the men and Griffin's snoring. To Danaka's surprise, the innkeeper had allowed Griffin to enter. Here in Ashfeld they were far more liberal than Tomellburg.

Danaka sat staring at her cup. It was made from clay and full to the rim with pale ale. She had never tasted it before; her uncle would drink it but only occasionally when Heidi let him.

"What do you know of Dalackis?" Danaka raised her cup, admiring the golden liquid. The froth released a complex fruity aroma that she could not make out. Slowly she took the ale to her lips; it was bitter and strong. It dried her mouth and sent a shock down her body, causing her face to twist.

Duro took a huge gulp from his jar; unaffected, he wiped the excess from his mouth before replying, "He is an eastern god. His followers mainly reside in the Eastern Isles and the Desert Realm but the faith has spread as far as Dagen. They believe Dalackis made the world. From his wings he spawned the land, the animals, then finally you and I."

"They are not all bad, are they?"

"All men are evil, it is in their nature." Duro took another big swig from his jar. Ale poured down his face.

Danaka looked him up and down; his eyes looked heavy and a faint mist had begun to form over them like an autumn fog. That was his third jar. "So, are you evil?"

"I have done some cruel and terrible things in my life." He brought the jar back to his lips, gulping it down until it was empty. He looked up and pointed his finger towards Danaka; it hovered from side to side. "But if you were to ask me if I could relive those moments again, would I change the decisions I took? Then I would answer, no." Duro's words were slurred and his eyes rolled to the back of his head.

"Why?"

"Because some people deserve to die."

Danaka did not know what to say in reply; instead she took another swig from her cup. This time it tasted better, enticing her to take another swing. Loud heavy footsteps banged against the wooden floor. Rings of mail clattered together as the loud steps made their way across the room. Danaka turned to see a man of average height. A dull helmet covered the majority of his face, metal plates fell from the crown of the helm and down to his jaw. He was clad in mail with a boiled armless leather tunic strapped to his torso. Standing alone at the bar, the man banged his hand twice, trying to get attention the barman's attention while he was half asleep. The noise thudded and echoed. He then unclipped his helm and lowered it to the bar. Danaka could see his hair was light brown, scruffy and curly; an ungroomed beard covered his face.

Duro slowly rose from his seat; he swayed slightly, taking in a big breath of air. "Malcolm Reymor! I have been looking for you."

Chapter 18
Souls of Broken Men

"Fuck me!" Princess Arrabella groaned and moaned. The pleasure tingled through her body; she thought of nothing but the Prince of Valanor, his defined well sculptured body, her fingers sliding over every groove and muscle. Her hands squeezing his buttocks as he thrust inside of her again and again, harder and harder. She gasped, begging for more; waves of satisfaction began to take hold of her senses. Arrabella rolled over onto her front, arching her back, widening her legs. "Gabriel!" she called as more pleasure coursed through her veins, and her body began to twitch. Her calls of ecstasy heightened.

"If only this was real," she whispered. Arrabella was on her bed, naked and alone. Her fingers had been doing the work that was meant for Gabriel, her body ached for him. It had been over an hour since she had attempted to seduce the prince but he had not come. She continued to imagine; her thoughts of such a moment had been in her dreams and Arrabella knew how she wanted it.

"It could be real," a sly murmur slid out from within the shadows.

Arrabella jolted. Turning over, she covered her naked body with her arms. "Who is there?"

Out of the darkness stepped Leylan. A grin filled his face from ear to ear. The red light from the hanging lanterns only highlighted his sinister demeanour. "Fear not beautiful princess, it is only I."

"How did you get in here?" Arrabella demanded.

Leylan smiled before replying casually, "Through the door; you should keep it locked. You never know what foul creatures are lurking within these halls." Leylan approached the princess, standing over her while she sat on the bed. "I see you didn't entice Gabriel to come taste what you have to offer." With his knee, Leylan forced open the princess' legs ever so slightly.

"You're a brave bastard. At the click of a finger, I could have you pulled limb from limb."

Leylan pulled the princess up to her feet; he began to whisper as his lips hovered above hers, "I live life on the edge; the thrill of what-ifs and what-could-be excites me, the greater the risk, the mightier the reward." He ran his fingers between her breasts, wiping away the perspiration.

"What reward do you desire tonight?"

"A princess."

Princess Arrabella smiled, and her heart began to rage within her chest. "Tonight I will not be your princess and I will not be royalty, I…"

"You'll be my slave. To punish as I see fit." Leylan pulled the princess' arms apart, revealing her breasts. A dark desire filled his eyes. He bit down on her nipple, his teeth pressed into her flesh.

Arrabella gasped and moaned as she squeezed his head closer to her bosom. Leylan broke free from her grasp and shoved her onto the bed; he threw his blue robe to the ground. The princess opened her legs and watched as he climbed onto her like a man possessed by the devil himself.

Leylan forced himself inside her; pain and pleasure screamed its way through the princess' body. Arrabella watched Leylan, as a demonic fire raged within him. With each thrust she could feel his hate and venom, yet it excited her. She was at his mercy.

Suddenly she felt herself thrown onto her front, her face pressed hard against the bed. Leylan yanked back on her hair, his body violently pounding against her buttocks. Arrabella grimaced and then gasped; her eyes rolled to back of her head. "Again, again!" she commanded.

He is no Gabriel but tonight... tonight he will do! Arrabella screamed.

****

"Why are you walking so slowly?" Lucian quickly descended down the pale white steps. "It must be down here!" The clanging of his armour rattled loudly.

Lassander casually strolled behind his brother, holding his helmet beneath his arm. The hot morning sun glared down from up above. "You said this last time. Are you sure you know where you're going?"

"Do you doubt me, brother?" Lucian eagerly jogged ahead, peering around the corner.

"As a matter of fact, I do actually. We have been up since dawn looking for this place." Lassander sighed. "All that wine you had has played with that tiny mind of yours." Lassander stood behind his brother. Looking down, he could see a walkway. It was wide, slanted and cobbled, white buildings standing either side.

"No, it is here; last night he told me so. Follow the white steps till you reach the cobbled ground."

"I thought you liked women, brother, now you're imagining men also. Antilion has had an effect on you I didn't see coming." Lassander was getting restless; he was tired and hungry. For hours he and Lucian had been wondering the lower level streets of the capital, an area they had been advised to avoid. "*Thieves, murderers and carnal sinners lurk in lower depths of the city,*" the drunken Antilion captain had said as Akeshan wine stained his beard.

"It is there!" Lucian called before he sprinted off.

Lassander jogged after his brother, who stood waiting outside a wide four storey high building. The walls were red and the door black.

"The red house of desire." Lucian's eyes widened, a cheesy grin filling his narrow face.

Lucian slowly pushed the door open; it creaked softly as they both entered. Inside was a wide-open space decorated with long purple cushioned seats. A bar stood at the back; beside it was an arched doorway where red silks dangled down. It was empty.

"Looks like no one is home," Lassander said as his eyes scanned the room.

"No, he said it was open from dusk till dawn, the house that never sleeps." Lucian sighed with disappointment.

"Hello boys!" a camp voice called out. "My you are early, eager devils!" A skinny man clad in a rainbow-coloured dress appeared. Bright red blusher was applied to his cheeks and large hooped earrings clanged together as he moved forward, flaunting his body. "Call me Elsa."

A panic-stricken Lucian backed away, almost cowering behind Lassander.

"Oh, don't be frightened." Elsa began to giggle. "The house of desire has a menu to satisfy all appetites." He began to brush his long blonde wig back away from his face; each hand gesture he made was big and flamboyant. He moved forwards, eyeing Lucian up and down. "Hmm I like."

"I bet you do!" Lucian replied as he arched away.

Lassander tried his best to conceal his laughter. He raised his hand to cover his mouth, revelling in his brother's predicament.

"What brings you to Elsa's house of desire?" Elsa ran his finger along Lucian's cheek.

"Women, women!"

"Oh, I see," Elsa replied slowly. "How do you like your women, sir knight?" He thrust his hips forward, revealing a bulge between his legs.

"Without a cock!" Lucian pulled away.

"Ha, I'm only kidding with you. Elsa, she is such a trickster!" Elsa flicked his eyelids before raising his hands in the air and clapped in fast succession. "Girls!"

Suddenly women began to emerge from behind the red silks. Lucian's eyes began to widen and happiness filled his baby face. Every type of woman you could imagine, some were tall, others slim then there were large breasted ladies, young and old. Some had skin as dark as the night sky and others as pale as the moon. The ladies of pleasure were dressed in nothing but nipple tassels and coloured silk which fell freely from around their waists. They arched their bodies and honed in their glare towards the Valorian princes.

For once Lucian struggled to speak. "Brother, come!" He stepped forward, excited.

"You enjoy them for me, I will wait here." Lassander sat himself down on one of the purple loungers, placing his helmet beside him.

"Oh, please choose, we can accommodate your wildest of desires." Elsa ran his hands down the curvy body of the Etorion girl.

"I have a wife." Lassander shook his head.

"Well, I see no wife," Elsa replied.

"She is here." Lassander pressed two fingers to his heart and tapped twice. He looked up at Lucian. "Enjoy yourself, brother."

Lucian put his arm around a large breasted girl; the two kissed softly. Her body was slim and appealing, her hair dark and her skin pale. "I won't be long," he added as he squeezed her buttocks. A girl next to him with skin as smooth and appealing as caramel ran her hands around his waist, kissing his neck. Lucian looked up. "Actually, I may be a while." The three disappeared behind the red silks; giggles and laughter soon followed.

Lassander smiled, seeing his brother happy made him content. Yet he felt a deep sadness within him; he held two small stone carvings in his hand. They were of his wife, Melaina, and son Zander. He missed them deeply. Without them by his side, part of his soul was missing. He kissed both stones and placed them inside his breastplate.

As time went by, he watched as punters entered, each man different from the last. Some poor, others rich, yet each had a carnal desire of their own. Some had unspeakable requests while others just wanted love and intimacy. That is what Lassander missed: watching the sun rise while he held his wife in his arms. "Soon," he told himself, "I shall hold you again."

****

King Aristian stretched out. His body felt stiff and his head pounded. *Too much wine!* The feast had been a success; the food was good, the entertainment joyous and the wine, yes, the wine had gone down exceptionally well. The wise king raised his hands to his head, as if to command the drums to stop beating within his skull.

The morning sun shone brightly through his balcony. A soft breeze blew his red and greens silk curtains ever so gently. His chambers were large, he had a bed wide enough for four people; thick oak beams were at every corner. He had slowly risen and feasted on bread, cheese and water. His stomach felt bloated and hard, and the food made him feel sleepy once again. In the far corner stood Beyorn. As always, the beast of Golgia was silent; he watched and he listened.

He looked over towards his bed, and the king felt alone. He remembered he would sit in this very seat, watching as his dear Sonja brushed out her long blonde hair. The king smiled to himself. She would never allow her hand maidens to do it. Queen Sonja knew what she wanted and how she wanted it done.

The entrance to his chambers was open. Outside Sir Dolfan Greenway called, "Your Majesty, the High Council wishes to enter."

King Aristian breathed deeply; his eyes felt sore and head tender. He was in no mood for council but he knew why they wished to enter and he was a King. His subjects came before any of his aliments. "Let them in."

Like slippery snakes, the High Council entered. As always, Lord Peyton was at the front, his gold silks sparkling in the rays of sun. Lord Dellio Greenway was in green and the king's cousin, Attico, wore red.

"Your Majesty," the lords spoke as they simultaneously bowed their heads.

Lord Attico spoke first. "We must speak, the matter is of the highest importance. This cannot keep happening; we have had five attacks in three days."

He was small and round, his dark hair retreated from his forehead and two chins lay around his throat.

"And this is just in the Capital; my reports state killings have been happening all over Allamantya, in Ethilbar, Ashfeld and Doldayne, they all have been hit," Lord Dellio Greenway added. He was the elder brother of Sir Dolfan yet they were anything but alike. Dellio was thin and weedy, his voice soft. His hair was long and as bright as fire.

"The culprits?" The king replied.

"They disappear, like grains of sand in the wind." Lord Dellio stepped forward.

"Yet even grains of sand shall fall somewhere, my lords." King Aristian rose from his seat.

"Examples must be made! Pull them from their holes, burn their cities to the ground; show them the true might of Allamantyan steel!" Lord Attico shouted. His eyes were deep and dark; they were possessed by greed and power.

"I agree the culprits should he made an example of, but where are they? I will not condemn an entire nation for the acts of a few." King Aristian's eyes moved from left to right. "I see Lord Mortimer Judaus is yet to return; how do you think to govern my lands when you cannot even keep track of your own council?"

"He has most likely fled with some young girl! His carnal tastes do not please me." Lord Dellio's face twisted.

Lord Peyton spoke for the first time, gliding forward. "He gave his word he shall return. His blood is of old King Avindel. He loves this land. Matters in the east are of our upmost concern; our people are being butchered by these heathen dogs. We shall not stand by while they suffer."

"The people of Eastern Isles, do they not suffer also? Count Baldwin of Ezzar writes to me daily, he tells of the horrors the brotherhood of Ralmalaur commit. Hundreds die by the day."

Baldwin Anglar ruled the Eastern Isles from the province of Ezzar since its conquest in 170 G.D. Aristian trusted Baldwin; he was an old and honest knight. He respected all faiths unlike his high council.

The king breathed deeply. "My father's empire was forged on the blood of his enemies but my empire shall be built by turning those enemies into friends."

It seemed an age that the king had spoken with his council; he had wanted them gone. His head hurt and he had no time for spineless men whose words were as weak and untrustworthy as thin ice. Yet it was Antilion tradition that a king rule with four of the most wise and noble lords by his side. He was not one break his country's tradition but that did not mean he had to enjoy their company.

"Brotherhood of Ralmalaur," he muttered under his breath. *Why must they come now?* When all in the world looked as though it was falling into place, something must come along to destroy all prayers for hope. For the past months the followers of Ralmalaur had been terrorising his land, murdering his people. This was not open warfare; they would not stand and face his soldiers on the battlefield. They would attack at night, killing both women and children. He did not know how long Count Baldwin, the governor of the Eastern Isles could hold out.

It is my fault! The king banged his hands on the table. His father, King Alector, had been the first Allamantyan ruler to bring the Eastern Isles to heel. He had succeeded where all others had failed. His armies conquered the unconquerable, destroying the enemy in their homeland, bringing their cities to ruin. King Aristian watched as success and power destroyed his father's sense of reason. King Alector's overconfidence would lead to his downfall. Drunk on his victory, he led the largest Allamantyan invasion of Valanor, accumulating in the most brutal and costly defeat in his nation's history. King Alector's shame would make way for his son's legend. When the old have fallen, the young shall rise.

King Aristian learnt from his father's mistakes; he did not allow himself to become overconfident, he reasoned every step he took. He vowed never to take what was not his own through war. He sought peace and allowed the people of Akesha, Yorno and Brundea to settle freely in Allamantya. Yet now some repaid his kindness with blood and death. The high council had warned the king to not let them through the gates at Hamon'dor, yet their words fell upon stubborn ears. *There is good and bad in all men.*

The rattling of mail and armour rang inside the king's head. "Your Majesty," a deep voice followed. Behind it was Prince Daemar. His left hand, as always, lightly perched on the tip of his sword. "You summoned me?"

"Has there still been no word from Princess Drusilla?" The king sat in hope of a reply that would warm his heart.

"There has been nothing." Prince Daemar's voice was saddened. He too missed his elder sister.

Five years ago, Prince Varden Redmond, Drusilla's first born, was killed in trial by combat. The killer judged innocent by the gods was banished from the realm. Five years he was to wander in the wilderness of the Allamantyan Empire. In the harshest and most forgotten breadths of the world he was to suffer for his actions. The killer's name was never to be uttered in the king's presence.

"Why does she not come?" Daemar added. "Her family is here."

"Grief destroys a person's soul. Our family have been cursed for what we did." Aristian's head sunk into his hands.

Prince Daemar approached. "We did what was needed, our father was weak."

"My wife, your wife and Drusilla's son. We have all lost those who we hold dearest. The gods punish sinners with a vengeful fury." King Aristian felt low; his sins always weighed heavily upon his aging shoulders. He wore a crown that was never meant for him and, along with his siblings, he had murdered his father, a man whose mind had become plagued by devils.

"I lose no sleep over what we did. 'For the good of the realm,' we said. If I could relive that moment, it would be I who held that pillow to his face. I would gladly take this burden you bear."

The king looked into his brother's eyes. "All I do, I do for my family and my people. You must swear something to me."

Daemar dropped to his knees.

“Swear that you will not kill Prince Gabriel?”

Daemar’s dark eyes seemed to contemplate the king’s words. Hesitation took hold of the prince. His hand gripped tightly. “I swear that my sword or any that I command will do him no harm.” His words were unwilling but his oath unbreakable.

Chapter 19
The Warrior Code

Between each step, only pain and death awaited Garroway and his children. Many hours had passed since they had been reunited, but in a flash, the beautiful green fields of Allamantya had vanished. Now only black rock and stone lay before them. The dark mountains of Hamon'dor were treacherous, yet they were the quickest path to the Kingdom of Antilion. Sir Dillian Howard was the man who could take them through the mountain gate. Strangers would not be allowed to pass at a time like this. The air was thin and cold; the black cloaks the assassins wore were wrapped tightly around their bodies.

Garroway and Lilah walked with their horses side by side, behind them the others followed loyally. No words were spoken as they knew they must tread carefully; one false move and they would fall to their death. One hundred feet below them was rock as sharp as spear heads; rubble of broken stone echoed and screamed as it fell from the pass and down the mountain side. A faint mist hovered above them as if the heavens themselves lay on the other side.

"How long until we reach the gate?" Garroway did not want to speak too loudly, an avalanche was the last thing they needed.

Sir Dillian Howard was a few metres ahead, he too walked with his horse. "In an hour we will reach the Hamon springs; we will wait there for the cover of darkness."

"Why will we need the cover of darkness?" Lilah, as always, questioned everything.

"So as to not arouse suspicion, we need to approach the gate from the Steps of Avindel and not the mountain pass. Only those loyal to royal family know of the existence of where we tread."

"Why would a knight be entrusted with such information?" Lilah whispered into Garroway's ear.

"Fear not my love. Trust in me." Garroway smiled.

The narrow pass they followed began to widen, until upon the mountain top they saw a magnificent sight. The cold air uncharacteristically began to warm as if only fire lay before them. In between the black rock and broken stone lay pools, circular pools of magical blue water. Hot stream rose high into the sky.

"By will of Dalackis, what is this place?" Lothar's single eye began to expand. Taking in the once in a life time experience. He knelt down and placed his fingers in the water. "It's hot!"

"This is the Springs of Hamon'dor. The gods of the White City kept it warm so the ancient King Avindel would not freeze and could live on to found the Kingdom of Antilion."

"A perfect place to rest." Garroway looked up through the mist; the last shimmers of light had begun to fade. Darkness was coming.

Five pools lay on the mountain top. Light, as if shining from the sun, rose up from the pools. The largest pool at the centre was where most of the assassins had decided to rest. Lothar, Caelan, Naleac, Roak, Valdar, Uriah and Zaira had sat facing one another, allowing the warm steaming water to cover their naked bodies. Rhodesha and Toran were in a smaller pool, away from the group. They could not be seen through the mist but Rhodesha's moans certainly made the others aware of their presence. Only Maarax and Sir Dillian had not taken refuge in the magical blue waters. Maarax as always was alert; he sat on a rock looking out across the mountains, admiring the snow filled tips.

At the far edge of the mountain, Garroway lay in a pool. The water was mix of blues, purples and greens. It swirled and bubbled. The feeling of it against his old skin instantly relaxed him. His aching muscles tingled as he closed his eyes. *When this is all over, every day shall be as wonderful as this moment.* As he opened his eyes, a beauty more magnificent than all the gold in the world stood before him. Out of the mist came Lilah; she wore nothing but the red hair on her head. Her athletic frame and curvaceous hips excited him as much today as they did the first time he laid eyes upon them. The light that shone from the pools only enhanced her magical beauty.

Lilah slowly lowered herself into the rainbow-like waters. Garroway sat up as she stood over him. At that moment he was at her mercy; his heart began to race. He was a slave ready to do whatever she commanded. Lilah slid her fingers through his thick silver hair. Garroway began to kiss down her stomach, tasting the sweat and taking in her scent. Garroway raised his hands out of the water and up her legs, feeling the smoothness of her thighs before he grabbed hold of her buttocks and pulled her down towards him. The water splashed as she sunk into its magical depths.

"The priests say the gods created all men equal. I disagree." Lilah admired the warrior before her, the man who had changed not only her life for the better but that of their ten *children*. She slowly ran her fingers over Garroway's face, feeling the texture of his stubble and that of his scars.

"Why?" Garroway asked as he squeezed her tightly before softly kissing her neck.

"Because they made you mightier than all the rest."

Garroway's excitement pressed hard against her leg. Lilah slid her hands down his chest, feeling the grooves of his torso before she dunked her hands into the depths of the water. Underneath, she took him tightly in her grasp. Garroway breathed in deeply before she bit into his lip; in that moment he pulled back her hair and grabbed hold of her breast with his right hand feeling her nipple rotating in his palm.

Garroway instantly knew Lilah was ready for him; he could feel her heart pounding and her body was ripe with excitement. He needed her and she needed him. Lilah lowered herself more. Garroway felt himself slide inside her, the warmth tingled through his body. They were connected. Their bodies, their hearts, their souls became one. A sensation of pleasure exploded throughout their bodies. Lilah began to scream, digging her nails into Garroway's back.

****

"You look excited old man!" Lothar laughed as he leant out of the pool. The hot water dripped from his face and into his beard.

Sir Dillian was sat beside them on a rock, looking out across the mountain top as Lilah rode Garroway as furious and intensely as one would ride a horse into battle. "Sin doesn't excite me, heathen."

"Heathen, he says?" Caelan smiled as he bobbed up and down in the water.

"Who decided what is sin?" Naleac joined in.

"If fucking and drinking is sin then I be the biggest sinner of all." Lothar looked back at his brothers and sisters and laughed. "Cesaril says, 'The mortal life is short, so live and enjoy every moment for one day you will look back and realise you haven't lived at all.'"

"Don't quote that devil shite to me. There is only one faith. 'The gods gave us swords so we can protect our holy mother and cast out the devil and his followers.'"

"Be careful, old man, for I am a devil and sin is in my blood." Roak appeared out of the mist, steam steadily rising from his naked body.

Sir Dillian stood up and backed away. Lothar and the others all began to laugh.

Uriah was uncharacteristically quiet; he sat in the warm waters listening. He watched as Zaira turned and began to step out of the pool; the water stopped below her belly button, teasing him. Her breasts were round and perky, her body toned and appealing. "Ever since I was a child, I wished to feel gold beneath my fingertips." Uriah looked down, watching the water rise and fall around her waist.

"Some treasures are not for the eyes of man." Zaira smiled as she grabbed hold of her cloak and wrapped it around her waist.

"A treasure hunter never stops until he has claimed his prize."

****

Rhodesha panted, breathing in deeply as she tried to catch her breath. Her heart beat wildly within her chest, her body tingled from head to toe. She was arched forward, leaning out of the hot pool. Peering back, she admired her man. The hot steam rose around him, sweat poured down his rising chest. Slowly Toran pulled himself from inside her. Rhodesha ached and twitched; she could feel his warm seed inside her.

Having Toran back at her side made her feel complete. It had been twelve years since they first met. Rhodesha remembered it clearly. Garroway had won Rhodesha in a game of dice, saving her from a life of misery and slavery. Garroway, Lilah and Lothar would take her with them from town to town; it was a happy time. On the banks of the river Tyma they regularly visited a brothel. Rhodesha liked it there; the women were always kind to her, feeding her sweated apples and honey water. It was there she first laid eyes upon the man who would claim her heart.

Toran had first appeared on the top of the old wooden stairway. Tall and broad he towered above any man she had ever seen, yet Toran was not a man, only a boy. Curly ginger hair as wild as the boy himself fell down to his neck. His eyes would scan the room as if it owned it yet besides that powerful glare, she saw laughter and love.

Even though Toran claimed he had, Rhodesha knew he never saw her that day, his eyes looked straight through her as he scanned the hundreds that filled those walls. At that moment she did not exist to him, but he did to her, and every day after, she would love him so.

"What do you want from life?" Rhodesha asked.

Toran lowered himself into the hot waters and pushed himself towards her. A wave of magical colours crashed against Rhodesha's breasts. "I want what any man would desire, gold and the love of a good woman." He stared deeply into her eyes. "Today I have one of them," he planted a kiss on her lips, "tomorrow I will have both."

Warmth swarmed her body as she ran her hand across his face. She turned so he could hold her in his arms, leaning back she could feel the hardness of his chest. "What about having a family?"

"I have one." Toran pointed across the silver tinted mist towards his brothers and sisters. "I go where Garroway goes. We owe him our lives."

Rhodesha breathed deeply as she held his huge hand in her own. She knew Toran spoke the truth; her life had been a living hell before Garroway had saved her. Each day had been more painful than the last; it was he who had given her a reason to live.

****

With the dark cloak of night resting heavily above, the assassins and Sir Dillian Howard began their descent down the mountain slope. The warmth of the magical pools had vanished and just cold air and grey mist floated around them. The slope was steep and as slippery as ice.

Garroway had commanded them all to be silent and alert. Be ready for anything or anyone. No one could fault his love for his children. There was one flamed torch for every second person. The flames flickered and crackled, lighting up the darkness that surrounded them.

The slope wound down the mountain side, like a snake that had wrapped itself around a tree. The path was thin and unnoticeable from the ground. As the mist began to fade the mountain gate of Hamon'dor revealed itself. Forged into the rock were two huge towers, each standing over one hundred feet high. They stood vigilant over the pass, silent but god-like in appearance. They were made of black stone and red mortar, which dripped like blood. The ramparts stuck up like spikes with flames flickering from the top. In between the two monstrous towers lay a thirty-foot wide gate, manned by rows of armoured guards, each alert and peering down towards the Steps of Avindel. The mighty drawbridge was lowered; numerous soldiers patrolled the ground level. Each dressed in thick armour that covered their entire bodies. Green and red plume fell from their helmets.

Garroway and the others quickly stepped out from the cover of the mountain rocks and onto the Steps of Avindel just out of sight of the guards. The path was wide, wide enough for over ten men to walk at one time. It was flanked either side by mountains as far as the eye could see. Beacons of fire were spread along the path, lighting up the road and making anyone who approached easily visible to the soldiers at the gate.

"All of you, cover your faces, hide your weapons and say nothing." Sir Dillian looked nervous. He wiped the sweat from his palms.

"Do as he commands." Garroway mounted his horse and covered his face.

The others did as they were ordered. Each sat silently; the only noise they could hear came from their beating hearts. Sir Dillian raised his hand and signalled them to slowly make their way towards the gate, which became even more intimidating the closer they got. The horses' hooves crashed against the rocky ground, echoing through the mountains.

"Halt, who goes there!" a soldier shouted from the drawbridge.

Sir Dillian pulled on his reins. Garroway could hear the old man mumbling prayers, trying to boost his courage. *If this knight fails us now, I swear he will be first to taste the kiss of the Titans Bitch.* Although he looked calm, Garroway felt as nervous as he had ever felt. He did not like this feeling; usually their missions did not involve a third party. They would hunt their prey and kill it without mercy then move on to claim their reward.

"Show yourself!" The soldier began to sound agitated.

Garroway looked Sir Dillian up and down, as if ice had consumed his body. The old man froze. The five soldiers from the drawbridge began to cautiously approach them; they dipped their spears and walked forwards. Looking up, Garroway noticed archers appearing on the ramparts, their arrows pointing towards them. If anything went wrong, Garroway and his children hadn't a chance. Suddenly, Sir Dillian kicked into his horse and moved forwards, meeting the soldiers half way. Garroway listened intensely, but the voices were muffled and broken. He gripped his reins hard, his heart thumped loudly. He could feel the unrest behind him, the assassin's horses moved back and forth, stamping their hooves on the ground. *If there is a god, get us past this gate, I beg you.*

Sir Dillian leant forwards from his horse, handing one of the soldiers something. The man stepped back and they all bowed their heads. He then returned to his seated position and raised his hand, signalling the assassins to join him. A loud bang echoed and thundered. Metal screeched and turned as the portcullis began to slowly rise. Once the gate was clear, the assassins slowly began to cross the drawbridge, the hooves banging against the wood. Each kept their heads down and refused to make eye contact with the soldiers.

As they passed through the dark gateway, lit up by only a few torches, Garroway noticed the murder holes; inside he saw the faces of the men peering out of the darkness. They looked dirty and tired; no souls lay behind their cold eyes. If the signal was given, in seconds he and his children would be dead. No matter how well he had trained them, none would live. Along the fifty-metre passageway lay another gate. This one, however, was open. Two large fire braziers burned brightly. *Head to the light,* he told himself. The sound of the horses, the crackle of the fires and the rustle of mail echoed through the tunnel. If there was a hell, it would be like this, a place as dark and loveless as this.

"Travel safe, my lord," one of the soldiers said as Sir Dillian passed through the second gate.

Garroway rode between the fire braziers and out of the passageway. In that instant his heart eased its beats and huge gulp of fresh air filled his lungs. He felt free. He kicked into his horse and followed Sir Dillian down the dirt road and away from Hamon'dor. He could not say how long they rode for but the mountain pass was no longer in sight when they stopped. Only broken ruins surrounded them now, red stone that was old and weary.

"The sun will rise soon, we must rest." Garroway stopped and dismounted.

His children did the same, each collapsing onto the grass or resting against the red stone.

"This is the old castle of the great King Kalidar. The Lion fortress it was called, before it was pulled down on the orders of his son, Alector. If ever a son hated his father so, it was he." Sir Dillian ran his hands along the broken stone, feeling the rubble between his fingertips.

"Why would he hate his father so?" Naleac pulled back his hooded cloak. Beads of sweat poured down his cheeks.

"Alector's elder brother, Nymar, was a sinner; he filled his bed with the company of men, casting aside the words of the White City and his right to the throne. Kalidar was a powerful and proud king, one who did not take insult lightly. So he had his son put to death, allowing the throne to pass to Alector, who thanked his father by destroying his most prized possession, the Lion fortress."

"You Allamantyans live by too many rules. They hold you back! You should be set free to enjoy whatever life throws at you. A bit of cock here or there never hurt anyone." Naleac patted Sir Dillian on the backside.

"Don't touch me, sinners!" Sir Dillian turned to Garroway, "If these dogs truly are your children it will be on your head when they burn in hell."

"There is no hell," Garroway replied.

"What do you believe, Father?" Caelan asked.

All the years Garroway and his children had fought and bled together, never once had Garroway spoken of an afterlife or the gods. He sat himself down, wiping the sweat from his brow. "I have always questioned the gods, but who am I to say whether they exist or not? Was it the will of the gods that I came to find the finest eleven people who ever walked this land? I don't know. Or is it the will of the gods that good men die and evil shall go on living? But an old man once told me what he believed and I think it better than all the rest."

"Tell us," Caelan demanded.

Valdar spoke no words but he lowered his cloak and locked his eyes on Garroway. Slowly the others moved in closer. Even Sir Dillian looked curious to hear what the old warrior had to say.

"When I die, I believe I will enter a great hall. Long tables filled with ale, wine, meats and fruits will await me. Beside those tables will be the people who, in my life time, I have come to love and cherish. They will bid me to take my place beside them. When my time comes and I enter such a place, I believe it is there I will await you all." Garroway smiled as he looked at each of his children. No words could be used to describe the love he felt for them.

"Let that time be far from now." Lilah planted a kiss on her man's head.

"All of you, sleep. We will ride at daybreak."

Garroway could not sleep. He lay on the grass, his head resting on his saddle. Lilah, as always, lay across him. The soft snores and heavy breathing of the others filled the air. He stared into the night sky and the stars, like eyes, peered back at him. Looking up he could see Lothar standing on the ruins above him. "Can't you sleep, old friend?"

"My mind wanders tonight." Lothar held out his curved sword, the shining blade twinkled in the star light.

Garroway slowly eased himself up, trying his best not to wake Lilah. He rose and climbed up the ruins until he stood with his old friend. This man he had known for more years than he could count. First, they had bled together during the prince's war, a small engagement fought between Brundea and Yorno. He was his first companion, his first dragon.

"What troubles you?" Garroway asked.

Lothar looked along his blade. "Do you remember the battle of the Weeping Widows?"

"I do, we chose the wrong side that day." Garroway laughed. "I caught two arrows in the ass and you one in the testicle if my memory serves me well."

Lothar didn't laugh. He replied solemnly, "It is the night before I speak of, do you remember that old man, Karim? He used to carry that broken sword. He told us he knew his time was up and he would not live to see the sun set on the morrow. And by his own words it was true, he got himself killed." Lothar paused and placed his sword back in his scabbard. He turned to Garroway, "I will die in combat, of this I am sure. Death in bed does not sit well within the warrior code."

"After a life time of war, maybe dying in peace isn't such as bad thing."

"I hope you can enjoy that peace for me, old friend." Lothar turned away and looked out into the night sky. "I believe I will await you in that great hall." He dropped down from the wall and walked away into the darkness.

A crunching of foot on stone brought Garroway to attention. He turned quickly. Out of the shadows Sir Dillian appeared, his body wrapped tightly in his black cloak. Garroway climbed down to meet his suspicious ally, his cold appearance and sleazy demeanour made him uncomfortable to be around.

"You call them all your children?" Sir Dillian asked, his curious eyes looked Garroway up and down. "But they are not of your blood. If the time came, would you really die for them as a real father would?"

"I would die for each of them ten times over." Garroway leant forwards towards Sir Dillian's face; the smell of Jasmine made him queasy. "You claim to love Allamantya but I doubt you would really give your life for this land."

"Allamantya is a mother to us all. A son shall do whatever is necessary to save her."

"When the time comes, we shall see if you are ready to spill your blood." Garroway turned his back and headed towards his sleeping Lilah.

"Come try again, if you can handle the shame brother." Caelan lowered his spear, admiring his victory.

Naleac rose to his feet, his pride dented. "Let's go!" he yelled as he jumped forward with his sword.

The steel crashed together as the brothers began to exchange blows. Naleac was on the front foot, forcing his brother back. Caelan deflected the blows, twisting his spear in front of him., trying not to allow Naleac to get too close, for then he would have him at a disadvantage.

"I told you Caelan was the stronger." Toran looked to Uriah and smiled.

"The fight is not over yet." Uriah flinched and ducked, as if he too was fighting.

"Three coins on Caelan," Roak placed his arm around Uriah's shoulder and pulled him close.

"Make it four." Uriah smiled.

Caelan twisted and moved, avoiding his brother's wild swings. One of the attacks was so close it severed one of his dreadlocks. The thick bead of black hair fell softly to the ground.

"Ha, one piece at a time!" Naleac began to gloat. The white of his teeth shone in the morning sun.

The loss of his hair seemed to spur Caelan on; he charged forward, thrusting out with his spear. His first attack caught his brother off balance, and he stumbled back. The second, he brought his spear around and caught Naleac in his stomach, winding him. He followed it up by sweeping his legs and knocking him back to the ground.

"You will never learn." Caelan smiled as he danced around him, playing to the crowd.

Lothar, Maarax and Roak began to cheer, clearly enjoying the contest. If two brothers fought, often it was these, always trying to outdo the other at any chance they got.

As Caelan took his eyes off his brother, Naleac realised this was his chance; he shot to his feet and lifted his sword up. Without space to defend himself, Caelan attempted to pivot but Naleac saw it coming and manoeuvred himself directly in his path. With the base of his sword, Naleac caught his twin directly on his chin. The impact of the blow took away his legs as his body crashed heavily to the ground. Naleac jumped over him and placed his sword on his chin. Victory was his.

"Four coins if you don't mind, brother." Uriah's grin spread across his face as he lifted his eyebrows up and down in quick succession.

Roak placed four coins in Uriah's little pouch and walked towards Naleac, "You cost me four coins!" Roak grabbed hold of Naleac and playfully lifted him off the ground. Instantly, Caelan flipped himself up from his back and onto his feet. He launched himself onto Roak's back and tried defended his brother. The three began to wrestle. Speed against power.

Garroway smiled as he approached the group. Watching the twins fight reminded him of the first day he ever laid eyes upon them. It had been a cold morning in Dagen; the sea crashed heavily against the shore. On the wet sand lay an old woman, her long black and grey hair swayed in the water. Her skin was pale and her eyes as white as a ghost. Beside her were two young boys, beautiful strong boys. They were fighting, punching and kicking at one another. As Garroway, approached them they instantly stopped. They turned and stood united, shoulder to shoulder. They showed no fear as they looked up at him. Their green eyes sparkled in defiance to this stranger who looked down towards them. It was their strength and loyalty to one another that had impressed Garroway so much, they would become his seventh and eighth dragons of Dagen.

By now Roak had both Caelan and Naleac in headlocks; his huge black muscles bulged from his arms as he squeezed them tightly. He began to laugh, his loud deep voice booming out.

Garroway knelt down and leant into Caelan's ear, "When you have a fight won, never give your opponent a second chance. For it could cost you your life."

The assassins, led by Sir Dillian Howard, rode across the rich open Antilion plains. Vast fields of green grass grew as tall as five feet, only to be brushed aside so feebly as the horses made their path. The air was warm and sun magnificent. As they descended down the hill, on the horizon they could see the palace, the ancient citadel and capital of all Allamantya. The huge white walls looked spectacular even from this distance. Across the last few metres of the field was a narrow forest filled with bushes and trees. A narrow dirt path cut between the forest and the open plains that lay on the far side. It was there they all dismounted.

"This is the place." Sir Dillian spread out his arm. "You will await them here."

Garroway admired the land, both the trees and long grass; it gave them the cover they needed. It was a good place for an ambush.

"How many will there be?" Lilah approached the old knight.

"Not many, maybe twenty. But if you are as good as your reputation boasts then it should be an easy task."

"I could kill twenty Allamantyan knights while I fucked a whore and drank my wine," Lothar laughed as he unsaddled his horse.

"And he is a one-eyed old man, so imagine what a good looking, two-eyed man could do." Naleac tapped Lothar on the back.

"This is where I shall leave you and by god's grace you will be triumphant." Sir Dillian pulled his horse away from Garroway.

"Leave no trace, leave no evidence, leave no witnesses." Garroway remembered the words, they echoed throughout his mind over and over. Oh, that wind, how it howled, like a woman screaming before the fatal blow, he heard it loud and clear. "Wait! You told me last night you would be willing to die for this land." Garroway looked towards Toran and nodded. "I am now going to put that to the test."

Sir Dillian turned, and before he knew it, Toran's arm shot out; with lighting speed it extended and gripped hold of him by throat. The Iron Bull's fingers began to tighten, squeezing away his rotten life. The old knight shuddered at the impact; his face was frozen with shock, his eyes ripe with fear. He began to claw helplessly at Toran's arm, he slapped and beat away at it, yet there was no effect. He whimpered and cried, frantically kicking out. The assassins stood around him and watched, emotionless. Their eyes locked onto the carnage that was taking place. Dribble began to fall from Sir Dillian's lips; it ran from the sides of his mouth and over Toran's hand.

Slowly Toran's fingers began to break through his skin, the flesh split as they slid into his throat. Sir Dillian let out a pathetic blood curdling cry, a high-pitched squeal as Toran's fingers clenched together. A sickening crunch exploded. They grabbed hold of his jugular; Toran suddenly twisted his hand back and forth. Sir Dillian began to choke on his own blood. The muscle tore as Toran yanked his arm back. Blood sprayed out, covering him in beads of red.

Sir Dillian dropped to his knees, his hands trying to the cover the gaping hole that now lay in his neck. He gasped for air as his life began to bleed out before him. Toran lowered his blooded hand; in his fist he held the old man's throat. The blood and tissue began to seep through his fingers.

Uriah knelt down beside him, looking into the old man's eyes. "Do you believe in your gods now?"

Sir Dillian slumped forwards. Crashing hard against the grass, his eyes widened further and the blood began to slowly ease out of the hole in his throat. He was dead.

Garroway looked to his *children*. "Move his body. Then prepare yourselves, for the moment has come." He then turned and drew his spear and looked along the path between the narrow cluster of trees and towards the White palace. "They sleep quietly in their beds; they think they are safe yet little do they know what hunts them."

Chapter 20
The Hunter and Its Prey

Where is she? Princess Tilia was saddled and ready to go. The morning sun was beautiful; the hot rays lit up the green grass beneath her horse's hooves. Tilia and her Valorian escort had been waiting in the palace courtyard for Princess Arrabella to arrive. Today was the day they were to go hunting. Tall white walls surrounded them. Sir Kaian Vadius and Sir Dejax Felios both looked restless as they stirred in their saddles.

Princess Tilia wore a well fitted red leather vest. It was cut low down her chest and her arms were free. It allowed her good movement when using her bow. Along her legs she wore a free-flowing red dress. Her long blonde hair was tied back in a bun. She felt most comfortable when saddled on Flame and in her hunting clothes.

A servant, riding a brown horse, charged towards her at full haste. "Your Highness, Princess Arrabella is not well but if you do not mind, I am to escort you to the Diamor Meadow."

A deep disappointment filled Tilia's heart. In way she had been expecting this. She nodded, signalling the servant to lead the way. All night the princess had looked forward to her day of hunting and bonding with her soon-to-be sister. But at least she would get to hunt. As they made their way across the mighty stone bridge, away from the palace and towards the city, the magnificent views meant nothing to her. In this moment her fears were beginning to come: the Antilion royal family were not accepting her. *Maybe Leylan is right, people want me for my crown, not my heart.*

While in the depths of her self-pity, Princess Tilia could see King Aristian; he was clad in long green robes and his sparkling golden crown was tightly rest upon his aging brow. He was mounted an on fine grey steed. "Princess," the king smiled, "why are you up so early?"

"I was meant to go hunting with Princess Arrabella but she is not well," Princess Tilia replied.

"It is rare to find my daughter awake at this hour." The king moved his horse closer to Tilia's before leaning forwards. "She cannot handle her wine. If you have no objections could I please ride with you? I have had a long morning talking with my high council. I think a long ride is much needed."

Tilia smiled. "Of course, we are heading to the Diamor Meadows. Do you hunt there often?"

“I am not one for hunting, but I will give it my best. But please don’t embarrass me too much. We have all heard of your skill with a bow.”

King Aristian and Princess Tilia rode along the outskirts of the city, down the long, cobbled steps and away into the beautiful Antilion countryside. The vast green landscape and clear blue skies were bright and magical. Rich coloured patches of the purple and orange flowers littered the fields. The column of horses made their way casually through the plains.

“Your Highness, look up ahead!” Sir Kaian called out.

On the horizon a herd of deer were running free; they were muscular and tall. Beautiful animals enjoying their freedom, the ground began to rumble slightly. Peaceful vibrations tingled throughout Princess Tilia’s body. Seeing such a magnificent sight, Tilia suddenly did not feel the urge to kill. She did not wish to stain this beautiful land with blood.

“What does Andros think of me?” Princess Tilia asked, her heart beginning to thump. Her small hands began to shake softly; she painfully awaited the king’s reply.

“I cannot read Andros’s mind but he is not like most men. As a child he was inseparable from his mother; women have this unique warmth that I believe can help him. After the first moment I saw you, I knew you were the one.”

The princess was taken aback by the king’s words. It was the last thing she expected; Tilia began to loosen the grip on her reins. She looked the king directly in the eye; his old face suddenly looked young as the bright rays of sun shone down from the heavens. His wrinkles began to disappear and he smiled. He looked like a man who rarely smiled; someone who could make others feel happy but he had no happiness of his own.

King Aristian continued, “My father would always tell me, ‘Every kingdom needs a king.’ It was one of the few things me and my father could agree on, but every king needs a queen. It takes a special kind of woman to be queen; they in a way must be mightier than their king. She must council him when he is lost, comfort him when he is sad and hold him when he is weak. I believe this woman is you; you are the queen that the Allamantyan Empire and the Western realm so desperately needs.”

The hunting party headed away from the open plains and towards a large cluster of trees. A narrow dirt path cut through the centre and on the other side tall strands of grass rose high. King Aristian said he once hunted Antilor boars along this forest, although he warned her that their ferocity had once killed two of his group. They were twice the size of traditional boars and had four tusks. Tilia was eager to test her skill against such dangerous animals. Sir Kaian tried to persuade her to hunt the deer but she would have none of it. They made their way underneath the shaded passage, trees and bushes flanking them either side. Bright single rays of light burst from above the trees and through the leaves.

Up ahead, a lone figure clad in a long black cloak emerged from within the bushes. It walked to the centre of the path; the image looked all more the harrowing as it moved slowly through the rays of golden light. It suddenly stopped, turning to face them. It stood still and had no fear of the oncoming horses and armoured soldiers.

"Step aside!" Sir Kaian Vadius ordered. He turned to the king and princess. "I will make sure it moves."

Princess Tilia pulled on her reins and the hunting party stopped. She watched as her sworn sword rode ahead. Tilia could not hear what was spoken but it was clear Sir Kaian was demanding the figure move out of the way. King Aristian was still talking, yet she zoned out, focusing on what was happening up ahead. Something didn't seem right; maybe it was her woman's intuition.

Unexpectedly the black clad figure launched into the air; he jumped like a rabbit, revealing a long, curved spear. Sir Kaian reared up on his horse to defend himself but it was too late. The spear came slashing down, slicing into his neck, removing his head. Fountains of blood sprayed out from Sir Kaian's stump; his body, stiff as a board, fell from his horse.

Panic and horror took hold of Tilia; she froze, unsure if what she had just seen was real. Shouting and rumbling thundered beside her. The Valorian soldiers, led by Sir Dejax Felios, charged forwards, ready to protect her.

"Sound the horn!" King Aristian screamed.

The trumpeter lifted his horn to his lips, blowing with everything he had; the call briefly rang out only to be cut short as an arrow found a way into his throat. The impact launched the soldier back from his saddle, knocking into the king. Aristian's horse brayed and whined, rising up onto its hind legs, kicking out wildly. The sudden movement caused the king to lose his grip; his feet dropped from the stirrups and he fell from his saddle. His body crashed hard against the ground; he yelled in pain as his body twisted and bent against a thick root sticking from the dirt.

Tilia quickly dropped down from her saddle. Just as she fell to the ground, an arrow thudded against the large oak tree to her back. Her horse Flame startled and rode off into the forest. Tilia collapsed beside the King who was clearly injured from his fall.

****

The black clad figure threw his cloak from his back, revealing Garroway. He lifted his spear into the air. "Kill today, so we may live tomorrow!" he yelled at the top of his voice. Today his children would put those words to the test.

Like a pack of wolves, the assassins surrounded the Valorian soldiers. They emerged from the trees and bushes like hungry animals. Each of them was calculated hunters, bred on blood and battle. They honed in on their prey, killing without mercy, without compassion. Garroway stood at the back as his children swarmed forwards. Lilah stayed by his side.

The soldiers of Valanor formed a semi-circle, two rows deep, protecting their princess. They stood side by side, shield to shield, brother to brother. Their bravery was to be respected but it did them no good against Garroway and his children. The assassins smashed against the shield wall, like a tidal wave of terror, hacking through them like a farmer's sickle through wheat. The noise of steel on steel rang out through the forest; the sound of death would soon follow.

As always, Toran and Roak were first into the fray; they swung their mighty broadswords, hacking and killing as they made way for their *brothers* and *sisters*. The men of Valanor screamed and wailed as the assassin's blades cut through flesh and shattered bone. One Valorian soldier was almost cleaved into two as Toran's sword exploded against his hip, his body split, his guts spewing out onto the ground.

Garroway yelled, "Now!" For he had seen the opening Toran and Roak had made with their immense power. It was now time for the others to be unleashed; Maarax fired his bow with deadly accuracy taking down any man his hawk eyes laid their glare upon. Caelan, Naleac and Valdar broke through on the Valorian left flank, destroying their shield wall. One soldier, however, put up a valiant defence as he traded blows with Valdar, even slashing the assassin's breastplate before Naleac came to his brother's aid, thrusting his sword through his back, killing him instantly.

Uriah and Zaira followed behind Toran, taking care of his leftovers. Uriah spun his short swords in his hands, smiling as a Valorian spearman charged him. At the very last second, Uriah side rolled to his right, jumping up and thrusting his blades into the soldier's exposed side. He pulled his swords free, covering himself in the man's blood. A loud wooshing flew past Uriah's head, making him flinch; the force lifted his long hair from his back. He turned to see a spear embedded into a soldier's chest, pinning him to a tree.

"Even now you need your sister to watch your back!" Zaira shouted as she flew past Uriah and pulled her spear free.

The chaos continued as the assassins fought with a demonic fury. Like beasts ravaging a herd they slaughtered all that stood before them, as screams rang out through the forest. The green grass turned red as the Valorian soldiers painted it with their blood.

"No surrender!" one of the soldiers yelled defiantly, his sword shaking in his hand. He charged forwards only to receive an arrow in his gut. The impact stopped him dead in his tracks, and he gasped for air. Yet the only thing he got was Zaira's spear across his throat.

The assassins were relentless, butchering Valorian soldiers like cattle, for they knew behind that shield wall of blue lay their prize: one hundred and twenty thousand Allamantyan gold coins to take one life, a royal life.

Rhodesha and Lothar exploded on the panic-stricken right flank. Some of the Valorian soldiers with bravery in their hearts stood their ground, refusing to accept their fate. Once the assassins were in close, the soldiers dropped their spears and drew their swords, fighting to the last. Lothar lunged forwards, striking one man in his breastplate; he withdrew his sword and pivoted to his left, avoiding an oncoming attack before returning with a venomous counter of his own that struck the soldier across his jaw, ripping it from his face.

"This is easier than fucking a whore in a brothel," Lothar laughed as he turned to exchange blows with two Valorian swordsmen. He cut one across his chest and the other tasted his blade through his stomach,

"Less talking and more killing!" Rhodesha interrupted as she charged forwards, killing without mercy. Her sword screamed for blood. None of the Valorian soldiers thought of glory, just survival as Rhodesha challenged them. Her speed and athleticism were outstanding, pivoting from right to left, jolting back and forth, killing was as easy for her as it was drawing breath.

Toran roared as he crashed his sword against a soldier's shield, the impact lifted the man off of his feet and, as he landed, Roak thrust down with his blade. Metal shattered and bone broke as Roak's sword pinned the soldier to the ground. Like a wild bull, Toran charged forwards, stampeding into the second shield wall. The crash echoed as his body slammed its way through; the Valorian soldiers flew into the air like bits of sand in a strong wind. Roak followed behind, swinging his sword, killing those who stood around him.

The sound of battle raged through the forest; the bloodied blades of the assassins clashed with the gleaming Valorian swords. No mercy was given, only death. Clanging of steel, the breaking of bones and the screams of the dying painted this once green paradise with the sound of hell.

The assassins pressed forwards; they would claim their gold with blood. The Valorian shield wall was broken, shattered like glass. The soldiers fell back, some fled for their lives, while others, who still clawed for breath, moved back towards their princess. They encircled her, their sword hands shaking as the assassins like hungry lions closed in.

Garroway slowly moved behind his children; like a soulless demon he stepped over the dead. His eyes burned with a thirst for blood and gold. The dying Valorians pleaded for their lives. Lilah, who was by Garroway's side, took care of the wounded with her spear. Gut wrenching slashing and stabbing rendered the injured silent.

Only ten Valorian soldiers remained, each dripping with sweat and fear. They bunched in tight, trying as best as they could to protect their princess. Sir Dejax, bloodied and injured, stood at the centre. The assassins stood opposite; they had barely broken into a sweat. The dragons of Dagen smiled as the blood of their victims dripped from their faces.

"Fight on! No surrender!" a Valorian soldier yelled as he broke rank.

Caelan dived forwards, skewing the man with his spear. His *brothers* and *sister* followed, obliterating the remaining nine soldiers with ravenous terror. Arms and heads were severed and bodies hacked to pieces as the assassins finished off the last remnants of the Valorian guard.

A silence fell over the forest; the screams were no more. A soft wind blew through the trees, signalling the end of the carnage. The assassins slowly parted, allowing Garroway to step forwards. On the floor were both the princess and the king. Aristian was clearly hurt; he clutched at his ribs as he defiantly forced himself to his feet.

"Stay behind me," the king ordered as he ushered the princess back. He dragged a sword from the ground before straining himself upright, his sword uneasily wavering in his right hand. "Cowards!" he spat.

"You are brave, old king, but that will not save you or her today." Garroway turned his back and walked away. "Kill them." His words were soft and slow.

King Aristian yelled with defiance. He stepped forwards, swinging his sword. Zaira opted to meet him head on, both blades met in the air with a resounding 'clang'. The king drew his sword back and unleashed another assault; he may not have been the warrior his brothers were, but he was willing to die like one. Zaira easily parried his attack and then grabbed hold of the king's sword hand, squeezing it tightly. Caelan and Naleac pounced like cats thrusting their weapons into the king's side. Aristian screamed in agony as the blades cut into his flesh.

Princess Tilia jumped up, grabbing the king as he fell back into her arms. His blood poured from his wounds and over her hands.

"Finish her," Toran ordered, pointing towards Uriah.

Tilia looked up as Uriah rushed forwards, his short swords held aloft, ready to inflict the final blow, yet at that last moment Uriah hesitated. Tilia closed her eyes and squeezed the king to her bosom, awaiting their fate.

A mighty roar exploded, like a dragon fixated with rage. Birds flew from the branches and tiny animals scattered to their burrows. Upon the brow of the hill amongst the trees the mighty Beyorn appeared. He charged forwards to the king's aid, growling like a monster unleashed from the deepest darkest depths of hell. He swung his brutal battle axe above his head as he stampeded towards the assassins.

The assassins looked up in shock. For a moment they were all spellbound.

"The beast of Golgia," Garroway whispered.

Behind Beyorn, the Allamantyan cavalry appeared, clad in shining silver armour and glorious green tunics. They brandished their swords and lances as they descended down the slope.

Lothar took one step forwards. He and Garroway exchanged a glance. "I choose today!" Lothar said. He spun his sword in his hand before shouting to the skies, "Valla eskalar Yorgala." He sprinted out to meet Beyorn head on.

The mighty beast of Golgia swung out with his axe. Lothar forward rolled, avoiding the attack. Both men turned back to face one another, exchanging blows; sparks flew from their steel as their weapons scraped against one another. Beyorn's huge axe missed Lothar's head by millimetres as he ducked and crouched to avoid been cleaved in two. The one-eyed Lothar lunged upwards, off the ground; he glided through the air like a hawk. Beyorn however caught him mid-jump. The beast's huge hand grabbed Lothar by his throat, a grip as powerful as an anaconda. The impact jolted Lothar back; his sword fell from his hand. Beyorn held the helpless Lothar above his head and roared, before slamming him hard to the ground. Dirt and leaves rose in the air as his body impacted with the dried earth.

Lothar gasped in shock, winded. Beyorn then proceeded to ram his fist into Lothar's chest, causing blood to spray from the assassin's mouth. The beast raised his foot above Lothar's head before forcing it down onto his face. At the moment of impact, Lothar's head exploded like melon; bits of brain and skull sprayed across the ground.

Garroway looked on in horror. Allamantyan cavalry swarmed through the trees and past Beyorn, charging straight towards him and his children. He screamed one word, "Run!"

Chapter 21
A Man Without Honour

Danaka's body tightened, gulping hard as she swallowed the last part of her ale. She watched as Duro unsteadily walked forwards, swaying from side to side. The wood creaked with each step he took. Malcolm Reymor appeared to be slightly confused as he watched Duro approach him; he looked him up and down before a smile began to spread across Malcolm's bearded face. He extended his arms and embraced Duro like brother. Duro's arms however hung by his side.

"Duro! You old sour puss," Malcolm squeezed him tightly, "when did you return?"

Duro stepped away. "A month ago. Sit with me at my table."

Both sat themselves down, Sir Malcolm beside Danaka. He was a big man and scruffy, smelling of old leather and ale. His scent made Danaka flinch as she subtly began to move her chair away from him.

"Two ales!" Malcolm roared, raising his hand in the air. "It has been too long, old friend!" He smacked Duro on his arm.

"It has been five years." Duro lifted the last of his ale to his lips, his eyes never left Malcolm.

"Give me those." Malcolm grabbed the two jugs from the bartender and placed them on the table. "I work as a tax collector now. My boss is Lord Ruskforn Derry, miserable old cunt. I miss being captain of the guard at Jade Stone. The fun we had, aye!" He laughed as he drank down his ale. The froth dripped from his jug and settled in his beard. Malcolm's eyes turned to Danaka; he observed her like a man would a painting. He wiped the ale from his mouth. "This your wife, Duro? I am shocked, you were never the marrying type. You turned down Princess Evelyn to marry a commoner?"

"She is not my wife."

"This one is pretty but that would have been a bad decision, friend."

Danaka frowned; she was about to reply when she calmed herself. *Bad decision? Who does he think he is? He isn't exactly anything special himself.* Danaka looked at Duro. Considering the two were old friends he did not look too pleased to see Malcolm.

"I heard you fought with our eastern mountain allies against the Samorans." Malcolm coughed loudly before spitting on the floor.

"Aalafar and Roldur have long since fallen." Duro's eyes moved towards Danaka; they exchanged a glance before he looked back to Malcolm. "So they never got round to knighting you then?"

"After, eh, you know, after what happened." Malcolm paused, before taking another swig of ale. "Things were never the same again at Jade Stone. House Redmond stopped the trade coming in and your father and mother dove deeper and deeper into despair so I had to move on to pastures greener." Malcolm looked uneasy; he rubbed his hands on his leather tunic. "It saddened me deeply when your father died."

"I did not see you at his funeral." Duro looked Malcolm straight in the eye.

Malcolm paused. "I wanted to go but with my work here I did not have time." His words were uneasy and rushed; he quickly changed the subject. "So what brings you to the shithole that is Ashfeld anyway?"

"You."

Malcolm smiled uncomfortably. "Me? How did you know I was here? The last you saw of me was at Baron's Bay, when you were banished to the east."

Duro slowly placed his jug on the table and turned to Malcolm. His voice was slow and his words strong. "Sir Claris told me."

"Sir Claris?" Malcolm hesitated; feeling uncomfortable, he began to scratch at his beard.

"Dying men usually have quite a lot to say but calm yourself." Duro poured himself some more ale. "It is not you who I hunt, you did not cut Darion down; I was sat beside you, remember? Where is your cousin, Castel Damari?"

Malcolm began to stutter. "He doesn't work with me anymore."

"That is not what I asked. Sir Claris told me you two worked together here. Where did he go?"

"He is my cousin, I cannot just tarnish my honour by betraying my kin." Malcolm attempted to stand from his seat.

Duro shot up, grabbing Malcolm by his tunic and dragging him back down. "I came here for blood and I'm yet to have my fill of it."

Malcolm winced as Duro forced his head onto the table. The jugs of ale shuddered as his face collided with the wood. He struggled to reply, "Was a prince's blood not enough?"

"Only when all those who deserve to die are dead, shall my sword rest."

The punters in the tavern began to uncomfortably stare over as Duro continued to press down on Malcolm's head. They started to mutter amongst themselves but none did anything to intervene. Danaka however pushed her chair back away from the table. Griffin stirred from his sleep.

"You swore to the king that your quest for vengeance ended when Prince Varden died. So you are truly a man without honour?" Malcolm grimaced as Duro bashed his face against the hard wood.

"I discarded my honour the day Darion decided to die for his."

"Okay, okay, last I heard Castel was working as Marshal Borin DeGrey's champion in Doldayne."

Duro slowly released Malcolm from his grasp. Danaka felt a little uneasy but violence seemed to follow Duro around like a bad smell so she was beginning to get used to it.

Malcolm rose to his feet, slightly unsteady. "So it is true then, what the rumours say. That it was you who killed Amber Blackstone?"

Duro frowned and took another swig from his jug. He did not reply.

Malcolm turned to Danaka. "Be careful the company you keep, little girl. For this one rapes and kills women."

Danaka watched as Malcolm collected his things and left the tavern. An awkward silence seemed to spread across the room. Duro said nothing as he sat sipping his ale and even Griffin was quiet. Danaka leant down and stroked his warm fur. As Danaka observed Duro, she began to think, *it is true I know nothing of this man or his past. He can be cold and distant but something draws me to him. We both have a sadness that dwells over us.*

The room was damp and dark; a double bed with stained white sheets was at the centre. To the right was a large window which looked out onto the street below. Danaka pressed her fingers against the glass. Outside it was dark, only a few lanterns lit up the street. She could see a few drunken men staggering around outside; they were shouting at one another but she could not make out the words they said.

Griffin began to sniff around the room, climbing over the bed and then near the old burnt out fire place, before finally curling up in a ball. Duro stumbled into the room; he dropped his things to the floor and collapsed onto the bed. His jug of ale crashed to the floor, spilling out everywhere.

"Oh, great!" Danaka yelled. "That's it, take up all the bed and make a mess everywhere."

Duro spread out across the bed; his dark hair was messy and over his eyes. Sitting beside him, Danaka smiled as she brushed the few strands of hair away from his face. She then began to run her fingers down his well sculptured face. His stubble was rough and sharp but his jaw felt strong. He began to stir and she quickly pulled her hand away.

"Not yet, not yet," Duro mumbled to himself as he rolled over.

Danaka leant forward. "What did you say?"

"He calls to me, from far across the river bank." Duro began to chomp at his lips, his eyes slowly opened as if he was waking from a dream. "He bids me to take my place beside him. Every night I see him, he calls out to me. So I play for him." Duro slowly raised his flute to his lips; the sound was broken and out of tune. "I want to cross the river." Duro suddenly grabbed Danaka's hand, squeezing it tightly.

"Why don't you go to him?" Danaka could feel the roughness of his palms.

"No… Not yet, I have things to do." Duro's eyes closed slowly and his grip loosened.

Danaka brushed his hair back and ran her hand down his arm. "Sleep."

She lay beside Duro as he slept. Danaka could not see him as it was so dark but she could hear his heavy breathing. She didn't know why but with him so close she felt safe. Her body began to relax as she pressed her head back against her thin pillow. A small tear was in the side and feathers had started to seep out. She thought about how different her life was; it had only been a few days but she felt free, her life was not confined to one place. Now she could explore, see new things and meet new people, but it was not without its dangers. She thought back to the words Duro told her. "*This world we live in, is a loveless place, unforgiving and uncaring. There is no gold at the end of the rainbow.*" At the time she believed what he had said, even now she did, but one day she would prove him wrong. "I will find that happiness, that gold," she whispered to herself before closing her eyes.

Bright light, of both red and yellow, began to fill the room; its powerful glow flickered against the wall. Danaka stirred from her sleep; a dark fog seemed to form over her eyes. Through the crackling and distant calls she could hear a woman screaming. Then Griffin began to bark, loudly. He ran towards the door, clawing at the wood.

Danaka quickly sat up. The room was hot, sweat oozed from her body. She jumped out of bed and headed towards the window. The wooden floor was roasting, the heat burnt through her thin sandals. Each step was more painful than the one before. Outside was chaos, mighty red flames had consumed the buildings opposite her, the fire roared as it wrapped its fiery arms around the charred wood. Below in the street, a woman was on her knees screaming; her arms were in the air as if she was calling for help from the gods. Out of the shadows a man appeared clad in black; he pulled out a knife and slit her throat. He threw her body to the ground and ran down the street. To Danaka's horror it was happening everywhere, figures in black armed with swords, knifes and meat cleavers were attacking people. Turning away from the window, she could see dark smoke seeping from underneath the door.

"Shit!" Danaka ran towards the bed. "Wake up! Wake up!" She grabbed hold of Duro's shoulder and began to shake him. "We need to go!" Duro barely moved as he replied with nothing more than a loud snore. "How can you sleep, you big oaf!" Danaka stepped back and clenched her fist and with all her might she lamped him across his cheek. A stinging pain shot through her hand, her knuckles twitched and throbbed.

Duro shot up, dazed, holding his cheek as he looked around. He closed his eyes as he moved his hands over the top of his head, his voice was groggy and low. "I feel like there is a battle going on inside my head."

"There is one going on outside!" Danaka paused before she calmly added, "Oh, and the tavern is on fire."

"What?" Duro staggered to his feet and looked around the room. "We need to move."

"Yes, that would be smart." Danaka pulled Griffin close to her. She watched Duro sway back and forth as he moved; he almost fell back, sliding against the wall before regaining his balance. Danaka looked at him with disgust, "Are you still drunk?"

Duro dropped down and grabbed his sword; he half strapped it to his back. It fell loose down his side. "Move aside," Duro coughed and pushed Danaka away. He raised his hand and held it to the wood of the door; he turned to Danaka and nodded.

Danaka closed her eyes as the door flung open. A strong gush of hot air crashed against her body; she began to cough, clawing for breath. She breathed deeply but the dry air she took in burnt her nostrils. The stinging sensation made her eyes water.

"Stay close to me." Duro grabbed Danaka by her arm and pulled her behind him.

The flames were raging; they had taken over the bar area and were creeping up the banister. The fire screamed as it consumed everything in its path. Danaka could feel her skin burning, the heat was unbearable. Duro pulled her forwards. The fire was overpowering, the red flames were so bright, they forced her eyes shut. Suddenly the panels beneath her feet gave way, they crumbled and snapped. Duro jumped forwards as Danaka fell. He grabbed hold of her wrist, just about stopping her falling to her death. He yelled in pain as his arm overextended. Duro squeezed her wrist as tightly as he could.

Danaka screamed as she dangled above the raging hell below. Her heart pounded as she looked down. The fire had burnt away the tables and chairs, a charred black body lay engulfed in flames. "Pull me up!" she screamed. Danaka could feel Duro's sweaty palm sliding from her wrist.

Duro let out a roar as he lifted her up, pulling her to safety. She did not escape from the fire at Tomellburg to die in one at Ashfeld. She choked as the smoke and ash filled her lungs. Duro picked her up and flung her over his shoulder. Disorientated and shocked, she looked up, seeing the world covered in burning red flame. To her horror, through the fire and over the broken walk way, she could see Griffin stranded. He was barking and backing away as the flames came towards him.

"Stop!" Danaka cried out, begging Duro to put her down. Once on her feet, she screamed, "Griffin!" It was as if her child was stranded, she wanted to jump the hole and hold him in her arms.

"Step back!" Duro pulled her away from the hole.

"Get off me; I am not going without him!"

"You would not reach the other side." Duro pointed down towards the raging flames.

The gap was now consumed with fire, it crackled and exploded as wood panels broke and fell away.

"Come here, boy!" Danaka beckoned him towards her. Yet all he did was back away, barking at the flames before whining. The black smoke began to rise, hindering their vision.

The whole inn was riddled with fire; if they did not get outside soon, they would be trapped. Suddenly Duro grabbed Danaka by her dress and forced her towards the end of balcony. The fires raged below her. She scrambled back clawing at his arm, in total shock as to what was happening.

Duro turned to Griffin and yelled out, "Save her!"

Griffin growled, locking in on Danaka. He stepped forwards then crouched, launching himself off the crumbling walkway. Just as he jumped, it gave way. The wood collapsed, resulting in a deafening crash. Griffin's athletic body stretched out, his sable fur shone in the red light produced by the fire. The flames rose up, flickering just below his paws as he flew over the hole and landed by Danaka's feet. Before Danaka had anytime to embrace her companion, Duro dragged her down her burning stairs and towards the exit. Griffin sprinted alongside them. Everything around them was burning fiercely, even the door was ablaze. Duro fought his way through the flames. He kicked down the door and they all collapsed outside. They gasped and clawed for breath. Smoke began to seep out of the open door way and into the alleyway.

Danaka looked up, and through the darkness, she could see Ashfeld had turned into a living hell. Buildings all around her were covered in flames; people screamed and pleaded as they saw their homes and businesses going up in smoke. Once again, she saw another black hooded figure appear from the shadows; it glided like a ghost and skewered a woman as she attempted to throw water on the flames. The sword burst out of her chest, spraying the cobbled floor red, killing her instantly.

"Get up, we need to move." Duro's voice had an air of panic. Something she had not heard before.

He leant down and pulled Danaka to her feet. They moved down the alleyway and away from the main street. She looked back as they started to run. She could see the lady on the floor, a puddle of blood had now encircled her. People ran over her like she didn't even exist.

Suddenly Duro stopped, and Danaka crashed into his back. He felt has hard as a stone wall. Three silhouettes stood at the end of the alleyway, faceless shadows, blocking their path. The red flames burning brightly, shone out from behind them. The fire crackled and hissed. Screams filled the streets. People sprinted back and forth, chaos had erupted like volcano. In their hands the three shadows held swords.

A panic began to take hold of Danaka, "It's Hazar!" she yelled as she stepped back. Somehow those shadows were more frightening than the burning buildings.

"Get behind me," Duro replied as he stood in front of her.

Griffin growled loudly, snapping violently.

"Duro, I am sorry it has come to this." It was Malcolm who spoke as he stepped forth from the darkness. He was clad in a thick breast plate and rings of mail covered his arms and legs. "Did you really think I would give up my cousin so easily? These are my friends, Aron and Tristos."

Both men, who flanked him either side, walked forwards. Tristos brandished his sword, swinging it back and forth. His hair was ginger and had a patch over one eye. Aron who stood on the left was the taller; he had dark hair and a patchy beard. He moved more casually as he rested his sword over his shoulder. Each was dressed in boiled leather and had thin rusted mail covering their arms.

"I am glad you have friends," Duro drew his sword, "no one should die alone."

"Three against one, does that remind you of anything?" Malcolm smiled.

"He is not alone!" Danaka drew her sword.

Malcolm, Aron and Tristos all began to laugh. Griffin growled louder.

"With all this going on," Malcolm raised his hands and pointed towards the riot, "No one will ask questions as to how two strangers wound up getting themselves killed."

Anger consumed Duro, his eyes burned with hate. He gripped his sword tightly and lowered himself into his fighting position. "If they get past me, run to the street and don't stop till you are far from this place." He stepped forward.

Malcolm, Aron and Tristos charged them, yelling as they approached. From a low fighting stance Duro brought up his sword; he intercepted all three of their attacks, his blade slashed against theirs. He carried the greater power as he knocked them back. He, in turn, lunged forward and caught Tristos with his elbow, dropping him instantly. He turned quick as Malcolm came at him, their swords crashed together. Exchanging blows, Duro forced him back. Duro however lacked the finesse and skill that had taken him to victory over Sir Claris. He swayed and stumbled, losing his balance. He moved his sword from his right hand to his left, clearly injured from when he caught Danaka. Malcolm swung violently at him. Duro ducked just in time as the sword glided above his head; sparks flew as the steel screeched against the stone wall to his back.

Duro pushed out away from the wall, standing toe to toe with Malcolm. His attacks were venomous. With each powerful blow Malcolm was able to deflect he staggered back. Aron, gaunt and long limbed, appeared behind Duro and grabbed hold of him. Duro kicked out, hitting Malcolm in the chest knocking him back. Duro then instantly snapped his head back, smashing it into Aron's face and then swung him from his back like nothing more than cat. Aron flew through the air and onto Malcolm. Tristos however crawled to his feet, blood pouring from his nose; he lunged at Duro and plunged forward with his sword. Danaka stepped up and deflected the blow. The sword vibrated in her hand and it almost fell from her grip.

Tristos yelled like a man possessed as he charged at Danaka, lashing out. Danaka lifted her sword up, deflecting the attacks raining down towards her. Tristos's sword slashed against her own, his blows were strong but wild. Danaka could see them coming, but she could do little more than to hold her sword up to defend herself. Duro's training went out straight out of her mind.

Duro, seeing her predicament instantly tried to come to her aid. Malcolm and Aron however had other ideas as they once again charged him. Both swung wildly with their swords; each had no skill, just the intent to kill. Duro stood his ground and three exchanged blows. With the fires raging behind them, they were three mighty silhouettes with glistening swords fighting for their lives.

Alone, Danaka retreated straight back. The alleyway was too narrow; she was unable to use angles to manoeuvre around Tristos. Her feet began to build up speed as she stumbled back. Her body thudded hard against the cobbled walk way and her sword flew from her hand. The blade screeched along the stone and away from her grasp. Tristos smiled as he brought his arm up, his sword was high in the air. The steel flickered in light from the flames. A psychotic look filled Tristos's face as if the pleasure of killing Danaka excited him. She closed her eyes, waiting for him to deliver the final blow.

Griffin charged forward and launched at Tristos. With his lion-like strength he locked his jaw around Tristos's arm and dragged him to the ground. Tristos shrieked as Griffin snapped and tore at him like a rag doll, pulling him from side to side. Tristos let out blood curdling screams as Griffin tore off chunks of his flesh, almost ripping his arm off from the elbow down. Tristos kicked out and swung wildly, but Griffin stepped back, avoiding the attacks. Tristos's arm was held together by nothing more than a few strips of skin. He screamed as he attempted to crawl away. Griffin eyed up his prey, before pouncing once again. This time his teeth sunk into Tristos's neck. Bone twisted and broke as Griffin dragged his limp body along the ground and into the darkness.

A hard thud, followed by a deafening scream, brought Danaka's attention back to Duro. She turned and saw his sword through Aron's stomach. Aron grimaced in pain as he pulled it free before throwing his body to the ground. Malcolm backed away, fear gripping hold of him.

"I see why they never knighted you." Duro panted loudly before spitting on the floor.

Malcolm leant forwards, wiping sweat from his face. "By now Darion had screamed like a whore."

Duro sprinted forwards; bringing his sword up from his waist. Malcolm cowered back, feebly trying to defend himself. Duro's sword crashed against his foes with an intense strength. Malcolm's sword arm swung from side to side as he gave ground. Fear had spread across his face as he was forced against the wall of the alleyway. One mighty brutal attack from Duro brought Malcolm's sword crashing to the ground.

"Please, please! Don't! Forgive me!" Malcolm pleaded like a scared child as Duro pinned him to the wall.

"It is the gods who forgive, not I." Duro instantly pressed the tip of his sword against Malcolm's chin, before forcing it upwards. Malcolm's eyes expanded violently, and blood sprayed from his mouth as the blade exploded out the top of his head. Brain matter and blooded bone decorated the wall behind him.

Danaka retched at what she had just witnessed, her stomach twisted and throbbed. Griffin appeared behind her, blood smeared across his sable fur. She pulled him close, relieved he was safe.

Duro removed his sword from Malcolm's chin. "Up with you girl!" He paused slightly before yelling, "Move now!"

Startled, Danaka quickly rose to her feet. Looking back, she saw a group of black cloaked figures coming down the alleyway from the main street. Their bloodied blades glistened in the moonlight. Danaka sprinted with everything she had. It felt as if she moved on air. Her feet never seemed to the touch the ground. Through the flames and smoke, past the pleas for help, she forced her way forwards, around the bend into the wide-open space where Elio had rallied his followers. Danaka headed for the small barn in the corner, where the inn keeper had taken Duro's horses.

The two horses brayed and panicked, rearing up on their hind legs and kicking out. The barn was ablaze. Flames had engulfed the hay and the old wooden frame. Duro cut them free before dragging his chests away from the fire. Danaka turned back towards the smoke; in the darkness she could hear sword cutting into flesh and the pleas for mercy before finally the screams of the dying. Then suddenly, everything, went silent; only the sound of fire crackling away over chard wood could be heard. Then the figures emerged through the smoke, faceless monsters. Eight men clad in black appeared, their swords dripping with blood.

Danaka froze, unable to move, unsure what to do. The monsters closed in, circling her like a pack of wolves. Suddenly she felt her feet lift from the ground, she began to hover. She felt the holy hand of angels of Ollaria'h against her skin, lifting her, guiding her to heaven. Fields of green and beautiful rivers of blue replaced the raging fires of Ashfeld. Danaka hovered like bird as she saw nothing but a paradise. A golden-haired prince rode a steed of the purest white. His eyes sparkled like the stars on the night sky. Flames of red soon engulfed her paradise burning it away like an old painting.

Danaka looked down; the ground beneath her feet was moving. A strong grip pulled tight against her stomach, looking up she saw Duro. His bloodied arm squeezed her tightly. He charged through Ashfeld upon the back of his great horse, behind she could see the smaller horse following loyally. All around, the city was burning; through the smoke and fire she could hear those horrible rhythmic chants that Hazar had been chanting.

"Yakash Mudra! Yakash Mudra!" the calls echoed out over and over.

Duro pulled hard on the reins. His horse brayed, its hooves knocking against the cobbled ground. "Climb up," he ordered.

Danaka did as he commanded; she dropped to the ground. Duro then extended his arm; she took it before he pulled her onto his saddle.

"Hold me tight, don't let go."

Danaka slid her arms around his waist. His body felt hard and strong. Wet stains of blood ran down his tunic. Looking up, she saw the last remains of Ale and Tits tavern burning away. Down the bottom of the street and through the smoke, more black cloaked figures began to appear, spread out in a single line. "There are too many! They are going to kill us."

Griffin suddenly began to bark furiously. His muscles tightened as he snapped his jaws at the figures as they moved closer.

Duro drew his sword; Danaka could feel his heart beating in his chest.

"I have no intention of dying today!" Duro kicked into his spurs, and his horse instantly took off at full speed. Duro held his sword arm out to his right; the bright blade glistened in the flames. Duro yelled powerfully, no fear was in his voice as he let out his battle cry.

Danaka wanted to close her eyes but she could not; she was compelled to watch as they drew closer to the hooded figures in front of her. She could see Griffin charging alongside them. Suddenly rows of half-dressed soldiers began to appear to her left. Some were topless but held spears and shields; others wore boiled leather and rings of mail but without helmets. They had clearly been woken by the chaos that had befallen Ashfeld. The soldiers took the black cloaked murderers by surprise, hitting them on their left flank. Duro however did not slow down he crashed straight into the men head-on. Danaka held tight as the impact thudded hard throughout her body. One of the cloaked men flew back, his limp body sliding against the broken slabs. Duro swung his sword out, from right to left; one of his attacks caught a man across his chest, his black cloak split as blood sprayed from his wound. He screamed in agony as he fell to his knees. Four men blocked their path. Duro's horse reared up, kicking out.

"Mudra!" a murderous voice screamed out.

A figure appeared out of the darkness. It was a woman. She ran as if she was possessed by the devil, a bloodied knife in her hand. She crashed into the side of their horse, her eyes blood red. At the moment of impact, Duro let out a cry of pain. Danaka was startled. Losing her grip, she frantically clung on, grabbing his tunic to stop herself falling. Duro instinctively retaliated, his sword smashing into the woman's head. Her black hair turned red as her skull split like rotten fruit. Duro kicked back into his spurs and they kept going. He did not stop. They charged through the chaos, leaving a path of destruction behind them until they passed through the gatehouse and over the drawbridge. Once safely on the other side, Duro pulled on his reins. His smaller horse stopped instantly. He looked exhausted but also happy to be away from the terror.

Danaka looked back. Screams echoed through the smoke as it seeped through the entrance of Ashfeld; yellow and red flames shone out through the darkness. "Griffin!" she screamed. Then, as if by command, he appeared through the smoke, he belted towards them at full pace. He charged straight past Danaka and Duro and did not stop. She watched as he ran across the field and away from the city.

Duro turned his horse and followed him. Danaka breathed deeply, she was safe. *Well, at least for now.*

Chapter 22
Hell Awaits All Sinners

Aristian was frozen; an eternal sea of darkness lay before him. His body felt cold as he continued to fall deeper and deeper into the shadows. He suddenly appeared at a great gate. Raging blood red flames roared all around the dark iron beams. As mighty as the flames were, they offered no warmth, just a heartless cold that could produce nothing but sorrow. Within the fire he could see his father's chambers; he lay stricken on his bed. Three shadows lingered around him like vampires ready to feast upon his blood. Aristian's heart began to sink, for he knew what he was being shown; the shadows slowly began to reveal themselves. He could see Daemar and his sister Drusilla; at the centre he could see himself: young, ambitious and ready for power.

His younger self held a pillow to his chest, he approached his father slowly. Rhythmically the three spoke over and over, "*For the good of the Realm*," before Aristian held the pillow to his father's face. It had to be done; his mind was plagued by devils. He wanted another war, more killing. The Kingdom of Allamantya would fall if they didn't do this terrible act. It was one life to save thousands.

The flames consumed Aristian's vision, it disappeared into the darkness. "*Sinners perish in the fires of hell,*" the white priests would say. Aristian knew his time had come, the gods were punishing him. A cold fiery mist approached, whirling and raging. Gargoyles and harpies appeared, giggling and screaming as their long branch-like arms stretched out, grabbing hold of his limbs like he was an eagerly awaited meal. They dragged him towards the shadows, into a world that knew no happiness, to the fires of eternal suffering. His father, the old King Alector awaited him, sitting upon a throne of thorns, blood dripping from his pale face into his grizzled long beard. "*The son who killed his father, the devil and his children await thee!*" His father laughed with a demonic evil; fire and smoke fell from his lips. Pain and death pierced each word he spoke.

"No!" Aristian screamed.

"Please, Your Majesty, stay calm," a soft voice spoke.

Pain coursed through the wise king's body; he felt cold and tired. He wanted to sleep, to close his eyes and rest beside his dear Sonja in the halls of the White City. Yet all that awaited him was the fires of hell.

"Cover the wound!"

"Hold him down."

Shouting and screaming echoed through his mind. Slowly his eyes opened, bright yellow light filled his eyes. For a moment he thought he was passing from this world towards the White City.

"Your Majesty, can you hear me?"

As the king's vision cleared, he could see an array of faces standing over him. His long green robes were stained with blood.

"Is he going to die?" A panic-stricken but soft voice screamed out.

"We must get him back to the capital."

The king slowly faded back into darkness.

More visions of fire and devils filled the king's nightmares until eventually he woke. He was lying within his warm bed; the soft sheets offered little comfort as his body raged with pain. Each breath sent ripples of agony down his spine. Huddled around him, he could see his three children and Princess Tilia.

"He is awake!" Andros shouted. He dropped to his knees, taking Aristian's hand. "How do you feel? The wisemen say they have stopped the bleeding."

"I have seen better days my son, but I do not feel I will be leaving this world just yet." The king grimaced as he spoke. "Where is Tilia, is she safe?"

"I am here Your Majesty." Princess Tilia stepped forward, her eyes heavy with tears. "I prayed you would come back to us."

"I thought I had lost you." Arrabella's voice was broken, rare compassion and suffering filled her words. She pushed Tilia aside to get towards her father. "Did you see who they were?"

"I can picture them; they weren't of the Western realm."

"Daemar believed they may be from the Eastern Isles. Beyorn killed one – his skin showed the eastern complexion." Andros turned towards his sister.

"No, some were white also." Tilia wiped a few tears from her eyes.

"Father, why would they want to harm you?" Princess Arrabella squeezed her father's arm.

The High Council suddenly entered the room; *the harpies have returned from my nightmare,* the king watched them slide into his chambers. One by one they surrounded him, their potent aroma of arrogance, greed and power angered him.

Lord Peyton the gold spoke first, "My king, by the grace of the gods you are safe."

"How dare those savages strike our king, we should've burnt the Eastern Isles to the ground!" Lord Dellio's feeble voice gave out a pathetic roar.

"Your Majesty, we have found Lord Mortimer Judaus." Lord Attico sounded guilty.

Princess Arrabella slowly stepped away from the bed.

King Aristian looked up. "Where is he?"

"Dead!" Prince Daemar entered; his voice was loud and filled with anger. He pushed the High Council away from the king's bed. "I found your dear councilman. Even in death his body reeked of Jasmine. His throat had been torn from his neck. What confuses me is why he was dressed in a coat of white armour? And why was he so close to the attack?"

The High Council, for once, looked lost for words; they stuttered and froze.

"It was nothing to do with us!" Lord Attico's words were cursed with fear.

"He said he was going east, it is all he said!" Lord Dellio began to shake as if he stood outside on a winter's morning.

"Take them!" Prince Daemar ordered. Suddenly Allamantyan soldiers entered the room dragging the councilmen out as if they were nothing more than petty criminals. They screamed and hollered their innocence but it was to no prevail. Prince Daemar followed behind.

King Aristian was in shock; he never trusted the High Council but he never once believed they could be behind such an attack. They swore an oath of allegiance to the king; they were religious men, they would not break their word.

"I never trusted them! Traitors!" Prince Andros spat. "I will have them torn apart."

"Yes, it must've been them!" Princess Arrabella joined in. "This is all too much; we should postpone the wedding. Father, you need to rest."

The king's eyes, once again, began to feel heavy; a weight of darkness was beginning to fall over them. He could hear Andros agreeing eagerly with his sister. The king wanted to smile as it was the first time he had heard them agree on something. Slowly the voices began to fade away, coming and going like a soft wind.

That was until Princess Tilia piped up, "No, the wedding should go ahead as planned." Her voice carried strength just like a queen's should. "It is what your father would want, it is what I want. We came here for a wedding and that is what we will have."

King Aristian looked towards Princess Tilia, and he smiled. In that moment she became the queen in everything but name. The king's eyes dropped and his nightmares of hellfire could begin once again.

****

Andros slipped away. He knew the best places to hide. As a child he would often be alone. He would travel down the palace stairways, into the mountain tunnels. He would delve deeper and deeper until no one could find him. He would often sit in the dark, just him and the flames for company. He could watch them for hours, flickering and burning. The soft crackling would often excite him but, as much as he loved them, they could open the doorway to his darkest desires.

Yet today he had not come here for excitement or for the flames, he had come to be alone. His heart raced within his chest, he struggled to breathe. Anger filled his muscles; he paced up and down within the mountain tunnel.

"Bastards!" he screamed. "I will have them eaten by dogs!" His voiced echoed over and over. Andros loved his father more than anyone in this world; he was the only one who understood him.

The prince could hear the sea crashing loudly, the echo emphasised its power. The ocean breeze blew gently down into the cave, the air felt cool and refreshing yet it didn't calm him. Andros could feel someone watching him, burning eyes that hawked his every move. "Who is there?" he yelled.

Only three people knew of this place. His father, Lyon and there was a third, but the third was dead. A soft voice called back from within the darkness of the cave, "Murderer."

Andros stepped back. "No, no. I'm not, it wasn't me. It wasn't me!"

"Killer."

"Hell awaits you."

The voices began to echo, booming out within his head. Andros held his hands to his ears, tears of both pain and anger trickled down his bony cheek. "It is happening again!" he screamed, "I didn't do it, I didn't!" Andros knew that death lingered in this cave; the hard rock and wet sand had lay witness to the evil that had taken place here.

"What didn't you do? Andros, are you okay?" Lyon N'Dai appeared down the stairway and into the cave. His voice was soothing, taking away the calls from within the shadows.

Andros turned. "How dare you taunt me! I am to be your king!" He stormed towards Lyon, grabbing hold of him by his white and red tunic. He proceeded to rain feeble pathetic slaps towards his lover. Lyon offered nothing in resistance until Andros dropped to his knees, collapsing into the sand.

"My prince, what is wrong? I thought I would find you here. I have just heard Lord Mortimer Judaus was acting as a guide for those assassins. Your uncle is rounding up the finest swords and is preparing to go after them. I will not let this act go unpunished!"

Andros began to laugh through his tears. "You will be going? You are as much a swordsman as I. You have never tasted battle; you are knight in name not deeds."

"You know not what I am capable of! Soon you shall see the lengths my love will go. I would kill for you."

"I will be married tomorrow, your love is wasted."

"The wedding goes as planned?" Lyon gasped, as if a dagger had been thrust through his heart.

"Tilia and my father wish it so." Andros rose to his feet.

"No, you are mine. You cannot marry her!"

"I am no man's! But you are mine and mine alone to have." Andros looked past Lyon to the bright flames from the torch. They beckoned to him. "Right now, I command you to take me!" The beautiful golden red flames crackled and hissed. It was as if they spoke to Andros, opening the doors to the sin that lay within him.

Lyon's smooth face was heighted by the red glow; his eyes sparkled, drawing the prince in. For years they came to this cave, the only place they could be alone. The fires along the rocks would fuel Andros's excitement, compel him to sin.

Andros moved his hand up Lyon's leather trousers squeezing the young knight's crotch. "Give it to me. I want it."

Lyon hesitated, as if somehow Andros had begun to frighten him. Yet the prince dropped to his knees and forced his way into Lyon's trousers; he then proceeded to take the knight within his mouth. Andros knew in the eyes of the gods he was condemned to hell. The white priests would say, "*Hell awaits all sinners*," but at this very moment he welcomed the devil's flames. He could feel the darkness roaring inside of him, a demonic violence-fuelled energy raced throughout his body.

"Murderer!" a whisper echoed throughout the cave.

"No!" Andros screamed as he scrambled to his feet. "I'm not, I'm not!" He crashed against the jagged walls, his face scrapping against the sharp rock, drawing blood. His hands dug into the cave, his mouth drooped open as tears fell from his cheeks.

"Andros, my love. What is wrong?" Lyon frantically tried to grab hold of him.

"It wasn't me!" The prince's squeal screeched against darkness before he fled up the stairway.

****

King Aristian peered around his chambers. Finally, it was empty. Since waking for the second time he had had visitor after visitor. King Vincinicus had been there the longest, offering fifty of his finest men to accompany Prince Daemar in hunting down the assassins. The hot sun shone through his silk curtains. The yellow beam of light was warm yet his body felt cold, his pains ached throughout his aging body.

Slowly his chamber doors squeaked open, King Aristian breathed deeply. To his surprise the Prince of Valanor entered. He wore shining deep blue armour. Silver lined decoration formed the outline of a man's torso upon his breastplate. As mighty as the prince looked, for once he walked without confidence. His steps were short and slow, he even peered down towards the floor.

"Gabriel, I didn't expect to see you." King Aristian attempted to sit up.

Prince Gabriel bowed his head. "Your Majesty, ever since I came here, I thought you to be my enemy. Yet today you were willing to give your life to save what I hold most dear in this world. I will never forget this. You have my spear from this day until the end of my days. I swear it."

Aristian beckoned the prince to sit beside his bed. "The rumours say you are undefeated in battle?"

Gabriel smiled as if the king's compliment fuelled the young prince's ego and thirst for glory. "I have fought in eleven battles and victory has always been mine."

"How can you truly enjoy the sweetness of victory, if you are yet to taste the bitterness of defeat?"

"In my mind there can only be victory, there is no room for defeat. In an hour I will ride out with Prince Daemar. Together we will hunt these assassins." The prince sounded excited by the prospect of clashing steel with an unknown foe.

The king dared not question the headstrong prince anymore. He was glad Gabriel had shown an allegiance to him but he wished he didn't have to taste an assassin's sword to get it.

Ever since his children had left, many thoughts had weighed heavily on the king's mind. First of all, the betrayal of Lord Mortimer Judaus and the supposed implication of the other members of the High Council. Why would the assassins kill Lord Judaus? It was clear it was to silence him, remove the witness. Nothing was clear in his mind except one thing.

"I want you to listen to me." Aristian stopped speaking as he began cough, his hand held his wound as his face was filled with pain. "There is something I must tell you."

Gabriel leaned forwards.

"I do not believe those assassins came for me. They were here for Tilia."

Chapter 23
We Stand and We Fight

"Run!" Rhodesha screamed to her *brothers* and *sisters.* "Don't stop!"

All her life she had been running. From the moment Rhodesha could remember, she would run. She had been born a slave to Samoran masters, working from before the sun rose to long after it had fallen. Her masters decided when she ate, when she slept, when she shat. This was not the life for her, so she ran and she kept running. Garroway had shown her how to stand, how to live and how to love. Today, however, she needed to run and to run faster than she had ever run before.

After the arrival of the Allamantyan cavalry, the assassins had fled. During the chaos they had scattered like birds, running for their lives. Garroway had told his children never to be caught out in the open against heavy cavalry, to use the land to their advantage. A warrior had more than just his weapon: "*The smartest warrior shall live longest,*" he had said. Yet now they were stranded, caught like rats in a trap.

The ground rumbled violently, a deafening sound of horses and armour. Rhodesha dared not look back. As fast as her legs could carry her, she bolted into a field of long grass; it raised high above her head. She disappeared into the green abyss, out of sight and, for the moment, into safety. Rhodesha stopped, drawing breath. She could hear the crashing of horses' hooves and grinding of mail rubbing against metal; she knew they were close. Gripping her sword tightly, she could feel the smooth handle within her palm. Someone was approaching. Rhodesha dropped down into her fighting stance; she readied herself. Like a tiger awaiting its prey, she honed in, ready to kill.

Charging like a wild buffalo, Roak came bursting through the grass, his bright white eyes bulged from his head, the sun reflected off his shinning black body. "Come on!" he yelled as he stampeded past.

Four heavily armoured knights charged forwards, their breasts of iron sparkled. Rhodesha turned and sprinted after her brother. Her speed was greater and, before she knew it, she was beside him.

"You run like an old man!" Rhodesha smiled as she looked at her brother.

Suddenly beams of light appeared as the long grass was no longer in front of them, then the ground disappeared from below their feet. Rhodesha and Roak both fell, they crashed into a bright blue stream. The water seeped into Rhodesha's nose and down her throat; for a moment she was disorientated and lost grip of her sword. She wiped the water from her eyes as she scrambled to her feet. The heavily armoured Allamantyan knights began descending down the gap in the long grass and into the stream. Rhodesha knew it was futile to run. The stream was long and wide, the bank on the other side was open and clear, a perfect killing ground for armoured horse. Along with Roak, she stood up straight. The water crashed gently against their legs. They gripped their swords and awaited their fate.

Like a god sent down from the heavens, Garroway appeared, gliding through the air. His spear, the *Titans Bitch*, held aloft, the blade sparkled. Its craftsmanship was stunning; it was forged for one purpose and that was to kill. He unleashed the devil's fury as he cut through the armoured knights. The spear spun within his hands, each move was precise and he killed as he pleased. His speed was unrivalled by the mortal man. In seconds, the horses were riderless and the knights lay dead in the stream, the cool blue water turning red. Before Rhodesha and Roak had any chance to thank him, more Allamantyan cavalry appeared at the far end of the bank.

"Go! Head back to the Lion fortress!" Garroway commanded before he turned and meet the Allamantyans head on. He charged without fear; it was as if he welcomed death with open arms.

Reluctantly, Rhodesha and Roak left their father. As they sprinted down the stream, the water crashed heavily against their knees. The droplets resembled sparkling diamonds. Rhodesha could see her father surrounded by knights, his spear flashing out from side to side. She wanted to go back. Her father had saved her life as child, how could she abandon him now? Yet along with Roak, she continued down the stream before heading through a dense woodland area. Both collapsed behind a large tree, clawing for breath.

"Are they following?" Roak panted desperately, his naked chest rose and fell.

"I can't see anyone."

Suddenly the ground began to rumble once again. Looking back, Rhodesha could see a vast number of knights and mounted men at arms; they were scouring the forest. *Garroway please be safe!*

Seeing the soldiers so close, she and Roak dropped down beneath the tree into a large ditch; the roots grew thick and strong, pulling away the earth. They were able to hide beneath them.

"Any sign of them?" one of the knights yelled.

Rhodesha held her breath, she dared not move. She could feel the sweat running down her cheek and her heart thumping beneath her breasts.

"I saw two of them head this way," another replied.

"They can't have gone far. Keep looking. Ten gold coins to the man who brings me their heads." The knights rode off, chewing up the dirt as they charged away.

When the coast was clear, Rhodesha and Roak made their way carefully through the forest. They treaded softly; their eyes ever watchful. It was not safe; at any moment those knights could appear. Rhodesha knew the Allamantyans were no match for her or her brother on foot. She had once killed five Dagari warriors single handily. She did not doubt her skill with a sword, for fifteen years she had been trained by the greatest warrior who ever lived.

Rhodesha suddenly felt sick. *We are the Dragons of Dagen, how can this happen to us?* She began to feel agitated and nervous. She had fought hundreds of times and, no matter the odds, they had come out victorious. Yet today, in the blink of an eye, her life had unravelled. Lothar was dead, killed by the biggest man she had ever seen. She wanted to scream Toran's name. Two tears fell from her dark eyes. If she had believed in the gods, she would be praying, begging them to keep Toran and the others safe. She breathed in deeply, attempting to stay calm. In the face of the death she had no fear, but where Toran was concerned, she was as anxious as a mother away from her new born baby.

"We shouldn't have left him," Rhodesha said sorrowfully.

"Garroway can handle himself. He commanded. We go, we do not disobey." Roak kicked at the dirt.

The sound of grunting and shuffling echoed through the trees. It caught Rhodesha and Roak's attention; they stopped dead, drawing their swords. She focused ahead, her grip tightened. *I will not die today!* The clanging of metal and the screaming of death soon followed. She eased her grip and slowly followed the noises; beyond bushes they saw a familiar face.

In the clearing, Zaira was alone, fighting toe to toe with an Allamantyan knight. The bodies of three men at arms decorated the dry earth. Zaira's free flowing blonde hair glided elegantly as she moved from side to side. The plaited side of her hair was stained with her enemy's blood. She was fast and elusive; her taut body was built for combat. The knight was clumsy; he plodded forwards, swinging wildly. She was teasing with him, smiling. Like a cat, Zaira played with her prey.

Seeing Zaira fight in such a way reminded Rhodesha of when she had first laid eyes upon her ten years ago. Garroway and his children had ventured east, to the Dagari city of Hunhelm, where he had been paid to kill a Samoran exile who had been stirring up trouble. This noble had been known for having a taste for young blonde girls. This man, however, made a grave mistake when he had tried to force himself on Zaira; she ripped off his testicles with her bare hands and watched him bleed out.

Zaira had sworn, "*No man shall defile my body with his hands of filth.*" Zaira fought with fire and fury against his bodyguards, teasing them with her speed. It was then Garroway knew she would be the twelfth and final Dragon of Dagen.

Suddenly Zaira thrust forward, as if her teasing had begun to bore her. She rammed her spear through the knight's breastplate. His yelp echoed from within his iron helm. He collapsed to his knees with an almighty thud; he was dead.

"Zaira!" Roak ran towards her and the two embraced.

"Have you seen the others?" Rhodesha asked frantically.

Zaira stopped to take a breath. "I saw Toran and Lilah heading into the long grass. I lost them. The others I have not seen. We must move, these knights are everywhere."

In that moment Rhodesha's body eased. Toran was not alone and, as far as she knew, he was safe, but what of the others? Leaving Garroway weighed heavily upon her shoulders.

The three began to head east, trying as best as they could to retrace their steps. Along the way they found dead Allamantyan soldiers but no sign of the others.

"This is the way," Zaira said as she looked ahead through the tress to an open plain.

They stopped at the forest's edge and peered out. The field was wide and empty; on the other side lay a rocky mound. Beyond those mounds was the Lion fortress and potential safety.

"As a boy, all I knew was chains and the hot taste of a whip against my back. Garroway freed me from those shackles; he gave me a family, a life." Roak's voice was low.

Rhodesha knew Roak's story. Like her, he had been born in Etoria. Captured as a child by Samorans, he worked for years as a slave. He and three of his Etorion kinsmen were being transported along the Desert of Bones when he broke free yet, instead of fleeing, he fought back, attempting to free his fellow slaves. Garroway saw him and, impressed by his bravery and strength, he freed him. *"Come with me and you will never feel the hold of a chain or the kiss of a whip again, I promise you."*

"Across this field we shall find him." Zaira placed her hand on his muscled shoulder.

"I will repay his kindness, I swear it!" Roak slapped his hand across his chest.

The field was a perfect killing ground for cavalry, so they needed to get to the other side as quickly as they could. The three of them began to jog, moving with haste but not wasting unnecessary energy. The hot sun was bright; it reminded Rhodesha of Samora, a place that only gave her sadness and eternal suffering.

Slowly the grey dried mounds of rock on the horizon drew closer. Rhodesha smiled. A loud trumpet rang out, a powerful tune that stung into Rhodesha like an arrow; it removed her smile instantly. Back on the forests edge, rows of Allamantyan cavalry appeared.

"Oh fuck!" Roak stopped in shock.

"Run!" Rhodesha screamed.

With everything they had, the assassins bolted for the rocky mounds. They moved so fast it was as if their feet never touched the green grass beneath them. Adrenaline fuelled their burning muscles as they forced themselves away from the oncoming danger. None of them dared look back, but they all knew death was close behind. Roak and Zaira reached the mounds first, climbing up the loose gravel with a desperate desire to live.

Rhodesha followed behind, scrambling clumsily. She slipped, scrapping her knees against hot stone. An anger rose inside of her as she stood up straight. "We are Dragons of Dagan, I will run no more. We stand and we fight!" Rhodesha yelled defiantly, she knew it was futile to run. She slowly drew her sword, the steel shining as it was exposed to the light. Along the blade she could see her reflection; beside her, she imagined Toran, his strong arms holding her tightly. *I will see you again, I will not die today.*

The Allamantyan cavalry formed up in rows of two, three armoured knights at the front, their glorious armour gleamed in the bright sun. Simultaneously, they drew their swords before they began to charge forwards. The ground rumbled and the air crashed; like thunder ahead of the storm they approached.

Roak and Zaira walked back towards Rhodesha, standing either side of her.

"You look scared, little sister." Roak smiled as he turned to Zaira. He placed his long, curved sword across his shoulders.

"Scared of what those lonely knights will do to a big handsome boy like you?" Zaira replied as she spun her spear in a figure of eight.

"Yes, this body of mine has been known to excite both men and women."

"Not this woman, big brother."

The assassins stood side by side. If today was the day Rhodesha was to leave this world then dying beside her family would be a fitting end to a life that had experienced so much. The Allamantyan cavalry drew closer and closer, a raging tide of green and red. The dried earth and dust rose up around the horses' legs. The armour and swords flickered in the bright sun. Rhodesha knew the Allamantyan soldiers would fight with a hellfire fuelled by vengeance but they had never faced Dagari Dragons before. The only advantage the assassins had was the terrain. The armoured knights and horses would struggle to manoeuvre on such uneven ground.

By now the cavalry were only a few metres away; the world began to rumble as if the gods themselves were shaking the ground beneath their feet. The noise was deafening but Rhodesha, along with Roak and Zaira, unleashed a mighty battle roar; they would not die in silence. The three of them stepped forwards to meet the soldiers head on. They had lived together, bled together and maybe today they would die together.

The soldiers charged up the rocky slope. Rhodesha slashed out with her sword; her first blow caught a soldier across his chest, removing him from his saddle. The assassins fought without finesse and without honour, just with a savage animal instinct to survive. They stayed low and moved around the legs of horses, causing the animals to panic and pull backwards. The riders tried to steady their unruly beasts but instead they found themselves in the dragons' killing range. Roak pulled a soldier from his horse and rammed his sword through his mail covered chest.

The sound of steel against steel and braying horses screeched across the Antilion plains. The assassins' moment of success was short-lived as the power of the Allamantyan riders forced them back; they retreated, fighting as they gave ground. Suddenly Roak found himself stranded, surrounded by swinging swords. He turned, and in flight, he felt a hot blade slashing across his back. In agony he fell to his knees before succumbing to the loose gravel. He began to slide down the slope; the cavalry saw their moment and began to ride over him. The hooves crashed hard against his body.

"Bastards!" Zaira screamed with vengeful anger. She launched herself off her feet and charged towards the thick of battle.

Rhodesha watched helplessly as her brother and sister disappeared into a wave of horses and men. She felt the moment of death drawing near. The Allamantyans surrounded her. Four soldiers had dismounted and advanced up the slope; a heavily armoured knight in shining silver plates of iron was at the front. She wanted to fight beside her siblings but dying alone on the peak of this mound would have to do. The soldiers closed in like pack of hyenas yet Rhodesha showed no fear as she met their attacks with speed and cunning. Sidestepping and pivoting, she countered and killed. In seconds, two men at arms lay dead, bleeding out on the hot stones.

The knight attacked, he swung towards Rhodesha who, at the last moment, turned her head, causing his sword to taste nothing but air. She lashed out, her sword scraping against his kite shaped shield, broken bits of wood spraying outwards. Out of nowhere a spear smashed against her head. Her ears rang out and a flow of blood poured into her eyes. Rhodesha's feet slid on the unruly ground as her body gave way. Disorientated, her vision blurred and her body loose, Rhodesha collapsed to her knees. The knight and two soldiers closed in, ready to kill.

"Toran," Rhodesha whispered. She felt the warm blood running down her face and over her lips. The hot sun shone down against her back, her hand rested against her lower stomach, a tear rose in her eye before falling from her cheek. She thought of the baby she would never see.

Savage screams of death soon followed, the noise of steel cutting through flesh and bone filled the hot dry air. The wailing of the dying emphasised the merciless attacks that raged upon that rocky mound of earth. Rhodesha's vision began to clear. To her surprise she could see Toran in all his magnificent glory, his huge broadsword cutting through his enemies. Caelan and Naleac were beside him; with spear and sword they vanquished the Allamantyan soldiers.

Slowly Rhodesha's vision began to darken once again.

Bright light shone down from the heavens; through the leaves and branches of the trees, spear-like rays of golden sun impaled the earth. Rhodesha slowly opened her eyes; she could feel a gentle touch against her face. Beside her was Toran, his large well-sculptured face had a large warm smile painted across it. His sparkling golden tooth blinded her for a moment.

"Rest, your Toran is here now." With a small rag in his large hand he began to wipe the blood from her face.

His touch soothed her; she sat up and rested herself against his strong body. His huge arms held her with a gentle but firm grasp, in this moment she felt nothing but happiness.

Rhodesha could hear familiar voices; around her were her *brothers* and *sisters.* Valdar sat on some red stone ruins, sharpening his sword; his usual angry expression validated his nickname of Valdar the Vicious. The twins, Caelan and Naleac, stood chatting away; Lilah and Maarax had climbed high on the decimated walls looking out into the forest. She instantly knew where she was: The Lion fortress.

"Roak? Zaira? Where are they? Are they okay?" Rhodesha pushed back away from the safety of Toran's chest.

"It will take more than a few Allamantyan swords to kill me!" Zaira's voice was soft and groggy.

Zaira sat behind Rhodesha, resting against the red ruins. Beside her was Roak, who lay snoring away. Both looked battered and bruised but well enough.

Rhodesha's happiness suddenly began to turn to a deep sickness; she scanned the ruins wildly. "Garroway, where is he?"

"He hasn't returned, nor has Uriah." Toran's voice was solemn.

Suddenly the assassins stood over her, peering down.

Rhodesha breathed deeply. "I saw Garroway."

Lilah pushed to the front. "Where? Is he alive?"

"I don't know. He told me and Roak to go; he stayed alone to face the Allamantyan cavalry. I shouldn't have left him!" Tears began to stream down her face.

Lilah seemed to freeze, as if her life had been destroyed before her eyes.

"You abandoned him!" Caelan's voice shot with anger.

"Coward!" Naleac added.

Toran roared, "She is no coward!" His huge hand grabbed Naleac by his leather tunic, lifting him from the ground. Caelan began to defend his brother, raining blows against Toran, who seemed immune to the attacks. Suddenly voices began to rise and explode like a volcano. Lilah frantically tried to restore peace to the raging violence that had begun to erupt.

For years the assassins had bled and killed to defend one another. They were more than *brothers* and *sisters*; forged in battle they had a bond stronger than blood. Yet now, in the foreign land, all was beginning to unravel; the Dragons of Dagen had turned on one another.

Chapter 24
Only Death Can Lead to Immortality

Princess Tilia stumbled down the corridor like a zombie; her body was present but her mind was not. Her soul relived the horrors at Diamor meadow; she could hear the screams of her dying Valorian guard. So many men gave their lives so she might live. Never had Tilia seen so much blood and death; she pictured the last moments of her sworn sword, Sir Dejax Felios, as he stood bravely facing down the assassins before they hacked him to pieces.

Her heart raced and her hands quivered. Tilia's legs gave way as she crashed against the stone wall. *No, stand. I will be a queen. No one will see me fall.* She forced herself onward and through the crowds of lords and ladies. All stared at her like an animal in a cage. Once out of sight, she closed her eyes, hoping to wipe the horrors from her mind but she could not. The screams still clawed inside her head. While the chaos had been taking place, Tilia had been so calm. While battle had raged around her, Tilia had shown a bravery she never knew she possessed. She'd cradled a dying King Aristian in her arms and thought nothing of her own safety. Now reality had set in, she knew what had just happened was real, it wasn't a nightmare.

After leaving King Aristian's chambers, her condition began to worsen; she moved from one hallway to another like a ghost, all the while trying to avoid contact with anyone. Before she knew it, she was outside in the palace gardens. Blossoming purple and yellow flowers decorated her path, perfectly pruned hedges and bushes surrounded her and immaculate golden pebbles lay beneath her feet, yet she felt nothing for their beauty. All she could see was a cloak of death and sadness.

A sandy coloured fountain lay at the centre of the garden; the water glistened like crystals as it rose into the air before falling elegantly. Sitting against it, Tilia peered into the pool. The ripples of water showed the faces of those who had died. Sir Kaian's bloodied face stared back at her; his cold eyes demanded why he should die and why she had lived. Her small quivering hands were drenched in the king's dried blood; she lowered them into the fountain, the cool water swashed against her skin. Slowly, the sparkling blue water began to turn red; in seconds it lost its magical glow.

A clash of voices drew her attention; she turned and at the far edge of the garden she saw two figures. The first was Princess Arrabella. She was flustered and upset. Beside her stood Sir Lyon N'Dai. The two looked as if they were arguing. Tilia felt the urge to hide; she dropped down behind the fountain, out of sight. Sir Lyon paced frantically beneath a garden archway. Purple and red flowers decorated the smooth oak. His hands clawed at his head. Tilia watched as the two began to bicker; the crashing of the water masked their words. It wasn't long before Sir Lyon stormed off.

Just as Tilia was about to rise, Leylan appeared. The Valorian snake slithered his way out of the bushes, latched onto Princess Arrabella and pulled her towards him. Tilia began to shake; a tingling feeling she couldn't be free of crawled its way along her flesh. Leylan stared in Tilia's direction, a dark grin spread across his face. Tilia knew he couldn't see her but his sinister eyes burned with a deep darkness; she could always feel them on her even when she knew he wasn't present.

After a while Arrabella and Leylan left separately. *Why would Arrabella embrace him? I must warn her.* Tilia needed to tell Arrabella to get her to keep her distance from Leylan. She would not let what he had done to her happen to someone else. *But what if he tells everyone what had happened between us?* Tilia began to panic. Leylan always told her no one would believe her, her lies would bring down her family, her honour and even her right to rule. "*Whores do not sit upon a throne ordained by the gods,*" he often would say.

I must tell King Aristian, he will believe me! Tilia rose with defiance in her heart. She frantically moved through the palace hallways towards the King's chambers. When she arrived, to her surprise, the guards outside were nowhere to be seen – the corridor was empty. As she approached the door, she could hear a panicked voice. She knew it to be Andros'.

"Father, I hear his voice. Through flame and shadow it calls to me. He wants me! The devil he claws at my flesh, the darkness it is there, I can feel it."

"You must fight it! Good and bad reside in all men. The holy men taught you to use the light, refuse to be consumed by shadow!" King Aristian's voice rose only to be cut off by waves of pain.

"Why has it returned? Why? Why?" Andros's voice whimpered into a wail.

"You're to marry tomorrow! Rise up, fight it. After you are wedded, the holy men will see to you."

"I can feel him watching me, even now. Where ever I go he is there."

Tilia began to shake. The rumours she feared were becoming a reality. She ran down the hallway as fast as she could; she needed to escape, to be far from this place. Everything seemed to watch her, from the paintings to the dead animal heads that hung from the walls. The eyes peered into her soul. *What am I marring? What have I done?*

She continued to run, she would not stop. As she turned down another endless hallway, she felt hands grab hold of her. They were strong, their grip tightened on her arms. Although strong they didn't hurt her, yet Tilia fought to be free, pulling as hard as she could to be set free from her chains.

"Tilia, Tilia!"

"Get off me!" She fought but to no avail. The arms that held her were warm. The body that produced so much strength offered protection. As her cloud of fear subsided, she could see Gabriel standing over her. His sparkling eyes showed a glisten of panic, she could see his concern.

"Are you okay?" Gabriel loosened his grip.

Tilia jumped forwards, holding him tightly. Gabriel held her like a brother should. In this brief moment she felt safe: the Leylans and the Andros's of this world could not harm her now.

"There's something I must tell you," Tilia spluttered, her words crashed into a wave of panic.

"Stay calm, it is okay. I'm here now you're safe."

"No, no it's not that." Tilia pulled away.

"Listen, the assassins can't get you now. Daemar is hunting them down, I will be there. They'll pay for what they did to you."

Tilia froze; a deep anger began to rise. "Men, all you care for is war! " She pushed Gabriel back.

"Abandoning your sister when she needs you most!" King Vincinicus shouted, his loud voice bouncing down the hallway. "You care more for personal glory than your own blood."

"I'm not a coward who hides behind his crown; I will not let others fight my battles."

Tilia felt helpless and alone. Her father and brother began to argue as they always did, each one refusing to yield to the other. In seconds it was clear both had forgotten she was there, each trying their best to be louder than the other. Suddenly Gabriel turned, storming off; tears began to well in her eyes. She wanted to scream, to call him back, she needed him.

Her father shouted a hail of obscenities before lifting a flagon of Leylan's wine to his mouth. His violent retching soon followed. "He is no son of mine! From this moment, he is dead to me!"

Tilia stood silent, watching as Gabriel disappeared out of sight. A horrible chill slithered down her arms as if the god of death had grabbed her soul. She tried to wipe the thoughts from her mind but something told her she might never see her brother again.

****

An anticipation of battle filled Gabriel's heart. His skill with a spear would provide his right to enter the White City. Every time he fought, it was for his people and his country but also his own personal glory. To test his ability against a rival was what he lived for; *the greatest warriors shall never die.*

Gabriel honed his finest armour, a pure white breastplate, golden shading of a male torso embedded on the front. Under his left arm he held a tall open-faced helmet; a fountain of golden plume fell freely. He gripped his spear tightly; all he could hear was the crunching of pebbles beneath his feet as he slowly walked beneath the palace walkway towards the courtyard. The hot Allamantyan sun was bright and glorious; the gods gave him their blessing. Fifty mounted Valorian soldiers awaited him on the other side.

"Gabriel!" Prince Arteus's voice echoed through the tunnel. He eagerly appeared and grabbed Gabriel by the arm. "I wish to ride with you but my father says I cannot. I want to fight."

"You must do as your father commands. Your time will come." Gabriel looked the boy prince in the eyes; he could feel his anger, his readiness for battle. He reminded him of himself. As a young Valorian prince, he would beg his father to allow him to face their Etorion enemies. "Have no fear; they will pay for what they did to your father, I swear it."

"Are you not afraid?"

Gabriel paused; Arteus stood unwavering, awaiting his answer. He looked everything like a warrior prince should: broad shoulders, strong arms and his armour fitted him like a glove. He noticed Arteus was so very different to his elder siblings; he was darker and, in some ways, simpler. He had no ego, no ambition, just a love for his father and a readiness to prove himself a man.

Gabriel took Arteus by the back of the neck. "Fear resides in all men but to die facing down your enemies is the greatest end any warrior can ask for. Fight bravely, fight with honour, so that in your last breath the gods' eyes will be fixated upon you. In that final moment, you will earn your right to enter the hall of fallen heroes." He released him and walked away, only to stop and shout, "Only death can lead to immortality!" His voice echoed out over and over through the tunnel.

The Antilion palace courtyard was filled with beautiful Valorian blue. High walls of untainted white stone surrounded the mounted soldiers; they had formed a semi-circle, all looking towards the tunnel. Gabriel walked out, and his countrymen's eyes locked onto their warrior prince. Gabriel could feel their overwhelming sense of pride and valour; it fuelled his ego and thirst for glory.

Dismounted at the front were his cousins, Lassander and Lucian. Beside them were the Valorian knights, Sir Hyandrei Milo and Sir Evandinor Linos. Each clad in sky blue breastplates and greaves. Both held their helmets under their left arms. "My prince." They said, bowing their heads simultaneously.

"Lassander, you and Sir Hyandrei will stay here. Guard Tilia. Keep her safe. Lucian you will ride with me."

"Cousin, I will give my life to protect her, you know that." Lassander placed his fist across his heart.

"I prey to the gods it doesn't come to that."

"Aye, me too. I quite like living. I have become fond of it over the years." Lassander turned to Lucian. "Keep out of trouble, I enjoy having you both around."

Gabriel, Lucian and Sir Evandinor mounted their horses. The sound of armour rattled across the courtyard.

Lucian replied, "Fear not for me or our prince. He has the mighty Lucian to protect him!" He began to laugh as he pulled his horse close to Sir Hyandrei, his voice becoming soft and hoarse. "If I fall, will you do one thing for me? Tell your wife I love her!"

Sir Hyandrei called out, "You didn't really fuck my wife, did you?"

Gabriel pulled away, and his mounted soldiers followed instantly, moving as one impenetrable unit. The mighty crash of horses' hooves against the cobbled ground echoed out like thunder, as the Valorians made their way down the slopes of city. The eyes of the populace watched in amazement. The bright rays of light magnified the beauty of the white walls, red thatched houses and the mighty statues that lined the streets. With each passing moment, Gabriel's burning desire to have his name carved into the minds of the mortal man increased; he was ready, this was his time.

Just as Gabriel passed out of the city and onto the Heldrium plain, he could see a large cluster of Allamantyan soldiers. He instantly knew they outnumbered his countrymen by at least three to one.

"We have been awaiting you, little prince. I was beginning to feel fear had gotten the better of you." Prince Daemar's arrogant tones angered Gabriel. He breathed deeply, trying not to bite. The Allamantyan prince was clad in a deep dark suit of armour; on his breastplate was the carved image of the red sword of Tyranian. A long forest green cape clung to his shoulders. "Your numbers are few, were your kinsmen afraid of the dangers ahead?"

"It is the quality of those who ride with you, not the quantity, old man." Gabriel eyed his new Allamantyan allies. He saw Marshall Varrone DeVeil, Sir Rolan Bonhuer and an array of knights he didn't recognise. Beyorn, the beast of Golgia, stood beside Daemar. The huge bulk of a man was as harrowing as anything Gabriel had ever seen. The bear's eyes raged with vengeance; they burned as deep as red flame. Drool formed at his mouth like a rabid dog.

Daemar pulled his horse, signalling his men to follow. A mighty rumbling crashed against the earth as Allamantyan horsemen charged across the Heldrium plain. Gabriel nodded to Lucian who drew his men alongside their allies. Gabriel knew this was his moment, his destiny was calling.

Chapter 25
A Fallen Dragon

The dagger cut into flesh, tearing muscle and breaking bone. Uriah retracted his weapon; he killed quickly and quietly. He stood alone with his back to a thick oak tree. An Allamantyan soldier slid down his body, the man's blood painting Uriah's chest red. The woodland was swarming with soldiers and knights, each looking to claim their own bit of glory. Uriah needed to keep moving, to get back to the Lion fortress in the hope his brothers and sisters were awaiting him.

After Lothar tasted the foot of Beyorn, chaos had erupted. Upon Garroway's orders the assassins had fled. Uriah had become separated from the others when a horde of Allamantyan horsemen rode him down like a wild animal. He was able to escape, heading into the forest for cover. As Uriah moved carefully, stopping every now and then behind trees and bushes, he couldn't help but think of Lothar, his old friend. A great warrior and even better drinker, it didn't seem real that he would never speak with him again; he was gone forever.

The beast of Golgia! Big as a fucking bear. Uriah gulped. All in his years of fighting he had never seen a man or animal as big as Beyorn. *But we are dragons and dragons eat bears.* With as much haste as he could muster, he powered along the winding stream, finding nothing more than floating bodies and crimson coloured water. All the while he kept his eye out for the beast; he could sense he was being hunted. *I have no intension of tasting bear foot this day!* He gripped the hilt of his dagger.

After walking for what seemed an age, Uriah slumped against a tree. His long hair was soaked with sweat, sticking to his face and neck. He had chosen a spot which was situated on the brow of a steep woodland hill. Waves of heat rose from the hot dried dirt, the trees around climbed high into the sky and the bushes were dense. The terrain offered great cover as he took a well-deserved rest. Everything seemed quiet, nothing but the singing of summer birds filled the forest.

Why did I hesitate? Uriah pictured Princess Tilia looking up at him, helpless, unarmed and at his mercy. It was not because she was a woman, for he had killed his fair share over the years, no matter the life, blood for gold. Tilia had cradled the king in her arms, awaiting her death without fear. It was as if her stare of defiance had held back his blade.

The blood of his enemies dripped from his leather breast plate; it fell like soft rain against his hand. He slowly ran his fingertips over the dark sticky matter, staring at it intensely. It took him back many years ago, to where his recent nightmare had ended.

The young Uriah froze, fixated with fear. He stood within a room of blood; an aura of death hovered around his head like an unwelcome mist. His hands were covered as if they had been painted red. His mother's screams seemed to echo over and over. She was pinned helplessly to the bed; her naked body was being slashed to pieces by a large brute wielding a jagged blade. The attacker was aroused, as if the blood and screams were exciting him, the harder he cut the more violent he thrust. He hacked at her body like she was a cow being carved up for a feast. Uriah wanted to help his mother, he tried to move but he couldn't. Toran at sixteen was still bigger than a man twice his age; he forced Uriah aside and charged the monster. He threw the man to the ground and pounced on him like a ravenous beast. With his mighty hands, Toran began to pound the brute's face. With each blow, the sound of bone shattering could be heard, and a pathetic whimpering soon followed. Toran proceeded to ram his thumbs into the man's eyes, and he squealed like a stuck pig as they exploded like grapes. Slowly, as chaos reigned around him, he turned to the doorway. It was there he saw a young Garroway. Hair as black as night and eyes as bright as the stars in the sky…

The breaking of branches and rattling of hot mail brought Uriah back to the real world. Down the hill and through the trees he could make out a small band of Allamantyan soldiers; they appeared and disappeared behind a row of thorn bushes. Four or five, he wasn't sure, but he knew he couldn't run. They would catch up with him sooner or later. Uriah rose and breathed deeply, awaiting their arrival. His mind once again played back to that room of death, the deep crimson coloured walls and the sickening cries of his mother. He wanted the thoughts gone from his mind, but once they were there, he couldn't remove them.

Uriah felt a presence behind him; he swiftly lifted his hand to one of the swords strapped to his back. A strong grip latched onto his wrist, forcing his hand downwards, locking the sword back into his scabbard. He turned ready to fight only to be pinned against the hard oak behind him.

"I taught you to be alert at all times."

When the haze cleared, Uriah's heart opened. Garroway stood before him. His yellow sorrowful eyes beamed out like two great suns. They embraced.

"I am being hunted, I counted four." Uriah pulled away and pointed down the slope.

"No one hunts you now, my son." Garroway wiped the blood from his spear. "There were five, not four. You must rest."

****

Garroway and Uriah sat side by side. Up above, thick branches held a roof of leaves which sheltered them from the flesh burning sun. Uriah seemed at ease, Garroway could sense it. A father knows the shield of safety he provides his son. He ran a wet stone across his blade, and the scraping sound screeched through the forest. Uncharacteristically, Garroway was emotionless; he stared coldly at his weapon.

"Father, do you fear for the others?" Uriah asked.

"No, they are safe, I can feel it." Garroway never looked up.

"What is wrong?"

"The Beast of Golgia, I had heard tales of a monster born from those dark western mountains. As tall as three men, as fast as a charging horse and as strong as a bear, they said. Unfortunately, the tables were turned."

"But you fear no man?" Uriah questioned, his voice uneasy.

"Lothar feared no man and look at his fate. Fear compels men to become greater than they could ever be, but he is the biggest man I have ever seen."

Uriah shuffled before turning to Garroway, "Many years ago, I cried to my mother because Toran had beaten me, the reason I cannot remember. I told her I wanted to be as big and as strong as him. She replied, 'The bigger the man, the smaller his brain. Use what the gods have given you.' So if what my mother says is true then that Beyorn must be the biggest fucking idiot in this cursed land." Uriah giggled as he closed his eyes.

Garroway stood over Uriah, guarding him. He would let no harm befall his son. *I failed Lothar, I'll not fail you.* Meticulously, he scanned the forest. In a way, he hoped Beyorn and the others would come. For then they would feel the full wrath of the *Titans Bitch*. It was the first time in many years he had felt anger; a deep burning lust for vengeance roared inside of him. *I know you're out there, I can feel you.* The wind blew softly, rustling the leaves and the bushes. In his mind he imagined Beyorn storming through the forest, breaking down trees and anything that stood in his way. *When our paths next meet, you will taste the steel of my vengeance.*

After an hour's rest, Garroway and Uriah continued their journey towards the ruins of the Lion fortress. Garroway was quiet; he had no time for words, his mind was on his children and vengeance. Although he had known Lothar since his youth, fighting together in wars all over the Calhorion world, it was an incident back in Dagen that came to mind. It occurred down the murky streets of Ryks in the city of Colladrya. Hekron, a troublesome blood collector, had vowed Garroway's head after a feeble quarrel over a woman. Garroway and Lothar had not long returned from Samora, spending away their well-earned coin on whores and ale. During the night, Garroway had fallen ill. A cold fever had swarmed his body, he was bed bound and immobile. As darkness crept in, so did Hekron and his band. Lothar however had stood over his brother defending him with his life. It had been six against one. Lothar killed four, but the two who survived lived the rest of their lives as cripples. He lost an eye in the process but gained a brother for life.

A dragon may fade but his memory never shall!

"Oh fuck!" Uriah shouted. His hands frantically patted his body as if he was covered in ants.

Garroway turned quickly, his spear ready.

"My coins, my bag of coins! I've lost it!"

Garroway smiled. "You will lose more than your coins if we linger here much longer."

"I hope whoever finds it, drinks and fucks himself into an early grave! Lucky bastard."

The two picked up the pace. Garroway had perfect eye for detail. He remembered everything: the trees, the leaves and even the dried dirt. He knew exactly where they were. Through the forest, agitated voices seemed to flow like an angry wind, each one was familiar. As the trees cleared ever so briefly, red rocky ruins opened up before them.

Past the ruins, Garroway could see his children; Toran was fighting with the twins as Lilah begged them to stop. Rhodesha and Valdar were shouting; this was not their usual banter. An aura of anger swarmed them. Each made enough noise to bring the entire Allamantyan army down upon them.

"Stop!" Garroway commanded. He looked down from the ruins with disgust. "I raised you all to stand by each other's side; you are brothers and sisters. Do not falter now." He dropped down as elegantly as a cat.

"Garroway!" Lilah called as she ran to him.

He held Lilah to his body; her warm skin eased any aches that plagued his muscles. Seeing all his children safe filled him with a brief happiness. The assassins happily closed in. Toran embraced Uriah, picking him up like a small child and squeezing him.

"Father, what are we to do?" Naleac asked.

"Do we run or do we fight?" Caelan added.

"That beast of Golgia is the biggest cunt I've ever seen; I don't wish to face him!" Valdar spat.

"If it is death that frightens you, have no fear. I'll protect you. Like a valiant knight protecting his wife." Uriah paused slightly before looking Valdar up and down. "My, what an ugly wife you would make."

"We head back to Baron's Bay; the ship that brought us here should still be there. We return home to Dagen." Garroway held Lilah close to him.

As commanded, his children began to collect their things, no questions asked, no orders refused.

"Is it not better to die facing your enemies than with your back turned?" Lilah whispered softly into his ear.

"It is better to live, my love." Garroway planted a kiss on her blood red lips

The assassins moved swiftly; they covered ground like a pack of wolves. Now they stood at the foot of the mountain gate of Hamon'dor; the mighty ramparts rose high into the blackened sky, stars glistened on the sea of darkness. Garroway and his children were hidden beneath the strands of high grass. They watched and listened, their weapons gripped tightly. Each honed in like hungry beasts awaiting their meal.

Garroway turned. "I command you to conjure all your anger, all your hatred. Remember Lothar, your brother, his face and his name. Kill like you have never killed before. The acts you carry out this night will curse their nightmares from this day forth. We are dragons and we have a thirst for blood."

Out of the darkness the assassins swarmed the mountain gate; steel and vengeance poured out from within the shadows. Allamantyan screams rang out from the stone walls and down into the mountains. With a cold brush, the gods of death painted this night.

Chapter 26
Raging of the Storm

The fires and smoke of Ashfeld were long out of sight. Danaka, Griffin and Duro headed south, passing the great Meridian Lake before crossing the open plains of Ardenia. As far as the eye could see were fields of green grass. They had ridden all night and most of the morning to make sure they were out of danger. After a few hours rest, they continued south to city of Doldayne.

Danaka was quiet, yet it was not the horrors that she had laid witness to that plagued her mind, but what Malcolm Reymor had said the night before. *"Be careful the company you keep, little girl. For this one rapes and kills women."* She could hear his words even now. She eyed Duro as he walked ahead. *If he wanted to rape me, he would've by now.*

"Did you rape Amber Blackstone?" Danaka blurted out, instantly regretting it.

Duro stopped. "I knew your silence wouldn't last. No, I killed her."

Danaka froze, shocked at his casual reply. "Who was she?"

"My brother's wife." He grimaced as he turned away.

Danaka, you idiot, you should've asked why he killed her! Danaka tugged on the reins.

Duro had been walking ever since they made camp. Danaka wondered if she should ask him to ride. He dragged his feet and arched forwards like an old man. As they passed through a clearing of trees, a wave of screaming and shouting drew Danaka's attention. To her right she could see three young lads being beaten by a group of mail clad soldiers. Women wearing long grey cloaks attempted to save the boys, slapping and kicking at the soldiers. One man turned to an elder woman and smashed her in the gut with his shield, flooring her instantly. Four soldiers on horses began to laugh.

One woman was screaming in a language Danaka didn't understand. By their complexion she could tell they were from the Eastern Isles.

"Murder women and children, will you? Not so brave, now you face real men!" A tall, brutish looking solider pinned one boy to a tree; he then proceeded to ram his head into the boy's face, painting it red.

"This is for Ashfeld, you Yornish cunt!" another yelled as he kicked a boy to the ground.

"It wasn't them, innocent!" The elder woman pleaded from the dirt.

"We've never been to Ashfeld!"

Danaka watched on in horror; she desperately wanted to help the boys. "What should we do?"

"Nothing, this does not concern us," Duro replied.

The tallest of the young lads attempted to fight back but it was to no avail, the Ashfeld soldiers beat him to the ground. The mounted horsemen dropped down and began to sling ropes around their necks before hoisting them up onto three horses. Their mothers wailed and pleaded, screaming for Dalackis to save their children.

A mounted knight, clad in plates of snow-white iron, appeared. His mail and armoured rattled together, singing a horrible tune of death. Danaka instantly recognised his attire as that of the Guardians of Thelonia, the religious order that had taken control of Tomellburg. "In the name of Aristian, King of Allamantya, I condemn thee for treason against his people and the faith of Ollaria'h. By the law of Tyranian, God of all, I sentence you to hang by the neck until you're dead." The knight slowly trotted up and down, looking the boys in the face.

The tall boy uttered two words, "Falahail Delaghara!"

Duro pulled the reigns of his horses. "Come, there is nothing left to see here."

Danaka turned and closed her eyes; the slashing of a whip, then a loud thud, was soon followed by a heart wrenching wail. In that moment, she knew the boys were dead. Her heart sank; she knew those boys were innocent, they were being punished for the crimes of others.

They travelled most of the day before Duro ordered them to stop. The sun was beginning to fade; clouds had begun to form on the ocean above. A huge tree stood alone, surrounded by vast Allamantyan fields. The branches hung low, each decorated with an assortment of green tinted leaves.

"Dismount and draw your sword." Duro pulled out his sword.

Danaka did as he said; she dismounted before pulling her sword free.

"You almost got yourself killed yesterday; you need more training."

"What? Got myself killed? I saved your life back there!" Danaka angrily stepped forwards. "If it wasn't for me, you'd have burned in that inn, then it was me who…"

Duro attacked without warning; his sword clanged against Danaka's, the shock violently rippled up her arm. She stumbled backwards but was able to keep her balance. *Bastard!* She gripped her sword before replying with two high attacks followed by low one. Duro parried each before side stepping. She turned quickly, looking to cut off his retreat, lunging forwards with her sword. The two blades met in a union of anger. Danaka and Duro pressed together; his chest was directly in her eyeline, beads of sweat rested peacefully on an arch in his muscles.

A sudden wince pain shot through Danaka's stomach and up her back; she struggled for breath as she fell to the grass. In that moment she knew Duro had hit her to the ribs; it wasn't a malicious punch but enough to wind her.

"Your sword isn't your only weapon. Use your free hand whenever you can." Duro shook his head.

Once up, Danaka attacked. She was angry. She was no longer thinking of what Duro was doing but of what she wanted to do next. Her swings were fast and accurate. Duro seemed slower than before but he defended well enough.

"You are fighting with your emotions, stay calm." Duro turned his sword side on and patted her backside as she stumbled forwards.

"I saw the way you fought Sir Claris, you were filled with rage that day!" Danaka came forwards with a rapid succession of slashes. "What had he done to you?" She continued to attack relentlessly.

Duro angrily pushed her back. His attacks were hard; they now carried more power than the previous ones. He grunted, his eyes darkening as he swung his sword. Danaka flinched as he backed her up against the oak of the tree; his face pressed against her own, he stared deeply towards her.

"He killed my brother."

With all her might, Danaka wacked him in the ribs and, like a sack of potatoes, he dropped to his knees. Griffin barked loudly as if applauding her. Duro stifled in pain as he clutched his side. Danaka looked at her fist. *What a punch!* Along her knuckles she could see blood. Looking down, Duro's white poplin tunic turned red. He collapsed back onto the grass, blood draining from an open wound.

Danaka flew to his side, ripping open his tunic. A deep gash lay beneath his ribs. "Why didn't you say something? You have too much pride to ask for help." Danaka pressed against the wound trying to stop the blood.

"I thought I stopped the bleeding when we rested." He let out a groan. Darkness began to spread across the sky, and a cold wave swept across the grass. Trickles of rain started to fall, every second they crashed harder against the ground. "There's a storm on the way."

"I can see that!" Danaka intentionally pressed harder on the wound, causing Duro to yell.

Duro began to cough; he slowly raised his blooded fingers to Danaka's face. They hovered for a moment before his eyes rolled into the back of his head and his hand slumped downwards.

"No, no. Don't you die on me!" Danaka was filled with a heart stopping panic; she frantically tried to stop the bleeding. Duro began to whisper as his eyes opened slowly. Danaka leant in as his warm lips pressed softly against her own. A tingle swept through her body followed by a wave of happiness.

"There is a man I must see in Doldayne before I die." Duro fell back.

The storm roared as the rain crashed down from the heavens. Danaka had used all her might to help lift Duro onto his horse; she sat behind him attempting to guide Otis away from the oak tree. Seconds later, the tree was engulfed in a white light. Flames obliterated the leaves and glided down the branches. The winds howled as they tried to look for cover. Duro swayed in his saddle, drifting in and out of consciousness. Danaka tried her best to hold him tight.

They travelled in total darkness; the only light was offered by flashes of lightening that sliced through the sky. Danaka was soaked through, her body shivered as the cold rain hailed angrily against her. Griffin resembled a drowned rat as he trudged alongside Otis.

"There must be somewhere we can take shelter," Danaka quivered, wiping the rain from her face. A wrath of thunder shook the earth, and seconds later a streak of lighting exploded on the horizon, white flames shooting outwards. In that brief moment, Danaka saw a cave beneath a mound of cliffs and scattered rocks. "*Beyond the darkness, there is always light.*" She remembered the words the holy men of Tomellburg used to spout. *Maybe for once they spoke something useful!*

Danaka moved with full haste, the light from the moon for a moment seeming to guide her to safety. She dismounted, pulling Otis and the smaller horse over the scattered rocks and around the mighty boulders. Griffin was the first into the cave; he was desperate to be sheltered from the storm.

Once inside, she tried over and over to make a fire, trying to burn left over kindling and sheets from Duro's chest. Eventually the flames obeyed, taking hold and producing the much-needed warmth. Allamantya was known for its sudden season changes; summers always ended with a mighty storm that laid waste to the beautiful countryside. The cave was wide but it didn't descend far into the cliff face. Duro shivered as he lay by the fire. Every now and then, he would utter names, four in total. Sir Claris Moon, Sir Castel Damari and Amber Blackstone, but it was Prince Varden he mentioned the most. His voice turned to pure hatred when he called that name.

Danaka had been able to stem the bleeding using the essence of lavenal she had taken from her farm. Next, she had cauterised the wound. The scream Duro let out hurt her more than any blow she had taken. Danaka had learnt this from her aunt Heidi, who had once patched up her uncle after he was attacked by a wolf.

The night seemed endless, the wind screamed and rain poured. The deafening noise of thunder exploded without warning. Danaka huddled next to Duro. As she ran her fingers down his face, she thought back to that kiss. *Did he mean it? Did he think I was someone else?* She kissed his forehead, hoping he'd recover soon.

She drifted into a sleep, dreaming of her mother in fields of green. Eventually, Danaka woke, the storm still attacking viciously outside. Peering towards the darkness of the caves entrance, she felt a presence – a dark evil lurked outside. Within the raging of the storm something approached. Griffin rose up, growling. A flash exploded, the white light blinding her for a second. Griffin jumped out of the cave. Swallowed by the darkness, he disappeared. A sickening yelp soon followed.

"Griffin!" Danaka screamed as she stumbled after him.

As she approached the eternal darkness, three figures emerged out of the gloom. Their soulless eyes told a story full of hate. Danaka's heart stopped, her stomach twisted.

"I knew we would find you." Hazar raised his head. A smile filled of chipped and broken teeth filled his face.

Before Danaka knew it, Kalos and Zedir had thrown her to the ground. They punched and kicked at her, laughing as they did it. Zedir even attacked Duro who was still half conscious.

"Leave him!" Danaka pleaded.

Kalos rammed his fist into Danaka's mouth. All went dark, blood filled her throat. As she awoke, she found Hazar on top of her, a short blade in his hand.

"Yakash Mudra!" Hazar pressed his face against Danaka's, his breath reeked of death. The emptiness in his eyes revealed the evil that lay within him. "I will carve the wings of Dalackis into your flesh before sending you to meet him. There you will be reborn, pure and faithful to the one god."

"Why do you do this?" Danaka asked as she struggled. "I have done you no harm!"

"You ask me why?" Hazar gripped her throat, his thin fingers sinking into her neck. "I had a wife, two daughters. Then your Hethelyon knights, your swords, your gods came to Yorno. They burned my village, raped my children and butchered my wife. Dalackis, in his wisdom, saw fit to save me. For thirty years I waited. Cesaril, the lawgiver, has now answered my calls sending the Brotherhood of Ralmalaur. Falahail Delaghara!"

"Falahail Delaghara!" Zedir and Kalos repeated his words.

"On the wings of death, my people will have their vengeance."

Suddenly a bright white light flashed before Danaka's eyes. A fatal beam of silver shone out from the darkness. It was followed by a loud thump. Kalos's head had slid from his shoulders, crashing to rock between his feet. His mouth hung open; a frozen image of shock was imprinted on his face. Out of the storm, a silver haired warrior flew in, spear in hand. Zedir turned and received the blade through his fat belly; he screamed as he fell to his knees. The warrior kicked him to the ground beside Kalos.

A heartbroken Hazar looked at his fallen brothers. "Mudra!" he screamed as he quickly placed his knife against Danaka's throat. As she felt the sharpness of the blade against her skin, a fountain of hot blood sprayed against her face and chest. Hazar called out in agony as he clutched at his armless shoulder; he fell back against the cave wall, blood falling from his stump like a water fall. Danaka lay in shock, her body was painted in Hazar's blood, and between her legs lay his severed arm. She crawled back, kicking it away.

Hazar growled and spat as he slid back towards the cave's entrance. "Mudra, Kalgara! Dalackis curse you. Rakali da—" His words were cut short as his head was removed with one swift attack.

A band of black cloaked shadows slowly appeared out of the darkness.

The silver haired warrior walked towards Danaka, extending his hand, "My name is Garroway, and you have no reason to fear me girl."

Chapter 27
Kings Hope and Queens Dream

Princess Tilia's night was plagued with nightmares and endless thoughts of terror. The few times she was able to drift off, her dreams were either filled with assassins, Leylan or of her crazed husband-to-be. She tossed and turned; in the shadows she could see Leylan watching her, just like he would do when she was a child, standing at the foot of the bed, before his snake-like arms slithered along her legs.

Her father had her room well-guarded. Lassander and Sir Hyandrei stood vigilant on her balcony, two other soldiers stood outside her door and Cassandra was asleep at the far side of the room. Even with so many people close, she felt alone. She had considered getting on her horse and fleeing Antilion, heading back to her home in Verdina. Yet, after all her worrying, she was compelled to stay.

The morning was warm but not as hot as the previous days. She sat on her balcony peering out over the vast city, then beyond towards the waterfalls and to Hamon'dor. Her mind wondered, drifting from one place to the next. Cassandra chirped away as usual but Tilia rarely replied. Tilia wore a dress of the purest white; pearls decorated the seam. It rose just around her breasts then perfectly clung to her waist and upper legs. It was a beautiful Valorian wedding dress yet it didn't match the ugliness of the occasion.

"I'm so excited Your Highness; I can't wait to see how jealous Princess Arrabella will be. You look stunning." Cassandra bobbed up and down, brushing her hair. "You are everything she is not. I don't like her."

Armoured rattled as King Vincinicus and his entourage marched in. "Wine, give me the wine. Where's my beautiful daughter?"

Tilia held her tongue, trying her best to show the enthusiasm her father was displaying. Even before she embraced him, she could smell his traditional wine flavoured odour.

"You are beautiful, what more could a father ask for!" King Vincinicus took the wine from Leylan's hand and gulped it down. He turned to his followers. "Beautiful, isn't she?" He roared loudly and they all eagerly agreed.

Leylan watched her silently; Tilia avoided eye contact with him as much as possible.

"I wish Gabriel could be here," Tilia replied solemnly.

"Don't mention his name! He is dead to me!" Her father began to choke, regurgitating Leylan's wine.

His words sadden Tilia greatly. She knew her wedding was never going to be for love but today darkened her heart as much as her mother's funeral had. Eventually King Vincinicus and his followers left. Leylan was the last to leave, his poisonous glare taking in every inch of her.

It was Valorian tradition for a princess to be escorted to her wedding by her sworn swords, but with Sir Kaian and Sir Dejax meeting their untimely end, Lassander offered to escort her. They slowly made their way out of the palace and across an inclined narrow stone bridge, Tilia looked over the edge. In her dreams she jumped, gliding down to the majestic blue waves below.

"Andros is a lucky man, Your Highness." Lassander spoke truthfully although his eyes looked heavy with worry.

"Lucian will return." Tilia held her cousin's hand.

They continued across the bridge and towards the Gods Tower. The grand stone tower rose into the pale blue sky out of sight. The knights of the order of Hethelyon stood vigilant along stone walkway, ordained in golden suits of armour with a pure snow-white silk cape. They served no king, only god.

A cold breeze blew across her face, and a shiver fluttered down Tilia's spine. Up ahead, past the holy soldiers, was a royal purple carpet; the silver trim sparkled like jewels. It ran up the stairs and to the golden doors of the holy temple. Hundreds of Antilions, who flanked either side, began cheering with wild enthusiasm.

"Your strength and bravery is unrivalled; you make every Valorian proud." Lassander kissed her hand. Maybe he could sense her fear as he added, "My mother told me, 'Kings hope and queens dream.' Believe in your dreams and they will live."

Tilia knew she must walk the steps alone. Slowly she placed one foot in front of the other as she made her ascent to the top. The applause was deafening; white petals fell softly around her feet. Once at the top, she looked back over her people, raising her hand. The crowd's cheers rose even louder, shaking the holy stone. Chants of "Tilia" boomed out.

At the foot of the Gods Tower was the Holy temple. Two knights of Hethelyon stood at the entrance. Tilia admired each perfectly-placed stone as it ventured upwards towards the heavens. She could feel the eyes of the gods upon her.

"They call your name now, but would they if they knew the truth?" From behind a pillar, Leylan appeared. His eyes were red with anger.

"Move from me; soon I will not be yours to haunt." Tilia knocked passed her bastard brother.

Leylan pulled her by the arm, his narrow fingers pinching into her skin. "When Andros takes you tonight, will he know your secret? Will he think you the innocent virgin princess or a devil's whore?" He whispered the words into her ear before slithering back behind the pillar.

Before Tilia had time to panic, the golden doors burst open, and she was greeted with an explosion of cheers and joyous applause of instruments. The fate of the Western realm lay on her shoulders. *I will not fail you.* Slowly she stepped forwards, following the purple carpet down the aisle. Either side were rows of wooden seats, each one littered with family members and royal guests.

Prince Andros awaited her; he awkwardly paced up and down, rubbing his hands frantically down his red and green silks. King Aristian sat by her father; he was bound to a chair of wheels, and tears welled in his eyes. He seemed the happiest in the room.

A white robed priest began his ascend down the holy steps. "When the God, Tyranian, wed the Goddess Alcea, their love created everything you see today: the sea, the land and the mountains." His voice was dull drool. He was thin and old, wearing a headdress seamed with gold. "We, as people, are shards of that purest love, so as to honour them we take into marriage. It's the holiest of unions between man and women. A wedding is more than two bodies, it's two hearts and two souls. Before us here we have two royal hearts, wholesome and strong."

Andros took Tilia's hand; his was ripe with a cold sweat. Tilia could feel their panic swelling together in a whirlpool of fear. The priest continued to recite passages from the holy book but Tilia began to think back to Lassander's words, *Kings hope and queens dream. My dreams are nightmares and it is those that live.*

"Do you give your heart and your soul?" The priest asked in his monotone voice.

"I do," they replied together.

"Will you offer love and protection?"

"I do."

"Do you vow to honour one another from this day until the end of days?"

"I do."

"With the gods as my witness, you are now man and wife."

The audience roared into an ovation and, for a moment, Tilia felt the stones of the temple shudder. Andros leant in and they kissed; he felt awkward and cold. As their lips touched, a huge gush of wind ripped open the golden doors. The crowd gasped and screamed. The wind squealed as it flew in like a harpy, blowing out all the candles that lined the holy steps.

Andros stuttered backwards as if trying to hide behind Tilia. Guards battled against the wind but were able to force the doors closed. An eerie silence spread across the temple; an unspoken fear seeped from one guest to another.

Hours had passed since the wedding; by now everyone was drinking and feasting heavily. The violent winds that interrupted the union were now long out of memory as guests laughed and rejoiced together. A storm was raging outside; the wind whirled and the rain crashed, yet no one seemed to care that the summers had ended. The hall was packed, doubling the festivities that were displayed when Tilia first arrived in Antilion. Everyone seemed so happy, even Lassander was smiling as he drank his wine with Sir Hyandrei. King Aristian smiled at her from across the room; his aging face seemed content.

The King had the lords of the high council released. He believed them innocent, but Tilia didn't trust them. They sat alone drinking until Lord Peyton the Gold approached her saying, "You are the greatest thief this kingdom had ever seen, for you have stolen the hearts of every man in this room." His words were kind but his eyes were not.

"Dance, we want a dance," King Vincinicus boomed.

"The prince and the princess must dance!" the crowd demanded.

Before Tilia had any chance to react, she was pushed to Andros's chest. The guests formed a circle, an unbreakable wall of people.

Violins began to play a soft tune and a vocalist began to hum sweet innocence. Andros took her hand and they started to move to the music. They stared at one another; his face was emotionless and hard. Beads of sweat littered his skin, yet he felt as cold as winter snow. A hollow void lay within his icy blue eyes; it was within that moment Tilia knew she was dancing with the devil. Once they stopped, the guests cheered; hands clapped together with indescribable enthusiasm. Only one guest stood still. Sir Lyon N'Dai looked on as if his world crumbled around him. He disappeared into the crowds, taking his sadness with him.

Once the feast and celebrations had ended, Tilia made her way to her chambers. She lay alone in the marital bed, her heart pounding. The hearth laden with fire burned fiercely across the room. Even with the intense heat her hands trembled as she wiped the sweat from her brow. Lifting the bed sheets, she examined her own naked body, pinching little parts of skin and feeling her breasts. *I hope I don't disappoint.* Cassandra had shown her the art of pleasing a man, *but all men are different.*

The chamber doors creaked open. Andros crept within the low light. He stood awkwardly at the end of the room; slowly he undressed all the while avoiding eye contact. His body was weedy; his long limbs were gangly and uncoordinated. The wind howled and the thunder crashed. His face was consumed by shadow. Tilia wanted to scream as she saw visions of Leylan in the darkness. His devilish eyes lusting over her naked body, his arms outstretched wanting to latch onto her. The flames from the hearth crackled loudly like devils laughing at her horror.

Out of the shadow and into the light Leylan's face disappeared. Andros stood beside the bed. He wiped his palms on his thighs before pulling off the quilt, exposing Tilia's naked body. Andros looked her up and down before quickly jumping in beside her.

The two lay staring at one another; there was no romance or lust just an awkward silence that lasted an age until Andros uttered the word, "Goodnight."

Tilia looked up as she felt him turn away; her body eased slightly. She felt as if her ordeal was over when, in fact, it was just beginning.

****

It was a cold morning, and the storm had raged all night. Rains attacked the palace walls and a winter chill had swept through the hallways. The summers were over. Andros rose early, eager to distance himself from his new bride.

The prince relaxed in his bath tub, and the silk-like steam rose from the bubbling water; he could feel it burning into his flesh but he liked it. The hot water calmed his mind; it eased the darkness that dwelled within him. "More water," he demanded. His skin had begun to redden but he didn't care, he wanted it hotter.

Andros was surrounded by a glistening haze that encircled him, he couldn't see his new wife but he could hear her chatting away with her handmaiden across the room. Her soft delicate voice was irritating him but the hot water quelled his anger. Through the mist, a young blonde-haired lad approached, one he had never seen before. The boy emptied a jug of water into the prince's bathtub. Andros's cold eyes never left him, watching his every move with sinful glare.

"Tell me your name," Andros demanded.

"Jarrell, Your Highness."

"You will pour my bath whenever I command."

Through the steam, Andros could feel flames watching him, their crackle whispering sins into his ears. He closed his eyes, trying to ignore the words.

A scream echoed down the hallway. Andros opened his eyes, peering towards the door of his chambers. The scream was soon followed by another; this one was louder and more harrowing than the last. A clambering of footsteps charged past his room. A commotion was building outside. Andros robed himself and was helped out of the bath by Jarrell; he quickly made his way down the hallway, pushing his way past the crowds of lords and ladies that had begun to form. He knew where the crowds were heading; his heart began to race, a sickness boiled deep in his gut. He could feel something horrible, as more screams wailed along the crowd.

"Move, move!" Andros demanded as he pushed a lady to the ground. He fought his way to the front and into his father's chambers. A stinging of death shot Andros like a thousand arrows. He screamed but no words fell from his lips; an eerie silence grabbed hold of his throat, squeezing it.

King Aristian, his father lay, stricken on his bed. His face was pale as snow, eyes rolled to the back of his head and his mouth drooped open. Death swirled around the room.

On the king's balcony sat a single black crow; it fluttered its wings and cawed loudly.

"The king is dead," Lord Peyton proclaimed. "Long live the king!"

Andros fell to his knees.

Chapter 28
A Whisper on the Wind

The sound of death lingered in the darkness; the memories of fallen heroes screamed from in between the cold walls of Hamon'dor. Gabriel treaded softly, stepping over the bloodstained bodies that littered the dim lit corridors.

"Are there any left alive?" Prince Daemar shouted, his voice echoing out over and over.

Gabriel had seen his fair share of battles and death but nothing as harrowing as this. Limbs and severed heads were scattered amongst the butchered bodies, crimson blood rivers flowed from one room to another. The stench was sickening; in front sat a young boy, his back perched up against the hardstone wall. He was late teens at best, his face was pale and his eyes close as if he was sleeping peacefully. As Gabriel's eyes lowered, he saw the horrors: the boy's hands clutched at his gut, his intestines seeped from his stomach like red snakes.

Even Lucian was quiet. The harsh reality of what he saw seemed to silence the overconfident prince. Gabriel continued along corridors, the massacre he was witnessing seemed to worsen, the bodies began to pile up and, in what looked like the commander's chambers, he found an old knight pinned to the wall with swords.

"It is the same on the battlements, they are all dead!" an unknown voice yelled.

"What is it we hunt?" Lucian asked rhetorically. He gulped hard.

Each darkened hallway offered nothing but death; each body was mutilated beyond recognition. Gabriel slid his fingers over the bloodied walls, he encircled the blood beneath his fingertips. It felt warm. *They're close, a few hours at best.*

"One's alive! Over here, he lives!"

Gabriel turned quickly, eagerly following the call. The hallways flickered with beams of yellow and red. Soldiers brandishing torches poured out of the rooms and down the corridors. Gabriel forced his way through the bustling crowd. He found Prince Daemar on his knees, cradling a dying boy.

"They came with the moon, demons out of the shadows," the boy spluttered, blood spraying from his mouth. "The first scream seemed so far away and then, before I knew it, they were all around me. One moment they were in front, then behind. They were everywhere!"

"Calm yourself." Prince Daemar patted the boy softly. "How many did you see?"

"I saw only shadows." The boy sprung up, his eyes widened as if he saw a phantom. "I can see them now, demons from hell, laughing as they hacked us to pieces. You're all going to die! They are not men; the devil has sent them here!"

The crowd of soldiers began to mutter amongst themselves. Gabriel could smell their fear.

"The boy is lucky to be alive." Lucian leaned forwards for a better look.

"They left him alive on purpose, to strike fear into the men." Gabriel moved away from the crowd. He was not scared; he knew not the meaning of fear. He was ready, eager to test his strength against these demons from the shadows.

The boy screamed one final scream before he closed his eyes, never to open them again.

It was still dark when they left the massacre at Hamon'dor. The stars seemed to glow red, the gods telling the world that blood had been split that night. Everyone seemed quiet, just the sound of armour and horse could be heard as they passed through the Steps of Avindel. The rattle and clatter echoed through the mountains. It was hard to believe that a few hours earlier they had just been in the warm paradise of Antilion and now they rode in cold shadows of Hamon'dor.

Once out of the pass, they made their way along the open plains. Prince Daemar had brought Yeltai with him, a Roldorian tracker from the Desert Realm. He could trace exactly where the assassins had been. He would feel the dirt around his fingertips, press his ear to the ground and even taste the earth. After a while he came to believe there were eleven of them. They were heading east; Prince Daemar assumed the assassins would be heading to the nearest sea port, either Baron's Bay or Petty Stone Valley. He wasn't willing to guess so they continued following Yeltai's tracking.

Lucian rode beside Gabriel, and the prince noticed him watching Beyorn with the utmost intensity. Beyorn walked alongside; he held his huge battle axe in his right hand. He was near as tall as the prince even with Gabriel saddle atop his horse.

"I heard after Beyorn saw King Aristian bleeding out in the dirt, he cut down a tree with one swing of that axe." Lucian gulped hard as he looked the beast of Golgia up and down.

"Trees don't fight back," Gabriel replied.

"Yes, but they don't fall down when I hit them with my sword!"

Gabriel had heard many tales of Beyorn, the beast of Golgia. He read of his ferocious battle against the Golgian mountain king, Dercindorik. Beyorn challenged his king to trial by combat to prove his loyalty to King Aristian. It was said he cleaved Dercindorik in two, from head to groin.

For the most part, Gabriel was silent. He would listen to his cousin's nervous chatter but rarely did he reply. The sun was high in the sky; he knew at this very moment his sister, Princess Tilia, was now married. The alliance was complete and she was now the wife of an Allamantyan. He felt hint of guilt; he had promised he wouldn't abandoned her and how he would stand by her side when she needed him. Yet here he was chasing his own piece of glory. He imagined her walking down the aisle, her fine white dress and that innocent smile on her face. He knew she would make a beautiful wife.

"*You will regret this boy; until the day you die, you will have wished you had stayed.*" He heard his father's loud drunken voice; the words dwelled on his mind. Had his father foreseen something? Is Tilia okay? The questions rang out over and over. His heart raced and he began to feel helpless and sick. *No... No! She will be fine; she is strong and she is a queen now!*

The Allamantyan and Valorian soldiers rested; all had dismounted. Some lay on the pasture while others walked around chatting and stretching their legs. A few guards were placed throughout the camp but for most part all were calm and relaxed as they knew the enemy was to the east.

Gabriel sat alone. He rested against a large oak tree, the long branches and thick leaves sheltering him from the sun. He was surrounded by a vast ocean of Allamantyan grass; it spread as far as his eyes could see. Just out of the shade were Lucian and Sir Evandinor, both sat on the grass sharpening their swords. He didn't want to rest; every moment they stopped the assassins got further away. He was restless; he could feel his muscles twitching.

"What do they feed him? He looks bigger every time I see him!" Lucian pointed towards Beyorn, who strolled across the plain. His huge bulk of a body seemed to block out the sun, his long strides thudded against the ground.

"I heard he eats his victims," Sir Evandinor replied as he watched the beast walk by. The knight was clad in sparkling Valorian blue; he had receding black hair that fell to his neck and his worn face exceeded his years.

"Anyone dumb enough to face him deserves that fate; I will be keeping my distance. There are many women in Valanor praying on my safe return."

Marshall Varrone DeVeil and Sir Rolan Bonhuer appeared, the latter speaking first, "Someone sounds scared. I fear we chose the wrong allies for this fight."

"Maybe they are better off at home, cooking our meals and keeping our fires warm," Marshall Varrone spat on the grass between Lucian's feet.

"The only thing I'll be keeping warm are your wives' beds," Lucian shot back.

Sir Rolan launched a vicious open hand slap across Lucian's face; the impact screeched, the force knocking him back and against the grass. "Insolent dog!"

In a flash, Sir Evandinor jumped to his feet. Lucian soon followed and the four lunged for their weapons.

"Stop!" Gabriel commanded as he casually strolled out from beneath the oak tree. As he moved out of the shadows, he felt the hot sun glide across his skin. "Put away your weapons." Lucian and Evandinor sheathed their swords and stepped back. Gabriel eyed up his competition. DeVeil was clad in thick armour; a yellow tunic with a black war lion was on his chest and he was already breathing heavily. Sir Rolan was also dressed in armour and his sword hand twitched nervously. Neither wore helmets, revealing the fear in their eyes. *Heavy armour and old faces, easy work.* He extended his spear towards DeVeil's chin.

"If you're fighting anyone today it will be me but I have one request." Gabriel began to spin his spear in front of him.

"Condemned men are always granted one last wish," Sir Rolan laughed anxiously.

"When you reach the gates of the White City, tell the gods it was Gabriel who sent you to meet them." Gabriel lowered into his fighting stance; when his Allamantyan foes made their first move, it would be their last.

The ground rumbled and armour rattled violently as Prince Daemar charged his steed between them. "The enemy is out there!" He growled pointing east across the plain. DeVeil and Sir Rolan backed away. Daemar's voice softened. "Gabriel, would you come with me."

The two princes walked side by side through the camp until they stood alone on the field. For a moment, Gabriel thought Daemar was going to challenge him to single combat. Daemar had a fierce reputation; he was the finest sword south of the Flentian Mountains. However, to Gabriel's disappointment, no challenge came.

Daemar stood silently for a while, first looking to the sky and then to the horizon. "This is a different type of war; they will not stand and face us openly." Daemar turned, facing Gabriel. "I sometimes think how different my life would've been if my wife and son were still alive. I was married at sixteen, widowed by seventeen."

Gabriel stayed silent.

"Two years later your grandfather invaded so I took up arms and rode with my brothers to the Pass at Falentis and then my legend was born. Maybe if my wife and son had been alive, I would've thought twice about facing death. I did not choose this life! But this is the life I lead. For different reasons we hunt the same enemy: one for family honour, one for personal glory."

Gabriel still offered no reply.

Suddenly the sky roared, a deafening god-like explosion ripped across the land. A dark cloud began to sweep across the heavens. All the light in the world began to fade as cold shadow engulfed the golden rays of sun.

Prince Daemar looked up to the blackened clouds. "The rains are coming."

Gabriel peered out across the vast plain; a storm raged on the horizon. Bolts of blue lightening shot down from the heavens. A strong breeze blew towards him, the hairs on his arms began to rise and a shiver crept down his spine. A calm voice followed, one Gabriel recognised, it danced softly through the air, more a whisper on the wind. It said only one word, *treachery.*

Chapter 29
Desolation

Hazar's warm blood trickled down Danaka's face, into her mouth. The hot taste of copper made her gag as she coughed and spat. Out of the darkness the ten shadows moved closer and closer, none spoke a word as they surrounded the fire.

"Stay calm," Garroway said as he offered Danaka his hand. "All we want is shelter."

Danaka hesitated before nodding; she crawled backwards to Duro, holding him in her arms. He groaned as she held him; he felt wet and cold. Looking up, she watched as Garroway and his group made themselves comfortable, laughing and joking as they threw down their black cloaks and sat around the fire. They were a formidable-looking bunch but strangely Danaka didn't feel in any danger.

"We are heading east; do you know of the fastest route to Baron's Bay?" Garroway turned to her. Beads of rain littered his scared face; his solemn eyes were heavy with an unquestionable weight.

"Sorry, I don't know these parts well." Danaka felt herself holding Duro tighter. She was surprised as Garroway proceeded to introduce his family; he called them his children. Danaka knew they were not blood relatives and, as always, her inquisitive mind called for questions. *Stay quiet you fool; it is safer to keep your mouth shut.*

"Look what I have here," the mighty Toran boomed as he came in from outside. In his arms he cradled Griffin.

"Griffin!" Danaka called.

"He will have a few bruises but he will be fine. Tough bastard this one." Toran lowered him beside the fire.

Danaka stroked his wet fur as he whined, the fire lighting up his sable coat.

Uriah began to laugh. "Toran, look who it is." He held Hazar's severed head aloft, turning it left and right, getting a good look. "Not as chatty now, are you?" He laughed once more before he casually tossed the head over his shoulder into the storm. A couple of thuds signalled its departure down the rock face.

As the night drew on, the storm continued to rage but it wasn't long before Garroway's children were fast asleep. Their snores were almost as loud as thunder that shook the cave violently. Danaka had watched the entire group and it was clear all were dangerous individuals but only one scared her: Valdar. Valdar the vicious, she heard one call him. His dark eyes lingered on her like she was a piece of meat; his lip would twitch as he looked her up and down. Valdar's gaunt bony face gave him a skeleton-like appearance.

Eventually however Danaka slept, her body cuddled against Duro. She could feel his body easing up the closer she was to him. It wasn't long before muffled voices woke her.

"We should take her, she will be useful," Valdar whispered into Garroway's ear. "You know I traded in slaves, we regularly imported them in from Petty Stone Valley. She would fetch just the price we need for a ship home."

Danaka dared not open her eyes fully; her heart began to thump. She gripped Duro's hand tightly, her other squeezed the hilt of her sword. *No one is selling me as slave!*

"At least take the horses. We are dragons, we take what we need to survive."

It seemed an age before Garroway replied, he must've been thinking hard on Valdar's words. "Not today, get some sleep."

Danaka felt Valdar walk away and sit down beside the fire. For a moment she lay still, listening to the crackling of the fire and the whistling of the wind. Slowly she sat up; Garroway held Lilah in his arms and stared into the flames. It was clear he couldn't sleep, his thoughts raged like the storm.

"Where are you from?" Danaka asked.

"Dagen, I grew up in a town called Hell." Garroway laughed quietly. "An aptly named place. Murderers and rapists were as common there as fruit on a market stall."

His description made Tomellburg seem like heaven. Danaka watched him closely, his silver hair glowed red in the flames. "Is that where you are heading?"

"Yes, back to Hell. Some say love is the greatest of gifts but it is also the mightiest of burdens. For once you love, your life is never your own. There were eleven pieces to my heart." He looked over his sleeping children.

Danaka counted only ten.

"You are a brave girl."

"I'm not brave," Danaka replied.

Garroway smiled then spoke, "You stood before your enemies and you fought. You faced death and pleaded for the life of another, not your own."

"I was scared, not brave."

"All those who are brave are scared." Garroway pointed to his children. "I fear each day, not for myself but for them. If we had met many years ago, maybe your life would be very different to the one you lead today. Good night Danaka." Garroway lay back, kissing Lilah's head before closing his eyes.

The sun had only just begun to rise; Garroway and his band were already making their way down the rock face. The rains had stopped but the morning was cold, their breath hovered from their mouths like autumn mist. Duro, wrapped in a grey blanket, sat at the cave entrance watching them leave. His pan flute played a soft tune. Danaka stood over him, her hand against his muscled shoulder.

Garroway stood on a rock, shouting up to Duro, "You should be grateful, it is not often a man finds a woman like her."

Duro sat silently, but for once his silence told a thousand words. It was as if he knew exactly who they were and what had happened last night. He stood up,

"Head east until you reach the Silver spear river, cross it then follow the coastline. There you will find what you seek." Duro headed back into the cave and began to saddle his horses, he was once again quiet. As they began to descend the rockface he turned to Danaka and spoke, "Thank you."

The trio headed south. Danaka looked back to see Garroway and his children disappear forever. Duro seemed to have regained some of his strength but he was far from his old self, he winced every now and then but he was not a man to complain. Danaka rejected his offer to ride, so she trudged ahead up front. Griffin seemed to be suffering too; he walked slowly alongside Danaka, sniffing at the muddy grass.

For the first time in days, Danaka felt safe. Hazar and his followers were gone; she felt bad feeling happy that someone was dead. Danaka breathed in the cool fresh air and smiled. For hours they trekked along the mud and swamp-like grass. Fallen trees littered the way; great beams of oak were shattered and broken. Some were frazzled and charred. What was once a summer paradise had become a desolated hell.

They continued through the fallen trees until they passed through a small town that had been decimated. Wooden builds had been laid to waste by the ferocity of the storm. Muffled sound of tears hovered along the cold air. People smeared in mud attempted to clear away the debris that covered the ground. A few black crows cawed, singing a song of death. The storm had destroyed everything in sight; a cold wind blew gently through the carnage.

Danaka had been told by her aunt she had been born on the Fist of stone, a small cluster of isles east of Allamantya. When she was only two, the summers of 184 G.D ended and came with it the great storm of Calorah. It destroyed the isles, ripping out the ground, consuming it with sea and stone. When the rains and wind stopped almost all who lived there were dead. It was commonly known now as the Isle of the dead. Danaka was then taken in by her aunt when she moved to Tomellburg.

The ground slowly began to rumble, the puddles shuddered and rippled, the birds taking flight.

"The storm, it's back," Danaka said as she looked up towards the grim sky.

"That is no storm," Duro countered.

Armoured horses poured down from the hills and through the scattered and broken trees. An array of shining green and glistening blue surrounded them. "Make way for Prince Daemar of Allamantya and Prince Gabriel of Valanor," a loud voice shot.

The muddied people of the town began to flee, taking shelter in their broken homes. Danaka froze as the horses charged around her, the noise painfully crashing against her ears. Mud and water covered her from head to toe. Griffin barked furiously.

"We search for a band of killers," a knight, clad in sparkling plates of iron, spoke as he rode forwards, raising the visor of his helmet. "They attacked our king, wounding him gravely. Have you seen who we hunt?"

"I have seen nothing but mud and rain," Duro replied bluntly.

The torrent of knights moved on without a single word, the noise was deafening as they roared by, drenching Danaka. She tensed up, feeling the cold water and mud running down her back. *Bastards!*

As the horses began to clear, a single rider stayed behind. He was clad in a breast of pure white decorated with gold; he approached slowly removed his shining helmet. "My name is Gabriel, Prince of Valanor." His blue eyes sparkled as he leant down from his horse. "What is your name?"

Danaka looked up at the Prince, his long golden hair brushing her face. She had seen him before but she couldn't recall when or where. "My name is Danaka," She was compelled to reply.

Gabriel stared at her, his eyes gracefully lingering. "I shall remember the name." He kicked into his spurs and rode off. A wave of summer followed him as he charged through the puddles and over the destroyed earth. Danaka felt like she heard an angel sing as he disappeared into the forest.

The light of day had begun to wane. Across the muddied plain lay an isolated two storey farmhouse; it was surrounded by drooping hills and a cold wind. The old wood showed its years. A painting of its constant battle against the elements, the straw roof riddled with decay abandoned the house with the gentle breeze.

"Stay here." Duro drew his sword and entered.

Danaka stood quietly, she knew it was empty. The area was drained of colour, cold shades of brown and yellow lingered before her eyes. It was the opposite of her house back in Tomellburg, which had been a vibrant welcoming feast of colour. After hearing Duro's call she entered, seeing the remains of a once beautiful home. Whoever lived here had abandoned this place long ago. Little remained inside. A single dining table lay on its side. Broken pots, dirtied cloths and rotting food covered the cold floor. A broken stairway led to a single room upstairs. The cold wood creaked in the wind.

Duro descended the stairs, then pulled the dining table upright and placed his sword upon it. "We will spend the night here; most things of use have been taken but there is a bed you can sleep in."

Danaka tried to make the most of her new home; she cleared away debris and helped Duro board up the entrance. The horses were taken to a small room at the rear to shelter them from the next wave of the storm.

A small fire crackled in the hearth. Duro sat beside it, running a wet stone against his sword. Danaka sat against the floor, and Griffin snored beside her. She pictured the house as if was her home: warm flowers on the window ledge, the smell of food roasting over the hearth and a child running happily from one room to another. She even imaged a husband, a man to call her own. Danaka's eyes lingered on Duro; first they were filled with admiration then with anger as his steel screeched a cold tune, one that reminded her of death.

"When does the killing end?" Danaka asked quietly.

"Only one more must die," Duro replied in the same whispered tone.

"Then will you be happy?"

Duro took the wet stone from his sword. "This is not how I thought my life would be; it is definitely not what my father had planned. He was so happy when he told me I would marry Princess Evelyn, the niece of King Aristian. I wish I could've shared his happiness; she looked like a crow without feathers. I told him, 'I would marry only for love, not power.'" Duro hesitated. "I destroyed my family that day."

Danaka sat up. "What happened then?"

"With my marriage refusal, and my father's family honour ruined, Darion was arranged to wed Amber Blackstone; a lesser arrangement but important none the less. She may have been a lady, but a wife she was not." Duro placed his wet stone on his blade, forcing downwards. Eternal sadness filled his eyes.

Danaka wanted to hold him but she rose and quietly headed upstairs, not wanting to pry too much. Half way up Duro spoke again.

"We were inseparable as children; he followed me everywhere." Duro smiled. "My little shadow, I called him. I told Darion I'd always protect him, keep him safe. He had a soft heart; he fell in love with his wife almost instantly. He worshipped the ground she walked on but, like I said, she may have been a woman but not a wife." Duro's wet stone pressed harder against the steel.

"How did he die?"

Duro turned to the flames. "It was three against one. He was never a fighter; it was I who had the talent for killing. I should've been facing them not him. Darion came home one night to find Sir Claris Moon, Sir Castel Damari and Prince Varden Redmond in bed with his new wife. Varden wanted vengeance for my refusal of his sister. Legally they called it a trial of sword and honour."

The flames seemed to burn brighter, crackling louder, and then the storm returned with the fury of the gods.

Chapter 30
Blood, Rain and Steel

The rain was heavy; it crashed onto the muddy ground with fierce intent. Garroway sat looking out of the window; he watched the storm rage through the night. He couldn't sleep, the enemy was close, he could feel it. He had spent so many years as the hunter, being the hunted didn't sit well with him. The assassins had arrived at Baron's Bay the day before, and each of his children were weary from days of travel. Garroway was alone with just the sound of the rain and snores of his children for company.

Outside, the town was silent; there was not a soul in sight. Garroway smiled as he looked over at his children. Each one he loved more than words yet without Lothar, his oldest friend, life did not produce the warmth it once had. *I will see you again old friend.*

Garroway thought back to Valdar's plan of selling Danaka to the slave ships at Petty stone valley. Maybe he should've accepted his plan. She would've brought in a fine price and paid for their trip back to Dagen. Baron's Bay however was closer and none of them had known the exact route south. Something told him deep in his gut he had made the wrong decision.

"Father, you must sleep." Rhodesha moved from her bed and sat beside him.

"I once went three days and nights without sleep at the Battle of the half moon." Garroway held her hand.

"There is something I must tell you." Rhodesha looked down, her hand cradling her stomach. "No one knows but…"

"I know all things." Garroway smiled the happiest of smiles. "I hope you carry a girl and she grows up to be as beautiful as her mother." He kissed her forehead.

"I know how to take life but I don't know if I am ready to raise one."

"All you need is love, for it is the greatest of gifts. You will make a wonderful mother."

Toran stirred. "Falahail Delaghara."

"When did he learn to speak ancient Ulkarian?" Garroway looked over at his son.

"Ever since we came here, he has been dreaming and muttering words in his sleep. The quicker we leave here the better."

Ulkarian was the ancient tongue of Dalackis, the Winged God. Not even Lothar, who had followed the eastern faith, knew much of the old words.

Ulkarian language was said to have been brought down from the heavens by Cesaril the lawgiver. Garroway watched his son uneasily.

Rhodesha rested her head on Garroway's shoulder; it briefly took his mind away from his troubles. It wasn't long before she was asleep. He lowered her softly before moving over to Lilah. He smelt her thick head of red hair; it reminded him of home. *I long to feel the sand of Dagen beneath my feet.* He lay beside her, taking her in his arms. He wouldn't sleep but he longed to feel her body against his.

"This place is wetter than a whore's cunt," Valdar blurted out. "The quicker we get to that ship the better."

"It's like their gods are pissing on us," Caelan added.

"Better than being shit on, I guess," Uriah replied as he moved to avoid a leak that was dripping on his head.

It was early but everyone was up. The rain still poured heavily outside; thunder rumbled before bursts of light opened the skies. The assassins stood at the doorway to the inn, each ready to take that final walk to the harbour. Garroway stood silently, his eyes scanning the muddied streets of Baron's Bay. The town was deserted, not a living creature was in sight, just rain and mud. He could hear his children chatting away.

"Zaira," Uriah asked as he paced up and down, a large smile painted on his face. "We don't know if we shall see the sun rise on the morrow or the feel the warmth of Dagen again. Will you not give a man one final request before his body becomes food for the crows?"

"What would a condemned man wish for, Little Uriah?" Zaira stood sharpening her spear. Her aesthetically pleasing body teasing him with each arch and curve.

"Don't you remember? I wish to see what no man has seen before."

Zaira signalled him to move closer. The others began to giggle and laugh. Once Uriah was in front of her, she seductively pulled up her leather skirt.

Uriah became engulfed in a golden light; he slowly turned back to the others, "If I die today, I will die happy."

Garroway banged his spear on the wooded floor. "It's time, we move."

The assassins stood outside; everything was silent except for the rain and the thunder. Garroway signalled them to move; side by side they slowly began to walk down the street. The muddied puddles were deep and thick. Rain like this was never heard of in Dagen.

"Maarax, keep that bow to the rooftops." Garroway extended his arm to the skies above.

Each assassin watched the windows, the alleyways and the rooftops. The enemy could be anywhere. Old wooden buildings that swayed and creaked flanked them either side, narrow walkways were situated every fourth building. The town was old and cramped; disease lived within the rotting wood.

"There is nothing but ghosts," Valdar said uneasily.

When they came to the end of the street, it veered to right and at the bottom was the harbour. Once again, the street was silent; there was a single ship waiting at anchor. It wasn't large or fancy. A trading ship but big enough to take them home and to safety.

"We've made it, there she is." Uriah slapped Toran on the back.

"Not just yet, little brother." Toran gripped his broadsword.

Thunder crashed above them like a mountain tumbling upon the ground. It was loud and deafening; the fright made Roak draw his sword. Lighting split through the sky like a sword through flesh.

"We might be safer here than out on the sea." Lilah looked out towards the raging ocean.

"I'd rather die out there than in this fucking shit hole of a country." Valdar wiped the rain from his cruel face.

"Here or there, death is death. I shall die when I decide my time is up." Uriah stepped up upon the harbour deck.

"No one dies today," Garroway replied firmly.

The sea crashed onto the harbour walls, followed by the echo of thunder.

"There are as many people here as there are coins in my back pocket." Uriah patted his back side.

The ship was empty; it just bobbed up and down on the stormy sea.

"Head back to the inn," Garroway ordered.

As commanded, the eleven moved quickly back along the muddy streets. Then, suddenly, the sound of a horn filled their ears. Long and frightening it called out, bringing them all to halt. Thunder bellowed again, this time louder than before; the ground shuddered beneath their feet. The town began to rumble, a rhythmic tune of marching played throughout the streets. Up ahead, Allamantyan soldiers approached in a squared formation. Either side, rows of cavalry rode out of the narrow walkways; they positioned themselves in front of the infantry. Another tuned played, this time from behind, and a band of Valorian horseman rode up to their rear.

"We're trapped." Valdar drew his sword.

Front and back, the soldiers began to march, the haunting sound of horse and armour closed in. "Lay down your weapons! There is no escape, we have you surrounded."

Garroway turned to his children; the rain trickled down his scared face. "If today be the day death finds us, do not go so willingly. Fight for your brothers and your sisters. You are the finest warriors I have ever known; we do not fear death, death fears us!" Garroway spun his spear.

His children roared in approval before forming a circle; they were ready, ready to show the Western realm the might of Dagari steel. Garroway could feel the patter of the rain on his face; he watched the water running down his blade. Soon it would be red with the blood of his enemies.

The Allamantyans continued their slow loud march, their mail covered feet crashed against the puddles. Suddenly they stopped.

Toran beat his hand on his chest then boomed, "Come on then, you cunts!"

"We haven't got all day!" Uriah added. "I have a ship to catch."

"In a few moments you will be dead; lay down your weapons." An Allamantyan knight barked as he rode to front of his men.

"We are dragons of Dagen, we don't die so easily." Garroway turned Maarax, "Let it begin."

Maarax drew back his bow and loosed his arrow; it whistled through the air and stuck into the knight's face, killing him instantly. At that moment, a horn of battle sounded, and the first wave of Allamantyan infantry charged forwards with an eagerness for death. Maarax fired in rapid succession, each arrow killing with pin point accuracy.

"Now," Garroway commanded.

In seconds, the assassin's unleashed their fury; their blades hacked and slashed like starved animals hungry for blood. They killed with an uncontrollable anger, blood sprayed across the rain and into the mud. Soldiers screamed as they tasted the full flavour of Dagari steel. Garroway unleashed his spear, swinging it with both hands. The blade, curved and ever sharp, cut its way through mail and bone. The wall of assassins held firm against the might of Allamantya. Swords and spears clashed, in a mighty battle of blood, rain and steel.

Toran and Roak hacked wildly; their swords obliterated the Allamantyan shields, smashing them into shards of broken wood. With their shields broken, they were lambs to the slaughter. Toran roared as he slashed downwards, his immense power cleaved his man in two; from head to groin Toran's blade emptied his guts into the mud.

The first wave was massacred, butchered without mercy. Bloodied bodies smeared the wet mud. The ghosts of the fallen would haunt these streets for years to come. A horn signalled the call of retreat. The wounded clambered back to safety, their courage smashed to pieces like the limbs of their fallen comrades.

"Is that all you have!" Toran stumbled forwards, he hacked at the wounded and those who attempted to flee. Alone and out in the open, he held a severed head aloft, roaring like a lion. "Fight me! I am the Iron Bull."

Rhodesha screamed, "Toran, get back here!"

"They are attacking from both sides." Caelan pointed to the Valorians.

The Allamantyan cavalry formed up in rows of two, and the Valorians did the same. They intended to attack simultaneously, wiping out the assassins in one mighty charge. The horn sounded, signalling the call for battle once more. The ground and sky rumbled as the horses ascended down the muddied streets, a deafening onslaught of thunder.

"Toran!" Rhodesha broke rank running to her man.

Before Garroway could intervene, Toran was swamped by the onslaught of heavy horse. The Iron Bull dropped the first rider with a swing from his broadsword, the second he dragged from his saddle with his bare hands before pinning him to the mud with the tip of his blade.

"Get out of there!" Garroway yelled helplessly.

Toran pulled Rhodesha out of the muddied street and onto the old rotten walkway, escaping death. Infantry pursued them relentlessly. Toran was able to smash down a door to the nearest building and they both disappeared inside, the soldiers following in after them.

Garroway wanted to help them but he couldn't. The cavalry smashed into them like a tidal wave; the force was immense as armoured horses poured down the street. The thunder of battle echoed through the rain. They were trapped, attacked on both flanks and heavily outnumbered. The assassins didn't fight for honour or for glory but for their brothers and sisters. Survival would be the greatest victory.

The horsemen charged up and down, swinging with their swords. Zaira and Lilah were able to duck and pivot, avoiding the brutal embrace of death. Both pulled a knight from his saddle, butchering him in the mud.

Maarax unleashed two arrows, the second saving Uriah from the kiss of steel. He, however, caught a fierce slash from a Valorian rider; a chunk of his shoulder left his body as he spun one hundred and eighty degrees, losing his bow. Another rider charged passed, ripping his sword across Maarax's chest. "Father!" he called before he felt a lance through his back.

Garroway watched helplessly; he had only been a few feet away from him but there was nothing he could do. Maarax slumped to the ground with an almighty thud. Anger filled Garroway's heart; his blood began to grow cold. He gripped his spear and fought like a man possessed. A surge of energy coursed through his body and then, fluent like the days of old, he took down a knight with one swipe of his spear, then another to his left who caught the blade directly in his chest. "Kill, kill them all!" he screamed as he fought on.

The battle was chaotic, screams of death screeched as lighting flashed from the darkened skies. The armoured knights were bogged down by the thick mud, some lost their balance and collapsed. Roak and Naleac pounced, cutting their throats and leaving them to bleed out, no quarter asked, none received.

"Die, die!" Valdar lost control of his senses as he climbed on top of a knight and repeatedly stabbed him in his throat. A lake of blood spread across the mud. The street was crowded with brutality, packed together, shoulder to shoulder. The death of Maarax fuelled the ferocity of the remaining assassins; they killed harder and crueller than ever before.

Zaira ducked, a sword gliding above her head. She countered by thrusting her spear upwards and through a Valorian's chest. Uriah, who was beside her, forward rolled in between two soldiers; he raised his swords, slashing them both across their stomachs. As both stood stunned, clutching at their guts, Zaira sliced outwards, ripping open their throats. The knights had come here in search of glory yet all they found was the fastest route to the White City.

Just when it seemed victory was near, a band of Allamantyan reinforcements arrived; they were fresh and ready for battle. They swarmed the left flank, taking Zaira and Uriah by surprise. Uriah was dropped by a barrage of spears and shields; he lay helpless in the mud. Zaira stood over him, defending her brother with everything she had. She killed two before tasting rusted steel across her wrist; the impact shattered her bone, almost severing her hand. It was held together by the thinnest of skin as she valiantly tried to fight on. Zaira lunged wildly, missing her attack as a knight skewered her through her stomach. Blood sprayed outwards as the sword exited out her back, a second entered her side. Uriah screamed a deafening scream; it roared up to the heavens as Zaira fell into his arms.

Garroway had been called a god of battle, a taker of souls, yet today he was a demon. Blood dripped from his face yet none of it was his own. He deflected two attacks easily before ending matters with a brutal thrust to a knight's chest. The force launched the man off his feet as Garroway glided through the air with him, ending with the knight on his back and Garroway standing over him.

Lilah and the twins were fighting side by side, back to back. Parrying and fighting with everything they had. The enemy were everywhere, like a swarm of ants they surrounded the assassins hacking and stabbing. Lilah was smeared with the blood of her enemies; her spear was as deadly as the lighting above, striking with faultless accuracy. Like a cobra her spear shot forwards, smashing a Valorian through his mouth; his teeth shattered as the blade exited his head.

The thunder boomed as steel met steel. Everything Garroway had taught them was coming to fruition; *he who fights hardest shall live to see tomorrow.* As rain turned to blood, a wall of dead began to line the muddy streets. Garroway stabbed and slashed; for a brief second, he admired his work. A severed head flew high into the air before falling down onto the chest of the knight's crippled body.

Caelan glided like a piece of fine silk in a gentle breeze, his spear tasting blood. He and Naleac moved like a mirror image, killing was as easy as breathing for these two. Caelan forced his spear through the chest of a fallen knight. He looked up and smiled at Naleac, his green eyes twinkling in the rain before he broke rank and headed towards the Valorians at the far end of the street.

****

Gabriel waited eagerly at the bottom of the street, his muscles twitching. Lucian and Sir Evandinor flanked him, five Valorian horsemen were behind. His countrymen were being slaughtered by the assassins, he could hear their screams. Gabriel desperately wanted to clash steel with these warriors from the east. Daemar had ordered he stay away, fighting only when necessary; he reluctantly agreed but his patience was wearing thin.

"I have never seen so many killed by so few." Lucian sat uneasily in his horse.

A single assassin made his way down the street; he screamed as he marched forwards, "My name is Caelan, who will face me?"

Gabriel smiled, *finally a warrior worth fighting.* "He is mine." He lowered his spear, holding it out in front of him. He watched along the blade as Caelan charged closer and closer. He was on foot whereas the prince was on horseback; he would allow his man to tire. Running in this mud was no easy task. Suddenly Gabriel kicked his spurs and charged full speed. His eyes never moved from his target. The rain crashed hard onto his armour, pattering against his helmet.

As the prince drew closer to his target, his horse suddenly reared up, letting out a deafening scream and Gabriel was thrown from its back and into the mud. Before he had time to react to what had happened, Caelan was on top of him, thrusting downwards with his spear. Gabriel rolled to his left, his face sliding through a brown puddle; it would be the last thing he ever saw if he didn't get to his feet and quick.

Caelan stopped attacking and stepped back, breathing heavily. "You will die standing, up with you."

Gabriel, a little shocked and confused, stood up. He pulled his muddied helmet from his head, dropping it to the ground. "You will see the face of the man who kills you."

Caelan placed his foot under the prince's spear and kicked it towards him. Mud splashed in Gabriel's eyes and in a flash Caelan was on him. Gabriel just about grabbed hold of his spear and deflected the lightening attacks that were raining down towards him. The two spears clashed together as the warriors lunged at one another. The attacks were god-like in speed; neither took a backwards step as they fought like lions. The collision of the steel made Gabriel's hands shudder; the vibrations shook up his arms and into his shoulders. He watched as Caelan stepped back. *He needs to rest; I will not give him that chance.* Gabriel attacked, first low then high, keeping the assassin off balance. Caelan stumbled backwards before taking a gulp of air. They exchanged again, spear against spear, god-like speed collided in a whirl of majestic beauty. Gabriel forced him back; he could feel the assassin's blows lacked the power and finesse of before.

Slowly they circled one another; Caelan's shoulders slumped and his breaths could be heard between the beating of thunder. Suddenly, like a cat, Caelan sprang upwards towards the prince, both his feet leaving the ground. Gabriel parried the first attack; the second however came from the right. The base of Caelan's spear smashed against Gabriel's cheek, snapping his head sideways. Gabriel crouched as he rode the attack, spinning his body three hundred and sixty degrees before slashing upwards. The blade of his spear ripped across Caelan's stomach, cutting through boiled leather and flesh. Caelan stumbled backwards, clinging to his wound as blood and entrails seeped from his body. He dug his spear into the muddied earth to keep himself from falling.

"You are done, surrender." Gabriel smiled, admiring his victory.

Caelan spluttered and groaned. "I'd rather fight and die than kneel and live."

"So be it." Gabriel shot forwards, moving like a hunter towards his prey. His spear glided along the rain and cold air as it struck Caelan in his exposed neck; the blade cut through flesh as it exploded out the back of his head.

The weight of the attack held Caelan upright. He choked and gasped for air; his green eyes slowly began to close as blood dripped from his mouth. The crash of horse and armour suddenly came up behind Gabriel. Lucian and the others surrounded him. Gabriel pulled his spear free, allowing Caelan's body to fall. Blood trickled from a cut above the prince's eye, his first wound. Gabriel's beautiful white horse lay dead, an arrow lodged in its neck. Its coat had been painted red with the kiss of battle. He turned towards the chaos at the centre of the street. "We end this now."

****

Valdar crawled along the mud, the rain washing away the blood that covered his pale shaven head. He forced his sword into the ground as he climbed to his feet. He screamed one word, "Bastards!" as he charged forwards, meeting the next attack of cavalry head on. He took one rider from his horse before tasting Allamantyan steel across his breastplate. Golden sparks flew from his chest as the impact took him from the ground; he disappeared down a muddied slope out of sight.

As the Allamantyans took the assassins from the front, the Valorian horseman smashed into their rear. A knight swung out with his shield, catching Naleac on his head, dropping him like a sack of potatoes. The impact of the attack forced the assassins apart; their circle was shattered. Lilah and Uriah backed away, defending themselves from the raging Valorian cavalry.

Roak was separated from the others; a rider stuck him with his sword as he charged past, another with his spear. The blade slid into his back, sticking between his shoulder blades. Roak let out a mighty roar before turning and slashing outward killing an oncoming knight. The first swing caught the man on his chest, Roak's next severed his arm and the third opened up his throat. Another rider caught Roak with his lance, the blade tearing through his shoulder. Three Allamantyan men at arms surrounded him, spearing Roak simultaneously. He let out a battle cry that defied the heavens; he attacked like a raged dog. He snapped and shattered the spears that skewered his body. His blade ripped and hacked, killing all three. Once his sword had tasted its final drop of blood, Roak fell to his knees, never to rise again.

Garroway, Uriah and Lilah were the last three standing; the fallen bodies of their loved ones united them in one valiant attack. They moved together as one impenetrable force, they killed with every ounce of energy they had remaining until nothing but the dead surrounded them. Another horn sounded a last call for battle. The remaining soldiers of the Western Realm retreated to the front of the street; they all dismounted, forming up in rows of blue and green.

I have failed you; despair befell Garroway as he saw his children in the mud. *I swore to lead you to safety yet death is all you found. No more will die!*

Uriah helped a wounded Naleac to his feet, who in turn called out wildly for his fallen brother, Caelan.

"Go, all of you!" Garroway pointed to the narrowest of alleyways.

"I will not leave." Lilah grabbed hold of his arm. "I cannot go on without you!"

Garroway pulled Lilah close. "No matter what happens I will always be with you." The rain crashed hard against Garroway's face, masking his tears. "We will watch the sun rise together." He kissed her one last time; her lips felt soft. In that moment Garroway was in a field of corn, Lilah in his arms as the warm sun blessed them with its golden beauty. The roar of thunder brought him back to hell; he saw Lilah and Uriah helping Naleac down the alleyway and to safety. Garroway would stay, he would fight and maybe he would die.

Garroway stood alone; he tore the tunic from his chest. The rain collapsed around him, splashing against the mud and puddles. Tiny droplets ran down his face and between the grooves of his muscles. He gripped the *Titans Bitch*, "Once more, old friend, once more into the hell of battle."

The soldiers charged forwards. Their feet sunk into the muddy ground as they inched closer and closer. Closing his eyes, he took in a deep breath. He lowered his spear towards his enemies, the curved blade dripping with blood. In a flash, he stepped forward, lashing out with his spear. He carried the fury of the gods with each blow he struck. As the men surrounded him, he hacked them down one by one, like thin branches they snapped and fell. He pivoted and manoeuvred forward, avoiding the oncoming blows before returning with destructive hell fire of his own.

A soldier let out a blood curdling scream as he clawed at his neck. Fountains of blood sprayed from the huge gash in his throat. Garroway stepped around the dying man, his feet splashing in the muddied puddles. He deflected the swords descending down towards him; sparks flew as the steel smashed together. Sidestepping, he slashed, killing without mercy. For every one he killed, he knew that would be one less that would pursue his children. A burning rage fuelled his desire to kill; he felt no pain, no remorse as he murdered his way through the helpless men who stood before him.

The soldiers' shields offered little defence as they were smashed and broken. The might of Garroway's strength could not be stopped, his spear span in his hands, twisting and turning before shooting out like snake. The knights swung wildly with their swords, stabbing nothing but air; with each mistake they made, Garroway made them pay.

"Gods have mercy!" a knight yelled, as he frantically tried to crawl away from the monster that was pursing him. Garroway walked over to the knight, his face cold, his eyes burning with hate. In a flash he severed the knight's face in two.

Garroway swung out with his spear; the blade cut through two men at arms like butter. Their bloodied lifeless bodies crashed to the ground. Garroway stopped, breathing deeply. His heart pounded in his chest; looking back he could see the street was littered with the dead and the dying. Mutilated men screamed as they clambered at their stumps. Emotionless, he wiped his face, removing the blood and rain that blurred his vision. Looking down, he noticed his chest was split; blood seeped from his wound, yet he did not feel any pain.

Two rows of soldiers still stood before him; it seemed for every one he killed, two would take their place. The men slowly marched forwards, shoulder to shoulder, their spears pointing out like the horns of a bull. Suddenly they stopped; their rhythmic steps were rendered silent. All that was left was the rain pattering softly against their cold iron.

“I am a dragon of Dagen, born of the warrior code. Beyorn! Where are you, Beyorn?” Garroway screamed. Anger and malice had taken hold of him.

A mighty roar let loose, like a dragon coming forth from its cave. The soldiers began to part; slowly stepping out of the shield wall was the beast of Golgia. The rain crashed hard against his muscles; he gripped his huge double edge battle axe in both hands. The steel glistened in the few strands of the light that shone down from between the clouds. His long dark hair stuck to his shoulders; his eyes burned with vengeance. Droplets of water formed in his beard. Beyorn slowly walked forwards; his steps mirrored the thunder as it rumbled from the sky. His breath was visible as he exhaled, the rain sprayed from his mouth. Like a wild animal, he grunted loudly.

Garroway smiled, eager to test himself. He stuck his spear into the mud and then pulled his long silver hair back, moving it away from his face. His nemesis approached; he was more beast than man. Slowly they began to circle one another. Garroway moved on the balls of his feet. He would not rush Beyorn; it would be foolish to make the same mistakes that cost Lothar so dearly.

The rain poured heavily, blue lighting split the sky, the thunder boomed. Beyorn roared. Garroway showed the white of his teeth.

Chapter 31
A Betrayal of Love

The tomb was cold; a deathly silence flickered along the candles that surrounded King Aristian's resting place. Deep in the crypts of the God's Tower, the Allamantyan king's body had been laid to rest. It was the most holy place in all of the Western Realm, a place so pure not even spiders spun their webs within its haloed walls. The cloak of darkness was everywhere, the torches along the walls offered minimal light.

King Vincinicus leant over the majestically carved tomb. It stood alone; eight steps of marble rose upwards encircled by golden candles. The stone was cold; he ran his figures over the sculptured face of his friend. *Only death is certain.* His mind wandered. He thought back to the morning they found the body, the cawing of the crow, the whiteness of his eyes and the bitter taste of death on the morning air.

"Death, only death." He took Leylan's wine to his lips before coughing; droplets of red sprinkled over the stone carved face. Vincinicus's mind was hazy; the wine did that to him. It cured his pain, helping remove his shame from memory. He slumped on the tomb steps, almost falling back. His hands rested on his large bloated belly. *I am the son of better men.* He took another swig of wine; it splashed across his beard and down his blue silks.

"You were a better man than me my friend; a toast to you and our ancestors. House Da'Menaeon!" Vincinicus raise his flagon and allowed the wine to fall into his mouth. His gut twisted as choked, he fell forwards banging against the marble steps. Laughing, he struggled to his feet. Blood and wine smeared his face. Vincinicus stared up to the darkness. "Good men fall while shadows live. I have seen so much death." He stumbled back up the steps and placed his bloodied hand on the stone face of Aristian and whispered into the ear, "Ollaria'h is it beautiful? Did the angels carry you on wings of gold?" His hand squeezed his flagon. "Death was forced upon you that night. I may be a joke of a king, a jealous father, but I know death. Who would want to murder you, great king?"

Slowly he made his way out of the crypts; outside the air was wet and cold. Vincinicus breathed deeply; he coughed, wiped his mouth, then concealed his bloodied cloth. Standing vigilant around the God's Tower were the Knights of Hethelyon; the rain crashed against their suits of gold.

A rainbow began to form on the horizon. Antilion was silent. The populace was mourning their great king. *My people will rejoice when the gods take me.* He took another gulp of wine until his flagon was empty. After stumbling down the steps, he stood on the bridge back to the palace. He peered over the edge; he saw jagged rock and waves of dark blue crashing against the mountain side. The ocean roared violently; the gods were angry.

He held the carving of his wife in his palm, the rain pattering against skin and stone. "Why did you leave me?" When alone, King Vincinicus was ripe with self-pity but in front of others he was able to cloak this sadness; *the greatest actor in all of Valanor.* Next to the carving of his wife he held another; it was almost identical. He stared at them both diligently. *So alike, so proud, so arrogant.* He squeezed both hoping to crush the stone within his mighty grasp. *You are not a god!*

Vincinicus knew the rumours at his royal court, that Gabriel was not his son. His wife had told all who would listen he had been fathered by the god of Ollaria'h. Most took this for madness yet others whispered she had taken another to bed. The thoughts angered him.

The sky groaned and rain began to fall. The king quickly made his way inside the palace. He stumbled around inside Aristian's chambers. The wind blew in from the balcony, the rain crashed heavily outside. He was determined to find something, evidence. The entrance to the chambers had been guarded; the guards said no one entered all night. Vincinicus glanced over the balcony; he saw nothing but smooth white stone and a sheer drop of one hundred feet, near impossible to climb, especially with the storm that was raging that night.

Whoever did this, knew the palace; maybe they were the ones who paid the assassins too. Angered by his failure, Vincinicus headed back to his chambers; inside he found Leylan seated on his chair. He was bastard to an Allamantyan mistress he had taken from the Flentian Mountains during one of his father's raids. He kept her; she warmed his bed when he felt low.

"Wine, give me wine boy," Vincinicus boomed as he entered. He had company so it was time to cloak his sadness.

Leylan, clad in robes of black, did as commanded.

"King Aristian – thoughts plague me of his death. I do not believe it was the gods' hands that took him." Vincinicus took the wine to his lips.

"He was old and old men die. Princess Arrabella told me he was ill; he had aged beyond his years since his wife died and he raised a son who fails to be a man."

The eyes of King Vincinicus contorted. "How do you know such things?"

"Women like to talk after making love." Leylan smiled.

Vincinicus banged his hands on the table, and the jugs of wine shuddered. "She is not for you! Keep away. She is a princess!"

Leylan raised his eyebrows, offering no fear of his father's words. "Just because she is born of royal blood does not mean she does not like to be fucked like a common whore, a filthy princess." Leylan laughed as he raised his wine.

The king lashed out; he smacked the goblet from Leylan's hands. The silver cup scraped against the marble floor. His small chubby hands grabbed Leylan by his silk yanking him forward. "You taint her honour. Bastards do not lay with royalty."

"What makes her royal blood greater than mine? If I bled her out right now, hers would be red just like any other."

King Vincinicus twisted in pain; he released Leylan and fell to the table. Blood began to trickle from his lips.

Leylan smiled and leant towards his father's face. "You do know Arrabella is not the only princess I have fucked. Oh, for years I visited the chambers of another."

The King roared, lunging upwards. His movement was cut short, stopping suddenly before raising his hands to his ears. His head began to pound, like a beating drum, over and over, louder and louder. He could hear a deafening spine-shivering scraping, like someone was hacking away at his skull with a hammer and chisel, breaking away the bone piece by piece. He fell forwards, crashing against the table. He tried to force himself up but his arms began to shake and his gut began to twist and turn. Vincinicus wrenched and choked as he crumbled back down to the wooden surface of the table. He coughed murderously before sliding onto the floor. Again, he gasped and spluttered, this time blood sprayed across the beautiful mosaic floor. His windpipes began to close and then open ever so briefly, teasing him with the taste of oxygen. He clawed frantically at his throat, digging his fingers into his jugular.

More blood sprayed from his mouth as he now began to gag; both phlegm and blood drained from his between his lips. Thick red veins began to surround the whites of his eyes then they began to swell. Again, he screamed in pain, gut wrenching pleas as his stomach began to burn, like red flame was cooking his insides.

"Poor father," Leylan calmly spoke as he walked around the table, before tipping his wine onto King Vincinicus. The deep red liquid crashed against his face, mirroring the blood that was already pouring from his mouth. "Gabriel said, "Wine will be the death of you," but you don't listen, do you?"

"Bastard!" King Vincinicus tried to yell, yet the words crumbled from his lips like an ageing rock. His throat began to tighten, his eyes began to darken as if a snake was sucking the life from his body, yet he forced the words from his mouth. He gripped his fist and banged it against the floor. "You paid those assassins, you killed Aristian."

"Oh, I dreamed of this moment." Leylan slowly knelt down, running his index finger over his father's shoulder and up to his crown. "Wrong, wrong. I do my own killing." Leylan took a deep breath. "I have been tainting your wine. I first tried Rathmol on your wife and it drove her mad. She died too quickly but I wanted you to suffer longer. It took me years but eventually I found Black Halis, a Brundean poison; it kills you from the inside, slowly." Leylan removed the king's crown, his voice lowered. "She told me what you would do to her."

In the midst of all his pain, King Vincinicus looked up at his bastard son.

Leylan leant forward, pressing his cold lips against his father's ear before whispering, "You kings are all the same, you take what you want. I saw the pain in her eyes, the suffering in her heart. You killed her." For once Leylan showed emotion in his voice, tears began to form in his eyes. He quickly wiped them away. “My mother, she told me what you would do to her, King Vincinicus, the rapist of women.”

“I–I–she was mine!” Vincinicus groaned as tears poured from his eyes.

“She was my mother!” Leylan screamed. Spit flew from his mouth and his face contorted. “Every night you left her room, I heard her cries. I saw her sadness. It was I who wiped away her tears. The day she died, she uttered a single word, ‘Vengeance’.”

The king choked and gasped, trying with all his might to take in as much air as he could. His face began to swell, his cheeks puffed outwards, his eyes were on the verge of exploding.

“No, don’t you die yet!” Leylan brought back his foot before ramming it into his father’s gut.

Vincinicus offered no reaction as he curled up; the pain that had consumed his body began twisting him, burning away his insides. His fist opened and he stared at the small carving in his hand. Smears of blood stained the grey stone. *Forgive me, my son.* It was an image of Gabriel he was holding.

“I made my mother a promise.” Leylan walked back round the table, sitting himself down. He poured a glass of fresh untainted wine before taking it to his lips. “As you die and breathe your last breath, I want you to know that I will destroy everything you hold dear. I will wipe your son’s name from the history books. Your beloved daughter will crawl at my feet and only when I have tired of her warming my bed, will I cut her throat.” A hollow smile filled his face; a single tear fell from his cheek. “Now, die quietly, old man.”

****

The flames crackled in the storm; Andros shuddered as the thunder rumbled outside. Tears filled his pale eyes as he moved from the hearth towards the balcony of his royal chamber. The cold wind swirled and howled. The rains fell violently, crashing against the white stone of the palace.

“Father!” he yelled across the night sky, the rain soaking his red robes. “I need you, I cannot do this alone!”

The gods replied with thunder and lighting, the latter forcing a cowering Andros back inside. He quivered as he fell before the flames; rain trickled down his face. *I lost a father but gained a wife.* Andros’s fist tightened.

A crash of thunder struck the prince to his core. He shook and quivered, turning to the flames for protection. Andros was always scared when summer ended; as a child the storms frightened him. He never liked the cold; he preferred the flames, feeling their warmth, hearing their soft crackle. Andros would cower under the dread of the storm. His mother would come to his aid and her words would soothe him. He remembered the night she passed from the mortal world, the raging of the flames against the stone, the howling and screaming. The thoughts both excited and sickened him; he blamed himself but he didn’t know why.

“Murderer.” a soft whisper crackled along the embers of red and gold.

"No!" Andros clambered to his feet, clutching a goblet that he then tossed into the flames.

His chamber door slowly squeaked open; the echo of clumsy steps soon followed. Under the low light Andros saw a familiar face, one that would usually bring both warmth and happiness to his heart. Today it brought only fear.

"Lyon, you mustn't be here!" Andros jumped up and unsuccessfully attempted to push his lover from the room.

"Oh, now you are married you no longer need me!" Lyon's slurred words were ripe with the odour of wine. "Scared your lovely Valorian wife will find me here, ha! I saw her praying in the great temple, praying for your father and her brother." Lyon stumbled forwards, pouring himself more wine. He lay back on the prince's bed. "Remember when we lay on these furs together, just you and I? I thought then I would be happy forever. How wrong I was."

"I demand you leave." Andros grabbed Lyon by the cusp of his leather doublet.

Lyon banished the prince's hands from him.

"How dare you lay a hand on me!" Andros slashed with his open palm; the sound of skin meeting skin violently echoed with the storm battling outside.

"Again, again! Punish me for the love I bear, my prince." Lyon proceeded to slap himself, tears of sorrow painted his cheeks. "We promised, we said we would always be together."

Andros watched with pity as Lyon sobbed. He wished to hold him but he knew if he did, he wouldn't be able to let him go. Andros owed Lyon far more than the knight could ever know. The priests had helped Andros forget the evil that plagued his mind, those dark days filled with blood, fire and sin, but it was Lyon that brought him back to the light. King Aristian thought it was the priests that cured his soul but it was the love of this man right here.

"I must live my father's dream. I will be the first King of a united Western realm." Andros knelt between Lyon's legs.

"You choose a crown over love." Lyon pulled a dagger from his belt and placed it in the prince's hand. "You must kill me; I do not deserve to live."

Andros froze, the dagger loosely dangled within his flaccid grasp.

"I know this palace like the back of my hand. You showed me the tunnels; I loved sneaking into your room so we could be alone. They were the only times I was happy. My world ended when your father married you to that foreign whore! Oh, I prayed she would die but the gods did not listen, but why would they heed the words of a sinner? Yesterday, as I watched you two dance, I felt my heart shatter. I drank until I couldn't drink anymore. I hid in the tunnels to be alone, reminiscing. Then I heard your father, I moved until I could see into his chambers. He was smiling in bed, laughing he was, laughing at me, how easily he took you from me. I waited until he was asleep then I entered."

Tears began to well in the prince's eyes.

"The king seemed so calm. I held the pillow then his eyes opened, he wanted to scream but I forced it down on his face." Lyon mimicked the actions. "I used all my strength; I hated and loved what I was doing. I just kept thinking what he had done, how he had ruined my life." A single tear fell from the knight's cheek. "His body twitched and kicked; when it stopped, I looked at his lifeless eyes. I felt his soul peering back at me; I hoped the harpies had taken him to the City of Fire." Lyon looked up. "Kill me."

Andros stood still, his cold eyes staring hopelessly, he never blinked.

Lyon couldn't contain himself any longer. "Kill me! Call in your guards and have them tear me limb from limb. Remove my head and roast it on your flames. Send me to hell to endure for my sins. I deserve it; I cannot live without you. Let the world know I was a sinner, a coward who killed an old man in his bed, but let them know the love I carried in my heart." Lyon collapsed, the weight of his guilt forcing him to his knees.

Andros clutched the dagger; the cold steel flickered in the light of the flames. Lyon continued to speak, but all Andros imagined was thrusting the blade into his neck, watching the blood drain from Lyon's body. Oh, he wanted to kill; his body craved vengeance, the fire whispered into his ears, commanding him to kill again. Andros breathed deeply. "Get up. You will live but your punishment will be to live without me. You will never see me again; I banish you from Antilion and from my presence. If your eyes take hold of me, I will have them burnt out; if your tongue calls my name, I will have it ripped from your mouth!" Andros screamed.

With Lyon's head hanging low, he left; his pride and dignity lay with his tears on the cold stone floor.

Andros stood alone; he felt a darkness slowly creeping over him, a voice called to him, it crackled from within the flames. His eyes twitched and hands began to shake.

Chapter 32
Duel of Titans

The whole world seemed to stop. Garroway moved softly. He encircled Beyorn, watching his every move. *You do not meet a beast like that head on; speed nullifies power, brain beats brawn.* The rain crashed hard, the thunder echoed. The gods awaited the battle to come.

"Tonight, I eat your heart!" Beyorn spoke devilish tone of death.

Garroway called him in, the beast responded. Beyorn charged forwards, his axe cutting through rain and air. Garroway sidestepped and pivoted, the cold steel missing his head by inches. *I will make him miss, make him tire.* Garroway moved on the balls of his feet, dancing along the mud, out of range.

Beyorn pounced, stampeding forwards with the force of a bear. Spear met axe, they exchanged blows. Garroway's spear shot forwards, the *Titans Bitch* just missing its target. Garroway used the tip and rear of his weapon, moving as he attacked. Beyorn blocked well as the two titans fought on even terms.

Garroway's speed kept him safe; he never stayed still for more than a second. Once he finished his attack he moved, never allowing Beyorn chance to counter. One mistake and death would claim him. Beyorn moved deceptively quickly for a man of his size. His attacks were not wild or uncoordinated, he had learnt well from the Allamantyan teachers.

The Allamantyan and Valorian soldiers began to chant and beat their shields, the gods responded with a flash of lightening and a roar of thunder, an orchestra playing the song of battle. Garroway danced to the tune, his movements were blessed with a majestic beauty. Each time Beyorn's axe hit the ground, the earth would shudder upon its impact.

The warriors exchanged blows; shining steel moved with lighting speed. Garroway brought his spear horizontal across his head to defend against Beyorn's monstrous attacks. The mighty axe came crashing down, the Golgian steel smashing through the shaft of the *Titans Bitch,* cleaving it in two.

Keep moving. Garroway compelled himself to move. He kept his balance and held onto the main body of his weapon. The spear now resembled a short sword. His legs ached, his muscles pleaded with him to stop. *If I stop, I die.* Garroway was not the warrior he used to be; he felt his aging body slowly giving way, but he was a dragon of Dagen and they do not die so easily.

Garroway spun the shattered spear in his hand. The bloodied steel was ready; he could no longer fight at a distance but he would do battle in close quarters now. They stepped forwards once again. Garroway ducked and rolled, slashing upwards, first cutting the beast along his stomach and then again across his back. Beyorn roared in pain.

The beast bleeds. Garroway smiled; he had drawn first blood. He attacked once more, slashing from left to right. His speed resembled a man half his age; fluent and beautiful, he bewildered Beyorn before cutting the beast across his shoulder, splitting his chest strap in two.

The thick mud made it hard for Garroway to manoeuvre; after his attack he stumbled but just about kept his feet. He however misjudged the distance and the beast's speed; before he knew it, he felt the grasp of Beyorn's fist around his throat. Death clawed its way through Beyorn's arm and around Garroway's neck; the beast lifted the helpless old warrior to the sky before ramming him downwards into the mud. The impact sent a shock through his body, he gasped for air. Looking upwards, he saw Beyorn's foot heading straight for his face. At the last second, Garroway side-rolled to safety. *I will not die as Lothar did.*

Garroway's heart raced and his body clambered for breath; his aging body wanted to give in but surrender was not in the warrior code. He climbed to his feet. Breathing deeply, he watched as the bloodied Beyorn stormed towards him, thunder echoed his charge. The beast of Golgia never once clawed for breath, he was restless in his attacks. Garroway took in a big gulp of air and met his foe head on. Warrior against warrior neither took a step back as they exchanged venomous blows. One mistake and Garroway would taste death. Garroway ducked, feeling the cold steel of Beyorn's axe gliding centimetres above his head. The old warrior countered, cutting at the beasts' legs. Beyorn let out a wild cry and unleashed a mighty right hand into Garroway's chest. The impact launched him from his feet and through the mud.

Garroway lay on his back; droplets of clear rain fell from the blackened sky, they patted softly against his face. He forced himself upright before crawling to his knees, blood pouring from his mouth. *Up, old man, fight!* He gasped and choked, desperately trying to breathe. His old body throbbed and burned with pain, his shoulders drooped and his legs twitched. Beyorn stumbled slowly forwards. *His wounds, they're slowing him down!*

With the last ounce of energy, Garroway mustered one final attack. He saw his chance, he jumped upwards, avoiding the deadly grasp of Beyorn and thrust downward at his adversary's exposed chest. The blade of the *Titans Bitch* skewered the beast. The broken spear embedded itself into his flesh.

As Garroway attempted to move out of range, Beyorn countered. He saw the fist of the beast heading towards him. Although he could see the attack he couldn't move, his aging reflexes betrayed him. The fist collided with his jaw, breaking bone and shattering teeth. Garroway's legs twisted and collapsed. As the bells rang out, another attack smashed against his face, then another. A broken and swollen Garroway slumped to his knees. Beyorn followed after him, the ground rumbled as the beast fell to his knees, the spear still in his chest. The two bloodied warriors stared at one another, they breathed deep and hard. The rain crashed against their wounded bodies. Blood and broken teeth fell from Garroway's mouth.

I can feel it, death is near. Garroway looked to the sky and the heavens began to open, golden light shining towards him. Through the heavenly glare he could see a great hall; rows of tables were filled with meats, fruits and wine. Along the centre table he could see his children. Lothar raised his goblet, smiling. Further along were Caelan and Zaira, each welcoming him. Opposite were Roak and Maarax, rich meats filling their hands. The head chair was empty, a tall throne made of pure oak. Garroway smiled; even in all his pain he felt content. *All these years I have eluded your cold touch, today is the day I allow you to find me.*

Garroway lifted his arms; Beyorn slowly climbed to his feet, he raised his axe to the sky. The rain fell softly through the ray of light. A broken smile filled the old warrior's face. Beyorn's axe fell, delivering the final blow.

I never knew death was so beautiful.

Chapter 33
To Live or Die

"Who dies first?" Toran boomed as he gripped his broadsword with both hands. A wave of Allamantyan men at arms poured through the broken door. Toran met them head-on; his mighty Dagari blade savaged the oncoming soldiers with a wild butchery. The rotting building was small; a narrow walkway was the only entrance. The compact location suited the assassins, only a few enemy soldiers could enter at one time. The bodies of the dead quickly began to fill the broken doorway.

Rhodesha fought alongside her man, she painted the mail suits of her enemies red. "Toran, pull back, there are too many."

Toran and Rhodesha moved backwards, allowing the onslaught of knights and soldiers into the building. They retreated as quickly as they could; they clambered out the back into the muddied alleyways of Baron's Bay. The storm smashed to the ground as thunder rumbled across the sky. Rhodesha wanted to be beside her brothers and sisters but now she had to think of Toran and her own survival.

The buildings of Baron's Bay were packed together; muddied streams caused by the storm flowed down the compact alleyways. Each alleyway was wide enough for one man. Rhodesha and Toran clambered forwards between the buildings, the mud rose above their ankles making each movement slow and twice as hard. They stopped as horsemen armed with kite-like shields and long spears moved along the wider streets.

"Half go that way, rest of you with me!" a commanding voice screamed through the rain. The charging of horse soon followed.

For a second, they seemed safe until Toran revealed himself, stepping out of the alleyway onto the wider street. "Bastards! Face the Iron Bull!" He beat his hand on his chest.

Rhodesha could see the fire of battle had consumed Toran; his lack of fear was perhaps his greatest weakness. The last two riders turned, lowered their spears and attacked. Toran roared, his ferocity matched that of a lion. His sword smashed through wood and mail, killing the first rider instantly. The second skewered Toran through his left shoulder, the spear slid through his leather tunic before shattering in half. Toran stumbled back then collapsed to his knees.

Rhodesha screamed, "Toran!"

The second rider drew his sword and attacked again; the rain crashed against his suit of mail. Toran was stunned, slumping forwards as he pulled the broken spear from his shoulder. The soldier raised his sword, ready to kill. Rhodesha dived forwards to save her man. Steel married steel as the thunder exploded; blue lightening lit up sky. The flash from the heavens temporarily blinded the soldier; in that split second Rhodesha took her chance, her sword slid underneath her attacker's, slashing open his side. The rider wailed as he fell from his horse.

Rhodesha quickly pushed the wounded Toran beneath a building, and the two lay, concealed in mud and water. They waited in silence; they saw and heard as armoured Allamantyan cavalry charged back and forth. When the coast was clear, they moved back towards the main street, climbing a set of old wooden stairs that clung to the outside of a tavern. Once on the roof, they lay down out of sight.

The sound battle roared down below. Toran pawed at his wound. Rhodesha crawled to the roof's edge and peered over. Dead bodies covered the muddied streets of Baron's Bay, rivers of blood flowed as the rains fell. An unimaginable horror plagued her eyes as she saw Garroway, her father, beaten and broken. Beyorn smashed his fists into his face over and over. She wanted to jump down and save him but she couldn't. Toran knelt beside her, his eyes welling as his fists tightened. They both watched helplessly as their father welcomed death with open arms. Beyorn's axe crashed against his shoulder, cleaving him in two.

Rhodesha's heart shattered and her body collapsed. Tears fell as she peered up towards the sky, a single beam of light fell from the heavens. She looked into its golden glow as she saw her father's spirit rise. Her hands began to shake; she felt nothing but pain, a darkness that could never end. Toran held her but for once it offered no comfort, she could feel his rage against the cold air that surrounded them. She didn't know how long they both lay on that roof, but by the time they rose, the rains had stopped.

Peering over the roof's edge, she could see four bodies hanging from a raised platform. Lanterns surrounded them, flittering light of red and yellow. The wind blew gently as the bodies creaked back and forth. She instantly knew who they were: Caelan, Roak, Zaira and Maarax. Below their hanging bodies was Garroway's severed body, skewered on a lance and left in the mud to rot. Her sadness turned to hate, her tears to vengeance.

"Uriah, can you see him?" Toran's once booming voice was seasoned with panic.

"I cannot; he and the others must be safe." Rhodesha scanned the muddied streets.

"I will kill them all!" Toran gripped his sword and attempted to stand.

"No, that is what they want." Rhodesha pulled him back.

Across the street, she had seen soldiers hiding in the alleyways. The bodies had been left to draw the remaining assassins out in the open. As much as Rhodesha wished to cover her blade with her enemy's blood she knew it was futile.

The sound of death ripped through the cold air. Rhodesha honed in on it like a shark to blood. A narrow walkway lead between the tavern and the next building. Glancing down, to her shock, she saw Valdar. He had pulled an

Allamantyan soldier from his horse before emptying his throat. Valdar was covered in mud and blood from head to toe; his blade stabbed and hacked at the dead man's body. His actions mirrored his name, Valdar the Vicious, perfectly.

"Valdar!" Toran shouted.

Valdar looked upwards, his dark hollow eyes filled with unimaginable pain. Rhodesha looked at her brother; without words she knew his next move.

In a flash, Valdar mounted the horse and charged into the street; he drew his sword and yelled, "There is still one here who draws breath. Let's be having you, you cunts!"

He rode up and down screaming, waving his sword above his head, before turning to the soldiers who poured out onto the street; he raged uncontrollably as he charged headlong into the face of death. His sword carried all his malice as it sent all who faced it straight to golden gates of Ollaria'h. He rode through the wave of Allamantyan knights and soldiers before disappearing out of sight.

"We must go," Rhodesha ordered.

The two quickly made their way out of town, trying their best to avoid being seen. They followed the coastline but there was no sight of Valdar, Rhodesha hated to think it but his chances of survival were slim. *Better he rest in the halls with our father.*

Toran didn't speak a word; he walked silently but Rhodesha could feel his wrath. He gripped his sword ever tight, the blade scraping against the wet stones beneath their feet. His eyes were a haze with dark mist, he never blinked.

Before long, night had fallen, and they both rested along the outskirts of the Ironwood. They had been following the same path they had taken during their journey back to Baron's Bay. Birds no longer sang, the sun no longer shone, just a cold darkness existed now. Rhodesha rested her head against Toran and closed her eyes. She dreamed of warm sand and blue skies. Along the beaches of Vathran, in western Dagen, her family danced and drank until their hearts' content. She sat on the sands, a baby in her arms. Her brothers and sisters came over, one by one, each kissing the babe. Eventually, those who had fallen disappeared, ghost-like silhouettes rising to the sky as they vanished forever.

"No!" Rhodesha screamed as she woke.

Toran was no longer beside her; he stood alone staring down the dirt path. He was flanked either side by trees. His mighty broadsword was held out before him. "They are coming."

The rumbling of armoured horse crashed against the morning sky.

Rhodesha scrambled to her feet. "We must move." She strapped her sword to her waist and moved towards the denseness of the forest before realising Toran was not following. Her stomach twisted.

Toran spoke in a haze, "Garroway said, 'From the moment we are born, death searches for us all, but we should decide the day it finds us.'" Toran drew his sword. "I choose this day!"

Rhodesha watched on helplessly. The man she loved more than life itself stood on the edge of death; he raised his sword pointing it towards the sound of armour and horse. The ground rumbled, the earth shuddered and the birds flew from the trees.

Toran stamped his feet and beat his chest wildly, spit flew from his mouth as he roared. Rumbling rose louder, the ground shuddered.

"Don't die today, live, live with me!" Rhodesha moved towards her man, her eyes never leaving him. "Toran, Toran. Live for your child!"

Toran lowered his sword and turned to her, his face frozen with shock.

"My love, we both need you." Rhodesha placed her hand on her lower stomach.

The sound of oncoming soldiers drew closer, the song of death following with them.

Chapter 34
Roaring Hearts and Thundering Skies

The storm roared through the night; rain crashed and the wind howled. The farmhouse creaked and swayed, Griffin barked and the horses brayed as the gods unleashed their fury upon the world. Danaka lay awake. Staring upwards, she thought of nothing but the hardship of Duro's life. In one night, she had learnt more about him than any of the others combined. He had suffered great loss but Danaka had suffered too. Her mother, who she'd never met, died on the Fist of Stone when she was a babe, her aunt and uncle had also passed, yet she did not hate the world as Duro did.

This little house, abandoned and decaying, allowed Danaka to feel safe; somehow, she felt at home in this place. With Hazar and his companions dead, she had nothing left to fear. The thought of leaving and heading out into the wilderness, trekking through mud, rain and who knew what else, did not appeal to her in any way.

Downstairs, she could hear Duro moving back and forth. *He's making more noise than the storm!* Inquisitively, she moved to the stairs to look. Duro wore nothing but his poplin tunic round his waist. The fire from the hearth painted his muscled body with a light of red and yellow. He lunged forwards, swinging his sword, thrusting and slashing. His attacks were uncoordinated as his blade scraped against the wall before embedding itself into the ground. Duro spun suddenly, clutching at his wound.

"You are in no fit state to fight," Danaka said as she moved into sight. "You must rest."

Duro, still clutching his side, replied, "I have no time, I must be ready. We leave at first light."

"I'm not leaving, I'm staying here." Danaka almost whispered her reply.

Duro replaced his sword with a shorter lighter one. He began to practice once again, swinging and moving. He swung wildly before grimacing as he stumbled forwards. The sword crashed from his hands, almost cutting into Danaka's bare feet.

"Stop!" Danaka commanded. "You can barely walk, let alone fight."

"I must be ready! Castel is a far greater foe than any I have faced." Duro dragged his sword from the floor before he began to swing it once again; the blade sliced through some old pots then decimated an old rocking chair, cleaving it in two.

With each vicious attack, every man that Danaka had seen die since she left Tomellburg, flashed before her eyes. The ghastly shriek of Sir Claris Moon screamed out as it tasted Duro's steel through his body, it echoed in her mind over and over, his blood painting the white marble red. Then, by a roaring wave of red flame, the massacre at Ashfeld burst into sight, hundreds of innocents dying, cut down by black cloaked shadows. Then, through flame and darkness, the pathetic begging of Malcolm Reymor rung out.

"Please, please. Don't! Forgive me," Malcolm pleaded.

"It is the gods who forgive, not I." Duro thrust his sword through Malcolm's chin.

The snap of a whip and the bray of a horse removed the flames. A cold fog clung to the base of a single tree where a young Yornish boy hung from a rope. His frail body swayed from left to right, the icy hand of death moving him back and forth.

The boy's skin had turned blue, slowly his eyes opened. *"He brings only death. He lives for blood; soon, soon it will be yours."*

The smashing of wood and clay brought Danaka back to reality. "I will not go!" she yelled.

A silence crept through the house. Duro turned slowly; the rain fell and the thunder let out a single boom across the night sky. He walked towards her. Danaka gulped.

"You are mine," he breathed deeply, his sweaty chest rose and fell.

"No!"

"By right of combat you are mine!"

"My life is no one's but my own!" Danaka rammed her hands against Duro's chest knocking him back.

She turned and fled into the rain. The storm fell against her body with an unrelenting power, she could barely see as the rain soaked her from head to toe. She stumbled forwards through the mud, anger blurring her mind. Before she knew it, she was out in the darkness.

"Danaka!" Duro called out, almost sounding pathetic.

In that instant, Danaka stopped. His words held back her legs, she couldn't move. Thump by thump her heart rose, her hands trembled slightly. She turned back. In the doorway, Duro stood, the light from inside beaming out like a torch in a cave. Slowly he moved towards her, forcing himself through the storm, the rain falling elegantly against his naked torso. An inch before her face he stopped, they stood staring into each other's eyes. Their chests rose and fell as they breathed deeply.

"That is the first time you've called me by name," Danaka whispered.

Duro lustfully stared back; his eyes took control of her soul. Suddenly he stepped forwards and pulled Danaka towards him and they kissed. Her lips met his in an explosion of passion; her body tingled with excitement as she felt the warmth of his tongue against her own. His strong hands tore at her dress, pulling it from her shoulders, exposing her naked body. The cool pearl-like drops of rain crashed against her skin. Duro sucked gently but firmly again at her lips. Danaka's knees quivered as their wet bodies embraced.

Duro hooked his arms underneath her legs and hoisted Danaka upwards. She, in turn, wrapped her legs around his waist as he carried her indoors. She continued to kiss him while running her nails along his sculptured back. Duro charged into the farmhouse; in one powerful swoop he removed everything from the dining table before dropping her against the surface. She stared into his dark eyes; the rain trickled down his black stubble and along his jawline. With her index finger, she slid it across his face and over his lips.

Danaka's heart raced and her stomach fluttered. As Duro kissed at her neck she couldn't help but beam and gasp. His mouth moved along her collarbone then across her breasts, his tongue encircling her nipples. Any embarrassment she felt about her body evaporated; every time he touched her, magic coursed between the two of them. Duro lifted her knees and pushed them against her shoulders. Slowly she felt his lips against her inner thighs; they moved inwards, closer and closer, teasing her with each kiss. Danaka raged inside, desperate for more. She needed him, she wanted him. Then, suddenly, she felt a god-like wave of pleasure as his tongue tenderly brushed between her legs, then again and again as it began to glide up and down. Danaka ran her fingers through his hair, scrunching it tightly as his lips massaged her clitoris. She screamed as loud and as powerfully as she could, the storm could not contain her. His mouth continued to send her into a realm of pleasure; her mind and body were transported to a paradise of unexplainable happiness.

Duro pulled away, standing over her. She stared up at him, helpless. Danaka was at his mercy, in this moment he could do with her as he pleased and she would obey. Her foot ran down his chiselled torso, her toes feeling every groove and muscle. Duro pulled loose his tunic from around his waist. Danaka sat up slightly, feeling how long and powerful he was. She squeezed it tightly in her hands as they continued to kiss. It felt smooth and firm; she quickly moved her hand back and forth. Her lips pressed against his scarred stomach, moving downwards until her tongue erotically encircled the tip of his cock. *I'm not the only one who can tease.*

Swiftly, she felt Duro's hand against her shoulder, as he pinned her to the table; she felt powerless against his dominance. Danaka could feel herself twitch and throb in wild anticipation. His hand pressed against her chest as he slowly began to slide himself inside her. As every inch entered, the gates of paradise opened further. Duro arched his body with an artistic beauty as he took her, he moved majestically. Danaka's hands caressed his body and her nails marked his flesh. Danaka began to scream uncontrollably with every thrust the pleasure rose. The bursts started gently before building in intensity. Wave after wave of pleasure exploded throughout her body, her legs shuddered and she gasped for air. Her chest rose and fell like waves on the ocean as she inhaled and exhaled furiously.

Spellbound, Danaka lay against the cold wood, staring upwards. A brief silence fell over them both as they looked at one another. The rain fell softly against the creaking frame of the house. Their eyes told the tale of what each desired. Duro flipped Danaka over, arching her over the table. She felt his fingers softly stroking down her spine, before he took her buttocks within his palm. He began to thrust, each one deeper and harder than the last. Danaka screamed louder and louder. The table creaked and banged. The sky thundered as their hearts roared. The gods of lust and love were alive this night.

Danaka lay with her head upon Duro's chest; she felt the slow deep thumping of his heart. He rested peacefully, his breaths were long and hard. Danaka couldn't remove the smile from her face, with each passing moment she relived her night of passion. She ran her fingers softly against his scarred torso. Each wound told a different tale, Danaka wanted to know them all.

The morning was cold but Duro's warmth was all she needed. A soft winter wind blew outside, the old wood creaked gently. Danaka didn't want to move, she wanted to stay in this moment forever. Yet soon she knew Duro would move on, heading south so he could quench his thirst for vengeance.

"I will not go!" Danaka uncontrollably burst out. She instantly attempted to cover her mouth but Duro began to stir. She admired him as his eyes slowly opened and he stretched out. He seemed happy; a hint of a smile formed along his lips.

For once they both were relaxed; the harsh reality of life lay beyond the banks surrounding the farmhouse but here, in this brief moment, life seemed simple and carefree.

"What did you want to be as child?" Danaka asked. Her voice was joyful, eager to hear parts of Duro's happier past.

Duro kissed her once and looked upwards as if he wanted to peer towards the sky. "I wanted to join the order of Hethelyon, to defend the faith of Ollaria'h and fight in the name of the gods." Duro sighed. "All my life I only ever asked the gods for only one thing, to defend my brother. When they abandoned him, I abandoned them."

With each word he spoke, Danaka wanted to hold him tighter. "This pursuit of vengeance must end; killing this man will not bring back your brother."

"Castel Damari, he is the last."

"Killing only breeds more killing."

Danaka rose; the talk of death began to devour her happiness. With her creative eyes, she looked the house up and down. The old cold wood turned warm and vibrant, flowers blossomed by the roaring fire. The smell of fresh bread filled her senses. Laughter of children rang out like royal bells as they played with their father on fields of green. Danaka smiled a hollow smile, one that told the tale of her failing dreams.

Danaka breathed deeply, she had to know. "Will you stay here with me? Give up your quest. We could make this into a home."

Duro sat up. "I've not had a home for many years; the stars have been the roof and the ground, my bed."

"Look, we could have flowers here," Danaka pointed near the hearth, "and sheep skin rug here; outside we can grow crops, we could have a few cows and then…"

"Breathe, breathe." Duro smiled.

Danaka approached him and knelt between his knees.

Duro ran his hands through her hair. "This world we live in is filled with so much hate but you've showed me that love can grow even in the darkest of places."

They began to kiss; the passion and desire for one another drew them together. Danaka's heart raged, her body yearned for him inside her once more. Duro pulled back and attempted to speak. Danaka held her finger to his lips. Peering into his dark eyes, she saw the soul of a good man, one twisted and moulded into the harsh life of a man without a home or a family.

"Give me your answer on my return, I will fetch us water from the well." Danaka kissed him one last time.

Danaka threw on her red dress and wrapped herself in a white sheet. As she made her way to the entrance, she could hear a soft tune from Duro's pan flute. For once, it was light and happy; the music brought a smile to Danaka's face. Griffin attempted to follow as she left the farmhouse but she closed him in; she didn't fancy him bringing all the mud inside. Danaka turned back, seeing her loyal friend peering out the window with his large friendly eyes.

The air was bitter and cold; it bit wildly against her skin. A faint fog hovered like floating silk above the muddied earth. She slowly trudged through the field of mud towards the well. Outside was quiet; no birds sang the morning song, just the winter wind that blew gently. The plain surrounding the farmhouse was wide and sloped downwards towards the house. The drooping hills to the back concealed the house and would be a perfect running ground to keep Griffin active. It would take a lot of work to make this place a home but Danaka wasn't shy of hard work.

Will he stay? Danaka asked herself over and over. With each step she took, the same question repeated itself in her mind. *Whether he stays or not, I'm not going with him!* Danaka yanked angrily on the rope as she began to hoist the bucket from within the dark depths of the well. The winch squeaked as the bucket slowly rose to the surface.

In the distance, she began to hear a familiar sound. The noise drew her attention; in the window of the house she could see Griffin. His head bounced up and down, he was barking with wild enthusiasm. It sounded just like back home in Tomellburg, when an unwanted guest would approach her farm. Suddenly, the warning took hold; a moment of fear wrapped its cold hand around her throat. The sound of horse against mud and water crashed heavily behind her. Danaka slowly turned.

Against the fog it appeared, as pale as death. As it galloped closer the goodness in the world evaporated. A skeleton-like figure leant down from its black steed; dark hollow eyes lay within the pale flesh of its rider. It was as if it had been unleashed from hell itself.

"Valdar?" Danaka froze in shock.

The cruellest and most frightful of all Garroway's children charged towards her with a wild fury, he roared like a mad man. Valdar's white flesh was stained with blood; his gaunt face eyed her like a hawk before the final attack. Danaka attempted to run but his long arm hooked around her waist, hoisting her upwards. She kicked and screamed but to no avail. Before she knew it, she was nearly at the brow of the hill. Danaka heard Griffin's helpless howl slowly fading away.

With one last burst of energy, Danaka screamed, "Duro!"

Chapter 35
God's Tears

The rain had slowly begun to ease, and the storm passed over, heading west. The streets of Baron's bay were a mess; the dead bodies of the Valorian and Allamantyan soldiers were drenched in blood, rain and mud. The stench of death would linger in those streets for years to come. Daemar had ordered that the bodies of the assassins be hung up and left to rot. He hoped it might draw out the survivors. He sent Beyorn, Marshall Varrone DeVeil and the wounded back to Antilion with news of their victory.

Gabriel, with his remaining Valorians, headed north along the coastline with his Allamantyan allies. They followed the tracks of what appeared to be three assassins. Yeltai, the Roldorian tracker, believed they were only a few hours ahead; one was injured too so their pace was slow. A strong breeze from the Calhorion Ocean blew in from the east.

"Many of those who died were my friends; it is sad knowing they will never see home again." Lucian spoke slowly as he looked out to sea.

Gabriel agreed; he reminisced about his clash with Caelan. One warrior against another, spear against spear. He was the finest he had fought. Gabriel ran his fingers above his eye; he could feel the wound, the mark where Caelan cut open his skin. *He was the first to lay a weapon upon me*. He peered back across his men; those who remained looked beaten and tired. The thundering of horses roared up behind.

Prince Daemar rode up alongside Gabriel. "Are you hurting little prince, looks like you'll have a scar."

"It will heal."

Daemar leant in close. "It is the scars you cannot see that never heal."

They continued north. The eastern winds grew harder and colder. The long fields of grass to their left arched heavily. Gabriel felt another storm was rising. The beach to his right was murky and wet, nothing like the paradise back in Antilion. The sea crashed hard, roaring loudly against the shore. Eventually, after hours of riding, they made camp. Daemar chose a spot surrounded by high dunes that sheltered them from the heavy winds. No tents were pitched; instead they placed spears into the sands and stuck sheets on top. If the assassins attacked, they needed to be ready.

The rains fell gently, beating a tender rhythm along the sands. Gabriel sat beside Lucian in their makeshift tent. His cousin was surprisingly quiet; he lay on his back staring upwards.

“I miss home; once this is over, I will ride back to Verdina. I want to see my mother again. I may find myself a wife, settle down; that will make her happy,” Lucian continued, gazing upwards, never blinking.

“Yes, it will.” Gabriel gripped his cousin’s wrist as he lay down beside him. Feeling relaxed, he closed his eyes, falling into deep slumber.

He dreamed of battle and victory, of death and glory, he was the prince who conquered. Suddenly he awoke from his dreams; darkness had fallen over the dunes. The rain pitter-pattered all around. Beside him, with his back turned, was Daemar. He sat silently, staring into the night.

“When the sun falls, do you see the faces of all the men you’ve killed?” Daemar spoke softly.

“I remember the dead more than I do the living.”

“The warriors curse, little prince.” Daemar held out his sword. Trickles of rain ran down the cold steel. A single horseman rode by, draining out their brief moment of solitude. The night seemed cold; death lingered on the eastern wind. Daemar extended his mail-covered hand, the rain patting softly against it. “A priest once told me, the rain is the gods crying because of the horrors that we do to one another.”

“Do you think the gods will forgive us for the things we have done?” Gabriel asked.

“Do we truly deserve to be forgiven?” Daemar stood up, “Get some sleep little prince.”

Gabriel lay back, closing his eyes.

“Ambush! Up, all of you!”

“They are everywhere, formation!”

Panic-stricken voices awoke Gabriel. The roaring of charging horses thundered against his aching head. The sun had risen and the rains had stopped. Slowly he sat up, his body weak and his mind disorientated. *The assassins, they are back!* Gabriel turned, looking for his spear. The sound of steel on steel and the wailing of death rumbled against the Allamantyan dunes. Across the rising sand, he could see his countrymen fighting for their lives, each man was half-dressed. They lacked helmets and breastplates but they fought valiantly none the less.

“My prince! Betrayal!” Captain Holar yelled as he charged forwards towards Gabriel. He was barely a few metres away when an Allamantyan horseman rode him down, the sword severing his head from the jaw upwards.

Betrayal? Suddenly his vision became clear; all around his Allamantyan allies were cutting down his men. Some were pinned to the sand, spears in their chests, killed in their sleep. Those left alive made a last ditched attempt at survival, fighting on the high ground of the dunes. Outnumbered, outflanked, they fought on.

Gabriel jumped to his feet, the massacre raging around him. Two Allamantyan soldiers approached him and with ease he cut them down. Like strands of wheat, their wilted bodies slumped to the wet sand. “Daemar! Where are you? Face me you coward!”

As if by command, Daemar appeared. He carried a shield in his left hand and his bloodied sword spun effortlessly in his right. He moved like a ghost through the chaos.

Gabriel eyed him with an uncontrollable anger; his mind honed in. His focus left the battle and latched onto Daemar. Gabriel stepped forwards, only to be met with a screeching of bells. His head rocked violently to his left. He felt blood spray down his face as he crumbled to his knees. The sound of the world drained out, the bells consuming everything. His vision blurred out but he could just about make out a horseman ride past. Gabriel's body felt heavy, his legs and arms began to sink into the sand. Daemar was still approaching. He fought with all his might to rise to his feet but he fell onto his back, he looked up, helpless.

"Traitor!" a loud droning voice called out. It echoed out long and hard.

Lucian and Sir Evandinor appeared, jumping over Gabriel's body, into the path of Daemar, both eager to defend their prince.

"Allamantyan dog! Face real Valorian steel."

Both attacked Daemar simultaneously; Lucian and Sir Evandinor wore nothing but their battle skirts. Each carried only swords. Daemar parried their attacks, side stepping and moving around them. He smiled, calling them in. Both replied readily, swinging out with their swords. Daemar moved with speed of a man in his twenties, he carried the weight of his armour well, moving fluently. In a flurry of violence, Daemar's sword clashed with Lucian and Evandinor in a ferocious exchange. Gabriel tried to rise, but still his body wouldn't allow it.

During the attack, Daemar hacked to his left; his sword slashed against Evandinor's exposed chest. Blood sprayed into the air as his body collapsed face-first to the ground. In that moment, Gabriel felt a tear fall from his cheek. He looked to the heavens; the shimmer of sun was rising on the greyed-out sky. *Give me the strength to defend my people; if I am your son allow me to rise!* It was the first moment in his life that he had begged, pleading with the gods to aid him. Yet they answered with nothing but the singing of angels, epic voices calling down from the clouds. It was all Gabriel could hear as his countrymen died all around him; screams were rendered silent as his soldiers died one by one.

Lucian, overzealous as always, swung wildly. Each attack, Daemar parried with his shield. He took the full force of the blows as he dropped down into a crouch. Gabriel attempted to scream, one final attempt to warn his cousin of the impending trap but it was to no avail. Lucian lunged in; Daemar easily blocked the attack and sliced at ankle height, severing his heels. Blood painted the sand, Lucian wailed in agony as he fell to his knees.

If Gabriel could've spoken, he would've begged for his cousin's life. Daemar stood over Lucian, his eyes never leaving Gabriel; he grabbed hold of Lucian's yellow hair and exposed his throat. Lucian's eyes welled with fear, the sudden realisation of his impending death. In a sadistic and slow manner, Daemar eased his sword across Lucian's neck, splitting it open like a piece of fruit. A waterfall of blood gushed across his chest. Daemar rammed his foot into Lucian's back, knocking him to the sand. Lucian's body twitched as he bled out.

"Why?" Gabriel somehow regained his speech.

Daemar approached slowly, before kneeling beside him. "Your thirst for glory will bring only ruin to our world; I will not let you destroy my brother's dream of peace."

"That is the last of them." Sir Rolan Bonhuer rode up, his balding head poured with sweat.

"Are you sure?" Daemar replied.

"The Valorians dine with the devil."

"I still breathe!" Gabriel answered defiantly.

"Yes, for now." Daemar swiped the blood from his sword. "Ever since you arrived, I dreamed of facing you. To humble your arrogance would've given me more pleasure than any woman, but I swore an oath. My brother made me swear not to kill you, so I keep his wish. I had hoped that assassin would've killed you in Baron's Bay, but even with the aid of an arrow he couldn't."

Daemar rammed his mail-covered fist into Gabriel's face. Pain scorched through his head; his vision blurred as everything became a fuzzy mess. He could feel the warm blood pouring from his mouth and nose.

"Bind him and strap him to a horse."

The voices around him began to rise and drain out.

"Take him south."

Angels appeared on the clouds, plucking away gently at magical harps. They looked so beautiful; tears of silver began to fall from the sky. Gabriel's eyes began to feel heavy.

"Sell him, a royal Valorian slave." Laughing soon followed.

Darkness consumed him, a never-ending dream of shadow.

Chapter 36
King Knows No Bounds

The flames flickered and crackled; they were so relaxing, so peaceful, yet so deadly. They burnt so brightly upon the great hearth. Andros was on his knees in front of the flames, as bare as the day he was born; he found the warmth pleasing, the heat burnt into his cool skin. Andros did not know why he was on his knees, why he was naked. All he knew was, he liked how he felt. He was submissive to the great flames in front of him, beautiful to watch but deadly to touch.

As Andros stretched his hands out beside him, he could feel he was kneeling on a great white fur rug. He ran his fingers through it and clenched his hands into a fist, grabbing the fur in his palm. He closed his eyes and remembered how he and Lyon would kneel together on this rug and talk all night. They even made love on it, on occasion, in front of the great fire. As Lyon would take him, Andros would admire the flames, they would excite him.

A sudden cold shiver ran through his spine, like an icy chill on a winter morning. He turned his head to see his great four poster bed, the one made for his wedding night. Beautiful wooden beams on each corner, hand-carved with the images of roses on one side and the sword of Tyranian on the other. However, it was not the bed or the beams that sent the chill down his spine but the body that lay sprawled out on the bed.

It was the body of a young lad. He was naked, face down, with his head hanging over the end of the bed. Andros quickly crawled over; he ran his fingers through the boy's thick blonde hair. He liked how it felt. He grabbed it tightly and pulled the head up. The boy's face was pale and cold. His hollow brown eyes were wide open; his lips were dark red. Andros leant forward and kissed them; he bit and sucked hard on his lips. He didn't know why he did it, or what compelled him to do so, but he enjoyed it. He could taste blood.

He ran his hands over the boy's cheek; his face was smooth but cold. He preferred the warmth of the flames to the glacial touch of this boy's skin. The neck was badly bruised, his skin had turned purple and black, showing the ruptured underlying blood vessels that ran across his throat and around up by his ears. Andros stood up and knelt onto the bed. He noticed a blood stain on the sheet; he followed it with his fingers and it ran up the boy's leg and onto his buttocks. They were splattered with blood; he touched it but it had dried, turning brown and hard. He remembered nothing of what he saw in front of him.

Who is he? Who is he? Who is he? He began to panic, his heart thumping inside his chest.

"He is Jarrell," a deep voice bellowed out from the darkness.

"What?" Andros quickly turned to see no one, just the fire burning at his hearth.

"*You know, the servant boy, the one who filled your bathtub,*" another voice called out, this time from the other side of the room; a softer voice this time.

He turned and once again saw no one, just a candle in the corner of the room, flickering peacefully.

"How did he get here?" Andros asked.

"*You had him brought to your room,"* the deeper voice replied.

"You greatly admired him, his youth, his looks," said the softer voice which was so elegant in tone.

"*It was his ass you wanted; you take what you want."*

Andros began to squeeze the boy's buttocks. He could feel himself hardening as he felt the cold skin beneath his fingertips. A sense of excitement ran through his body. He squeezed tighter and harder.

"*Yes, yes you like that!*" the deep voice roared loudly.

"No! No! I don't." Andros panicked and shuffled back to the head of the bed. He smacked his back against hard wooden headboard which briefly took his breath away. He gasped for air; Andros raised his hands and covered his ears as he placed his head in his knees.

"Not again, not again, not again," Andros said as he began to weep.

"Why do you cry, Your Majesty?" The softer voice sounded sympathetic.

"Because he has murdered... again," the deeper voice countered.

"No, No, No, No," Andros mumbled to himself, as he started to bash his hands against his head.

"*He is to be a king, why should he care?*"

"Yes, a king does as he pleases."

"A king knows no bounds."

"He answers to no man."

"No man may judge a king."

"Right or wrong."

"Murderer or saviour."

The two voices had become like one, clashing together like a wave on the mountainside. Andros raised his head and looked out at the body before him, looking at what he had done. It slowly began to come back to him, violent images flashed like lightening before his eyes. He remembered, now he remembered! But he wished he didn't. The kissing, the fighting, the crying, the screaming, the pleasure, the fire, yes, the fire.

"What should I do? Father, Father, Father, help me."

"*Your father is dead. Killed by your best friend,"* the soft voice said ever so slowly.

"By your lover; your father cannot save you this time," the deep voice added as if it was happy at Andros's despair.

"You are to be the king. Your father is gone. He sleeps. He sleeps in the White City. You live, you will rule."

"You give the commands; you get what you want. A king always does."

Andros stood up from the bed and wrapped himself in a long black cloak, trimmed with wolf fur. It felt warm around his naked body. He began to pace up and down in his room.

"Yes, Yes." Andros began to smile. "I am to be the king and who is that boy?" he asked rhetorically.

"*His name is Jarrell,*" the deep voice boomed.

"No one cares about his name or who he is!" Andros angrily clapped his hands together.

"*He was your servant, he must have a family.*"

"No one asked about the blacksmith's son," Andros quickly countered back. "He is gone, it's been five years and no one came looking for him. My father saw to that, no one knew but him and I."

For the first time in five years, Andros remembered that night. It came to him so clearly. He had taken the boy to his cave, deep in the mountains. He had promised to show him the flames that speak. Darkness had compelled Andros to take him, kicking and screaming. He drowned the lad in a puddle of seawater as he ravaged him.

"*Your father's dead.*"

"*Now you are to be the king.*"

It was cold outside; Andros could see his breath appearing like an autumn mist. The sun was beginning to rise on the horizon. Harsh and the cold, the morning breeze blew in from outside. Andros looked down between his legs.

"Very cold, yes very cold!" the soft voice giggled.

"More fire," Andros demanded. Logs fell softly against the flames, they hissed and crackled. Andros peered out across his kingdom; a cold darkness filled his eyes. Power and voices consumed his mind. "I am the king!"

List of Characters

House Da'Menaeon of Allamantya

- Aristian I, King of Allamantya, emperor of the Antilion Empire
  Andros, King's firstborn male and heir to the Allamantyan Throne
  Arrabella, King's first-born daughter, twin to Andros
  Arteus, King's youngest son
- Daemar, King's younger brother and commander of his armies
  Wife, deceased
  Son, deceased
- Danaus, King Aristian's elder brother, killed at the Falentis pass.
- Drusilla, elder sister to Aristian and married to House Redmond of Yardesa
  Edwin Redmond, husband.
  Varden Redmond, son deceased
  Evelyn Redmond, youngest daughter

Beyorn, beast of Golgia, King's Champion
Sir Dolfan Greenway, commander of red sword army
Sir Henry Shay, knight of the red sword
Sir Steffan Mace, knight of the red sword

- Marshal Latimor N'Dai, governor of Kathoros and Western Darnor
  Lady Dyana N'Dai, wife
  Sir Lyon N'Dai, eldest son.
  Sir Gerold N'Dai, youngest son.
  Sir Yandris Dellamoor, champion for House N'Dai
  Lord Wylliam Yorkus of Irontown, in service of House N'Dai
  Lord Glynn Harron of Arbor
  Sir Jenson Harron, son of Glynn Harron.
  Sir Wallace, knight in service of house Harron
- Marshal Varrone DeVeil, governor of Ardenia and Northern Darnor
  Sir Yalron DeVeil, eldest son.
  Sir Rolan Bonhuer, champion to House DeVeil
  Lord Ruskforn Derry of Ashfeld, in service of House DeVeil
  Malcolm Reymor, Ashfeld tax collector
  Marshal Boris DeGrey, governor of Southron
  Jaeron DeGrey, eldest son.

Sir Castel Damari, champion to House DeGrey

- Marshal Edwin Redmond, governor of Yardesa
  Princess Drusilla, wife of Edwin
  Varden, eldest son, deceased
  Evelyn, eldest daughter
- Marshal Guy Bailyn, governor of Oalandrium
  Lord Franco Tomell of Tomellburg, in service of House Bailyn
  Sir Claris Moon, Lord Tomell's champion
  Benedict Darris, Mayor of Tomellburg
  Harad Joyn, store keeper
  Walter, a drunk
  Irban, an Akeshan trader
  Sir Tomas, a knight in service of the Guardians of Thelonia
  Danaka, a farm girl who lives alone with her dog Griffin
- Members of the Antilion High council
  Lord Peyton Beldomir, the gold
  Lord Mortimer Judaus, the white
  Lord Dellio Greenway, the green
  Lord Attico Da'Menaeon, the red
- Order of Hethelyon, holy knights sworn to defend the faith of Ollaria'h and the God's tower
- Guardians of Thelonia, a splinter faction of Hethelyon, who spread the word of Ollaria'h through conquest.
- Baldwin Anglar, Count of Ezzar, governor of the Eastern Isles.
- Jerome Riordal, Lord of the Marsh
- Duro Bel'Rayne, wandering swordsman
- Sir Dillian Howard, mysterious knight.

House Da'Menaeon of Valanor

- Vincinicus II, King of Valanor
  Tilia, King's first-born daughter and heir to the Valorian Throne
  Gabriel, King's eldest true born son
  Leylan, King's bastard son, born to an Allamantyan woman
- Damidar, King's younger brother and commander of Imperial legions
  Marticus, eldest son of Damidar
  Emir, youngest son of Damidar
- Lorella, King's younger sister, married to Kassian Elkelmar
  Lassander, eldest son of Lorella
  Lucian, youngest son of Lorella
- Flarian nobles
  Cassius Jove
  Cato Balbus
  Gerhardt Linos
  Domiol Vude

Kaian Vadius, sworn sword of Princess Tilia
Dejax Felios, sworn sword of Princess Tilia
Cassandra, handmaiden of Princess Tilia
Sir Hyandrei Milo, commander of 8th legion of horse
Sir Evandinor Linos, second in command of 8th legion of horse
Sir Kanutus Jove, commander of 2nd legion of foot

Lords of Darnor

- Lord Devon Hohjan, ruler of Southern Darnor. Father-in-law to King Aristian
  Sonja, eldest daughter, married to Aristian, deceased
  Sir Terrell, eldest son
  Sir Godfrey, youngest son
- Lord Girard Lannis, ruler of Eastern Darnor
  Sir Morten Durand, Lords Champion

12 Dragons of Dagen

Garroway, leader, father of the group
Lilah, Garroway's woman
Toran, elder brother to Uriah
Uriah, younger brother to Toran
Caelan, spear warrior
Naleac, twin to Caelan
Roak, warrior born of Etorion blood
Rhodesha, lover of Toran, also of Etorion blood
Valdar, the vicious
Lothar, born of Yornish descent
Maarax, the archer
Zaira, golden haired warrioress